A
STUDY
IN
DROWNING

AVA REID

An Imprint of HarperCollins*Publishers*

For James
This is a love story.

HarperTeen is an imprint of HarperCollins Publishers.

A Study in Drowning
Copyright © 2023 by Ava Reid

www.epicreads.com
Library of Congress Control Number: 2023933636
ISBN 978-0-06-321150-6 (trade bdg.)—ISBN 978-0-06-335494-4 (special ed.)
Typography by Sarah Nichole Kaufman
23 24 25 26 27 LBC 9 8 7 6 5
First Edition

"I refuse mirrors," the Fairy King said. "I refuse them for you, and I refuse them for me. If you want to see what you are, look into the tide pools at dusk. Look into the sea."

FROM *ANGHARAD* BY EMRYS MYRDDIN, 191 AD

ONE

It began as all things did: a girl on the shore, terrified and desirous.

FROM *ANGHARAD* BY EMRYS MYRDDIN, 191 AD

The poster was as frayed and tattered as a page torn from someone's favorite book. Surely, Effy thought, that was intentional. It was printed on a thick yellow parchment, not unlike her drafting linens. The edges were curling in on themselves— either shyly or protectively, as if the parchment had a secret to hide.

Effy used both hands to smooth the paper flat, then squinted at the curling script. Handwritten, it was smeared in several places. It was further obscured by a water stain of no discernible shape, like a birthmark or a growth of mold.

> *To the esteemed students of the Architectural College,*
> *The estate of Llyr's national author EMRYS MYRDDIN*
> *is soliciting designs for a manor home outside the late author's*
> *hometown of Saltney, Bay of Nine Bells.*
> *We ask that the proposed structure—HIRAETH*
> *MANOR—be large enough to house the surviving Myrddin*

family, as well as the extensive collection of books, manuscripts, and letters that Myrddin leaves behind.

We ask that the designs reflect the character of Myrddin and the spirit of his enormous and influential body of work.

We ask that the designs be mailed to the below address no later than midautumn. The winner will be contacted by the first day of winter.

Three conditions, just like in one of Myrddin's fairy tales. Effy's heart began beating very fast. Almost unconsciously, she reached up to grasp at her knot of golden hair, tied back with its customary black ribbon. She smoothed down the loose strands that floated around her face in the drowsy, sunlit air of the college lobby.

"Excuse me," someone said.

Effy's gaze darted over her shoulder. Another architecture student in a brown tweed jacket stood behind her, rocking back and forth on his heels with an air of obvious irritation.

"Just a minute," she said. "I haven't finished looking."

She hated the way her voice shook. The other student huffed in reply. Effy turned back to the poster, pulse ticking even faster now. But there was no more left to read, only the address at the bottom, no signature, no cheery *best of luck!* sign-off.

The other student began tapping his foot. Effy reached into her bag and pawed through it until she found a pen, uncapped and clearly unceremoniously abandoned, the nib thick with dust. She pressed it against the tip of her finger, but no inkblot appeared.

Her stomach twisted. She pressed again. The boy behind her

shifted his weight, the old wood under him groaning, and Effy put the pen in her mouth and sucked until she tasted the metallic bite of ink.

"For Saints' sakes," the boy snapped.

Hurriedly she scrawled the address on the back of her hand and dropped the pen into her bag. She tore away from the wall, and the poster, and the boy, before he could do or say anything more. As she walked briskly down the hallway, Effy caught the end of his muttered curse.

Heat rose to her cheeks. She reached her studio classroom and sat down in her customary seat, avoiding the gazes of the other students as they shuffled to their places. She stared down, instead, at the bleeding ink on the back of her hand. The words were starting to blur, as if the address were a spell, one with a tauntingly short life span.

Cruel magic was the currency of the Fair Folk as they appeared in Myrddin's books. She had read them all so many times that the logic of his world was layered over hers, like glossy tracing paper on top of the original.

Effy focused on the words, committing them to memory before the ink could run beyond legibility. If she squinted until her eyes watered, she could almost forget the boy's whispered slur. But her mind slipped away from her, running through all the reasons he might have scoffed and sneered at her.

One: She was the only female student at the architecture college. Even if the boy had never so much as glimpsed her in the halls before, certainly he had seen her name on the exam results, and then, later, on the college roster in the lobby. Three days ago, some anonymous vigilante had taken a pen and turned her last name, *Sayre,* into something lewd, preserving the last two letters.

Two: She was the only female student at the architecture college, and she had placed higher than him in the entrance exam. She had scored high enough for the literature college, but they didn't accept women, so she had settled for architecture: less prestigious, less interesting, and, as far as she was concerned, monumentally more difficult. Her mind didn't work in straight lines and right angles.

Three: He knew about Master Corbenic. When Effy thought of him now, it was only in small pieces. The gold wristwatch nestled in the dark, thick hair of his arms. The adultness of it had shocked her, like a blow to the belly. Few of the boys at her college—and that's what they were, boys—had such thick arm hair, and even fewer had expensive wristwatches to nestle in it.

Effy squeezed her eyes shut, willing the image to vanish. When she opened them again, the chalkboard in front of her looked glassy, like a window at night. She could picture a thousand blurry, half-seen things behind it.

Her studio professor, Master Parri, was running through his usual introduction, only in Argantian. It was a new policy at the university, instituted only at the start of her first term, six weeks ago. Officially, it was out of respect for the university's few Argantian students, but unofficially, it was out of a sort of preemptive fear. If Argant won the war, would they impress their language upon all of Llyr? Would children grow up shaping its vowel sounds

4

and verbs instead of memorizing Llyrian poetry?

It might be a good idea for everyone at the university to have a head start.

But even when Master Parri lapsed back into Llyrian, Effy's mind was still turning, like a dog unable to settle itself down to sleep. Master Parri wanted two cross sections finished by the end of class. She had chosen to do a redesign of the Sleeper Museum. It was the city of Caer-Isel's most beloved tourist attraction, as well as the alleged seat of Llyrian magic. There, the seven Storytellers slept in their glass coffins, silently warding Llyr against threats and, according to some, waiting for the country's bleakest moment to rise again and protect their homeland. It was either provincial superstition or gospel truth, depending on who you asked.

Ever since Myrddin had been laid to rest, just before the start of her term, tickets had been sold out and lines for the museum wrapped around the block. Effy had tried three times to visit, waiting for hours only to be turned away at the ticket booth. So she had simply had to imagine how the Storytellers would look, penciling in the features of their slumbering faces. She had taken extra care with Myrddin's. Even in death, he appeared wise and gentle, the way she thought a father would.

But now, while Parri's voice rolled ceaselessly over her like low tide against the shoreline, Effy opened her sketchbook to a new page and penciled in the words *HIRAETH MANOR*.

After studio, Effy went to the library. She had turned in only one of her cross sections, and it wasn't very good. The elevation was all wrong—lopsided, as if the museum were built on a craggy cliffside instead of the meticulously landscaped center of Caer-Isel. The university buildings curled around it like a conch shell, all pale marble and sun-blanched yellow stone.

She never would have dreamed of turning in such shoddy work at her secondary school back home. But in the six weeks since she had started university, so much had changed. If she had come to Caer-Isel with hope, or passion, or even just petty competitiveness, it had all eroded quickly. Time felt both compressed and infinite. It rolled over her, like she was a sunken statue on the seafloor, but it tossed and thrashed her, too, a limp body in the waves.

Yet now the words *Hiraeth Manor* snagged in her mind like a fishhook, propelling her toward some purpose, some goal, even if it was hazy. Maybe especially because it was hazy. Bereft of vexing practical details, it was much easier to imagine that the goal was within her reach.

The library was no more than five minutes from the architecture college, but the wind off Lake Bala lashing her cheeks and running its frigid fingers through her hair made it feel longer. She pushed through the double doors in a hurry, exhaling a cold breath. Then she was inside, and the sudden, dense silence overwhelmed her.

On her first day at the university—the day before Master Corbenic—Effy had visited the library and loved it. She had smuggled in a cup of coffee and found her way to one of the disused rooms on the sixth floor. Even the elevator had seemed exhausted by the time it reached the landing, groaning and heaving and giving a rattle that sounded like small bones being shaken inside a collector's box.

The sixth floor housed the most ancient books on the most obscure subjects: tomes on the history of Llyr's selkie-hunting industry (a surprisingly lucrative field, Effy had discovered, before the selkies were hunted to extinction). A field guide to Argantian fungi, with a several-page-long footnote on how to distinguish Argantian truffles from the much-superior Llyrian varieties. An account of one of Llyr and Argant's many wars, told from the perspective of a sentient rifle.

Effy had folded herself into the most concealed alcove she could find, under a rain-marbled window, and read those arcane books. She had looked particularly for books on fairies, and spent hours thumbing through a tome about fairy rings outside Oxwich, and then another long-dead professor's ethnography on the Fair Folk he encountered there. Such accounts, centuries old, were written off by the university as Southern superstition. The books she had found had been spitefully shelved under *Fiction*.

But Effy believed them. She believed them all: the rote academic accounts, the superstitious Southern folklore, the epic poetry that warned against the wiles of the Fairy King. If only she could have studied literature, she would have written her own ferocious treatises in support of her belief. Being trapped in the architecture college felt like being muted, muzzled.

Yet now, standing in the lobby, the library was suddenly a terrifying place. The solitude that had once comforted her had become an enormous empty space where so many bad things could happen.

She did not know *what*, exactly—it was only a roiling, imprecise dread. The silence was a span of time before inevitable disaster, like watching a glass teeter farther toward the edge of a table, anticipating the moment it would tip and shatter. She did not entirely understand why the things that had once been familiar now felt hostile and strange.

She didn't intend to linger there today. Effy made her way up the vast marble stairs, her footsteps echoing faintly. The arched ceilings and the fretwork of wood across them made her feel as if she were inside a very elaborate antique jewelry box. Dust motes swam in columns of golden light.

She reached the horseshoe-shaped circulation desk and placed two hands flat on the varnished wood. The woman behind the desk looked at her disinterestedly.

"Good morning," Effy said, with the brightest smile she could muster. *Morning* was generous. It was two fifteen. But she'd only been awake for three hours, just long enough to throw on clothes and make it to her studio class.

"What are you looking for today?" the woman asked, unmoved.

"Do you have any books on Emrys Myrddin?"

The woman's expression shifted, her eyes pinching with disdain. "You'll have to be more specific than that. Fiction, nonfiction, biography, theory—"

"Nonfiction," Effy cut in quickly. "Anything about his life, his family." Hoping to endear herself to the librarian, she added, "I have all his novels and poetry already. He's my favorite author."

"You and half the university," the woman said dismissively. "Wait here."

She vanished through a doorway behind the circulation desk. Effy's nose itched at the smell of old paper and mildew. From the adjacent rooms she could hear the flutter of pages being turned and the slowly scything blades of the ceiling fans.

"Hey," someone said.

It was the boy from the college lobby, the one who'd come up behind her to see the poster. His tweed jacket was under his arm now, suspenders pulled taut over a white shirt.

"Hi," she said. It was more of a reflex than anything. The word sounded odd in all that quiet, empty space. She snatched her hands off the circulation desk.

"You're in the architecture college, right," he said, but it didn't have the tenor of a question.

"Yes," she said hesitantly.

"So am I. Are you going to send in a proposal? For the Hiraeth Manor project?"

"I think so." She suddenly had the very strange sensation that she was underwater. It had been happening to her more and more often lately. "Are you?"

"I think so. We could work on it together, you know." The boy's hand curled around the edge of the circulation desk, the intensity of his grip turning his knuckles white. "I mean, send in a joint proposal. There's nothing in the rules that says otherwise. Together we'd have a better chance at winning the contract. It would make us famous. We'd get scooped up by the most prestigious architectural firms in Llyr the second we graduate."

The memory of his whispered slur hummed in the back of her mind, quiet but insistent. "I'm not sure. I think I already know what I'm going to do. I spent all of studio class sketching it." She gave a soft laugh, hoping to smother the sting of the rejection.

The boy didn't laugh, or even smile back. For a long moment, silence stretched between them.

When he spoke again, his voice was low. "You're so pretty. You really are. You're the most gorgeous girl I've ever seen. Do you know that?"

If she said *yes, I do,* she was a conceited harpy. If she shook her head and rebuffed the compliment, she was falsely modest, playing coy. It was fae-like trickery. There was no answer that wouldn't damn her.

So she said, fumbling, "Maybe you can help me with the cross sections for Parri's studio. Mine are really bad."

The boy brightened, drawing himself up to his full height. "Sure," he said. "Let me give you my number."

Effy pulled the pen out of her bag and offered it to him. He clasped his fingers around her wrist and wrote out seven digits on the back of her hand. That same rainwater rush of white noise drowned out everything again, even the scything of the fans.

The door behind the circulation desk opened and the woman came back through. The boy let go of her.

"All right," he said. "Call me when you want to work on your cross sections."

"I will."

Effy waited until he had vanished down the stairs to turn back to the librarian. Her hand felt numb.

"I'm sorry," the librarian said. "Someone has taken out everything on Myrddin."

She couldn't help the high pitch of her voice when she echoed, "*Everything?*"

"Looks like it. I'm not surprised. He's a popular thesis subject. Since he only just died, there's a lot of fertile ground. Untapped potential. All the literature students are clamoring to be the first to write the narrative of his life."

Her stomach lurched. "So a literature student checked them out?"

The librarian nodded. She reached under the desk and pulled out the logbook, each row and column filled out with book titles and borrowers' names. She flipped open a page that listed a series of biographical titles and works of reception. Under the *Borrower* column was the same name, inked over and over again in cramped but precise handwriting: *P. Héloury.*

An *Argantian* name. Effy felt like she'd been struck.

"Well, thank you for your help," she said, her voice suddenly thick with a knot of incoming tears. She pressed her fingernails into her palm. She couldn't cry here. She wasn't a child any longer.

"Of course," said the librarian. "I'll give you a call when we get the books back in."

Outside, Effy rubbed at her eyes until they stopped welling. It was so unfair. Of course a literature student had gotten to the books first. They spent their days agonizing over every stanza of Myrddin's famous poetry, over every line of his most famous novel, *Angharad*. They got to do every day what Effy had time for only at night, after she'd finished her slapdash architecture assignments. Under her covers, in a pale puddle of lamplight, she pored over her tattered copy of *Angharad*, which lay permanently on her nightstand. She knew every crack in its spine, every crease on the pages inside.

And an *Argantian*. She couldn't fathom how there even *was* one at the literature college, which was the university's most prestigious, and especially one who was studying Myrddin. He was *Llyr*'s national author. The whole thing seemed like a terrible knife-twist of fate, a personal and spiteful slap in the face. The name in its precise writing hovered in the forefront of her mind: *P. Héloury.*

Why had she even thought this might work? Effy was no great architect; she was only six weeks into her first semester at the university and already in danger of failing two classes. Three, if she didn't turn in those cross sections. Her mother would tell her not to waste her time. *Just focus on your studies,* she would say. *Your friends. Don't run yourself ragged chasing something beyond your reach.* She wouldn't mean it to be cruel.

Your studies, her mother's imagined voice echoed, and Effy thought of Master Parri's disdainful glare. He had held up her one cross section and shaken it at her until the page rippled, like she was an insect he was trying to swat.

Your friends. Effy looked down at the number on the back of her hand. The boy's 0s and 8s were bulging and fat, as if he had been trying to cover as much of her skin as he could in the blue ink. All of a sudden, she felt very sick.

Someone shouldered roughly past her, and Effy realized she had been blocking the doorway to the library. Blinking, embarrassed, she hurried down the steps and crossed to the other side of the street, darting between two rumbling black cars. There was a small pier that overlooked Lake Bala. She leaned over the railing and rubbed at the third knuckle of her left hand like a worry stone. It ended there, abruptly, in a shiny mass of scar tissue. If the boy had noticed the absence of her ring finger, he hadn't said anything about it.

Pedestrians brushed past her. Other students with leather satchels on their way to class, unlit cigarettes hanging out of their mouths. Tourists with their wide-lensed cameras moving in an awkward, halting mass toward the Sleeper Museum. Their odd accent drifted toward her. They had to be from the southernmost region of Llyr, the Bottom Hundred.

Beneath her the waves of Lake Bala lapped timidly at the stone pier. White foam frothed like spittle in a dog's mouth. Effy sensed a dangerous frustration under the meekness of the tide, something fettered that wanted to be free. A storm could come on as quickly as an eyeblink. The rain would cause a sudden bloom of black umbrellas to rise up like mushrooms, and it would wash all the tourists out of the street.

Just faintly, through the ever-present rheum of fog, Effy could glimpse the other side of the lake, and the green land that lay there. Argant, Llyr's belligerent northern neighbor. She used to think the problem was that Argantians and Llyrians were too intractably different, and that was why they couldn't stop going to war and hating each other. Now, after living in the divided city for six weeks, she understood that it was the opposite problem. Argant was always claiming that Llyrian treasures and traditions were really their own. Llyr was forever accusing Argant of stealing their heroes and histories. The appointment of national authors, who would eventually become Sleepers, was a Llyrian effort to create something Argant couldn't take.

It was an archaic tradition, but dutifully followed, even if most Northerners didn't believe what Southern superstition said: that when Llyr's tanks rolled across that green land, when their rifles peeked up from the trenches they had dug into Argantian soil, it was the magic of the Sleepers that protected them. That when Argantian guns jammed or an out-of-season fog crept across the battlefield, that was Sleeper magic, too.

For the past several years, the war had been at a standstill. Occasionally the sky rumbled with the sound of distant gunfire, but it could easily be mistaken for thunder. The inhabitants of Caer-Isel, Effy included, had learned to treat it like the white noise of traffic, vexing but unavoidable. With Myrddin's consecration as a Sleeper, she hoped the odds might turn in Llyr's favor.

She had no choice but to believe in the Sleeper magic, in Myrddin's magic. It was the foundation her life was built upon. Though she had read *Angharad* for the first time at thirteen, she had been dreaming of the Fairy King long before that.

A spray of salt water kissed her cheeks. To hell with that

literature student, that Argantian, P. Héloury. To hell with Parri and those terrible cross sections. She was tired, tired of trying so hard for something she didn't even want. She was tired of being afraid she might see Master Corbenic in the hall or the college lobby. She was tired of the memories that swam behind her eyelids at night, those little pieces: the enormous span of his fingers, knuckles whitening as his fist clenched and unclenched.

Effy stood up and retied her hair. Overhead the sky had turned the color of iron, clouds swollen with ominous fury. The tram clanged down the street, louder than the nearing thunder—real thunder this time, not gunfire. She buttoned her jacket and hurried toward her dorm as the rain started to fall.

She staggered into her dormitory damp-haired, water dripping off her lashes and pooling in her boots. Effy yanked them off and hurled them down the hallway, where they landed with two empty thuds. Of course today would end with her getting caught in one of Caer-Isel's miserable autumn downpours, despite rushing to escape the rain.

Having exhausted a bit of her jilted fury, Effy hung up her jacket more calmly and squeezed out her hair.

The door to her roommate's bedroom creaked hesitantly open. "Effy?"

"Sorry," she said, a flush creeping up her neck. Her boots were still slumped at the end of the hallway. "I didn't know you were home."

"It's all right. Maisie is here, too."

Effy nodded, and went to retrieve her boots with a numb sort of embarrassment. Rhia watched from the doorway, dark curls askew, her white blouse buttoned haphazardly. Not for the first time, Effy had interrupted something private between Rhia and her paramour, which made the situation all the more humiliating.

"Are you okay?" Rhia asked. "It's wretched outside."

"I'm fine. I just didn't have an umbrella. And I also might be failing three classes."

"I see." Rhia pursed her lips. "It sounds like you could use a drink. What's that on your hand?"

Effy looked down. The rain had made the blue ink run all the way down her wrist. "Oh," she said. "I was mauled by a giant squid."

"Terrifying. If you towel yourself off, you can come in and have some tea."

Effy managed a grateful smile and went into the bathroom. Everyone had told her the university dorm rooms were disgusting, but when she arrived, she'd thought of it as sort of an adventure, like camping in the woods. Now it was just boringly, inanely gross. The grout between the tiles was filthy, and there was a sickly orange ring of soap scum around the edge of the tub. When she yanked her towel off the rack, she saw a preternaturally huge spider scuttle away and disappear into a crack in the wall. She didn't even have the energy to scream.

When she stepped back into the hallway, drier, Rhia's door was flung open, her room filled with soft yellow lamplight. Maisie was perched on the edge of the bed, steaming mug in hand, auburn hair swept up into a hasty bun.

"I saw Watson in there," Effy said, collapsing into Rhia's desk chair.

"No, I squished Watson, remember? That's Harold."

"Right," Effy said. "Watson went out in a blaze of glory." The black mess of him had taken ten minutes to scrub off the bathroom wall.

As Rhia filled Effy's mug, Maisie asked, "How come all the spiders are men?"

"Because then it feels more satisfying to squish them," Rhia said, flopping down beside her on the bed. Seeing her curled around Maisie like that, with such casual intimacy, Effy had the sudden sensation of being an intruder.

It was an eternal feeling, this sense of being unwelcome. No matter where she was, Effy was always afraid she was not wanted. She took a sip of tea. The warmth helped ease some of her discomfort.

"So I think I'm failing three classes," she said. "And it's only midautumn."

"It's a good thing that it's only midautumn," Maisie said. "You have lots of time to make it up."

Rhia played absently with a strand of Maisie's hair. "Or you could just quit. Come join us in the music college. The orchestra needs more flutists."

"If you can teach me to play the flute in the next week, consider it a deal."

She didn't say that frustrating as it was, architecture felt less like giving up than music would. The architecture college was the second-most prestigious at the university. If she couldn't study literature like she wanted, at least she could pretend architecture had been her first choice all along.

"Not sure that's entirely realistic, my love," Maisie said. She turned to Effy. "So what *are* you going to do?"

Effy almost told them about the poster. About Emrys Myrddin and Hiraeth Manor and the fresh drawing in her sketchpad. Rhia was impulsive and always full of wild ideas, including but not limited to *I'll teach you to play flute in a week* and *let's sneak up to the rooftop of the astronomy college*, but Maisie was almost annoyingly reasonable. She would have told Effy it was a mad thing to even consider.

Right now the possibility of Hiraeth Manor, the dream, belonged to her and her alone. Even if it was inevitable that it would come crashing down, she wanted to keep dreaming it a little while longer.

So in the end she just shrugged, and let Rhia try to talk her into taking up the organ instead. Effy finished her tea and said good night to the other girls. But when she got back to her room, she did not have the remotest desire to sleep. The itch of frustration and yearning under her skin wouldn't fade.

She sat on her unmade bed and picked up her battered copy of *Angharad* instead.

Angharad was Myrddin's most famous work. It was the story of a young girl who became the Fairy King's bride. The Fair Folk were vicious, shrewd, and always wanting. Humans were playthings to them, amusing in their petty, fragile mortality. The Fair Folk's glamours made them appear hypnotically beautiful, like a gaudily patterned snake with a deadly bite. They used their enchantments to make humans play the fiddle until their fingers fell off or dance until their feet bled. Yet Effy found herself half in love with the Fairy King sometimes, too. The tender belly of his cruelty made her heart flutter. There was an intimacy to all violence, she supposed. The better you knew someone, the more terribly you could hurt them.

In the book, the protagonist had her tricks to evade and ensorcell the Fairy King: bread and salt, silver bells, mountain ash, a girdle of iron. Effy had her sleeping pills. She could swallow one, sometimes two, and fade into a dreamless slumber.

She turned to the back flap of the book, where Myrddin's author photo and biography were printed. He had been a hermit and a recluse, especially in the last few years before his death. The newspaper articles written about him were stiff and formal, and he had famously refused all interviews. The black-and-white photo was grainy and taken at a great distance, showing only Myrddin's profile. He was standing at a window, his silhouette dark, face turned away from the camera. As far as Effy knew, it was the only photo of Myrddin in existence.

Any house that honored Myrddin would have to be similarly mystifying. Was there any other student at the architecture college who understood that? Who knew his works back to front? Effy doubted it. The rest of them just wanted the prestige, the prize money, like the boy in the library. None of them cared that it was *Myrddin*. None of them believed in the old magic.

Her sleeping pills lay untouched on the dresser that night. Instead, Effy pulled out her sketchpad and drew until dawn.

TWO

Storytelling is an art deserving of greatest reverence, and storytellers ought to be considered guardians of Llyrian cultural heritage. As such, the literature college will be the most exclusive of the university's undergraduate programs, requiring the highest exam scores and fulfillment of the most stringent requirements. Pursuant to that, it would be inappropriate to admit women, who have not, as a sex, demonstrated great strength in the faculties of literary analysis or understanding.

FROM A MISSIVE BY SION BILLOWS UPON THE FOUNDING

OF THE UNIVERSITY OF LLYR, 680 BD

"So you're really going," Rhia said.

Effy nodded, swallowing a burning sip of coffee. All around them, other students had their heads bent over their books, pens gripped in ink-stained hands, lips bitten in concentration. There was the grind and hum of the coffee machine and the sound of dishes clinking as tarts and scones were served. The Drowsy Poet was the favorite café of students in Caer-Isel, and it was a mere block away from the Sleeper Museum.

"I'm not trying to rain on your parade—or, Saints forbid,

sound like Maisie—but don't you think it's all a bit odd? I mean, why would they pick a first-year architecture student for such an enormous project?"

Effy reached down into her purse and pulled out a folded sheet of paper. Maneuvering around her coffee cup and Rhia's half-eaten pastry, she smoothed it flat on the table, then waited as Rhia craned her neck to read what was written in neat, dark ink.

Dear Ms. Sayre,

I am writing to congratulate you on the selection of your proposal for the design of Hiraeth Manor. I received a great many submissions, but yours was far and away the one I felt best honored my father's legacy.

I happily invite you to Saltney, to speak with you in person about your design. By the end of your stay, I would hope to have a set of finalized blueprints so we can break ground on the project swiftly.

To get to Hiraeth, please board the earliest train from Caer-Isel to Laleston, and then switch to the train bound for Saltney. I apologize in advance for the long and arduous journey. I will have my barrister, Mr. Wetherell, pick you up at the station.

With greatest enthusiasm,
Ianto Myrddin

As soon as Rhia looked up from the letter, Effy said in a rush, "I've already shown it to Dean Fogg. He's allowing me the next six weeks to go to Saltney and work on the house. *And* he's making

Master Parri count it as my studio credit." She tried to sound smug, though mostly she felt relieved. She wished she had been there to see Master Parri pinch his nose as Dean Fogg delivered the news.

"Well," Rhia said after a moment, "I suppose that sounds legitimate enough. But the Bottom Hundred . . . it's quite different from here, you know."

"I know. I bought a new raincoat and a dozen new sweaters."

"Not like that," Rhia said, with a faint smile. "I mean—back home, every single person believes the Sleepers are what's stopping Argant from just bombing all of Llyr to bits. Saints, my parents were convinced that there was going to be a second Drowning, before Myrddin was consecrated. Here no one believes in the Sleepers at all."

But I do. Effy kept the thought to herself. Rhia was a Southerner, and often spoke with disdain about her tiny hometown and its deeply religious people. Effy didn't feel right trying to debate her—and she didn't want to confess her own beliefs, either. That sort of superstition didn't suit a good Northern girl from a good Northern family at the second-most prestigious college in Llyr.

So Effy kept her true thoughts to herself, and instead said, "I understand. But I won't be there for long. And I promise not to come back smelling of brine."

"Oh, you're going to come back half a fish," Rhia said. "Trust me."

"Which half?"

"The bottom half," she said, after a moment's consideration.

"Think of how much money I'll save on shoes."

The library was blessedly empty, probably due in part to the cold. Mist rolled down from Argant's green hills and hung about Caer-Isel like a horde of ghosts. The university's bell tower wore its fog as if it were a widow's mourning veil. Students stopped smoking underneath the library portico because they were afraid of getting impaled by hanging icicles. Every morning the statue of the university's founder, Sion Billows, was caulked in a layer of new frost.

Effy had never gotten a call from the librarian about the books on Myrddin. Whoever P. Héloury was, clearly he was not relinquishing them anytime soon. The knowledge had eaten at her for three weeks, a low, simmering anger in the bottom of her belly. She practiced arguments with him in her mind, imagined scenarios where she emerged from these verbal spars preening and victorious. But none of that really eased any of her fury.

Today, though, Effy was at the library for a different reason. She took the elevator up to the geography section on the third floor. The room was crammed with a labyrinth of bookcases, which created many dusty, occulted corners. She pulled down a large atlas from a shelf and found herself one of those corners, right beneath an ice-speckled window.

She opened the book to a map of the island. There was the river Naer, which cut straight through it vertically, like the blue vein on the back of her hand. There was Caer-Isel, of course—with a footnote reminding her of the city's Argantian name, Ker-Is—a large piece of flotsam in the center of Lake Bala.

The official border between Llyr and Argant was a large steel fence, topped with coils of barbed wire. It gashed through the center of the city, almost right through the Sleeper Museum. Effy had gone to see it during her first week at the university, and the stark authoritativeness had stunned her. A number of gray-clad security guards were stationed along the fence, unsmiling under their fur hats. She had watched as a small group—a family—came up from the Argantian side and began the long process of unfolding papers and passports, the guards' movements brisk and the children's faces growing redder as they stood out in the cold. Above them, the two flags warred with one another, and with the wind: the black serpent on a green field for Argant, and the red serpent on a white field for Llyr. After a while, it had become too difficult to watch, and Effy had left in a hurry, feeling an odd sense of shame.

Her finger traveled down the map. Northern Llyr was verdant hills, a patchwork of sunlight and mist, pocked with squat trees and stone houses, small towns with narrow streets, and the largest city, Draefen. It was the administrative capital of Llyr, and the site of her family's townhouse, where Effy had grown up with her mother and grandparents. Draefen sat snugly in a valley between two mountain peaks, spanning both sides of the Naer. The sky was clouds and factory smog, and the line of the horizon was cut up with the crests of white sails, like the fins of lake monsters that no one from the North believed in anymore. She had thought seeing it, even as just a sketch on parchment, might make her feel homesick, but mostly she remembered the smells of oil and salt and fish guts. Effy's eyes moved past it quickly.

And then, south of Draefen, south of Laleston, the last town that anyone with good sense had reason to visit, was the Bottom Hundred. The southernmost hundred miles of Llyr were all ragged coastline and fishing villages, crumbling white cliffs and brusque, ugly beaches with pebbles that cut right through your boots. Even the illustration seemed hurried, as if the artist had wanted to be done with it and move on to something better.

The Bay of Nine Bells looked like the bite a dog had taken out of a rotted old piece of meat. Effy brushed her thumb along it, tracing the serrated outline of the cove. And Emrys Myrddin was from *here*, the very bottom of the Bottom Hundred, a place so dismal and remote, Effy could scarcely even hold it in her mind. It was so different, it might as well have been another country, she thought. Another world.

The sound of the door creaking open made Effy jump. She peered out from behind the bookcase and saw another student enter the room, peacoat held under his arm, still breathing hard from the cold. He put down his coat and satchel on one of the tables and moved toward her, and a chill shot up her spine. The idea of him coming upon her, tucked on the floor in her corner, was both embarrassing and strangely terrifying. Effy stood up and tried to move quietly out of sight, but he saw her anyway.

"Hey," he said. His voice sounded friendly enough.

"Hi," she said back slowly.

"Sorry—you don't have to leave. There's enough room here for the two of us, I think." He smiled, showing just the faintest edge of his teeth.

"That's all right," she said. "I was leaving anyway."

Effy tried to move past him, to return the atlas to its place on the shelf, but the boy didn't step aside to accommodate her until the very last second, so their arms brushed. Her heart jumped into her throat. *Stupid,* she chided herself immediately. *He hasn't done anything wrong.* Still—the air in the room suddenly felt solid and thick. She had to get out.

Then her eye caught the patch on his jacket. It was the insignia of the literature college.

"Oh!" she said, abruptly and too loudly. "You study literature?"

"Yes." The boy met her gaze. "I'm a first-year. Why?"

"I was just wondering . . ." She hesitated. She was sure the request would seem odd. But the morbid, bitter curiosity had pricked at her for so long. "Do you know any Argantian students in your college?"

He frowned. "I don't think so. Well, maybe a couple, in their second or third years. But it's not common. I'm sure you can imagine why. I mean, how many Argantians want to study Llyrian literature?"

Her question exactly. "So you don't know any of them by name?"

"No. Sorry."

Effy tried not to look visibly disappointed. She knew it was childish to make P. Héloury the avatar of all her bitterness. But it was just so wretchedly unfair. Argant had been Llyr's enemy for centuries. Why was it that an Argantian could study Llyrian literature, just because he was a man, but she couldn't because she was a girl? Why didn't it matter that she knew Myrddin's books back to

26

front, that she'd spent almost half her life sleeping with *Angharad* on her bedside table? That once she'd tried to fashion a girdle of iron for herself and laid boughs of mountain ash at the threshold of her room?

"That's all right," she said, but the chagrin crept into her voice anyway. The boy was looking at her with bewilderment, so she felt the need to explain. "It's just, I was trying to take out some books on Myrddin—"

"Oh," he cut in. "You're one of Myrddin's devotees."

His tone was disparaging. Effy's face warmed. "I like his work. A lot of people do."

"Lots of girls." An expression she couldn't quite read came over his face. He looked her up and down. "Listen, if you ever want to pick my brain about Myrddin, or anything else—"

Her stomach lurched. "Sorry," she said. "I really have to go."

The boy opened his mouth to reply, but Effy didn't wait to hear it. She just dropped the atlas on the table and hurried out of the room, blood roaring in her ears. It was only once she'd made it down the elevator, out through the library's double doors, and back into the biting cold that she felt she could breathe again. That same inner voice told her she was being childish, absurd. Just a few words, a narrow-eyed look, and she'd reacted as if someone had jabbed her with a knife.

Her vision was blurry for the entire trek back to her dorm. Rhia wasn't home, and her own room was nearly empty, everything packed away in the trunk that she would take with her to Saltney. The only thing left out was her copy of *Angharad*, dog-eared at the page where the Fairy King bedded Angharad for the first time. Beside it, her glass bottle of sleeping pills.

She poured one out and swallowed it dry. If she didn't, she knew she would dream about the Fairy King that night.

There remained one thing to do.

The door to her adviser's office seemed wider and taller than the rest of the doors on the hall, like one of the ornamental letters on an old manuscript, embellished and baroque and huge compared to the small, ordinary text that followed.

Effy raised a hand and laid it flat on the wood. She had meant to knock, but somewhere along the way her body had given up her mind's goal.

It didn't matter. From the other side there was a shuffling sound, a muttered curse, and then the door swung open.

A blinking Master Corbenic stared down at her. "Effy."

"Can I come in?"

He nodded once, stiffly, then stepped aside to let her through. His office was how she remembered it: so cluttered with books that there was only a narrow path from the door to the desk, dusty shutters pulled down so that only a knife of light squeezed through. Framed degrees lined the wall like taxidermy animal heads.

"Please," he said, "sit down."

Effy stood behind the green armchair instead. "I'm sorry I didn't make an appointment. I'm just . . ." She trailed off, hating the smallness of her voice. Master Corbenic's sleeves were rolled up to his elbows, exposing the swathes of dark arm hair and the golden watch glinting within it.

"It's not a problem," he said, though his words had a chill to them that made Effy want to shrink down and vanish through that tiny gap in the shutters. "I figured you would come back sooner or later. I heard about your little project."

"Oh." Her stomach knotted. "I suppose Dean Fogg told you."

"Yes. He's speaking to me again, miraculously." Master Corbenic's voice had grown even colder. "Saltney is a long way from the big city."

"That's what I wanted to talk to you about." She picked at the loose fibers on the back of the armchair. "Dean Fogg said I could have six weeks starting with the winter holidays, and he made Master Parri agree to count it as my studio credit, but I still—"

"He wanted your adviser to sign off on it," he finished tonelessly. His fingers, crumpling the white fabric of his shirt, looked enormous.

She drew a breath, steadying herself against the armchair. She had pulled out so much of the green thread that it looked like she was clutching a tangle of vines. But the armchair had been in tatters since the first time she saw it. At the beginning of the semester, whenever Effy came back from Master Corbenic's office, for hours she would find these small green threads caught in her hair.

Slowly, she reached into her pocket and took out the folded parchment. "I just need your signature."

There. She had said it. Immediately her chest felt lighter. The grandfather clock in the corner ticked past the seconds, each one plinking down like a droplet of rainwater on the floor. Her hand shook as she held the paper out to him, and for a while he said nothing, did nothing, until all of a sudden he lurched forward.

29

Effy took a stumbling, instinctual step back as he grabbed the paper from her hand.

Master Corbenic gave a low, short laugh. "Oh, for Saints' sakes. There's no need to act like a blushing little maiden now."

Her pulse was so loud and fast that she scarcely heard herself say, "You're still my adviser—"

"Yes, and isn't that a wonder—I was sure Dean Fogg would have dismissed you, or had me sacked."

"I didn't tell anyone," she managed, her face burning.

"Well, word still got around, didn't it?" Master Corbenic said, though he deflated visibly, leaning back against his desk. He ran one enormous hand through his black hair. "I met with Dean Fogg last week. He was apoplectic. This could have cost me my career."

"I know."

She knew it so well, it was all she had thought about, when he stood over her in that armchair. When he palmed the back of her head, when the weak sunlight glanced off his belt buckle, all Effy had been able to think about was how dangerous it all was. Master Corbenic was young, handsome, a darling of the faculty. He and Dean Fogg took tea together. He didn't *need* her.

But oh, he had made it seem like he did. "You're so pretty," he had said, and had sounded almost breathless. "It's agony to watch you come in here every week, with your green eyes and your golden hair. When you leave, all I can think about is when you'll come back, and how I'll survive seeing something so beautiful I can't touch."

He had held her face in his hands with as much tenderness as a museum curator would handle his artifacts. And Effy had felt her heart skip and flutter the same way it did when she read her favorite bits of *Angharad*, those permanently dog-eared pages.

"Is this all you need from me?" Master Corbenic slashed his pen across the page and thrust the parchment back to her, then huffed a lower, shorter laugh. "You know what I think, Effy. You're a bright girl. You have potential, if you keep your head out of the clouds. But a first-year student, taking on a project of this scale? It's beyond you. I can't fathom why the Myrddin estate would put out a call for students in the first place. And—I assume you've never been south of Laleston before?"

Effy shook her head.

"Well. The Bottom Hundred is the sort of place that young girls escape from, not go running off to. It would be easier to just stay here in Caer-Isel and try to get your grades up. If you need tutoring in Master Parri's class, I can help you."

"No," Effy said quickly, pocketing the parchment. "That's all right."

Master Corbenic stared at her inscrutably, the late-afternoon sunlight pooling on the face of his wristwatch. "You're the sort of girl who likes to make life more difficult for herself. If you weren't so pretty, you would have failed out already."

Effy left Master Corbenic's office with her eyes stinging, but she refused to cry. On her way back through the college lobby, she saw the class roster, her last name crossed out and replaced with *whore*.

After checking to make sure no one was coming, Effy tore the paper down, balled it up, and carried it out of the building. Her heart was pounding. *The Bottom Hundred is the sort of place that young girls escape from, not go running off to.* Perhaps she was running away. Perhaps she was making life more difficult for herself. But she couldn't bear it, the rush of floodwater in her ears, the haze that fell over her eyes, the nightmares smothered only by the annihilating power of her sleeping pills. She wasn't a Southerner, but she knew what it was like to drown.

She walked past the library and out onto the pier. She stood there, leaning over the railing, wind biting her cheeks, and then she threw the crumpled paper into the ice-choked waters of Lake Bala.

THREE

What is a mermaid but a woman half-drowned,
What a selkie but an unwilling wife,
What a tale but a sea-net, snatching up both
From the gentle tumult of dark waves?

FROM "ELEGY FOR A SIREN," COLLECTED IN *THE POETICAL WORKS OF EMRYS MYRDDIN*, 196–208 AD

Effy tucked her copy of *Angharad* into her purse. Her trunk was packed full of trousers and her new turtleneck sweaters and warm woolen socks. Rhia went with her to the train station.

"Are you sure I can't convince you not to do this?" Rhia asked.

Effy shook her head. Passengers milled past them in blurs of gray and tawny. Rhia was generous and open-minded and clever, and kind enough to never mention the rumors about Effy and Master Corbenic.

But she didn't know about the pink pills, the ones Effy kept at her side always, in case the edges of things started to blur. She didn't know about the Fairy King and had never read a single page of *Angharad*. She didn't understand what Myrddin meant to Effy, and she didn't understand what Effy was escaping from. Rhia was a Southerner—but *she* didn't know what it was like to drown.

A woman in a blue cloche shoved by and stepped on Effy's foot. "I'll miss you. Tell Maisie she can have my room."

"I will." Rhia chewed her lip, then managed one of her incandescently bright smiles as the train sang like a teakettle behind them. "Be safe. Be smart. Be sweet."

"All three? That's a lot to ask."

"I'll settle for just two, then. Your pick," Rhia said. She reached around Effy to embrace her, and for a moment, with her eyes shut and her face pressed into Rhia's fluffy brown hair, Effy felt calmer than the windless sea.

"That's far more reasonable," Effy mumbled. They broke apart as a mother trailing two ornery-looking children shouldered past them. "Thank you."

Rhia frowned. "What for?"

Effy didn't reply. She didn't really know. She was just grateful not to be standing on the platform alone.

The other passengers were breathing in clouds of white, belts and wallet chains jangling, high heels striking the tiled floor with a tinny sound. Effy dragged her trunk on board and watched from the window as the train pulled out of the station. She didn't look away until Rhia, waving, vanished into the crowd.

She'd meant to work on the train; she'd even brought her sketchpad and pen in her purse. But as soon as the train started down the bridge that led south over Lake Bala, her mind filled with a vague yet obliterating dread. The blank white page of her sketchpad and the bright midmorning light glancing off the lake made her eyes water. The woman sitting next to her crossed and recrossed her legs over and over again, and the sound of silk hissing against leather was so distracting, Effy couldn't think of anything else.

Northern Llyr spooled past her, emerald green in the winter. When she had to switch trains in Laleston, she shuffled off and crossed the platform in a haze, dragging her trunk behind her. Though she couldn't see outside, the air felt humid and thick, and there was rainwater trickling down the windows.

They arrived in Saltney just as the clock ticked past five. In Caer-Isel, even in winter, the sun would have still been holding stubbornly to the line of the horizon. In Saltney, the sky was a dense and dusky black, storm clouds roiling like steam in a pot.

As the last few passengers disembarked, Effy stood in a rheumy puddle of lamplight, staring down the dark and empty road. She didn't know where to go.

Her mind felt cloudy. Even though she'd read Ianto's letter so many times, now she couldn't remember the name of his barrister, who was supposed to pick her up at the station—Wheathall? Weathergill? No one had given her a number to call. And as she peered down the dimly lit street, there were no cars in sight.

There was only a row of small, dingy buildings, their doors and windows as black as mounds of dirt. Farther down, she could see a cluster of thatched-roof houses, rising out of the stubbly grass like broken teeth. There was the faint, distant sound of water breaking on rocks.

The wind picked up, and it seemed to blow right through Effy's coat and thick woolen sweater, lashing her hair around her face. She could taste the sea salt in it, grit gathering on her bottom lip. She squeezed her eyes shut, but a tremendous pain was sharpening in the center of her forehead, right between her brows.

There was only the wind and the cold and the dark, stretching out all around her, solid and endless. There would be no other trains before morning, and what would she do until then? Maybe no one was coming at all. Perhaps the whole project had been a farce, a joke played at a naive first-year's expense.

Or, worse: a ruse to lure a young girl to a faraway and dangerous place she'd never come back from.

Everyone had said there was something *off* about the whole affair. Something strange. Rhia had warned her; even Master Corbenic had warned her. And yet she had flung herself toward it like a sparrow against a windowpane, oblivious to the sheen of glass.

A panicked sob rose in her throat. Through the glaze of unshed tears, she could see a rectangular blur in the distance. She shuffled closer and it took shape: a telephone booth.

Effy picked her trunk back up and dragged it with her into the booth. With shaking fingers, she reached into her pocket and pulled out a few coins, cramming them into the slot.

She hesitated before dialing. One part of her wanted to slam the phone down; the other was desperate just to hear a familiar voice. So she dialed the only number that she knew by heart.

"Hello?"

That familiar voice split through the silence. "Mother?"

"Effy? Is that you? Where are you calling from?"

"I'm in Saltney," she managed thickly. "In the Bottom Hundred."

She could almost see the little pinch of her mother's brow. "Well, what in the name of all Saints are you doing there?"

At that, a strange hollow opened up in Effy's chest. She shouldn't have called.

"There's this project I'm doing," she said. "For the estate of Emrys Myrddin. A bunch of architecture students sent in designs, and they picked mine."

There was a stretch of silence. Effy could almost see her mother curled up in her armchair, one sip of gin still left in her glass. "Well, then why are you crying?"

Effy's throat felt very tight. "I'm at the train station. I don't know if anyone is going to pick me up, and I don't have a number to call . . ."

Her mother drew a quick, sharp breath. And then: the sound of ice clinking as she poured herself a new glass. "You didn't think to get a phone number before you went to some no-name town—what, six hours south of Draefen? I can't listen to this right now, Effy. It's just bad decision after bad decision with you."

"I know." Effy's hand tensed around the receiver. "I'm sorry. Can you ask Grandfather if he can—"

"You can't always expect someone to bail you out," her mother cut in. "I'm not going to ask Grandfather to drive six hours into the Bottom Hundred in the dark. Listen to yourself."

But Effy could only hear the muffled sound of the sea.

"I wouldn't be doing my job as your mother," she went on. "At a certain point I have to let you sink or swim."

Effy's cheeks were slippery with tears. The phone kept almost sliding out of her grip. "I'm sorry. You don't have to wake Grandfather. I just don't know what to do."

"First you have to calm down," her mother said briskly. "I can't talk to you when you're behaving like this. When you're having one of your *episodes*. Are you seeing things?"

"No," Effy said. Outside, the darkness pulsed and seethed.

"Do you have your medication?"

"Yes."

"Then take it. All right? Call me when you've calmed down."

Effy nodded, even though she knew her mother couldn't see. But she held on to the phone until there was a soft click on the other end and her mother's breathing was gone.

She let the phone slide out of her grasp, dangling on its cord. She pried open her purse and dug for the small glass bottle, uncapped it and poured out a single pill. It was the rosy color of an unopened flower bud, dead before it would ever bloom.

Effy clapped a hand over her lips and swallowed it, dry-mouthed.

It took several minutes for the furious drag of her pulse to slow. She'd gone through bottle after bottle of these pills since she was ten years old. It was inside the doctor's office that she'd first learned to call these moments of panic, these slippings, *episodes*.

The doctor had held the bottle of pink pills in one hand and wagged a finger at her with the other, as if he were admonishing her for something she hadn't even done yet.

"You have to be careful with these," he said. "Only take them when you *really* need them. When you start seeing things that aren't real. Do you understand, missy?"

She was ten, and already she'd given up trying to explain that what she saw *was* real, even if no one believed her.

Effy had looked instead at the tuft of silver hair curling out of the doctor's left ear. "I understand."

"Good," he said, and gave her a stiff, clinical pat on the head. Her mother had bundled the pills into her purse. They had left his office, walking into a damp spring morning, and under a flowering pear tree, her mother had stopped to blow her nose into a handkerchief. Allergies, she'd said. But her mother's eyes had been rimmed with red and when they got home, she had shut herself in her room for hours. She didn't want to have a crazy daughter any more than Effy wanted to be one.

Now her surroundings returned to her in pieces: the dark road, the puddle of lamplight, the houses with their shut windows and locked doors. Effy stepped out of the booth, dragging her trunk behind her, and inhaled the salt smell. The rush of waves bathing the rocky shoreline was loud again, oppressive.

She hadn't been outside for more than a minute before a swath of light beamed down the gravel lane. As it grew closer, the single beam of light cleaved in two, and a black car crunched to a halt in front of her.

The driver's-side window rolled down. "Effy Sayre?"

At once she was flooded with a staggering, breathless relief. "Yes?"

"I'm Thomas Wetherell, barrister for the Myrddin estate. I was instructed to pick you up at the station."

"Yes," she said again, the word pluming white in the cold air. "Yes. Thank you."

Wetherell frowned at her. He had slicked-back gray hair and an extremely clean-shaven face. "Let me help you with your trunk."

Once she was inside the car, Effy felt her body go stiff again, her short-lived relief curdling into fear. There were, suddenly, a hundred new worries in her mind. Mainly that she'd made an abysmal first impression.

In the bleary, rain-spattered window, Effy saw a muddled version of herself: nose pink, eyes puffy, cheeks still damp and shiny. She scrubbed at her face with the sleeve of her sweater but only succeeded in reddening her face further. The car clattered down the dark road, and a particularly nasty lurch sent her jolting forward, knees jamming up against the glove box.

Effy bit her lip on a curse. She didn't want Wetherell to think her a squeamish city girl, even though that was exactly what she was.

"How far to Hiraeth?" Effy asked, as they passed Saltney's handful of buildings. A pub, a small church, a fish-and-chip shop—in the Bottom Hundred, that was enough to constitute a town.

Wetherell frowned again. Effy had the sense that she would be seeing that frown quite a lot. "Half an hour, maybe more. Depends on the state of the road."

Effy's stomach churned. And then the car began to slant sharply upward.

Instinctively she grabbed the handle on the door. "Is that normal?"

"Yes," Wetherell said, looking at her with sympathetic disdain, something almost approaching pity. "We're going up the cliffs."

It was only then that she realized Hiraeth Manor would not be in Saltney at all. Even that flyspeck of civilization was nothing she could count on. Effy's heart sank further as the car jostled up the cliffside.

She was almost too afraid to look out the window. The moon seemed to keep pace with the car, painting the road and the moldering cliffs in a pallid light. They were white, ribboned with bands of erosion, grown over with moss and lichen and speckled with salt. They looked beautiful against the black enormity of the sea, its titanic waves striking the pale rock over and over again.

Effy was halfway to admiring them when the car jerked to a halt. In front of it, where the road curled up the cliffside, the road was suddenly awash with foam and dark water. She looked to Wetherell in horror, but he scarcely reacted at all. When the tide receded again, he drove on, tires sloshing through the newly wet dirt.

It was another long moment before Effy found her voice. "Is *that* normal?"

"Yes," Wetherell said. "We usually wait until low tide to drive into town, but the timing of your arrival was . . . unfortunate."

That was putting it mildly. As the car climbed farther up the hill, the roar of the waves grew dimmer, but a thick mist descended, shrouding the trees in white cloaks. The road narrowed, fog closing in on all sides. Effy's throat tightened.

"How much further?" she asked.

"Not very far now."

And then something burst from the tree line and the mist and out in front of the car. Effy saw only a flash of it. There was dark hair, tangled and wet, moving as fluidly as water. Where the head-lights caught it, she also saw a pale yellow curve of bone.

"Mr. Wetherell." She gasped as it disappeared into the mist again. He hadn't even let up on the gas. "What was that?"

If she hadn't just swallowed one of her pills, she wouldn't have asked at all. But Wetherell must have seen it, too. She *couldn't* have imagined it: the pink pills were for obliterating her imagination.

"Most certainly a deer," Wetherell said, in an offhanded way that seemed almost too offhanded. "The deer in the South have developed some peculiar adaptations. Webbed feet and scaled bellies. Biologists have speculated that it's evolutionary preparation for the second Drowning."

But Effy had seen no scales. She had seen a wild knot of hair, a crown of bone. She scrubbed at her face again. What would the doctor have said? Was it possible for two people to have the same hallucination?

The car made a strenuous, halting turn, and the mist seemed to cleave apart in front of it. Wetherell stopped right beside an enormous oak tree. Its branches heaved and bowed with the weight of dangling moss. He reached over and opened the glove box, removing a small flashlight. Wordlessly he clicked it on and stepped out of the car, even though Effy could not see a house rising out of the mist.

She heard him begin to drag out her trunk. Effy opened the door and followed him around to the back of the car. "Are we here?"

"Yes," Wetherell said. He dropped her trunk into the grass, which was so thick that it seemed to swallow the sound. "Just up this hill."

The mist made it difficult to see more than a few steps ahead, but Effy felt the incline in the soles of her feet. She trudged after Wetherell, his flashlight parting the mist. After a few moments of walking in silence, following only the faint outline of Wetherell's back, the fog thinned again. She could see that they were in a small, close circle of trees, the branches overhead knit together so thickly that no sky showed through.

A stout, clumsy shape emerged: a stone cottage with a thatched roof. It was so old that the earth had begun trying to reclaim it—grass was growing over the south-facing side, giving it the appearance of a large head with green hair, and vines were threaded through every crevice in the walls.

Wetherell stamped right up to the door and opened it with a blunt and businesslike shove. There was the rasp of metal against stone, like a knife being sharpened.

Effy couldn't help the choked sound that came out of her. "This isn't—this can't be Hiraeth?"

43

Halfway through the door, Wetherell turned and gave her that now familiar pitying look. "No," he said. "But the mistress has requested that you stay in the guest cottage. You can view the house tomorrow, when it's light."

The mistress. Myrddin's obituary had mentioned that he was survived by a wife and a son, but neither had been named in the article. She only knew Ianto from his letter, which hadn't spoken of his mother at all. Her skin prickling, Effy followed Wetherell inside.

He set down her trunk and began to fiddle with an oil lamp on the wall, which, after a moment, flared to life. Effy looked around. There was a small wooden desk in the corner, and a tub for washing, but the cottage was dominated by an enormous four-poster bed, which looked absurd against the crumbling, lichen-covered stone of the walls. It had a delicate, filmy canopy that reminded Effy of cobwebs. Its green velvet duvet was tucked under at least a dozen pillows, their gold tassels wilting like cut stalks of wheat.

Everything seemed worn out, somehow, weather-blanched and faded as an old photograph. It felt colder inside the cottage than out.

"No electricity," Wetherell said frankly. He lit a second oil lamp, hanging over the door. "But the taps work, if you're persevering."

Effy looked at the two rusted taps above the tub and said nothing. She thought of her mother's voice, crackling on the other end of the phone line. *Bad decision after bad decision.*

Wetherell finished with the lamp and handed her the box of

matches. Effy took them wordlessly. "Well, I'll send someone to fetch you in the morning."

"How far is it to the house?"

"A ten-minute walk, give or take."

"Depending on the roads?" Effy tried a fragile smile.

Wetherell looked back at her without humor. "Depending on a great many things."

Then he was gone, and Effy was alone. She had expected to hear him stomping through the grass, but everything was unsettlingly silent. No crickets chirping, owls hooting, or predators shifting behind the tree line. Even the wind had gone quiet.

After growing up in Draefen, with the sounds of the city playing on a relentless loop, cars always honking and people always shouting, Effy found the silence intolerable. It was like two daggers driven into her ears. She drew in a deep breath and let it out again tremulously. She could not allow herself to cry. Today's pill had already been swallowed.

Standing there in the cold, damp cottage, Effy considered her options. There were very few, and none of them good. She could try to stumble her way through the dark back to Saltney, but she would be at the mercy of the cliffs and the sea and whatever waited out there in the mist. She thought of the thing she'd seen dart across the road, and her stomach folded over on itself.

Even if she did make it down, there were no trains until morning. And then what? She would ride back to Caer-Isel, back to her decrepit dorm room, back to the spiders and soap scum, back to her terrible attempts at cross sections and boys who whispered about her in the halls. Back to Master Corbenic. Back to staring across the snowy courtyard at the literature college, full of envy and longing. She would call her mother to tell her the news, and her mother would sigh with relief and say, *Thank you for being reasonable, Effy. You have enough problems to deal with as it is.*

Just then, all of it seemed preferable to staying in Hiraeth. But she could do nothing about it until the sun rose.

She opened her trunk and changed into her nightgown, cringing at the feel of the icy stone floor against her bare feet. She opened up her other pill bottle and swallowed her sleeping pill without water, feeling too demoralized to even try the taps. She lit the candle on the bedside table, and extinguished the oil lamps.

Effy was about to crawl under the velvet duvet when a terrible fear plucked at her. She thought again of the creature in the road. It had not been a deer, but it had been nothing human, either; she knew that much. And it had *not* been imagined. She'd taken her pink pill. Wetherell had seen it, too. Even the doctor, with his medical tomes and his glass bottles, could not have explained it.

Anything could come bursting in, anything. Effy snatched up the candle and walked toward the door, her breath coming in short, cold spurts.

There was no lock, but the door was extraordinarily heavy and bolstered with metal. Iron. Effy ran her finger over the brace, and no rust flaked away under her touch. Everything else in the cottage was ancient, but the iron was new.

As Effy returned, haltingly, to the four-poster, a phrase floated up in her mind. *I waited for the Fairy King in our marriage bed, but he didn't know I was wearing a girdle of iron.* Angharad's words were so familiar, they were like the voice of an old friend. Few things could truly guard against the Fair Folk, but iron was one of them.

Effy knelt over her trunk and took out her copy of *Angharad*, flipping to the page where she'd underlined that passage in black pen. This was Myrddin protecting her, giving her a sign. Keeping her safe.

She tucked the book under the pillows and pulled the duvet up to her chin. The dark was heavy and still. It was utterly silent, save for the faint sound of water dripping. Wherever the water was, it sounded close.

She was sure she would never be able to fall asleep in this clammy, dense silence, but the sleeping pill did its work. Effy slipped quietly under, the memory of Angharad's words something close to a lullaby.

FOUR

We must discuss, then, the relationship between women and water. When men fall into the sea, they drown. When women meet the water, they transform. It becomes vital to ask: is this a metamorphosis, or a homecoming?

FROM *A MEDITATION ON WATER AND FEMININITY IN THE WORKS OF EMRYS MYRDDIN* BY DR. CEDRIC GOSSE, 211 AD

Effy woke the next morning to the sound of iron rasping against stone. The side of her face was wet and strands of damp hair stuck to her forehead. She wiped it dry with the edge of the green duvet. When she looked up, she saw a bit of the ceiling was soaked through—the sound she'd heard last night but couldn't locate. The nasty, stale water must have been dripping on her for hours while she slept.

She was just sitting up in bed, gagging, when light cleaved through the open door. Her whole body tensed, half expecting to see wet black hair, a yellow curve of bone. But it was just a boy standing on the threshold, his dark brown hair wind tossed and untidy, though not remotely wet.

Decidedly *not* the Fairy King, but an intruder nonetheless.

"Hey!" She gasped, yanking the covers up to her throat. "What are you doing here?"

He didn't even have the decency to look scandalized. He just backed up halfway out of the doorway, turning away from her with his hand still on the knob, and said, "Wetherell sent me to make sure you were up."

Already Wetherell appeared to have very little confidence in her. Effy swallowed, still holding the duvet to her chin, squinting at the boy, who stared determinedly outside. He wore thin-framed round glasses, slightly misted by the dewy morning air.

"Well?" Effy demanded, scowling. "I'm not going to change with you in here."

That, at last, appeared to offend him. His face turned pink, and without another word, he stepped outside and shut the door after him, more firmly than seemed necessary.

Still glowering, Effy got up and pawed through her trunk. Even her clothes felt somehow damp. She put on a pair of woolen trousers, a black turtleneck, and the thickest socks she owned. She tied her hair back with its ribbon. There was no mirror in the guesthouse, so she would have to hope her face wasn't too puffy and her eyes weren't too red. So far, she was zero for two on first impressions.

She shrugged on her coat and pushed through the door. The boy—university age, surely not much older than she—was leaning against the side of the cottage, a small leather-bound notebook in one hand and a pack of cigarettes in the other. He had a face that seemed both soft and angular at once, his glasses perched on a narrow, delicate nose.

If Effy had been in a more charitable mood, she would have called him handsome.

When he saw her, he put his cigarettes back into his pocket. He was still flushing a little bit, and resolutely made no eye contact. "Let's go."

Effy nodded, but his rudeness turned her stomach sour. The morning light, even through the trees, was bright enough to make her head throb behind her temples. Ungenerously, she shot back, "You aren't even going to ask my name?"

"I know your name. You haven't asked mine."

He was wearing a blue coat, flapping open at the front, that seemed, to her, too thin for the weather, and a white button-down shirt under it. His boots showed some scuffing. All of it made Effy think he'd been at Hiraeth for some time now. But he was not a Southerner; she could tell. His complexion was not quite pale enough, and he picked his way through the forest with a hedging delicacy that bordered on distaste.

Effy relented, her curiosity getting the better of her. "What's your name?"

"Preston," he replied.

A stuffy, prim sort of name common in Northern Llyr. The name suited him. "Do you work for the Myrddin estate?"

"No," he said, and did not elaborate further. He looked her up and down with a raised brow. "Aren't you going to bring anything? I thought you were here to design a house."

Effy froze. Without another word, she turned on her heel and hurried back into the cottage. She knelt beside the trunk and yanked out her sketchpad and the first pen she could find, then stomped out again. She no longer felt cold. Her cheeks were burning.

Preston had already continued down the path. She took three comically large steps to catch up with him, trying to account for the difference in the length of their legs. Though he had a slight, almost waifish frame, Preston had to be a head taller than her.

They went on in silence for a few moments, Effy's eyes still adjusting to the light. In the morning, the forest was less terrifying but even stranger. Everything was too green: the moss growing over every stone and up the trunks of the trees and the long, soft grass under their feet. Overhead the leaves rustled with a sound like the nickering of horses, and the morning dew on the leaves turned crystalline in the sunlight. For some reason, the way the light trickled in reminded Effy of being in a chapel. Memories of dusty pews and prayer books made her nose itch.

The path curled upward, leading them over fallen branches and broken rocks. Effy's legs were already aching when the trees began to thin. Preston ducked under a low-hanging branch, heavy with moss, and held it up so she could go through after him. The unexpected display of chivalry vexed her. Rather than saying thank you, she shot him a sulky glare.

And then, all at once, they were standing on the edge of a cliff.

The wind was blowing hard enough to make her eyes sting, and Effy blinked furiously. The salt-streaked stone of the cliffside tumbled down to a rocky shoreline, where the waves rolled in over and over again, drenching the pebble beach. The sea stretched out to the line of the horizon, choppy and blue gray and dotted with caps of white foam. Seabirds swooped through the iron-colored sky, water glistening on their beaks.

"It's beautiful," she said. Preston just stared ahead, frowning.

She was going to make a snippy remark about how standoffish he was being. But then she heard a sound—a terrible sound, like the wrenching of a tree from its roots, loud and entirely too close.

Effy looked down in horror: the rock was crumbling under her.

"Watch out!" Preston's hand closed around her arm. He pulled her to safety just as the outcropping where she'd been standing fell down into the sea.

The shattered rocks vanished beneath the water, each crash grim and final.

Effy stumbled back against Preston's chest. Her head was jammed under his chin and she could feel the throb of his pulse, the heat of his body through his shirt.

They both jerked away from each other, but not before she managed to get a good glimpse of his notebook, near enough now to read the name embossed on its cover: *P. Héloury.*

"Don't stand so close to the edge of the cliff," he snapped, buttoning his jacket shut as if he wanted to forget that—Saints forbid—they had ever touched. "There's a reason the naturalists are up in arms about a second Drowning."

"It's you," Effy said.

His eyes narrowed. "What?"

She felt breathless. She had spent the last weeks conjuring a wicked version of P. Héloury in her mind, a perfect amalgam of everything she despised. A literature student. A shrewdly opportunistic Myrddin scholar.

An *Argantian*.

"You're the one who took out my books," she said at last, the only words she could summon as her blood pulsed with adrenaline. The memory of standing in front of the circulation desk, the boy's number in bleeding ink on the back of her hand, filled her with a jilted anger anew. "On Myrddin. I went to the library and the librarian told me they had all been checked out."

"Well, they're not *your* books. That's the entire premise of a library."

Effy just stared at him. Her hands were shaking. She had practiced arguments in her mind against her imagined version of P. Héloury, but now that she was standing before him, all eloquent reasoning had abandoned her.

"What are you even doing here?" she bit out. "Pawing through a dead man's things so you can steal what you need for some . . . for some scholarly article? I'm sure you can write a paragraph or two about the coffee rings on his desk."

"Myrddin has been dead for six months now," Preston said tonelessly. "His life story is more than fair game."

The wind snatched at Effy's hair in a fury, nearly yanking it free from its black ribbon. Preston folded his arms over his chest.

His impassive reply made her stomach roil. She searched the morass of thoughts in her mind, trying to find something she could use, an arrow that could pierce his stubborn facade. At last, an idea.

With a trembling voice, Effy said, "How did you even get here? Argantian students with temporary passports can't leave Caer-Isel."

Behind his glasses, Preston's gaze was unflinching. She might as well have not spoken at all.

"My mother is Llyrian," he said. "Regardless, I could have gotten a scholar's visa. I'm here with permission from Dean Fogg. Collecting Myrddin's letters and documents for the university archive."

She hadn't noticed his very faint accent before, but she heard it now: the little catch in his throat before the hard consonants, his barely aspirated *h*'s. Effy had never spent so long speaking to an Argantian before. For a moment, she was fixated on the particularly delicate way Preston rounded his lips when he said his long vowels, but then she blinked and all her anger returned.

"I don't know why you care about Myrddin at all," she said. Unexpectedly, her throat tightened, on the verge of tears. "He's *our* national author. Not yours. Have you even read his books?"

"I've read them all." Preston's expression hardened. "He's a perfectly valid subject of scholarly inquiry no matter the background of the scholar in question.

She hated the way he talked, so full of aloof confidence. For weeks she had steeled herself for precisely this confrontation, but now they were arguing and he was *winning*.

Effy remembered what the librarian had said to her. "You want be the first to tell his life story," she said. "You're—you're just the academic equivalent of a carpetbagger." An Argantian trying to write the narrative of a Llyrian icon's life—of *Myrddin's* life—it was so aberrant that she was at a loss for further words.

"No one owns the right to tell a story," he said flatly. "Besides, I'm not pushing any particular agenda. I'm just here for the truth."

Effy took a deep breath, trying to untangle the various strands of her rage. Underneath the righteous anger she felt about an Argantian perverting Myrddin's legacy, there was something deeper and more painful.

What's the point in studying literature if you don't want to tell stories? She wanted to ask him, but she was afraid that if she opened her mouth, she might actually cry.

And then, over Preston's shoulder, she saw a figure pacing down the cliffside. He was enormously tall and clad in all black, and despite the wind, his dark hair lay flat upon his head, almost as if it were wet.

Effy thought of the creature in the road, and her chest seized. But by the time the figure reached them, she could tell he was an ordinary man—broad shouldered and square jawed and enormous, but mortal after all.

"I was beginning to worry you'd fallen right into the sea," he said. He was middle-aged, around forty. The same age as Master Corbenic. "The cliffs have been particularly unsound of late."

"No," Preston said. "We're fine."

"Then the sea is behaving itself today." The man's gaze flickered briefly to the seething gray expanse below. "You both know the rumors about the second Drowning, I'm sure. Have you been explaining our predicament to Ms. Sayre?"

Preston stiffened. Effy wondered if he would mention their argument. Well, it had been more of a verbal assault on her part. But what would that achieve, aside from making them look like squabbling children?

"I thought I would leave that to you," Preston said at last. Effy noticed the way he dug his thumbnail into the spine of his notebook.

"Excellent," the man said smoothly. He turned to Effy, his pale eyes gleaming. "It's very nice to finally meet you, Ms. Sayre. I can't express enough how pleased I am that you've agreed to come. I'm Ianto Myrddin. The late illustrious author was my father."

Under his stare, Effy felt her stomach swoop like the gulls. Ianto had a coarse, rough-edged handsomeness, as if he'd been born right out of the rough-hewn rocks. His knuckles pressed up beneath taut skin. When she shook his hand, her palm came away prickling, almost raw from his calluses.

"Thank you for inviting me," she said. "Your father—he was my favorite author."

It was an understatement, but she figured there would be plenty of time for gushing praise. Ianto smiled at her, highlighting the one crooked dimple that slashed his left cheek. "I could tell from your design. That's why I chose it, of course—it's something my father most certainly would have loved. Treacherous but beautiful. I suppose that characterizes all of the Bay of Nine Bells, doesn't it, Ms. Sayre?"

"Effy," she said. She had not expected to sound so dumbstruck, or for her knees to feel so weak. "Just Effy."

Beside Ianto, Preston looked very thin—and very uneasy. Effy didn't miss the way his throat pulsed when Ianto spoke.

"I'm going back to the house," Preston said. "I have work to get done."

"Yes, there's a stack of my father's letters waiting for you," Ianto said. "And for you, Effy, breakfast and coffee. I'm sorry you have to endure the guest cottage, but my mother insisted. She's very elderly. Fragile."

"It's not a problem," she said. Her voice sounded, to her own ears, oddly vacuous. She had the sudden and familiar sensation that she was underwater, the tide rolling ceaselessly over her. She had not taken any of her pink pills this morning.

"Well then." Ianto smiled again, and Effy felt the same way she had when the cliff had crumbled beneath her, the awareness of being at a great height pulsing in the soles of her feet. "Let me show you Hiraeth."

A faint morning fog was coming over the cliffside. It crept in pale and slow, like lichen consuming a dead tree. Out of the mist rose Hiraeth Manor, gray and black and green, as if it were an extension of the cliffs themselves.

Ianto led them up a stone staircase, the steps uneven and carpeted in moss. The wooden double doors were damp and moldering; Effy could smell the rot before she even reached the threshold. The brass door knocker was huge as a bullring and flaking with rust. Ianto had to jam his shoulder against the door several times to force it open, until at last the ancient hinges relented with a dismal and ominous groaning sound.

"Welcome," Ianto said. "Try not to slip."

Effy looked down before she looked up. The tile floor was scummy, like the surface of a pond, and the red carpet that led up to the staircase was thick with mildew. When she lifted her gaze, she saw the staircase itself, the wood termite-eaten and wet, cobwebs strung through the banister like weaving on a loom. Portraits hung askew over peeling wallpaper, which looked like it might once have been an attractive peacock blue, but water stains had turned it a grimy shade of gray.

"I—" she began, but stopped abruptly, unsure of what to say. The air tasted thick and sour. When she had recovered her faculty of speech, blinking profusely against the dust in the air, she managed to ask, "Has it been this way since your father passed?"

Ianto gave a huff that was half amusement, half dismay. "It's been in various states of disrepair since I was a child. My father wasn't much for home improvement, and the climate in the bay doesn't exactly make for easy upkeep."

There was a faint splash from her left. Preston had stepped through a small, filmy puddle. "I'm going upstairs," he said shortly. "I've wasted enough of the morning already."

Effy knew that was a hidden gibe at her, and she narrowed her eyes back at him.

"At least have some coffee." Ianto's tone did not suggest Preston had much choice in the matter. "And then perhaps you can help me give Ms. Sayre a tour. I imagine you're more familiar than I am with some parts of the house by now. My father's study, for example."

Preston drew in a sharp breath, but didn't protest. Effy felt no more pleased at the prospect of him tagging along, though for Ianto's sake, she tried not to show any obvious displeasure.

The kitchen was off the foyer—small, cramped, and tumble-down, half the cabinet doors hanging off their hinges. The white tiles were laced so thoroughly with filthy grout that they looked like crooked teeth in an old man's mouth.

Ianto gave Effy coffee in a chipped mug. The back of his hand was covered in black hair, just like Master Corbenic's.

Effy took one sip, but the coffee tasted as sour as the air. Preston held his own mug but didn't drink from it. His hand kept fluttering back to his pocket, and Effy remembered how he had stuffed his cigarettes in there. His fingers were long, thin, nearly hairless. Feeling heat rise to her cheeks, she tore her gaze away.

"I really should get back to work," he said, but Ianto was already ushering them into the dining room. There was a long table with a moth-eaten white cloth over it, the ends stained like the muddy hem of a dress.

An odd and very dusty chandelier dangled precariously from the ceiling. Effy had never seen anything quite like it before: shards of mirrored glass, carefully cut into narrow diamonds like icicles, light bouncing from one to the next in a rippling glimmer. It almost made it look like it was moving, even though the air in the room was oppressively still.

"That's lovely," Effy said, pointing up. "Where did you get it?"

"I think it was an acquisition of my mother's. I don't truly remember. I can't say we've done a lot of dining in here recently," said Ianto, and gave a short laugh that fell limply in the silence.

They passed through the rest of the rooms on the first floor: a pantry that even rats and roaches had abandoned, a living room that had certainly not seen very much living lately, and a bathroom that made even Ianto frown in tacit apology.

By that point, Effy's stomach was churning so viciously, she thought she might retch.

Ianto took them up the stairs, pointing out each of the portraits on the way. None were of real people—the Myrddin family had no aristocratic pedigree and therefore no ancestral heirlooms. Emrys had been the son of a fisherman. No, these were paintings of characters and scenes from Myrddin's books.

Effy saw Angharad in her marriage bed, pale hair strewn out among the pillows, iron girdle glinting at her waist. She saw the Fairy King, black hair streaming past his shoulders like a slick of fetid water, his colorless eyes seeming to follow her as she climbed. Effy paused mid-step, heart lurching. That hair, those eyes, the slender, jagged form like a gash in the fabric of the world—

"Mr. Myrddin—um, Ianto," she said. "I saw something last night, in the dark—"

"What's that, Effy?" Two steps ahead of her, Ianto's voice sounded distant, disinterested. But Preston was looking at her with an inscrutable expression, as if waiting for her to keep speaking.

"Nothing," she said after a moment. "Never mind."

The entrance to the upstairs landing was a wooden archway decorated with carvings. Intricate vines and seashell outlines surrounded the solemn faces of two men.

"Saint Eupheme and Saint Marinell," Preston said. Then he ducked his head, as if regretting that he had spoken at all.

Saint Eupheme was the patron of storytellers, and Saint Marinell the ruler of the sea and the patron of fathers. Ordinarily she might have been curious to see who Myrddin had chosen to bless his threshold. But now she only felt vaguely ill.

"I know you might think it blasphemous to have a portrait of the Fairy King beside the likeness of saints," Ianto said, breaching the archway. "But my father was a Southerner through and through. He never left this estate, did you know that? After the publication of *Angharad*. He took no interviews, gave no speeches. They called him mad, his critics, but he didn't care. He didn't leave this house until the Sleeper Museum came to load his corpse into their car. And—well, I won't bore you with the details. All I meant to say is that despite his thoroughly Southern upbringing, my father never sought to *humanize* or pardon the Fairy King in any way."

Effy thought of Myrddin's Fairy King: charming, cruel, and, in the end, pitiful in his corrosive desires. He had loved Angharad, and the thing he loved the most had killed him. She frowned. Surely there was nothing more human than that.

"I would suggest the opposite, actually." Preston spoke up unexpectedly, his tone cool. "Stripped down to his essence, as he is in the end when Angharad shows him his own reflection in the mirror, the Fairy King represents the very epitome of humanity, in all its viciousness and vulgar fragility."

That was how Angharad had finally slain him: by showing the Fairy King his own countenance in the mirror. There was a beat of silence. Ianto turned slowly toward Preston, pale eyes narrowing.

"Well," he said in a low voice, "I suppose you *are* the expert among us. Preston Héloury, student of Cedric Gosse, the university's preeminent Myrddin scholar. Or perhaps I should say Gosse's errand boy—I presume he's far too busy to pick through old letters in a house at the bottom of the world."

Preston said nothing after that, but around the spine of his notebook, his knuckles turned white. Effy stood still for a moment in shock. He had been bold enough, articulate enough, to voice precisely what she had only thought quietly to herself. She had absolutely no interest in letting him know it, of course, but it seemed that on the topic of the Fairy King . . . she maybe almost agreed with him.

Effy pushed it out of her mind. She didn't want to share any common ground with Preston, especially not when it came to *Angharad*.

Ianto led them down the hallway, naked glass bulbs flickering on the walls. The first door on the left was cracked open.

"The library," he said, turning to Effy. "I'm sure you'll agree there's the most work to be done in here."

Effy followed him into the room. A single greasy window poured light onto the overflowing bookshelves, the three-and-a-half-legged desk, the melted-down candles. A stained armchair peered out from behind one of the shelves like an old cat, ornery at being disturbed. The rotted wood floor creaked and moaned under their feet, heavy with so many stacks of books. They were overflowing the shelves and spilling onto the ground, spines ripped and pages torn out, sitting in puddles of their own bled ink.

It was several moments before Effy was able to speak. The question that rose to her lips surprised her. "Was it like this all your life?" she managed. "Did your father keep it this way on purpose—"

"Unfortunately," Ianto said in a clipped tone. "My father was a genius in many respects, but it often meant he had little care for the mundane, unpleasant tasks of daily life."

Should she have been taking notes? She felt woozy. Myrddin had been an odd man, a recluse, but there was no reason he had to live in such squalor. Effy could no longer see him as the enigmatic man in his author photo. She could only picture him now as a crab in its slippery tide pool, oblivious to being drenched over and over again by the water.

"Let's keep going," she said, hoping her voice did not betray how weary she felt. In her peripheral vision, she saw a little furrow appear between Preston's brows.

The door to the next room was closed. Ianto pushed it open, and Preston immediately pressed forward, lodging himself in the threshold.

"This is the study," he said. "I've been keeping my things in here."

What could he possibly have to hide? Maybe he was examining Myrddin's coffee rings after all. Maybe he had dug up Myrddin's dentures. Another wave of nausea washed over her.

"I'd really like to see it," Effy said. Sick as she felt, she didn't want to miss an opportunity to goad him. And his caginess had made her curious.

Preston eyed her with immense disdain, lips going thin. But as it turned out, there was nothing incriminating or embarrassing in the study: there was a ripped chaise, a blanket tossed over its back, that he had clearly been sleeping on, and a desk scattered with papers. Cigarette butts lined the windowsill.

It was neater than every other room in the house by miles, but it was still not as immaculate as she'd expected from the smug, pedantic P. *Héloury.*

As they left the study, the floor groaned deafeningly under them, and Effy lurched for the nearest wall. Momentarily she was certain the wood was going to collapse under her, just like the rock had on the cliffs.

Ianto gave her a sympathetic grimace, and she righted herself, cheeks hot. Her mother's voice thrummed in her mind. *Bad decision after bad decision.*

They came to a door at the end of the hallway, and Ianto said, "I would show you the bedrooms, but my mother doesn't want to be disturbed."

Myrddin's widow. Effy didn't even know her name; didn't know a single thing about her other than that she'd ordered Ianto to have her stay in the guest cottage. But she'd allowed Preston inside the house. Effy couldn't help but think the widow did not want her here.

She could feel the beginnings of panic buzzing in the tips of her fingers and toes, her vision whitening at the edges. She wished she had her pink pills, but in her rush she'd left them behind on the nightstand. *Preston's fault,* she decided, but she couldn't even imbue the thought with the malice she wanted.

"That's all right," she said. "I've seen enough."

All three of them went downstairs again, Effy gripping the moist, slippery banister all the way. She wanted nothing more than to leave this terrible house and its thick, briny air. But as Ianto led her back toward the kitchen, insisting upon scones and kippers, Effy's eyes landed on something she hadn't noticed before: a small door, its frame badly slanted and the wood at its base speckled with tiny white barnacles. Looking at it, she swore she could hear the waves more clearly, like an enormous pulse of blood from the heart of the house itself.

"Where does that door lead?" she asked.

Ianto didn't reply, but reached below the collar of his black sweater and produced a key, strung around his neck on a thin piece of leather. He fitted the key into the lock and the door swung open.

"Be careful," he said. He moved aside so Effy could see through the opening "Don't fall down."

The door opened onto a set of stairs, half submerged in murky water. Only the first few steps were visible. Salt smell curled into her nose, along with the peculiar scents of old leather and wet paper.

"Those were my father's archives, in the basement," Ianto said. "But several years ago, the sea level rose too high and flooded the whole floor. We haven't managed to get anyone to come all the way down here and try to drain it."

"Aren't there very valuable documents in there?" Effy was surprised at herself for asking such a question. It sounded prying, opportunistic, like something Preston might say. Maybe he already had.

"Of course," said Ianto. "My father was very protective of his personal and professional affairs. Whatever papers are down there, I'm sure they're properly sealed away, but they're impossible to reach, unless you fancy a very cold, very dark swim."

Effy watched the water ripple, bunching and then flattening like black silk. "Shouldn't the water have drained on its own? When the tide went down?"

Ianto gave her the same pitying look that Wetherell had given her in the car. "The cliffside here is sinking. The very foundation of the house is waterlogged. The whole Bay of Nine Bells, in fact. We are closer to drowning every year."

Effy hadn't realized how literal talk of the second Drowning was, more than mere Southern superstition. She felt ashamed for dismissing it now.

Above the stairs was another archway. The stone was wet and draped with moss, words etched on its surface between carvings of waves.

She read the engraving aloud, her voice tipping up at the end to make it a question. "'The only enemy is the sea'?"

And then, to her complete surprise, it was Preston who spoke.

"*Everything ancient must decay,*" he said, and it had the cadence of a song. "*A wise man once said thus to me. But a sailor was I—and on my head no fleck of gray—so with all the boldness of my youth, I said: The only enemy is the sea.*"

Effy just stared at him while he recited the lines, his gaze steady behind his glasses, his tone hushed and reverent. She recognized the words now.

"'The Mariner's Demise,'" she said softly. "From Myrddin's book of poems."

"Yes," he said, sounding taken aback. "I didn't realize you knew it."

"Literature students aren't the only ones who can read," she snapped, and then instantly regretted the razor edge to her voice. She'd shown her bitterness and envy too plainly. Perhaps Preston could already guess why she loathed him so much.

But all he said was, "Right."

His voice was short, his gaze cold and aloof again. Effy shook her head, as if trying to dispel the hazy vestiges of a dream. She wanted to evict from her mind that one fragile moment she and Preston had shared.

Ianto cleared his throat. "My father was always his own greatest admirer," he said. He waited for Effy to step aside and then shut the door, returning the key to his collar. "Let's all go eat some breakfast. I won't have you making a churlish host of me."

But Effy excused herself, insisting that she needed air. It wasn't a lie. She could scarcely breathe in that ruin of a house.

She clambered up the moss-laden steps and through the path onto the cliffside. This time she was careful not to stand too close to the edge. The crumbling white stone looked like the slabs of ice that floated down the river Naer in the winter: churning and fickle, nothing you could trust to hold beneath you. Effy squeezed her eyes shut against the biting wind.

Perhaps there had been no other applicants to the project at all. Perhaps she was the only student who had looked at the poster and seen a fantasy, while the others had seen the dreadful reality.

At last Effy understood: *this* was why Ianto had sought out a student. No seasoned architect would try to build a house on the edge of a sinking cliff, on a half-drowned foundation. Not even in reverence to Emrys Myrddin.

It's beyond you, Master Corbenic had said, and he was right. He was like a splinter she couldn't get out from under her nail. The memory of him stung at the oddest times, when she'd done as little as curl her fingers to reach for a coffee mug.

Far below, the waves gnawed at the cliffside. Effy could no longer see it as anything but consumption, dark water eating away at the pale stone. Her knees buckled beneath her and she sank hopelessly down onto the rippling grass.

The truth was, she had seen many fine and beautiful things underneath all the damp and rot, like chests of treasure waiting to be dredged up from a shipwreck. Plush carpets that must have cost a fortune, candelabras made of solid gold. But none of it could be salvaged from the rot and the rising sea.

It was the task of a fairy tale, the sort of hopeless, futile challenge the Fairy King himself might have set. In her mind, she saw that creature from the road. It turned toward her, opened its devouring mouth, and spoke: *Sew me a shirt with no seam or needlework. Plant an acre of land with one ear of corn. Build a house on a sinking cliff and win your freedom.*

She had never thought Myrddin would set a task so cruel. But she did not know this man, the one who had kept his own family trapped in a sinking, fetid house, the one who had let everything around him fall to ruin. The man she had spent her whole life idolizing had been strange and reclusive, but he had not been coldhearted. It all felt so terribly wrong. Like a dream she wanted desperately to wake up from.

It was Preston's voice in her ear now, his hushed recitation. *The only enemy is the sea.*

FIVE

Myrddin's reception is as curious as the man himself. Some critics accuse him of excessive romanticism (see Fox, Montresor, et al.). Yet *Angharad* is grudgingly accepted, even by his detractors, as a profound and surprising work. His admirers—and there are many, both critical and commercial—insist that the relatability of his work, the universalism, is intentional, reflecting a keen understanding of the human condition. In this manner, he is generally considered worthy of his status as national author.

FROM THE FOREWORD TO *THE COLLECTED WORKS OF*
EMRYS MYRDDIN, EDITED BY CEDRIC GOSSE, 212 AD

The next morning was cloud-dense and sunless, and Effy rose in a pale, rheumy gray light. She had not returned to Hiraeth yesterday, even at Ianto's urging, and had instead sat in the guesthouse, her mind running dismally through her few and narrowing options.

She tried the rusted taps above the tub, twisting them back and forth until her fingers ached and her palms were gritty with rust. At last she managed to get a slow drip from one of them, and cupped her hands under the trickling stream. It took the better part of an hour to scrub herself clean and wash her hair, but she refused to go into town filthy. She had that much dignity left.

When she was finished, Effy put her pill bottle in her purse and slid on her coat. She left her trunk ajar and abandoned. What did she need that couldn't be replaced? She considered it as she began her stumbling walk down the cliffs toward Saltney. Some clothes, her drafting linens, a cheap set of protractors and compasses. She would not miss any of it.

Effy had finally settled on a plan late last night, lying under the green duvet, waiting for her sleeping pill to do its work. As rancid water dripped onto the pillow beside her, she decided she couldn't afford to wait, or plead with Wetherell for a ride. She would leave Saltney first thing in the morning, and she would walk herself, the sea be damned.

The dark-haired creature be damned, too. She knew the stories, and she knew her own mind. The Fairy King did not show his face in the light of day. But she took one of her pink pills, for good measure.

Her plan had seemed sound enough until it started drizzling. Effy went on stubbornly, her boots scrabbling against the loose rocks, as the road turned steeper and steeper. The sprinkle of rain was enough to turn the packed dirt into mud, and soon every step was a labor, the muck sucking at her shoes. Water trickled down her face.

Her vision blurring, Effy stared determinedly ahead, trying to gauge how much of her journey was left. There was a sharp bend in the road, and the cliffs rose jaggedly above it, blocking her view of Saltney. She could see no smoke chuffing from chimneys in the distance, no thatched roofs along the horizon.

She rubbed at her cheeks. To her left the sea was lapping at the edge of the road, in broad tongues of salt and foam. A wave crested over the rock and washed the toe of her boot.

Panic was rising in her chest when Effy heard the rumble of a car engine behind her. A black car was clattering down the road, its windows speckled with raindrops, its hood sleek and wet.

Effy stepped aside to let it pass, but instead it slowed to a halt beside her. The driver's-side window rolled down.

Preston stared at her in silence for several moments, his arms braced on the steering wheel. His hair looked as untidy as it had yesterday, and his eyes were unblinking behind his glasses. At last, he said, "Effy, get in."

"I don't want to," she said mulishly.

Of course the rain chose that precise moment to pick up, the fat droplets catching on her lashes. Preston's gaze was flat with skepticism. "The road is all but washed away down there," he said. Then, in complete deadpan, he added, "Are you planning to swim?"

She glanced down the muddy road, glowering, and said, "Is this how you entice all the girls into your car?"

"Most girls don't give me the chance, since they're sensible enough not to try and saunter down cliffs in the rain."

Her face turned magnificently warm. She stomped around the other side of the car, cheeks flaming. In one furious motion, she jerked open the car door and plunked into the passenger seat.

She looked stubbornly forward as she said, "I object to the word *saunter*."

"Your objection is noted." His gaze didn't shift from her. "Put your seat belt on."

He was trying to humiliate her, to treat her like a child. "My mother doesn't even make me wear my seat belt," she scoffed.

"I don't suppose your mother spends a lot of time driving you down half-sunken roads."

She couldn't think of a clever reply to that. Preston had his seat belt on, and she was too cold and wet to argue. As she buckled herself in, she thought, *You are so insufferable.* She almost said it out loud.

They drove on in silence for several moments, the wheels of the car spinning hard against the muck. Every time the rain picked up, Effy's mood turned fouler. It was like the weather was mocking her, reminding her how stupid and helpless she'd been, and how Preston, dryly logical, had come to her rescue. She sank down in her seat, scowling.

The inside of Preston's car smelled like cigarettes and leather. It was not, as much as she loathed to admit it, entirely unpleasant. There was something almost comforting about it. She stole a glance at him, but his eyes were fixed determinedly on the road as the car wound down the cliffside.

"Why are you going into Saltney?" she asked.

He looked surprised to hear her speak. "I go to the pub to work sometimes. It's hard to focus in that house, with Myrddin's son breathing down my neck."

A flare of anger in her belly. "Maybe Ianto doesn't like soulless academics rifling through his dead father's things for little anecdotes to pad their thesis."

Preston's head snapped up. "How did you know it's for my thesis?"

Effy was so pleased her bait had worked, she had to keep herself from smiling. For the first time, she felt she had gained some ground, had some advantage over him. "I just assumed you had an ulterior motive. You were so uneasy when Ianto tried to show me the study."

"Well, congratulations on your powers of observation." Preston's tone took on a bit of bitterness, which pleased Effy even more. "But just so you know, not a single literature student would pass up the opportunity."

Not a single *literature* student. Was he trying to belittle her, to rile her? Had he guessed the real reason she despised him so much? Effy tried to hide her frustration and envy. "The opportunity to what? Write some gossipy little thesis and get a gold star from the department chair?"

"No," Preston said. "The opportunity to find out the truth."

That was the second time he'd said it—*the truth*. Like he was trying to make his self-interested scheming sound more noble. "Why did Ianto even invite you here?" she bit out.

"He didn't. Obviously he didn't object to the university creating a collection out of his father's papers, but he didn't invite me." Preston's eyes darted briefly toward her, then back to the road. "Myrddin's widow did."

The mysterious widow again, who hadn't even left the bed-chamber to greet Effy, who had insisted on marooning her in the guesthouse. Why was *she* playing patron to a scurrilous university student?

The car sloshed through a mess of salt water and foam, a wave that hadn't yet receded. A sudden stop sent Effy lurching forward, her seat belt catching her before she smacked her face into the glove box.

Still unwilling to concede, she righted herself and stared straight ahead in surly silence. She could have sworn she saw the ghost of a smirk on Preston's face.

As the car turned down the last bend in the road, he sobered and asked, "Why are you so desperate to get to Saltney?"

Her stomach knotted instantly. The last thing in the world she wanted to do was confess that she was planning to leave Hiraeth after only one day. Even in the face of such an impossible task, sur-render was humiliating. Doubly humiliating, because Preston had been living and working in that awful house for *weeks*, undeterred by the rot and ruin and sinking cliffs. Admitting the truth would mean accepting he was cleverer, more resourceful, more determined.

And it would be worse to tell him the deeper, more painful truth: that seeing Hiraeth had ruined her childish fantasy, ruined the version of Myrddin she had constructed in her mind, one where he was benevolent and wise and had written a book meant to save girls like her.

Now when she imagined him, she thought only of the crum-bling cliffs, the rocks falling out from under her feet. She thought of that drowned room in the basement, of Ianto saying, *My father was always his own greatest admirer.*

"I need to call my mother," she said.

It was the first lie that came into her head, and it wasn't a very good one. Effy's cheeks warmed. She felt like a child caught shoplifting, embarrassed by the clumsiness of her artifice.

Preston lifted a brow, but his expression didn't seem disdainful. "Does she know you're taking time off from your studies?"

His tone was casual, unassuming, but it stopped Effy's heart for a brief moment. They went to the same university. Different colleges, of course, but it was possible that they'd passed each other in the library, or while drinking coffee in the Drowsy Poet. Being the only girl in the architecture college was like being under a bell jar, everything she did closely scrutinized. The rumors had started so easily, and traveled so far. It wasn't unrealistic to imagine that he had heard about Master Corbenic.

Now that her mind had conjured the possibility, her belly pooled with terror and dread. She had the abrupt urge to fling open the car door and pitch herself into the sea.

She managed to calm herself and reply icily, "That's none of your business."

Behind his glasses, Preston's gaze hardened. "Well," he said. "I'll drop you off by the phone booth."

Mercifully, the rest of the car ride was short. By the time Preston pulled into Saltney, the rain had stopped, too. Dirty puddles pocked the road. The main street housed a church, made from the same crumbling white stone as the cliffs, a fish shop with a wooden sign hanging slanted above the door, and the pub, soft golden light gleaming from behind its rain-streaked windows.

"You can let me out here," Effy said. "I'll walk."

Preston pulled over without a word. Effy tried to open the door, but the handle just flapped uselessly. She pulled it over and over again, frustration rising to a fever pitch, her face burning.

"It's locked," Preston said. His voice was tight.

It was a petulant sort of stubbornness that kept Effy yanking at the handle, even though the door wouldn't budge. After several more moments, she heard Preston draw a breath, and then he reached over, fumbling for the lock.

His shoulder was pressed against her chest, their faces close enough that Effy could see the muscle feathering in his jaw. His skin was very lightly tan, and from this vantage point she noticed the faint scattering of freckles on his cheeks. She hadn't seen them before. There were two red marks where his glasses had dug in, tiny nicks that winged the bridge of his nose.

She wondered if they hurt. She almost wanted to ask. It was a strange thought, and she wasn't sure why it had occurred to her. Her heart was shuddering unsteadily, and she was certain Preston could feel it through the wool of her sweater and his coat.

At last the door clicked open. Preston pulled back, letting out a quiet huff. Effy only then realized that she, too, had been holding her breath.

Cold air wafted in from the open door, bringing with it the smell of the sea. She clambered out of the car as quickly as she could, her bottom lip stinging where she'd bitten it nearly to bleeding.

The train station was not far from the pub, but as soon as she started to walk, Effy's legs began to go numb beneath her. She watched from the street as Preston climbed out of the car, the collar of his jacket pulled up around his ears.

There was a pale flush painting his cheeks, and Effy was sure she wasn't imagining it. He gave her one stiff, tight nod and then vanished into the pub. While the door was briefly open, Effy heard the muffled music of the record player.

She turned toward the train station. There was no use waiting, she figured, if she was indeed going to leave. On the way, her left foot plunged into a puddle, soaking the hem of her pant leg. Already she missed Caer-Isel and coffee shops and Rhia. She even missed Harold and Watson.

Mostly, she missed paved streets.

There were no other cars aside from Preston's, and the street was dreary and empty. The train station was nothing more than a small ticket booth and a stretch of silent tracks, water beading on the booth's window and dripping off the awning.

She didn't know when the next train was coming, and there didn't appear to be any sort of schedule posted. Effy glanced over her shoulder, as if she might catch Preston watching her. But why would he care enough to investigate her lie?

Effy was only a few paces away from the station when she saw the telephone booth—its glass, too, misted thoroughly with condensation.

She wasn't sure exactly what made her enter it and pick up the phone. She owed no loyalty to the stupid lie she'd told Preston.

And yet she found herself dialing her mother's number again.

A very small part of her *did* want to hear her mother's voice. It was the urge that a dog had to nose the same old beehive, forgetting the fact that it had been stung before.

"Hello? Effy? Is that you?"

"Mother?" The relief she felt almost bowled her over. "I'm so sorry for not calling you back sooner."

"Well, you should be," her mother said. "I was frantic. I told your grandparents. Where are you?"

"I'm still in Saltney." Effy swallowed. "But I'm going to leave now."

There was a rustling sound; she imagined her mother shifting the receiver so it was cradled between her shoulder and her ear. "What made you finally change your mind?"

Finally was a little pinch of cruelty. It had only been one day. "I just realized you were right. I was taking on more than I could handle."

Her mother made a low, approving sound. There were the faint noises of cars rattling down the street in the background. Effy pictured her mother standing by the open window, telephone cord wrapped around her lithe body. She imagined the armchair in the living room where she used to curl up after school and do her homework; she imagined her grandparents shuffling about in the kitchen downstairs, cooking venison and mincemeat pies. She imagined her bedroom, with the same pastel pink wallpaper she'd had since she was a child and the stuffed bear she'd been too embarrassed to bring to university but missed every night.

"Well, thank the Saints," her mother said. "I can't handle any more trouble from you."

"I know," said Effy. "I'm sorry. I'm coming home now."

The words shocked her the second she uttered them. A moment ago, she'd been missing Caer-Isel, but she realized now that even if it was familiar, it wasn't safe. A beat of silence. Her mother inhaled sharply.

"Home? What about your studies?"

"I don't want to go back to Caer-Isel." The knot of tears rose in her throat so suddenly, it was painful to speak. "Something happened, Mother, and I can't—"

She wanted to tell her mother about Master Corbenic, but any capacity for speech abandoned her. It still only came back to her in flashes; there was no narrative, no story with a beginning, middle, and end. There was only the haziness of dread, the dry-mouthed panic, the nightmares that sent her jolting awake at night.

And she knew exactly how much sympathy her mother had for her nightmares.

"Effy." Her mother's voice was so razor-edged, it made Effy's stomach curdle. "I don't want you to come home. You can't. I have work and you're an adult now. Whatever mess you've made, you need to sort it by yourself. Go back to school. Take your medication. Focus on your studies. Let me have my life. You are taking your pills, aren't you?"

Effy wished, in that moment, that her senses would dull again. She wanted to go to that deep-water place, where she could hear only the churning of the waves above her.

But her mind wouldn't carry her there. Instead she felt acutely the cold press of the telephone against her ear, and the tightening of her throat, and the panicked, off-kilter beat of her heart. She lifted her hand to rub at the knob of scar tissue where her ring finger should be.

"I'm taking them," Effy said. "But that's not—"

She cut herself off. She meant to say *that's not the problem,* but wasn't it? At any point when she'd been in Master Corbenic's office, she could have run. That's what the boys in her college whispered: that she'd wanted it. After all, why else would she have stayed? Why had she never pushed him away? Why had she never said that simple word, *no?*

Trying to articulate the inarticulable fear she'd felt as she sat in his green office chair would lead her down the same road it always had. It would end with her mother telling her there was no such thing as monsters. That there was nothing watching her from the corner of her room, no matter how many nights Effy could not sleep under its cold, unblinking gaze.

"Haven't I done enough?" Her mother's voice was trembling faintly, like a needle against a scratched record. "For eighteen years it was just you and me, and by the Saints, you didn't make it easy . . ."

She considered reminding her mother that her grandparents had done just as much, that they had paid for her schooling, taken her on trips, helped with her homework, tended to her while her mother nursed her gin headaches or stayed in bed for days under a gloom of exhaustion. But Effy had listened to this record turn a

81

thousand times. There was no use saying any of that, no use saying anything at all.

"I know," was all she managed, in the end. "I'm sorry. I'll go back to school now. Goodbye, Mother."

She hung up before her mother could answer.

Effy stepped out of the phone booth, her boots crunching the wet gravel. She had expected to feel a tight cord of panic lace up her spine, but instead she felt oddly serene. It was the removal of choice that calmed her. There were only two roads ahead of her now, one of them well-trod and dark, the other half lit and waiting.

She had thought she could go down that dark road, but the more she thought of the whispers in the hall and Master Corbenic, the more she realized she could not bear it. That made her next decision easy. She knelt to roll up her wet pant leg and then stood and marched down the empty street, the train station blurring in her peripheral vision.

Effy hadn't gone more than a dozen paces when she saw someone coming down the road toward her. He was an older man with a weather-beaten face and a shepherd's crook, and there were a number of bleating sheep at his back. She couldn't count how many until he grew closer.

It was city-bred instinct that had Effy clutching her purse against her body, but the man paused more than an arm's length away from her, wizened fingers curled around the crook. His eyes were the color of sea glass, a matte and cloudy green.

"I know you aren't from here," he said, in a garbled Southern accent that Effy struggled to understand. "A pretty young girl alone on the cliffs up there—you haven't been reading your fairy tales."

Effy felt deeply offended. "I've read plenty of fairy tales."

"Haven't been reading them right, then. Are you a religious girl? Do you pray to your Saints at night?"

"Sometimes." Truthfully, she hadn't been to church in years. Her mother had only brought her out of vague obligation, citing her grandmother's faith and devotion to Saint Caelia, patron of maternity. The nearest chapel in Draefen was dedicated to Saint Duessa, the patron of blessed liars. Effy had sat there in a starched white dress, swinging her legs beneath the pews and counting the number of red bits in the stained glass windows. Once or twice she had caught her mother nodding off.

"Well, your prayers are no use," the old shepherd said. "They won't protect you against *him*."

The wind picked up then, brittle and cold. It blew the grass on the hilltops flat and carried the salt spray of the sea from the shoreline. One of the black-faced sheep bleated at her anxiously. There were seven of them, horns curled against their flat heads like mollusks.

Electricity sparked along Effy's skin. She lowered her voice and leaned closer to the shepherd. "Do you mean the Fairy King?"

The man did not immediately reply, but his eyes shifted left and then right, toward the hills and then toward the sea, as if he expected something to come rising or lumbering out of either one.

Effy thought of the creature in the road, its wet black hair and bone crown. She had seen it. Wetherell had seen it. Perhaps the shepherd had seen it, too. Her whole body felt like a live wire, blood running with adrenaline.

"Guard yourself against him," the shepherd said. "Metal on your windows and doors."

"Iron. I know."

The old man reached into his left pocket and dug around for several moments. Then he held out his hand. Cupped in his palm were a bevy of stones, white and gray and rust-colored, like the pebbles on the beach. Each one had a small hollow in its center, through which Effy could see the man's wrinkled, ancient skin.

"Hag stones," the shepherd said. "The Fairy King has many clever disguises. Look through these and you'll see him coming, in his true form."

He grasped Effy's wrist and pried her fingers open, then deposited the stones in her palm before she could protest. They were heavier than they had looked when the old man held them. She put the stones in the pocket of her trousers.

When she looked up again, the shepherd had turned around and was walking down the road, away from her, up toward the green hills. His sheep bobbed after him like buoys on the water. One paused in the road and looked back at her.

Her skin was still electric. Effy reached into her pocket and lifted one of the stones to her eye, peering through the hollow in the middle. But she only saw the sheep staring back at her, unblinking and frozen.

She lowered the stone again, feeling foolish. Fairy tales or not, back in Caer-Isel, she never would have stopped to listen to the ramblings of some strange old man in the street. She put the stones back in her pocket and wiped the sea spray off her cheeks. It occurred to her that she'd just been the exact opposite of pickpocketed.

The pub had a name, but the sign was so damp and wood-rotted that Effy couldn't make it out. She pushed through the door with more confidence than she felt. The hairs on her neck were stiff and risen from listening to the shepherd's words.

At once she was bathed in the pub's warm, golden light. There was a stone fireplace in the corner that crackled with a sound like twigs snapping under the tread of a boot. Above it, the mantel bore old sepia-toned photographs. The room was crammed with a number of circular tables and two booths in the far back corner. The wood on the booths was shinier, newer, clearly an effort at modernizing.

Behind the bar were rows and rows of liquor bottles, some of them clear, others green or amber, gleaming like hard candies. The record she'd heard earlier was still turning, playing a song by a supine-voiced woman Effy didn't recognize.

The pub was empty save for two older men sitting by the window—fishermen, judging by their thick sweaters and rubber boots—and the bartender, a woman about her mother's age, with hands that looked like they'd worked as many years as Effy had been alive. And Preston, whose untidy hair she spotted over the top of one of the booths. She darted around the nearest table so he wouldn't see her.

She had only been to a pub once or twice in her life, when Rhia had taken her. She didn't know any of the unspoken etiquette. She didn't drink, either. Alcohol, the doctor had said, reacted poorly with her medication, and Effy already had enough trouble discerning what was real.

The bartender gave her a pitiless, glowering look. "You going to order something?" she asked, her accent as incomprehensible as the shepherd's had been.

Effy took a step toward the bar. "Yes. Sorry. I'll have a gin and tonic, please."

It was her mother's drink of choice and the first thing that came to mind. The bartender raised a brow but busied herself fetching a glass. Effy felt her cheeks heat. It was only just past nine in the morning, but she hadn't known what else to order.

She let her gaze wander toward the fishermen, who had stopped their conversation to watch her, eyes small and keen under their bushy brows.

The shepherd's words thrummed in the back of her mind. *Look through these and you'll see him coming, in his true form.*

To religious Northerners, the fairies were demons, underworld beings, the sworn enemies of their Saints. To smarmy, agnostic scientists and naturalists, the Fair Folk were as fictitious as any other stories told in church. But to Southerners, fairies were a mere fact of life, like hurricanes or adders in your garden. You took precautions against them. You shut your windows and locked your doors. You didn't go overturning any large rocks.

Effy almost raised the hag stone to her eye again, but she would have felt stupid, here in open sight of the bartender and these men.

Besides, the Fairy King was vain until his very last breath. He would choose a more dignified disguise.

The sound of a glass being placed on the bar jolted her from her thoughts. The bartender looked at her expectantly.

"How much?" Effy asked. The bartender told her, and Effy dutifully counted out the coins. The fishermen were still watching. The bartender took the money and Effy picked up her glass. "What's the most popular drink here?"

"Usually scotch. But seeing as it's winter now, most people order hot cider."

Effy clutched her cold glass, flushing. As soon as the bartender went back to wiping the counter, she scurried away.

Once she was out of sight of the bartender, she considered her options. She could sit at one of the tables, in full view of the leering fishermen, or she could take the booth right next to Preston's and—what? Sip her drink in silence, while Preston worked on the other side, both acutely aware of the other's presence with only the thin glossy wood between them like a church confessional?

Effy could scarcely imagine anything more awkward. And after the episode in the car, she felt as if she needed to reclaim some of her lost dignity. Before she could lose her nerve, she marched toward Preston's booth and sat down across from him.

He startled at once, slamming his book shut. With the flush painting his cheeks and his darting eyes, he looked like a guilty schoolboy. She supposed that was what he was, only she didn't know what he had to feel guilty about.

"I guess you finished your phone call," he said.

"Yes," Effy replied. By Preston's elbow was a glass of scotch, half full, which made her feel less foolish for ordering a drink at nine in the morning. She still hadn't decided if she was actually going to take a sip, but she was glad she had it—it made her feel more like Preston's equal.

He slid his book back into his satchel, but not before Effy saw the title on the spine: *The Poetical Works of Emrys Myrddin, 196–208 AD.*

He caught her looking and gave a defiant look back. "One of *your* library books," he said. "I didn't mean to salt the wound."

She decided not to let him fluster her. "You must have just been reading it, then. 'The Mariner's Demise.'"

"It's not one of Myrddin's well-known works. I'm surprised you recognized it."

"I told you. He's my favorite author."

"The scholarly consensus is that Myrddin's poetry is generally middling."

Effy's face heated, anger curdling her stomach. "Why bother studying something you clearly find beneath you?"

"I said that was the scholarly consensus, not my personal opinion." Which of course he wasn't going to share. He was much better than Effy at keeping his cards close to the vest. His glasses had slipped a bit down the bridge of his nose; he pushed them up again. "And anyway, you don't have to love something in order to devote yourself to it."

He said it so offhandedly, she knew he hadn't meant to rile her, but that only made it worse—that he had to do so little to wound her so much. "But what's the point otherwise?" she managed. "You scored high enough on your exams to study whatever you want, and you chose literature on a whim?"

"It wasn't a whim. And maybe architecture is your life's passion, maybe it's not. We all have our reasons for doing what we do."

Another flare of anger. "I don't see any reason for studying literature unless you care about the stories you're reading and writing."

"Well, I study theory, mostly. I'm not a writer."

That crushed her like something caught in the tight, relentless snarl of a riptide. How could he be satisfied only *studying* literature, never writing a word of his own? Never getting to put to paper the things he imagined? Meanwhile, the banal reality of her own life made her miserable: sketching plans for things she didn't know how to build, drawing houses *other* people would call home. It was enough to make her want to cry, but she dug her fingernails into her palm to keep the tears from pricking her eyes.

"Well," she said at last, trying to match the cool flatness of his tone, "I can't imagine what an Argantian would learn from reading Llyrian fairy tales, anyway. Myrddin's *our* national author. You wouldn't understand his stories unless you grew up hearing your mother read them."

"I told you," he said slowly, "my mother is Llyrian."

"But you grew up in Argant."

"Obviously."

That earned her a scowl—it was the first time Effy had seen him appear chastened, defensive. But the small victory tasted less sweet than she had thought it would. Of course Preston was *aware* of his accent and his unmistakably Argantian surname. She remembered her conversation with the literature student in the library, who had echoed her question: *I mean, how many Argantians want to study Llyrian literature?*

Underneath it was a second, unspoken question: *What gives them the right?*

She didn't want to be like that boy, didn't want to be like *those* Llyrians, small-minded and bigoted, believing all the absurd superstitions and stereotypes about their enemies. No matter how much she disliked Preston, it wasn't his fault for being born Argantian, any more than it was her fault for being born a woman.

And Effy remembered the reverence in his tone when he'd recited those lines from "The Mariner's Demise." *We all have our reasons for doing what we do.*

Maybe there was a reason he'd attached himself to Myrddin. Maybe it wasn't just shameless opportunism. Suddenly, and against all odds, she actually felt sorry for goading him.

Preston lifted his glass and downed it in a single swig, without even grimacing. When he was finished, he glanced toward her untouched gin and tonic. "Are you going to drink that?"

Effy looked down at her glass, the ice melting, tonic water fizzing. She thought of her mother's bloodshot eyes after a night of drinking and felt vaguely nauseous. "No."

"Then let's go."

"What?"

"I'll drive you back to Hiraeth."

"I thought you were going to work here," she said. "What about Ianto breathing down your neck?"

"At the house it's Ianto, here it will be you." Preston caught the beginnings of an objection on her lips, and hurriedly went on: "It's not your fault. You just won't have anything to do in town except drink gin and stare at me while I work. I'm not happy to be the most interesting thing in Saltney, but regrettably I can assure you that that is the case."

"I don't know about that." Effy thought of the shepherd, the stones in her pocket. She decided not to mention any of that. Instead she said, "Not to wound your ego, but I saw some very interesting sheep dung on my way over here."

Preston actually *laughed*. It was a short, surprised little huff of air, but there was no malice in it, only genuine amusement. And Effy found—regrettably—that she liked the sound of it.

She returned her still-full glass to the bartender and followed Preston out into the street. It had started to drizzle again, and the water caught in his hair like tiny bright beads of morning dew.

Effy licked a drop of rain off her lips as Preston reached into his pocket and pulled out a pack of cigarettes. He put a cigarette in his mouth and lit it one-handed, the other hand braced on the driver's-side door. His long, thin fingers wrapped around the handle entirely.

"Can I have one?" she asked.

She wasn't exactly sure why she said it. Maybe she wanted to prove something to him, to make up for the glass of gin she'd left melting on the bar.

Maybe she was just distracted by the way his lips rounded gently when he smoked them. Effy shook her head, trying to dispel the unwelcome thought.

Preston looked as surprised as she felt. But without a word, he plucked out another cigarette, put it in his mouth, lit it, and passed it to her over the hood of the car.

Effy let out a short laugh of her own. "You don't trust me with your lighter?"

She was very pleased to see his cheeks pink. "I was trying to be polite," he said. "I won't make that mistake again."

They got into the car. Effy put the cigarette to her lips and inhaled, trying not to cough. She'd never smoked before, but she didn't want Preston to know that. She also didn't want Preston to know that she was thinking intently about how the same cigarette had touched his lips mere moments ago. Her gaze kept darting to his mouth, the way he held his cigarette delicately between his teeth while he drove.

The car wound up the hillside, cigarette smoke curling in the quiet air, the sea thrumming its ceaseless rhythm against the rocks. Perhaps it was the cigarette, perhaps the oddly comforting smell of Preston's car, but Effy felt a sort of numbing calm come over her.

She reached for the stones in her pocket anyway, running her finger along the hollows, as she was delivered to Hiraeth once again.

SIX

The Drowning was more than a climatological event. It came to define social, political, and economic history in the region, and gave rise to a distinctive and ever more salient subculture among residents of the Bottom Hundred. Somewhat paradoxically, it caused an upswing in Southern nationalism, a hardening of Llyr's North-South divide. It can thus be said that the Drowning structures the core of Southern identity, even nearly two centuries later.

FROM THE INTRODUCTION TO *A COMPENDIUM OF SOUTHERN WRITERS IN THE NEO-BALLADIC TRADITION,* EDITED BY DR. RHYS BRINLEY, 201 AD

The next morning was the first truly cloudless day in the Bay of Nine Bells since Effy had arrived, and she took it as a sign. As soon as she awoke, she dressed quickly and scampered up the path toward the house, her boots sliding in the soft dirt.

Below, even the sea appeared to be behaving itself, the waves a hushed murmur against the stone. Sunlight glinted off the white peaks of foam. In the distance, she saw two seals at play in the water, their gray heads pebble-small from her vantage point.

Yesterday's calm had given way to a fledgling determination. Sitting in the car beside Preston, tobacco smoke filling the cab, Effy had decided she would try. She could not give up before she even started.

You don't have to love something in order to devote yourself to it, Preston had said. In the moment she had chafed at his condescension, but now she realized—with some reluctance—that it was actually good advice.

And maybe she had been wrong about Myrddin in a few aspects, but that didn't mean she was wrong about everything. He was still the man who wrote *Angharad.* He was still the man who put iron on the doors of the guesthouse.

Angharad had once thought her tasks impossible, too. At first she had never believed she could escape the Fairy King.

Effy was no great designer, but she was an excellent escape artist. She was always chipping away at the architecture of her life until there was a crack big enough to slip through. Whenever she was faced with danger, her mind manifested a secret doorway, a hole in the floorboards, somewhere she could hide or run to.

At last the house came into view, starkly black against the delicate blue sky. Effy had her sketchpad with her original design for Hiraeth Manor and three pens, lest one or two of them run dry. She was panting with pleasant exhaustion by the time she climbed the mossy steps.

Ianto was waiting for her at the threshold. He looked pleased to see her, perhaps even relieved. "You look as though you're feeling better," he remarked.

"Yes," she said, feeling a fresh wave of embarrassment as she remembered how she'd fled from the house. "I'm sorry about not coming yesterday—I'm still, um, getting used to the air down here, I think."

"Understandable," Ianto said, generously. "You're a Northern girl through and through, I can tell. But I'm glad to see you looking less green." She didn't know whether he was commenting on her appearance or her attitude, until he added, "Your skin is a lovely color."

"Oh," she said. Her face heated. "Thank you."

Ianto's pale eyes were shining. "Let's begin, then," he said, and beckoned Effy through the doorway.

Effy shook off the slight feeling of unease and followed after him. She had been chosen on the strength and inventiveness of her original design, but that had been done before seeing Hiraeth itself. Ianto's initial entreaty had made it sound like there would be nothing but a large empty field waiting for her, ready to be filled with a new foundation. Not a dilapidated monstrosity. After returning from Saltney yesterday, Effy had sat down on the edge of the bed, sketchpad balanced on her knees, and tried to marry her initial vision with the ugly reality she'd seen.

The result was, at least to her novice's eyes, not half bad. She figured the plan would evolve over time—Ianto wanted a finalized design before she returned to Caer-Isel—but she could do it. She needed to do it.

Ianto led her into the foyer, which, despite the sun and cloudless sky, was still only half filled with gloomy gray light. The puddles on the floor were murky and salt-laced. Wetherell was standing by the entrance to the kitchen, looking stiff and dour and hard-edged. When she said good morning to him, he responded with only a nod.

Effy refused to let him temper her enthusiasm. "This is where I want to start, actually," she said. "The foyer. It should be flooded with light on a sunny day."

"That will be difficult," Ianto said. "The front of the house faces west."

"I know," she replied, reaching into her purse for her sketch-pad. "I want to flip the whole house around, if we can. The foyer and the kitchen facing east, overlooking the water."

Ianto assumed a pensive look. "Then the entrance would have to be along the cliff."

"I know it sounds impossible," she acknowledged.

Wetherell spoke up. "What it sounds is expensive. Has Mr. Myrddin discussed the financial constraints of the project with you?"

"Not now," Ianto said, waving a hand. "I want to hear the extent of Effy's plans. If we need to make adjustments, we can do that later."

For a moment Wetherell looked like he might protest, but his lips thinned and he sank back against the doorway.

"Well," she began carefully, "I did think about that. Cost and feasibility. Following my design, it would be necessary to demolish most of the current structure and set the new house back several acres from the edge of the cliff. Given the unpredictability of the rock, the uneven topography . . ." Effy trailed off. A pall had come over Ianto's face. His look of displeasure told her that their ideas were not, in fact, aligned. Had he not thought of an entirely new structure taking the place of the old?

Ianto's expression, the darkening of his eyes, filled her with a vague but terrible dread. She shrank back.

But he only said, "Will you come upstairs with me, Effy? I'd like you to see something."

Effy nodded numbly, immediately feeling foolish for being so afraid. It was the sort of thing her mother would have chastised her for—*nothing happened, Effy*. She'd been offered that puzzled scorn in lieu of comfort as a child when she'd run to her mother's room after having a nightmare.

After having the *same* nightmare, over and over again, that same dark shape in the corner of her room. Eventually she had stopped coming to her mother's door at all. Instead she read *Angharad* in the lamplight until her sleeping pills pulled her under.

Ianto led her upstairs, hand gliding over the rotted-wood banister. Effy followed, feeling a bit unsteady on her feet. As they passed the portrait of the Fairy King, she paused briefly and met his cold stare. She hadn't meant to do it. It felt like a taunt, a reminder that *this* version of the Fairy King was trapped inside a gilded frame, inside an unreal world.

But the real Fairy King was not muzzled like the one in the painting. And she had seen that creature in the road.

Effy gripped the hag stone in her pocket as she and Ianto reached the upstairs landing. Water was dripping off the carvings

97

of Saint Eupheme and Saint Marinell. Ianto was so tall that it dripped onto his shoulders and his black hair.

He didn't seem to notice. Living in a place like this, Effy supposed, you might begin to not feel the cold or damp at all.

"This way," Ianto said, directing her down the hall. The floor groaned emphatically beneath them. He stopped when they reached a small and unremarkable wooden door. "You left in such a hurry the other day, I didn't get to show you this. Not that I blame you entirely, of course. This house is not for the faint of heart."

The knob began to rattle and the doorframe began to shake, as if someone were pounding on the door from the other side. Effy tensed, heart pattering. She found herself thinking of Master Corbenic's office and the green armchair, its loose threads like reaching vines.

Ianto threw the door open. Or rather, he turned the knob and the wind did the rest, nearly yanking the door right off its hinges with a vicious howl. Effy stumbled back instinctively, raising a hand to shield her eyes. It wasn't until there was a lull in the wind's wailing that she was able to peer through the open door.

There was a narrow balcony, only half its boards fully intact, eaten away so thoroughly by mold and damp that the floor resembled a checkerboard: stretches of black emptiness alternating with planks of sun-blanched wood. It creaked and moaned in the wind the way Effy imagined a ghost ship would, tattered sails swaying to a banshee's song.

She looked up at Ianto in horror. She hoped he didn't expect her to actually set foot on the ruined platform.

As if able to read her thoughts, he thrust out his arm to hold her back. It was a large arm, black-haired, the skin under it as pale as the ancient stone.

"Don't go any further," Ianto said. "And ignore yet another testament to my father's negligence. I want you to look at the view."

Feeling safer behind Ianto's arm, Effy peered forward. Over the rotted wood was the cliff face, green and white and gray, dotted with eyries and smaller gull nests, feathers catching in the wind. Below it, the sea looked sleek and deadly, waves gnashing their teeth against the rock.

Effy felt the height in the soles of her feet and her palms turned slick. Before, when the cliff had broken apart beneath her, it had been so unexpected, she hadn't even had the chance to be afraid. Now she understood the danger of the rocks, the ocean's foaming wrath.

"It's beautiful, isn't it?" Ianto said. Even in the wind, his hair still lay mostly flat.

"It's terrifying," Effy confessed.

"Most beautiful things are," Ianto said. "Do you know why it's called the Bay of Nine Bells?"

Effy shook her head.

"Before the Drowning, the land stretched out further into the sea. There were dozens of small towns there on the old land— fishing villages, mostly. What have you been taught about what happened to them?"

"Well, there was a storm," Effy started, but she could tell it was one of those false questions that was like a hole in the floor. If you took the bait, you would fall right into it.

Ianto smiled at her thinly. "That's one of the misconceptions many Northerners have about the Drowning. That it was one enormous storm, a single night of terror and then its aftermath. But it can take a person up to ten minutes to drown. Ten minutes doesn't seem like a very long time, but when you can't breathe and your lungs are aching, it seems very long indeed. You can even die after you've been pulled from the drink, dry on land, water having rotted your lungs beyond repair. The Drowning of the Bottom Hundred took years, my dear. It started with the wet season lasting longer than it should and the dry season being less dry than it ought. A few cliffs crumbling, a marsh or two swelling past its margins—at first it was scarcely remarked upon, and certainly not taken as a warning.

"Have you heard the expression about the frog in hot water? If you raise the temperature slowly, he won't notice a thing until he's boiled alive. A soft-bellied Northerner might have seen the danger coming, but the Southerners practically had scales and fins themselves. The sea took and took and took, thousands of little deaths, and they endured it all because they knew nothing else. They didn't think to fear the Drowning until the water was lapping at their door.

"The lucky ones, the wealthier ones, with their homes set back further from the shore, managed to flee. But the waves rose up and swallowed everything, houses and shops and women and children, the old and the young. The sea has no mercy. In this bay there were nine churches, and they were all swallowed up, too, no matter how hard their supplicants pleaded with Saint Marinell. They say that on certain days you can still hear the bells of those churches, ringing underwater."

Effy turned toward the water and listened, but she didn't hear any ringing.

"The Drowning was two hundred years ago," she said. "Long before your father was born." She hoped it didn't sound disparaging.

"Of course," Ianto said. "But the story of the Drowning lives in the minds of every child who is born in the Bottom Hundred. Our mothers whisper it to us in our cradles. Our fathers teach us to swim before we can walk. The first game we play with our friends is to see how long we can hold our breath underwater. It's the fear we have to learn. The fear keeps the sea from taking us."

Effy remembered what Rhia had told her about the Southerners and their superstitions. About how they feared a second Drowning and thought the magic of the Sleepers would stop it. Watching the ocean barrage the cliffs, and hearing Ianto speak, Effy could understand why they thought such a thing. Fear could make a believer of anybody.

Strangely, she found herself thinking of Master Corbenic. When he had first placed his hand over her knee, she had thought he was being warm, fatherly. She hadn't known to be afraid. Even now, she didn't know if she was allowed to be.

"That's why my father built this house here," Ianto went on.

"He wanted my mother and me to learn how to fear the sea."

"Your mother isn't from the Bottom Hundred?" It wasn't the point of what Ianto had said, but the small detail stood out to Effy, who hadn't seen even a trace of the mysterious widow.

"No," Ianto said shortly. "But Effy, I hope you understand that to tear down this house would be an act of sacrilege. It would dishonor my father's memory. Perhaps I was unclear in my initial missive, and I apologize. This house cannot be leveled. I know that you have enormous respect and affection for my father and for the legacy of Emrys Myrddin, so I am confident you can rise to the challenge."

Did he believe, too, that Myrddin's consecration would stop another Drowning? That perhaps it would even reverse the damage that had already been done? Effy didn't ask; she didn't want to risk offending him. As she tried to decide how to reply, Ianto reached over and pulled the door shut. The wind's howling grew muffled, and her hair lay flat again.

"I'm ready," Effy said at last. "I want to do this."

She wanted so badly to do something valuable for once, to make something beautiful, something that was *hers*. She wanted this to be more than just an escape, wanted to be more than a scared little girl running away from imaginary monsters. She couldn't write a thesis or a newspaper article or even a fairy tale of her own—the university had made damn sure she knew that. This was her only chance to make something that would last, so she would take it, no matter how insurmountable the task seemed.

And when she went back to Caer-Isel, it would be to tell

Master Corbenic and her schoolmates that they had been wrong about her. She would never go back whimpering and kneeling. She would never sit in that green chair again.

She would have to put her faith in Myrddin once more. She would have to believe he would not set her an impossible challenge. She would have to trust, as she always had, the words written in *Angharad*, the happy ending it promised. So what about the million drowned men? So what about the rumors of another Drowning?

Her only enemy was the sea.

"Excellent," Ianto said, smiling his one-dimpled smile. "I knew I was right to choose you." He reached over and rested a hand on her shoulder, giving it a gentle squeeze. Effy froze.

Ianto did not stop staring at her, as if he expected her to reply. But all Effy could feel was the clamminess of his touch, the enormous weight of his hand. It sent her stumbling backward in time, back to Master Corbenic's office. Back to that green chair.

She couldn't speak for how heavy it felt. She felt as if she'd turned into an old doll, buried under cobwebs and dust.

When the stretch of silence became too long and too awkward, Ianto let her go. The intensity of his gaze dimmed, as if he had sensed her sudden terror. He blinked, looking a bit dazed himself.

"I'm sorry," he said. "Excuse me for a moment. I need to run some numbers by Wetherell. He's not going to be happy with me, I'm afraid. Please just wait here."

Effy didn't wait. Her head was throbbing and her stomach felt thick. Myrddin's strange ruin of a house creaked and groaned around her. Many years ago, before the first Drowning, the people of the Bottom Hundred had executed their criminals by tying them up on the beach at low tide. Then they all watched and waited as the waves came up. They brought picnic blankets and bread. They fed themselves as the sea fed the sinner, pouring water down her throat until she was pale and gorged.

Effy wasn't sure why she always pictured a woman when she thought of it. A woman with kelp-colored hair.

That was exactly the sort of barbarity the Northern conquerors claimed they were saving their Southern subjects from. Centuries later, it was the stuff of fairy tales and legends, all of it generally *Llyrian*, as if no conquest had ever occurred. As if whole villages had not been slaughtered in a quest to eradicate those unseemly traditions. As if stories were not spoils of war.

Effy walked slowly down the hall, one hand pressed flat against the wall for support. Her nausea did not abate as she paused outside one of the doors. It was the study on the other side, Preston's room. Curiosity, or maybe something else, compelled her to reach out for the knob.

She had always sat numbly inside the church confessional, trying to invent sins that seemed worth confessing but not so horrifying as to scandalize the priest. Now she had the unmistakable urge to confess. She wanted someone to know how Ianto had touched her—even if she was still trying to convince herself it had been nothing at all. A friendly gesture, a bracing pat on the shoulder. But didn't all drownings begin with a harmless dribble of water?

Effy hated that she couldn't tell right from wrong, safe from unsafe. Her fear had transfigured the entire world. Looking at anything was like trying to glimpse a reflection in a broken mirror, all of it warped and shattered and strange.

Preston had said all he cared about was the truth. Who better, then, to tell her whether her fear was justified? She felt, somehow, that he could be trusted with this.

All that time in the car and he had never touched her. In fact, he had moved about her, *around* her, in a very careful sort of way, as if she were something fragile he did not want to risk breaking.

Effy held her breath and opened the door slowly. It creaked like the rest of the house, an awful squeal like a dying cat. She was expecting to see Preston sitting behind Myrddin's desk, head bent over a book.

But the room was empty, and Effy felt a thud of disappointment. She let her gaze wander across the scattered papers and old books, the cigarettes lining the windowsill, the blanket thrown over the shredded chaise longue. She looked at the chaise for a moment, trying to imagine Preston sleeping there.

It made her smile a little bit to think about it. His long legs would dangle over the edge.

Feeling more curious and emboldened, she moved toward the desk. It had been Myrddin's, though she could no longer imagine him sitting there—Preston was all over it. His books were lying open like clamshells, water stains yellowing their pages. *The Poetical Works of Emrys Myrddin, 196–208 AD* was open to the page with "The Mariner's Demise." Effy traced her finger over the words, thinking of Preston doing the same. Had she imagined the reverence in his tone, or did he feel passionately about Myrddin after all?

There were papers strewn about, some balled up or folded, others just crumpled and then smoothed flat again. Many had ragged edges, as though they'd been ripped out of a notebook. Effy looked for Preston's notebook, but she didn't see it. His pens were scattered around, irresponsibly uncapped.

It was funny now, how she had assumed he would be fastidious and precise in all his work. Even *she* didn't leave her pens uncapped like some kind of barbarian.

Effy was aware that she was snooping, but she didn't care. She smoothed some of the papers flat. Most of them were written in Argantian, which she couldn't read, though she did pause to study Preston's handwriting. It was tight and neat, the same way it had looked in the library logbook, but not necessarily elegant. He had a funny way of drawing his *g*'s, two circles stacked like a headless snowman. Effy bit her lip because it seemed like a silly thing to smile at, even though it did charm her.

She unfolded another paper, this one written in Llyrian.

Proposed thesis title? Execution of the Author: An Inquiry into the Authorship of the Major Works of Emrys Myrddin
Part one: present theory of false authorship, starting with ??
Part two: cryptographic evidence—ask Gosse for samples
Part three: letters, diary entries—use nearest mimeograph, in Laleston?

The list went on for quite a bit longer, but Effy's mind stopped on the first line. *Execution of the Author.* With trembling fingers, she turned the paper over. Preston had drawn some aimless sketches in the margins and scrawled some slapdash words, repeating their way down the page.

She was staring at his marginalia in shocked disbelief when the door creaked open.

"What are you doing?" Preston demanded.

Effy crumpled the paper at once, heart pounding. "I could ask you the same."

Her voice sounded more certain than she felt. Preston had a mug of coffee in one hand, and his lithe fingers curled around it so tightly that his knuckles were white. That same muscle feathered in his jaw. Effy remembered how guarded he had been when Ianto showed her the study, how quickly he had put his notes away when she joined him in the booth yesterday.

Now she knew why he'd been so careful to hide his work.

"Effy," he said gravely. He still hadn't moved from the threshold, but his eyes were darting around behind his glasses.

"'Execution of the Author,'" she read aloud in a quavering voice. "'An Inquiry into the Authorship of the Major Works of Emrys Myrddin.' This is your thesis?"

"Just wait a second," Preston said, an edge of desperation to his words. Effy found she quite liked the idea of him *begging* her, and a little heat rose in her cheeks at the thought. "I can explain everything. Don't go running off to Ianto."

Her cheeks heated further. "What makes you think I would run to Ianto?"

Preston paced toward her slowly, letting the door groan shut behind him. Effy's heart was beating very fast. She remembered what the shepherd had told her, about the Fairy King in his disguises, and in that moment she thought she could see a bit of that wickedness in Preston, his eyes narrowed and his chest swelling.

Effy reached for the hag stone in her pocket.

In another moment, all the ferocity in him fizzled. He shrank back, as if tacitly apologizing for daring to approach her like *that*, and Effy's hand slid from her pocket. Preston did not make a very convincing Fairy King. Too stiff. Too scrawny.

"Listen," he said. "I know you're a devotee of Myrddin, but this isn't meant to disrespect his legacy."

Effy held the paper against her chest. "You think he was a *fraud?*"

"I'm just trying to get at the truth. The truth doesn't have an agenda." When she only stared back at him stonily, Preston went on. "'Fraud' has certain connotations I'm not comfortable with. But no, I don't think he's the sole author of the majority of his works."

Gritting her teeth, Effy wished he would just speak plainly for *once*. She struggled to keep her voice even as she replied, "Myrddin was a strange man, a hermit, a recluse—but that doesn't make him a fraud. Why would you believe something like that? *How* could you believe something like that?"

It was *Myrddin* they were talking about, Emrys Myrddin, the seventh and most recently consecrated Sleeper, the most celebrated author in Llyrian history. It was absurd. Impossible.

"It's complicated." Preston put down his coffee mug and ran a hand through his already-mussed hair. "For starters, Myrddin was the son of a fisherman. It's not clear whether his parents were even literate, and from what I can find out, he had stopped attending school by age twelve. The idea that someone of his limited education could produce such works is—well, it's a romantic notion, but it's highly improbable."

Effy's blood pulsed in her ears. By now, even the tips of her fingers had gone numb with fury. "You're nothing more than a typical elitist twat," she bit out. "I suppose that only the spectacle-wearing university-educated among us can write anything meaningful?"

"Why are you so interested in defending him?" Preston challenged. His gaze was cold, and even in her rage, Effy supposed it was deserved. "You're a Northern girl. Sayre isn't exactly a Southern peasant name."

How much time had he spent thinking about her surname? For some reason it made her stomach flutter.

"Just because I'm not a Southerner doesn't mean I'm a snob," she said. "And that just proves how stupid your theory is. Myrddin's work isn't just for superstitious fisherfolk for the Bottom Hundred. Everyone who reads it loves it. Well, everyone who isn't an elitist—"

"Don't call me a twat again," Preston said peevishly. "I'm far from the only one to question his authorship. It's a very common theory in the literature college, but so far, no one has done enough work to prove it. My adviser, Master Gosse, is leading the charge. He sent me here under the pretense of collecting Myrddin's documents and letters. I *am* here with the university's permission—that part wasn't a lie."

The thought of a bunch of stuffy, pinch-nosed literature scholars sitting around in leather armchairs and coldly discussing ways to discredit Myrddin made Effy feel angrier than ever. Angier than when she'd confronted Preston on the cliffside, angrier than when she'd seen his name written in the library's logbook.

"What's your end goal, anyway? Just to humiliate Myrddin's fans? They would remove him from the Sleeper Museum, they would . . ." Something truly terrible occurred to her. "Is this a grand Argantian plot to weaken Llyr?"

Preston's expression darkened. "Don't tell me *you* actually believe the stories about Sleeper magic."

Effy's stomach shriveled. Her fingers curled into a fist around Preston's crumpled paper. Of course *he* wouldn't believe in Sleeper magic, being a heathen Argantian and an academic to boot. She felt embarrassed to have mentioned it.

"I didn't say that," she snapped. "But it would be massively humiliating for Llyr, losing our most prestigious Sleeper. It would affect the *morale* of our soldiers, at the very least."

"Llyr is winning this war, in case you weren't aware." Preston spoke aloofly, but a shadow passed over his face. "They're even thinking about reinstating a draft in Argant—all men eighteen to twenty-five. It's not my aim at all, but it wouldn't be the worst thing in the world if Llyrian soldiers were to suffer a loss of *morale*."

Effy could hardly imagine anyone less suited to military life than Preston Héloury. "So you're a saboteur."

He scoffed. "Now you're being truly ridiculous. This isn't about politics, not in the slightest. This is about scholarship."

"And you think scholarship is completely removed from politics?"

To his credit, Preston seemed to genuinely consider this, fixing his gaze on some obscure point on the far wall for a moment. When he looked back at her, he said, "No. But ideally it would be. Scholarship should be the effort to seek out objective truth."

Effy made a scathing noise in the back of her throat. "I think you're deluded in even believing there's such a thing as *objective truth*."

"Well." Preston folded his arms across his chest. "I suppose we fundamentally disagree, then."

Effy's rage was starting to subside, leaving her shaky with the ebbing of adrenaline. She stopped to think more calmly.

"*Well*," she said, mimicking his smug tone, "I don't think Ianto would be very happy to learn that the university student he's hosting is actually trying to tear down his father's legacy. In fact, I think he would be furious."

She was glad to see Preston's face turn pale.

"Listen," he said again, "you don't have to do this. I've been here for weeks and I've hardly found anything of use. I'm going to have to give up the project and leave soon, unless . . ."

Effy arched a brow. "Unless?"

"Unless you can help me," he said.

At first she thought she had misheard him. If he had meant to fluster her, it had worked. When she recovered herself, Effy asked, incredulously, "*Help* you? Why would I ever help you?"

And then, without preamble, Preston said, "'I looked for myself in the tide pools at dusk, but that was another one of the Fairy King's jests. By the time it was dusk, the sun had cowed herself too much, drawn close to the vanishing horizon, and all that remained in those pools was darkness. Her ebbing light could not reach them.'"

He looked at her expectantly. Even as dazed as she was, Effy remembered the end of the passage. "'I slapped at that cold, dull water with my hands, as if I could punish it for disobeying me. And in that moment, I realized that without knowing it, the Fairy King had spoken truly: although the tide pools had not shown me my face, I had been revealed. I was a treacherous, wrathful, wanting thing, just like he was. Just as he had always wanted me.'" Effy paused, gulped down a breath, and then added, "And it's 'waning light,' not 'ebbing.'"

Preston folded his arms across his chest. "No one else in the literature college can do that. Quote *Angharad* word for word at the drop of a hat. And that poem, 'The Mariner's Demise'? Myrddin isn't known for his poetry, and that's a very obscure one."

"What's your point?"

"You clearly want to be in the literature college, Effy. And you deserve to be."

Effy could only stare at him. She had to remember to breathe, to blink. "You can't be serious. I have a good memory—"

"It's more than that," he said. "What do you think the other literature students have that you don't?"

Now he had to be toying with her. Hot, indignant tears pricked at her eyes, but she refused to let them fall. "Just stop it," she bit out. "You know the reason. You know women aren't allowed in the literature college. You don't need to play some cruel, silly game—"

"It's an absurd, outdated tradition," Preston cut in sharply.

Effy was surprised at his vehemence. He could have repeated the same platitudes that all the university professors did, about how women's minds were too insipid, how they could only write frivolous, feminine things, nothing that would transcend time or place, nothing that would *last*.

"I didn't think you'd care so much about a rule that doesn't affect you at all," she said.

"You should know by now that I'm not a fan of doing things just because that's the way they've always been done." Preston set his jaw. "Or preserving things just because they've always been preserved."

Of course. Effy's cheeks warmed. "So, what? I would get a paragraph in your acknowledgments?"

"No," he said. "I would make you coauthor."

That was even more unexpected. Effy's breath caught, her heart skipping its beats. "I don't—I've never written a literary paper before. I wouldn't know how."

"It's not hard. You already know Myrddin's works back to front. I would write all the theory and criticism parts." Preston looked at her intently. "If you went to them with a truly ground-breaking literary thesis, they wouldn't be able to come up with an excuse not to let you in."

113

Effy almost rolled her eyes—who called their own work *ground-breaking*? But she allowed herself, briefly, to imagine a new future. One where she went back to the university with her name beside Preston's on a *groundbreaking* thesis (maybe even *before* his, if Preston wanted to play fair and put their names in alphabetical order). One where the literature college broke with its outmoded tradition. She would never have to draw another cross section.

She would never have to see Master Corbenic again.

There was hope, blooming like a tender little flower bud. Master Corbenic, the other students—they couldn't win if she quit their game and started playing another.

But it would mean betraying Myrddin. Betraying everything she had believed her whole life, the words and stories she had followed like the point of a compass. *Angharad* had always been her true north.

"I can't," Effy said at last. She couldn't bring herself to elaborate further.

Preston exhaled. "Aren't you at least a little bit curious about Myrddin's legacy? Don't you want to find out the truth for yourself? He's your favorite author, after all. You could end up proving me wrong."

She snorted, but she couldn't deny the idea was appealing. "You really care more about the truth than you do about being right?"

"Of course I do." There was not an ounce of hesitation in his voice.

His intensity made her falter. As if sensing her will had wavered, Preston pressed on. "I can't tell you it won't be difficult, getting the department to change their minds. But I'll fight for you, Effy. I promise."

He met her eyes, and there was no subterfuge in his gaze. No artifice. He meant it sincerely. Effy swallowed hard.

"I did try, you know," she managed. "When I first got my exam score. I wrote a letter to your adviser, Master Gosse. I suggested thesis topics. I told him how much Myrddin's work meant to me."

Preston drew a gentle breath. "And what did he say?"

"He never replied."

Effy had never told anyone that, not even her mother. She looked down at her hands, still curled around the crumpled piece of paper. They were trembling just a little bit.

"I'm sorry," Preston said. And then he hesitated, running a hand through his hair. "I—that's terrible and cruel."

She said nothing, trying to ignore the tears pricking at her eyes.

"But I have faith in this project," Preston went on. His voice was softer now. "I have faith in you—in both of us." He stammered a little bit at the end, as if embarrassed by what he had said. Effy had never heard him trip over his words before, and for some reason it made her want to trust him more.

"But what about the Sleepers?" she asked, risking the possibility that Preston would just scoff at her again. "I know everyone at the university is a snooty agnostic who thinks they're too clever for myths and magic, but not everyone in Llyr feels the same. Especially in the South. They think that Myrddin's consecration is the only thing preventing a second Drowning."

"A single paper isn't enough to destroy a myth in one fell swoop,"

Preston said. "Especially not one that's had centuries to build. The Sleeper Museum isn't going to evict Myrddin the moment we step off the train in Caer-Isel with our thesis in hand."

He hadn't spelled it out precisely, but Effy knew what he meant: that truth and magic were two different things, irreconcilable. It was precisely what Effy had been told all her life—by the physicians who had treated her, by the mother who had despaired of her, by the schoolteachers and priests and professors who had never, ever believed her.

Effy had put her faith in magic. Preston held nothing more sacred than truth. Theirs was not a natural alliance.

And yet she found herself unable to refuse.

"Don't you think they'll have the same apprehensions I did?" It was her last line of defense. "Don't you think some of them will ask why a person with the name *Héloury* is so intent on destroying the legacy of a Llyrian national author?"

"All the more reason to have a blue-blooded Llyrian name like *Effy Sayre* on the cover sheet next to mine." Preston's gaze held a bit of amusement. "Consider it an armistice."

Effy couldn't resist rolling her eyes. "Is that *really* why you want my help?"

"Not just that. Ianto is shutting me out. He doesn't trust me. But he trusts you."

She remembered the way Ianto had laid his hand on her shoulder. How heavy it had felt, how it had pushed her back down into that drowning place. Without thinking, she blurted out, "So what do you want me to do? Seduce him?"

116

Preston's face turned strikingly red. "No! Saints, no. What kind of person do you think I am?"

Effy was flushing, too, unable to meet his gaze. Why had she said that? It was more proof that something was broken inside her brain, like a skewing of train tracks. She could never trust anyone's intentions.

"Do Argantians have a patron saint of truth?" she asked.

"Not exactly," said Preston. "But I'll swear by your Saint Una if it makes you happy."

Somehow, Effy found herself nodding. Her right hand was still clutching Preston's paper, so she stuck out her left hand, with its missing ring finger.

Preston took her hand and they shook. His palm was soft, his fingers long and thin. Effy usually didn't like shaking hands with people. She always held on past the point of comfort because she never knew when it was time to let go.

"I swear by Saint Una I'll help you," she said. "And I won't reveal you—us—to Ianto."

"I swear by Saint Una I won't betray you," said Preston. "And I'll fight for you. I promise your name will be there on the cover sheet, right next to mine."

Effy held on to him, their fingers locked. She waited for him to twitch, to shake her loose, but he didn't. The pad of his thumb was ink stained. She wondered if this was some sort of test, if he was trying to judge her mettle. Effy had never thought of herself as someone with much staying power.

Yet there was nothing challenging in his eyes, and Effy realized then that he was giving *her* the choice. It was a small thing, maybe not worth remarking upon at all. But very rarely did anyone allow Effy to choose.

Finally she let go. Preston's hand dropped to his side at once, fingers flexing.

"We'll start tomorrow," he said stiffly. "Can I have my paper back?"

Mortified, Effy released the page and set it down on the desk. The ink had bled a little onto her palm. "You should have written that one in Argantian, too," she said.

Preston gave her a thin-lipped look. "I know that now."

Back in the guest cottage that night, Effy's mind wouldn't stop turning. Even after she had swallowed her sleeping pill, she lay awake staring at the damp and moldy ceiling, thinking of the bargain she had struck.

Perhaps in the morning she would realize it was a foolish thing to do. Perhaps she would regret not leaving on the next train.

Perhaps she would regret betraying Myrddin.

But for the moment, all she could feel was a stomach-churning adrenaline. She rubbed at the nub of her ring finger. It was as smooth as a hag stone.

Effy rolled over, hair streaming out over the green pillowcase, heartbeat still quick. When she closed her eyes, she could see Preston's page of notes, blue ink against white. It was her name he'd scrawled aimlessly in the margins, repeating all the way down the page:

Effy
Effy
Effy
Effy
Effy.

SEVEN

Angharad is a difficult text to place. Certain passages read as lurid and vulgar, more befitting an erotic tale or a romance, while others have exquisitely rendered prose and great thematic depth. It is not uncommon to see housewives paging through their copies over a pile of laundry, or commuters hunched over their paperbacks on the tram. And yet it is just as common for *Angharad* to appear on the syllabi of the university's most advanced literature courses. No other book in Llyrian history can boast such universal appeal.

FROM THE INTRODUCTION TO *ANGHARAD: THE
ANNOTATED COLLECTOR'S EDITION*, EDITED BY
DR. CEDRIC GOSSE, 210 AD

When Effy first came to Hiraeth, she would never have expected to find herself, at the bright hour of seven in the morning, poring over a dead man's letters with Preston Héloury. Yet that was exactly where she found herself the next day.

"Well," Preston said, "I suppose you'll want to know where I've left off."

She nodded.

"I suppose I'll explain the basis for my theory, then. Myrddin's family were refugees of the Drowning," said Preston. "It would seem intuitive for his works to paint the natural world as inherently perilous, unstable, even malicious. Much of his poetry personalizes nature in that way—"

Effy cut him off. "'The only enemy is the sea.'"

"Precisely. But Myrddin's father was a fisherman, and his grandfather, too. Master Gosse was the first to bring up that apparent contradiction. Myrddin's family depended on the sea for their livelihood, yet it's only ever painted as a cruel and vicious force of evil in his work."

"That's not true," said Effy. "In *Angharad*, the Fairy King takes her out to see the ocean, and she says it's beautiful and free. 'Lovely and dangerous and vast beyond mortal comprehension, the sea makes dreamers of us all.'"

Preston gave her an odd look. It was the first time she'd seen him look bemused, quizzical. "Finish the quote."

"Hm." Effy racked her brain to remember the passage. "'I looked to the Fairy King behind me, and the ocean before, the two most beautiful things I had ever seen. They were both creatures of rage and salt and foam. Both could strip me to the bone. I wanted nothing more than to tempt their wrath, because if I were brave enough, I might earn their love instead.'"

"You really do know it cover to cover," Preston said, and this time, Effy was certain—there was admiration in his voice. "But I don't think that paints the sea in a very charitable way, either. The Fairy King is Angharad's captor. Myrddin portrays the sea as a trickster god, luring Angharad with its beauty, but always with the potential to destroy her utterly."

"He loved her," Effy said. She was surprised at the vehemence of her tone. "The Fairy King. He loved Angharad more than anything. *She* was the one to betray *him*."

She'd never had the chance to speak about *Angharad* like this, to defend her position, to present her own theories. There was something exhilarating about it, and Effy expected Preston to challenge her. Instead he stared at her for a long moment, lips pursed, and then said, "Let's move on. The metaphoric resonance of one particular passage doesn't matter right now."

"Fine," Effy said. But she felt let down.

"So anyway, Gosse published a paper discussing the irony of it, but he didn't make any specific claims about Myrddin's authorship. That was a few months ago, when Myrddin was freshly dead. Since then, scholars have really begun to dig into his background. Gosse wants first crack at it, but he didn't want to spook Ianto by coming himself—the intimidating effect of being the preeminent Myrddin scholar and all that. So he sent me instead." Preston frowned at this, as if expecting her to berate him again. "There's no schoolhouse in Saltney, as you saw. Myrddin had some informal schooling from the nuns, but that stopped definitively at age twelve. His parents weren't literate. We have several documents from the Myrddins—including the lease from their house—and they're all signed with a mark."

"Where is their house?" Effy asked. She thought of the shepherd retreating toward the green hills. "I didn't see very many homes down there."

"Oh, it's gone now," Preston said. "Several of the older homes in Saltney, the ones closer to the water, have already fallen into the sea. I almost don't blame the locals for their superstitions about the second Drowning."

She felt a thud of vague, confused grief. The house where Myrddin had grown up, where his mother had tucked him into bed at night, where his father had rested his scarred fisherman's hands—swallowed up and eroded, lost to the ages. Effy had listened for the bells under the water that morning, but she hadn't heard a sound.

Would she be responsible for further eroding Myrddin's legacy? Her stomach twisted at the thought.

"That still doesn't prove anything," Effy said. "Look at all of Myrddin's letters here. Clearly he could read and write."

"But *look* at them," Preston emphasized. He picked up the nearest one, its edges curled, paper turned yellow with time. "This is dated a year before the publication of *Angharad*. It's addressed to his publisher, Greenebough Books. Look how he signs his name."

Effy squinted at the page. Myrddin's script *was* quite careless, difficult to comprehend.

"'Yours sincerely, Emrys Myrddin,'" she read aloud. "What's wrong with that?"

"Pay attention to the surname," Preston said. "He spells it *Myrthin*, with a *th*. That's the Northern spelling."

Effy took the paper from him and ran her finger over the signature. The ink was old and faded, smudged in places, but the *th* was clear.

She didn't want to admit how much it baffled her, so she merely said, "It could have been a simple mistake."

"Strange mistake, to misspell your own surname."

"So what?" she challenged. "Being a poor speller hardly equates to illiteracy."

"Regardless, I don't think Myrddin wrote it at all. I think it's a forgery."

Effy gave a derisive laugh. "Now *you're* sounding as nutty as those superstitious Southerners you have so much contempt for."

"It's not unprecedented." Preston sounded almost petulant. "We've seen instances of literary forgery before. The trick of any good lie is just finding an audience who wants to believe it."

Effy chewed her lip. "Then who is the audience for Myrddin's supposed lie?"

"You said it yourself." The corner of Preston's mouth turned up into a thin half smile. "Superstitious Southerners who want to believe one of their own could transcend his common origins and write books that make even Northern girls swoon."

"I've never *swooned* in my life," she said crossly.

"Of course not," Preston said, completely straight-faced again. "But there are other people who stand to profit from the lie. Myrddin's publisher, for example—Greenebough makes a killing from royalties, even now. Half of Myrddin's appeal was this compelling backstory: the impoverished provincial poet who turns out to be a genius. There's a lot of money to be made off that myth."

Preston had a way of speaking with such eloquence and certainty that for a moment Effy found herself half-convinced, and too intimidated to argue. When the fog lifted, she was angry with herself for being so easily swayed.

"You're condescending," she said. "Not all Southerners are backwards peasants, and not all Northerners are snobs. I bet you hate it when people paint Argantians in such broad strokes. You know, most Llyrians think Argantians are cold, leering little weasels who believe in nothing but mining rights and profit margins. I can't say you're doing much to dispel those beliefs."

Even as she spoke, Effy regretted indulging the same old stereotypes. Mostly, she was frustrated with herself for failing to come up with a better argument against him.

"I don't see it as my duty to refute Llyrian clichés." Preston's voice was cold now. "Besides, it's a *fact* that the South is economically deprived compared to the North, and that deprivation is felt most acutely in the Bottom Hundred. It's also a fact that Llyrian political and cultural institutions are dominated by Northerners, and have been throughout history. That's the legacy of imperialism—the North reaps while the South sows."

"I didn't ask you to educate me about my own country," Effy snapped. "Statistics don't tell the whole story. Besides, Argantians did the same thing. Cut up your northern mountain villages into mining towns and coal tunnels, only you let your myths and magic fade into obscurity instead of celebrating them. At least Llyr doesn't try to hide its past."

Preston looked weary. "Some might call it celebrating; others would call it flouting a colonial legacy—oh, never mind. We can argue about this until the entire house falls into the sea. I'm not asking you to buy my narrative wholesale. But you did agree to help, so can you at least *try* not to fight me at every turn?"

Effy ground her teeth and looked down at the pile of letters on the desk. She *had* agreed, but she was finding it harder than she anticipated, what with Preston's snooty attitude. She would try her best to bear it, for now. Once she had secured a place in the literature college, she could spend the rest of her university career trying to undo the damage she'd done to Myrddin's legacy.

"All right," she said at last, scowling. "But you have to promise to be fifteen percent less patronizing."

Preston drew a breath. "Ten."

"And you think *I'm* the stubborn one?"

"Fine," he relented. "Fifteen, and you don't swear at me again."

"I only did that once." She was still convinced he'd earned it. But he was right; there was no use arguing with every breath.

Yet it all tasted bitter to swallow. She had abandoned her principles to get what she wanted, to improve her standing at the university, to earn some academic honors. To escape the sneers in the hallway, the whispers, and that green chair. What did that make her? No better than Preston, in the end. At least he was committed to the vaguely noble principle of *truth*.

Mortified by this realization, Effy fell silent.

Preston folded his arms across his chest. "Anyway. Before I came here, Gosse and I compiled a list of vocabulary used across all of Myrddin's work and cross-referenced that with his letters."

Immediately forgetting her previous promise, Effy blurted out, "Saints, how bloody long did that take you?"

"It's my *thesis*," Preston said, but the tips of his ears turned pink. "It turns out there's very little overlap between the vocabulary he uses in his letters and in his novels—specific phraseology that appears over and over again in his books but never occurs in his letters. If it didn't all bear the name *Emrys Myrddin*, you would never imagine they were written by the same man. And then there's the problem of *Angharad*."

Effy was instantly defensive. "What's the matter with *Angharad*?"

"It's an odd book. Genre-wise, it's hard to classify. Myrddin generally belongs to a school of writers credited with reviving the romantic epic."

"*Angharad* is a romance," she said, trying to keep her voice level. "A tragic one, but still a romance."

Preston hesitated. Effy could almost see him turning over their agreement in his mind, calculating how to moderate his tone by around *fifteen percent*. "Romantic epics are typically written in the third person, and always narrated by men. Heroes and knights whose goals are to rescue damsels and slay monsters. But the Fairy King is both lover and monster, and Angharad is both heroine and damsel."

"And of course you can't simply credit that to Myrddin being a creative visionary," Effy said, scowling.

"There are just too many inconsistencies," Preston said, "too much that doesn't sit quite right. And Ianto is so cagey about it. It only makes me more suspicious."

Effy looked down at the scattered papers again. "Don't tell me this is all you've managed to find out."

"I said I needed your help," he said, and he didn't manage to not sound miserable about it. "Ianto is keeping me in the dark. Wetherell was the one who gave me these letters. He asked around for them from some of Myrddin's correspondents, his publisher and friends. But there have to be more."

"More letters?"

"Letters. Diary entries. Rough drafts of bad poems. Half-finished novels. Shopping lists, for Saints' sakes. *Something*. It's like the man has been erased from his own home."

"He *has* been dead for six months," Effy pointed out. She thought again of what Ianto had said: *My father was always his own greatest admirer.* She'd heard a hint of resentment there.

"Still," Preston said, "I'm convinced Ianto is hiding something. This is an old, confusing house. There has to be—I don't know, a secret room somewhere. An attic, a storage area. Something he's not showing me. Ianto swears there's not, but I don't believe him."

Effy thought of the door with the pulse of the tide behind it. "What about the basement?"

Preston turned pale. "I don't see any use in asking about that," he said quickly. "It's flooded. And besides, Ianto guards that key with his life. I wouldn't even bother."

She detected a note of fear in his voice. She had never heard him sound even remotely afraid before, and she decided not to press him on it. For now. Besides, something else had occurred to her.

"The widow," she said. "You told me she invited you here."

"I've never seen her," Preston replied, looking slightly less pale and relieved to have changed topics. "Ianto told me she's ailing and prefers to keep to herself."

Effy couldn't help but wonder about her. Myrddin had been eighty-four when he died; surely the widow was not much younger. Perhaps *ailing* was a euphemism for *mad*. Men liked to keep mad women locked up where everyone could comfortably forget they ever existed. But Ianto hadn't seemed to harbor any malice toward his mother. Effy shook her head, as if to banish the thought.

"All right," she said. "But what do you want from me?"

Preston hesitated, and didn't meet her gaze. "Blueprints for the house," he said after a beat. "I'm sure they exist somewhere. Maybe Ianto showed them to you already."

"He didn't." And Effy hadn't even thought to ask, which was a bit embarrassing. "It would be a very reasonable thing for me to request, though. I can ask."

"Right. Ianto wouldn't suspect a thing." Preston's eyes flickered behind his glasses, but his expression was unreadable. "Just be careful. Don't—"

Effy sighed. "I'll be perfectly polite, if that's what you mean."

"I meant the opposite, really." Now Preston was flushed. "I would keep him at an arm's length. Don't be too . . . obliging."

Effy couldn't tell if he was trying to admonish her or warn her. Was it her he didn't trust, or Ianto? It made her skin prickle. Surely he didn't think she was so incompetent.

Preston looked so flustered that she knew there had to be something else he wanted to say, but couldn't. Effy kept her gaze on him to see if she could determine it, but she only succeeded in flushing, too. In the end, she merely replied, "I'll be careful."

"Good," he said, straightening up, his tone cool and clipped again. "And, of course, I'll be discreet. I take all my notes in Argantian so Ianto can't read them."

"Except for one," Effy said. She had spent all last night thinking about seeing her name scrawled down the margins of that page in Preston's precise, tidy script. *Effy Effy Effy Effy Effy.* Maybe it was just meaningless marginalia. Maybe it was something else. She didn't want to embarrass him, but she didn't think she could stand not knowing the truth. "Why not that note, too?"

"Most of what I write doesn't really matter." Preston's gaze was on her, unflinching, though his flush had not entirely faded. "It's just whatever errant idea goes through my head. I know I'll just throw them away later, so I don't have to bother translating them from Argantian into Llyrian. I suppose I thought that one was important."

It took Effy the rest of the morning to work up the courage to talk to Ianto. Over and over again, her mind replayed that moment where he'd laid his hand on her shoulder. She had slipped so quickly into that deep-water place. She paced the upper landing and shook her head, trying to cut the memory loose. *He's always been kind to you,* a voice said. Eventually she convinced herself that the gesture had been fatherly and nothing more.

Ianto was taking his tea in the dining room, under that perilously dangling chandelier. Cobwebs stuck to the empty candleholders like spun sugar, and the glass shards seemed to ripple, even absent of wind. When he saw her, he immediately rose to his feet and said, "Effy! Please sit. Can I get you some tea?"

She held the back of a chair in both hands. Instinctively she wanted to refuse, but she had come there with a purpose. Slowly, with her belly roiling, Effy slid into the seat.

"Sure," she said. "Tea sounds lovely."

"Excellent," Ianto said. He hurried off to the kitchen and Effy sat there, palms slick, trying to keep her mind from slipping away from her. Trying not to think of how heavy his touch had felt.

Ianto returned several moments later, carrying a chipped porcelain cup. He set it down before her. She took a small, experimental sip; immediately, unmixed sugar gathered like grit on her tongue. She put the cup down again.

"I was just wondering—" she began, but Ianto held up his hand to stop her.

"I feel I know so little about you, Effy," he said. "You're an architect, you're a fan of my father's, but surely there's more to you than that."

"Oh, I'm not very interesting," she said, with a short, uncomfortable laugh.

Ianto captured her gaze and held it. "You're very interesting to me. Are you originally from Caer-Isel?"

"Draefen." Effy rubbed the heel of her hand against her stockings. "I came to Caer-Isel to study at the university."

"A Northern girl through and through," Ianto said with a smile. "I could have guessed as much by your name." He squinted at her for a moment, as if trying to remember something. "You don't happen to be related to the banking Sayres of Draefen."

Effy felt her muscles relax slightly. These were easy questions to answer. "Yes. My grandfather is the bank manager. My mother is one of his secretaries."

"Clearly architecture doesn't run in the family. What inspired you to study it?"

Effy considered how to reply. She didn't want to express her true lack of enthusiasm for the subject, so she merely said, "I like a challenge."

Ianto gave a delighted chortle. "Well, you've taken up the right project, then."

Feeling more at ease, Effy took another sip of tea and tried to smile along. She even allowed herself to meet Ianto's eyes. They were very unusual eyes, she realized, almost colorless, like water. No matter how his expression changed, no matter whether he was smiling or frowning, his eyes seemed not to shift at all. It was like looking into one of the tide pools, the Fairy King's false mirrors.

Very abruptly, Ianto stood up. "You know," he said, "this is hardly the right atmosphere to have a lively conversation. Did you have a chance to visit the pub while you were in town yesterday? I'm sure you'd like another chance to return to civilization, such as it is in the Bottom Hundred."

And that was how Effy ended up back at the pub in Saltney, sitting across the table from Ianto Myrddin.

The windows of the pub were opaque with fog and rainwater left over from the earlier downpour, and the lights inside glowed sallowly. Ianto was smiling, making small talk with the bartender, who only looked as grim as ever.

Effy tried to order hot cider, but Ianto quickly procured two glasses of scotch instead. In an effort not to be rude, Effy feigned taking tiny sips and watched him over the rim of the glass. His damp hair brushed his shoulders, and his arm was braced over the back of the booth, as if to hold himself in his seat.

She set her glass down, fingers trembling slightly. She tried to look around the pub curiously, so as to give the impression that this was the first time she'd seen it.

"Thank you," she said. "You were right. This is lovely."

"It's nice to be out of the house," Ianto said.

His voice had taken on an odd tone, lower and raspier. Effy was sure she was just imagining it.

"I know it's no comparison to the fare in Caer-Isel," Ianto went on, his voice still slightly off pitch, "but the steak-and-kidney pie here is very good."

Effy was planning to politely tell him she didn't care for steak-and-kidney pie, thank you, but there was no use. When the bartender returned, he immediately ordered two of them.

Once she had shuffled away again, Effy cleared her throat. "So, about Hiraeth—"

"You said you're a girl who likes a challenge," Ianto cut in. "I can see why you threw your name in the hat for this project."

Effy drew in a breath. Clearly getting the blueprints was going to be more difficult than she thought. "Yes," she said. "And you know how much respect I have for your father's work."

It wasn't technically a lie, but it felt like one, considering the agreement she'd just made with Preston. She said a quick, silent prayer to Saint Duessa, folding her hands in her lap. The patroness of deception with good cause (arguable) was getting a lot of her solicitation lately.

"Of course," said Ianto. "But the task is monumental. I wouldn't blame you if you had to find some unfortunate orphan to bleed out."

Effy blinked, so taken aback that she was momentarily lost for words. "What?"

"Oh, you haven't heard of that old myth?" Ianto looked pleased, but there was something eerie under his smile. "It's a rite here in the South, dating back to the pre-Drowning days. Spilling the blood of a fatherless child on the foundation of a castle was supposed to ensure its structure was sound and strong. Blood sacrifice—I suppose you Northerners would think it very brutish."

As a fatherless child herself, Effy found it both brutish and oddly fascinating. Luckily, their food arrived before she could choke out a reply.

The steak-and-kidney pies were steaming, the same golden brown color of varnished wood. Effy picked up her fork reluctantly. Preston was asking quite a lot of her, to feign enthusiasm for kidney.

But to her surprise, Ianto didn't touch his food. He was looking at her intently. He said, "You've been spending time with the Argantian student lately."

Effy's heart stuttered. "Not really," she managed. "Only this morning. He's . . ." She fumbled for an innocuous descriptor, something that wouldn't be a lie. "He has interesting things to say."

"I don't get a good feeling from him." Ianto picked up his knife. The grease-marbled blade glinted. "He's a bit twitchy, isn't he? A strange, skittish young man. Perhaps it's the Argantian blood."

For some reason, Effy felt the need to defend Preston. "I think he's just dedicated to his work. He doesn't waste time on small talk or pleasantries."

"I suppose he's very much like my father, in that way." Ianto pointed his knife at her. "Go on, then. Eat."

Effy's heart skipped another beat. She sliced through the flaky exterior of the pie, steam wafting from the cut like a spirit escaping its vessel.

Ianto watched her without blinking, his watery, colorless eyes unreadable. When she was mid-bite, he said, "You're a very pretty girl."

The food on her tongue burned too much to swallow. She wanted to spit it out into her napkin but she couldn't bring herself to; she could scarcely bring herself to move. Her eyes welled, and Ianto just kept looking at her, gaze inscrutable and relentless.

She didn't think she looked pretty. At least, she had no idea whether she did or not. She was wearing stockings and a plaid skirt, with a white woolen sweater over it. It was the sort of outfit she'd worn during her first week at university. Before Master Corbenic. She regretted it now. The damp air had turned her normally wavy hair to curls and the curls to untended frizz. Because there was no mirror in the guesthouse, she hadn't been able to put on any makeup, or even check to see how large the circles under her eyes were.

It hurt so much to hold the steaming food on her tongue, but eventually it cooled down enough to swallow. Effy put her hand to her mouth. The tip of her nose was starting to get hot, the way it did when she was about to cry.

Ianto didn't seem to notice. His eyes were unyielding—and, she noticed, they looked clearer. Sharper.

"Your eyes. Your hair," he said. "Beautiful."

Effy dug her fingernails into her palm. She regretted coming here at all. But she didn't want to fail at her task. As much as it shocked her to realize it, she didn't want to fail Preston. So she met Ianto's gaze and gathered up as much of a response to the insipid flattery as she could muster.

"Thank you," she said. Her blush, at least, was not feigned. "That's very kind of you to say."

The door to the pub clattered open and three fishermen stomped in, carrying with them the salt smell of the sea. Even as the wind blew through the doorway, Ianto's black hair lay flat.

Effy had brought several of the hag stones in the pocket of her coat. Still holding her fork with one hand, she touched the stones with the other. Did she dare to take one out in front of him? Would her obvious terror ruin everything?

She couldn't wait any longer; she would only grow more afraid. So she blurted out, "I wanted to ask if you had blueprints for the house. That would really help me out a lot."

This, at last, unlatched his gaze from hers. Surprise flittered briefly across his face and then vanished, like a bird hitting a window and then fluttering crookedly off again. Unexpectedly, Ianto reached into his pocket and pulled out a folded sheaf of paper.

"There you are," he said.

Eager, Effy reached out to take it. Her fingers had only brushed the edges of the paper when Ianto suddenly grabbed her hand. His grasp was painfully tight, and she let out a small, shocked whimper.

"Ianto—" she started.

His face was as pale as the cliff stone and his eyes held no color at all. And then, as suddenly as he had grabbed her, he released her again, leaving Effy holding the papers. He rose from his seat with such abruptness that it was almost violent. His knife clattered onto the table.

"Let's go," he said. His voice came out through gritted teeth. When Effy only stood there staring, open-mouthed, he repeated in a snarl, *"Let's go!"*

Numbly, Effy got to her feet. She tucked the blueprints into her purse and hurried after him.

Back in the car, Ianto's gaze was trained unblinkingly at the road ahead, his enormous hands wrapped around the steering wheel.

Effy was afraid to shatter the heavy, constricting silence, afraid to imperil her precarious victory, afraid to provoke Ianto. She looked out the window instead, eyes tracing the path of raindrops sliding down the glass. Her fingers still throbbed where he had grabbed them.

The sea frothed angrily at the rocks, tongues of foam bathing the edge of the road. The water had a greenish hue today, like a witch's brew.

Still staring straight ahead, Ianto barked out, "Did you enjoy your meal?"

"Yes," Effy replied. The bites of steak-and-kidney pie sat queasily in her belly. Each bump in the road made her stomach churn further.

"Good. Not all girls are so grateful for chivalry, nor so humble about their own charms. In the cities up North, I've heard that women are starting to have very uncharitable views about men and marriage."

Effy swallowed hard. It was true that there were more women at the university than ever, and many of them left without wedding rings. Ten years ago, the only reason a girl went to college was to find a husband. Her grandmother still inquired about this every time she wrote, asking if Effy had met any nice young men. *No,* Effy always wrote back, *I haven't.*

The car lurched and jostled, making her heart clatter in her chest. In one last effort at civility, Effy asked, "Have you ever been married before?"

The car sloshed viciously through wet sand.

"No," he said. "Marriage is not for all men."

"I understand," she said, trying to be charitable. "My parents never wed."

There was a long stretch of silence, during which the wind wailed so loudly that the windows seemed to rattle.

Ianto was driving far, far more quickly than Wetherell had driven in the same car. Effy grasped the edge of the seat and bit down on her lip. The inside of the car smelled like brine and musk. It smelled like Hiraeth.

"Are you in a hurry to get back?" She nearly had to yell over the sound of the wind and the sand flying up to pelt the windows.

"Of course," Ianto said. But it was closer to a growl.

The tone of his voice pinned her there, like a needle through a butterfly wing. She was filled with a vague and ominous fear, fingers curled around the handle of her purse, blood racing and heart pounding. A bodily, animal instinct was telling her: *Something terrible is about to happen.*

"I'm sorry," she said. The air in the car felt extraordinarily stiff and heavy.

She had not taken her pink pill that morning, she realized.

Ianto's gaze shifted from the road, and she had not been imagining it earlier—his once turbid eyes were now glassy and sharp. Something manic was glinting in them.

"We spoke for an hour and you never told me what I really want to know," he said.

Effy wanted to tell him not to look at her, to keep his eyes on the road. The car was hurtling up the cliffside so quickly that her body was practically pinned to the seat.

Miserably, she managed to reply, "And what is that?"

Suddenly Ianto whipped his head around to check the road. And that was when Effy realized the car had no rearview mirror. The side mirrors were turned inward, invisible. If Ianto wanted to look behind him, he had to crane his neck backward.

How had she not noticed that before, when Wetherell was driving? Had there been mirrors then?

Her vision was beginning to blur. *Not here,* she begged herself. *Not here, not now.* She had the pink pills in her purse, but she

139

couldn't risk taking them out in front of Ianto. She couldn't bear the questions he would ask about them. The hag stones in her pocket bounced jaggedly with the rhythm of the car.

"Why did you really come here?" Ianto said at last. His voice was that same low, rasping snarl. "A beautiful girl like you doesn't need this project to pad her résumé. Any hot-blooded professor would give you highest marks in a heartbeat."

Her panic crested like a white-capped wave, and then Effy saw him. He was sitting in the driver's seat, where Ianto had only just been. His black hair was as slick as water. His skin was moonlight pale, and his eyes burned holes right through her, down to her blood, down to her bone. His fingers uncurled from the steering wheel and reached for her, nails long and dark and sharp as claws.

She wasn't wearing her seat belt, so when she flung the door open, it was easy enough to hurl herself out of the car.

EIGHT

The Fairy King had many forms, and some looked, on the surface, identical. Some days I could not tell if the husband who came to me was the one who would kiss my eyes closed with infinite tenderness, or if he would press me down into our bed and not care that I whimpered. Those were the most difficult days. When I could not tell the kind version of him from the cruel. I wished he would be a serpent, a cloven-footed creature, a winged beast—anything but a man.

FROM ANGHARAD BY EMRYS MYRDDIN, 191 AD

It took Effy an hour to reach Hiraeth, her legs numb beneath her, vision blurring and then sharpening in dizzying turns. Her hair was damp and plastered to her face, her stockings ripped to ruins. Also, she was bleeding.

Preston was standing at the top of the stairs, and when he saw her, he lurched down, taking the steps two at a time.

"Effy," he said, breathless, when he arrived. "Where did you go?"

"Where's Ianto?"

"He came back half an hour ago, alone." Preston gestured

toward the black car in the driveway. "I tried to ask him where you were, but he just brushed past me and locked himself in his bedroom—what happened?"

Effy coughed, trying to find her voice. Her lip was split and felt puffy, painful.

"I got them," she said at last. "The blueprints."

Preston looked at her as if she'd grown scales and fins. "No, I mean what happened to *you*? You're covered in blood and—well, dirt."

"The road is dirty," Effy said. She wasn't quite lucid enough to feel embarrassed.

Preston led her up the stairs and into the house. Ianto was still nowhere to be seen—a small miracle—but Wetherell glowered at them from the threshold to the kitchen. He looked as dour as ever, skin washed gray in the watery light.

The stairs to the second floor were more difficult. Effy leaned heavily on the railing as Preston watched her with a tight mouth, shoulders tensed as if he expected her to topple over at any moment.

The portrait of the Fairy King looked fuzzy and kaleidoscopic, the paint colors swirling into an unreadable blur. His face was a pale smudge, featureless.

Maybe this was her punishment for betraying Myrddin, for planning to trample all over his legacy. She choked out something that was almost a sob, too low for Preston to hear.

The Fairy King had never appeared to her in the daylight before.

When they reached the study, it took all of Effy's strength not to collapse. There was a bright, staccato beat of pain behind her temples. She looked around at all the papers scattered on the desk, the splayed-open books, and the battered chaise longue and felt, for some reason, a quiet thrum of relief.

"Effy," Preston said again, his voice grave. "What did you do?"

"I jumped out of Ianto's car," she replied.

Hearing herself say it out loud made the fog dissipate. She was suddenly aware of how mad she sounded. How mad she had *been*. She raised a hand to her mouth and felt her swollen lip, wincing.

Preston looked despairing. "How did the blueprints factor into that? I didn't think your mission would require such daring heroics."

"There was nothing heroic about it," Effy said. She was flushing profusely. "I wish there had been. Ianto had already given me the blueprints. I just—I couldn't stand to be in the car with him any longer."

That was all she could bear to tell him. What would Preston say if she confessed what she had seen—if she had really even seen it at all? It would be no different than it had ever been, with her mother and her grandparents, with the doctor, with the teachers and priests.

At best Preston would blink at her bemusedly, certain she was making some sort of joke. More likely he would scoff and secretly regret that he had tethered his academic future to some mad girl who needed pills to tell what was real and what wasn't.

Surely there was no worse ally than Effy in a quest to uncover *objective truth*.

But all Preston did was shake his head. "And he just left you there? Looking like—like this?"

As Effy had watched Ianto's taillights vanish in the distance, all she'd felt was relief. She'd been afraid he would pull over and drag her back inside. The vision of the Fairy King, his wet black hair and his horrible, reaching hand, was still playing on the inside of her eyelids.

"I don't blame him," she said, voice hollow. "It was a stupid thing to do."

Preston let out a long breath. "I really didn't think he'd try to take you out of the house. I'm sorry."

"What are you apologizing for?"

He blinked, glasses slipping down his nose. "I'm not sure."

If she'd been in a more coherent state of mind, hearing Preston admit to uncertainty would have pleased her. At last there was *something*, however trivial, that he didn't know.

Effy finally had the courage to look down at herself. Her white sweater was damp and smeared with mud. She couldn't see it, but she could feel her elbow throbbing under her sleeve, blood sticking to the woolen fibers. And though her skirt had emerged relatively unscathed, her hip ached.

Her stockings had suffered the worst: torn beyond repair, both of her knees scraped bloody and stinging enough to make her gasp. Flecks of dirt and tiny pebbles were caught in the mangle of her skin like flies trapped on flypaper. Her nose hurt and she was glad she couldn't see her face.

There had been no mirrors in Ianto's car. She was sure of that.

In fact, ever since she had arrived in Hiraeth, she had not seen her own reflection once. She could not even see herself in the mirror of Ianto's cloudy, roiling gaze.

"Here," Effy said weakly, thrusting her purse at Preston. "I have the blueprints."

Preston took her purse and set it down on his desk. He didn't open it or even peer inside. "Effy, why don't you sit?"

"Why?" A bolt of panic shot up her spine. "I don't want to."

"Well," Preston said, "that's going to make this a lot more difficult."

And then he knelt in front of her, and Effy was so shocked that she nearly *did* topple over. She had to put her hand on the desk to steady herself.

"What are you doing?" she choked out.

"If you don't wipe away the dirt, your cuts will get infected. Infections can lead to blood poisoning, which, if it remains untreated, will eventually necessitate amputation. And in a way, it would be all my fault if you had to have your legs amputated at the knee, because I was the one who asked you to get the blueprints in the first place."

He said all this with complete sincerity.

Effy took a breath—partly to steel herself, and partly so she wouldn't laugh at him. True to his word, Preston began delicately picking the pebbles from her wounded knees. His touch was so gentle, she felt only the faintest nips of pain. His eyes were narrowed behind his glasses, as focused as he'd looked when poring over one of Myrddin's books.

After a while he seemed satisfied that he had gotten out all the pebbles, and he reached up for the glass of water on his desk. Effy was still so baffled that she hardly reacted when he wet his shirtsleeve and began to dab at her gouged skin. That, finally, elicited a gasp from her.

"Ouch," she whined. "That really stings."

"Sorry," he said. "Almost done."

The pain was making her woozy again. Gingerly, she let her other hand rest on Preston's shoulder for balance.

He paused in his ministrations, muscles tensing, and looked up at her. They locked eyes for several moments, but neither of them said a word. After another beat, Preston looked down again, returning to his work.

Effy curled her fingers into the fabric of his shirt. His skin, underneath, was warm, and she could feel his muscles flexing. "How many skinned knees have you treated in your career as an academic?"

"I have to say you're my first."

She laughed, almost in spite of herself. "You're very strange, Preston Héloury."

"You're the one who jumped out of a moving car, Effy Sayre."

"It's only because I wasn't wearing my seat belt," she replied.

It was the second time she'd heard him laugh, and Effy remembered how much she liked the sound of it: low and breathy, his shoulder shaking just slightly under her grip.

In another moment, Preston got to his feet and said, "Let me see your hands."

Effy held them out. Her palms were scratched but not badly. It looked like she'd tussled with a rosebush. With her fingers splayed like that, the absence of her ring finger seemed glaringly obvious.

She hoped Preston wouldn't ask about it. That was another question she didn't want to answer.

"They look all right," Preston conceded. "I'm confident this will not be what does you in."

He had a little smear of her blood on his cheek where he'd raised his red-stained hand to adjust his glasses. Effy decided not to tell him.

"That's a relief," she said. "I would hate for you to be responsible for my untimely demise."

Preston laughed again. "I'd never overcome the guilt."

Effy smiled, but she could not stop thinking of the look in Ianto's eyes, the change in the tenor of his voice. Could she have imagined it all? Why had he hurried her out of the house, only to hurry her back again? He had driven so fast, with such determination, his words all snarled and low. Her brain had pulsed like a lighthouse beacon, every beat of her heart screaming, *Danger. Danger. Danger.*

She remembered how Ianto had told the story of the Drowning: how the inhabitants of the Bottom Hundred hadn't realized they were going to die until they were neck-deep in the water. If she hadn't flung herself out of the car, would she have drowned there?

Sometimes Effy had nightmares where she was sitting in Master Corbenic's green office chair, her wrists strapped to the armrests, black, murky water rising around her. She couldn't escape, and the water kept coming in—and worst of all, in those dreams, she didn't even struggle. She just gulped down the water as if it were air.

"Do you think he'll be angry at me?" Effy blurted out. "Ianto, I mean."

The amusement in Preston's eyes vanished. "Well . . . it's not the most tactful way to escape an awkward conversation, I'll give him that. What did he say to you?"

She drew in a breath. Where would she even begin with explaining it all? She certainly could not tell him about the Fairy King. Preston had been clear enough on how he felt about *Southern superstition*. Confessing to any of it would reveal her as precisely the sort of unstable, untrustworthy girl Effy was so desperate not to be.

"It was just an awkward conversation, like you said," she replied at last. "I overreacted."

"I'm sure he'll get over it," Preston said. But his expression was uneasy.

Now that Preston was satisfied that Effy would not perish of her injuries, and now that Effy's headache had begun to recede and her eyes had cleared, they unfurled the blueprints on the desk. By then it had grown dark, and only a pale trickle of starlight bled through the window. The moon was pearl white and not quite full, cobwebbed with lacy clouds.

Preston lit two kerosene lamps and brought them over so they could read by their orange glow.

The blueprints were very old. Effy could tell because they

were actually *blue*. A decade or so ago, traditional blueprints had become obsolete, replaced by less expensive printing methods that rendered blue ink on a white background. The blueprints for Hiraeth Manor were the bright sapphire color of her mother's favorite brand of gin. The edges were ragged and much of the ink was smudged and faded.

The first page showed a cross section of the house—far, far better than anything Effy could have dreamed of drawing—and the second showed a floor plan.

Preston squinted. "I can't make sense of any of this."

"I can." Effy was pleased that for once she knew something he didn't.

She drew her thumb down the page, tracing the outline of the first floor. There was the dining room, the kitchen, the foyer, and the horrifying bathroom she had not even been permitted to lay eyes on. Nothing out of the ordinary there. But when she looked for the door to the basement, she found nothing.

"Interesting," she murmured.

"What?"

"It doesn't look like the basement is in the blueprints at all," she said. "But, well, a basement isn't exactly something you can tack on at the last minute. It has to be part of the architectural plans from the very start. The only thing I can think is maybe this house was built on a previously existing foundation, one that already had a basement."

Preston's jaw twitched. "You mean there used to be another structure here, before Hiraeth? It's hard to imagine how that's possible. Even this house seems to defy the laws of nature."

"It wouldn't be so strange. The Bay of Nine Bells was ravaged by the Drowning, but that doesn't mean nothing survived." Effy looked down at the blueprints again, feeling certain of her theory. "It's easier to repair an existing foundation than to build something entirely new."

"You're the expert, I suppose," Preston said, though he sounded unconvinced.

It was curious, but it didn't solve any of their problems, since Preston had point-blank refused to go anywhere near the basement, and his face had turned pale at even the mention of it. Effy scanned the drawing of the second floor. There was the study, and the door out to the crumbling balcony, and then the series of rooms Ianto had forbidden her from seeing: his and his mother's bedchambers. The larger one had to be the master, and then on the left, Ianto's.

As was always the case when she came up, Myrddin's widow caught in Effy's mind like the prick of a needle.

"You've never met the mistress of the house, right?" she asked.

"No," Preston said. "I've never even spoken to her on the phone. She's old, and I imagine she values her privacy."

But a chill prickled the back of her neck. "If she values her privacy so much, she wouldn't have invited the university to poke around here."

He folded his arms across his chest and replied defensively, "I'm only looking through her husband's things, not hers. Whoever Mrs. Myrddin is, she's not relevant to my scholarly inquiries."

"But haven't you wondered—outside of your *scholarly inquiries*—why she's so reclusive?" All of it felt wrong, had felt wrong ever since she came to Hiraeth, and certainly ever since she saw the Fairy King. "When I've asked Ianto about her, he hasn't said much."

"We're not writing a thesis on Myrddin's widow, Effy. We should just be relieved she's staying out of our way."

Effy could think of at least five rebuttals, but in the end she just pressed her lips shut.

She looked back down at the blueprints. The private chambers, which Ianto had barred them from, consisted of two bedrooms and two bathrooms. Perfectly typical. All of it was perfectly typical.

Slightly demoralized but unwilling to admit defeat, she flipped over to the cross sections again.

There was the gabled roof with a very slight pitch, not large enough for an attic, or even a crawl space, as Preston had previously suggested. But along the eastern-facing wall of the house, just near Ianto's bedroom, there was a narrow strip of white space, something the architect had forgotten to fill in.

Only no architect worth their salt *forgot* to finish their cross sections (just Effy, and that was mostly apathy, not incompetence), so she leaned over the desk and squinted, trying to measure the size of the empty space against her thumb.

"What is it?" Preston urged. "Do you see something?"

"Yes." Effy pointed. "It's not in the floor plan, which is odd, but if you look closely at the cross section, you can see this little bit of white space. Judging by the relative scale of the drawing, it's just the size of a narrow closet and it's off Ianto's bedroom. I'd say it was a mistake on the architect's part, but I already know you don't believe in coincidences."

Though Preston looked affronted, he didn't argue. "Well, I can believe Ianto is hiding something of his father's in there. He's certainly cagey enough."

"But we can't go there *now*." It was already late; Ianto had retreated to his chambers, and the thought of confronting him again made Effy feel queasy. Whenever her mind was not otherwise occupied, it was immediately filled with the image of the Fairy King, one hand on the steering wheel and the other reaching toward her. She shook her head, trying to dispel the memory.

"No, of course not," said Preston. "But tomorrow morning Ianto will go out—he always goes down to church on Sundays; it takes about an hour. We can seize the opportunity while he's gone."

An hour. That was roughly as long as they had spent in the pub, and Ianto had been in such a vicious hurry to get back. Effy considered bringing it up, but what did it suggest, really? Nothing useful. Just her brain trying to make meaning out of the baseless terror that haunted her like a ghost.

Instead she said, "What about the *irrelevant* Mrs. Myrddin? You said she never leaves her chamber. She'll be there, even if Ianto won't."

Preston glanced askance at the door, as though he expected someone to come bursting through. "We'll just have to be quiet so that we don't disturb her."

"But what if we *do* disturb her?" Effy ventured.

"Then I suppose we'll have to lie," said Preston. He shifted a little as he said it, shoulders rising. "Just tell her Ianto sent us."

"That's not a very good lie."

"Well, you come up with something, then." He was very faintly flushed. "We'll meet back here tomorrow morning. Ianto will be gone by sunrise."

It still seemed like an extraordinarily bad idea. But Effy couldn't think of any alternatives. "All right," she agreed. "Meet here at dawn."

Preston nodded. As Effy turned toward the door—slowly, so as not to aggravate her gouged knees any further—she felt his gaze on her still. She looked back over her shoulder and saw Preston look down hurriedly, shuffling through some papers on the desk, embarrassed to have been caught watching her.

His flush had deepened. Effy found herself thinking about how lightly he had touched her, and how the pads of his fingers were still stained with her blood.

"Preston?" she said. Her voice sounded strange: small, wondering. Almost hopeful.

He glanced up. "Yes?"

"Thank you."

"For what?"

"For caring whether or not I die of sepsis," she said.

"Oh," he said. "Well, you can never be too cautious. People have died in much more banal ways."

"Thank you for giving me the chance to die of something interesting, then."

"As long as you don't throw yourself out of any more moving

cars." There was a slight quiver on the left side of his mouth, as if he were trying not to smile. Behind his glasses, his eyes were solemn. "There are far more interesting deaths out there."

Effy stepped out of the study and stood in the flickering glow of the naked bulbs that lined the hallway. The moment the door shut behind her, she felt suddenly cold and rooted to the ground, as if something invisible were holding her there. Her breath misted out from her mouth in pale wisps.

Yet it was not *panic*, the same way it had been when she'd seen the Fairy King. This was the opposite, in fact—an eerie and unnatural calm.

All around her there was a stunning, seething silence. The floorboards had stopped their groaning, and Effy could no longer hear the distant sound of the ocean rolling against the rocks, slowly dragging Hiraeth down toward the sea.

Preston was only on the other side of the door, but Effy felt so terribly alone, the house spreading out on all sides like reaching vines.

And then she saw it: a white glimmer at the end of the hall, as if someone had left a window open and the curtain was blowing. But there was no window, no curtain. There was the ragged hem of a dress and a flash of long silver hair. She caught just the end of each, and the heel of a bare foot, pressing up from beneath the surface of her phantom skin like a fisherman's tangled net and the fleshy sea-thing caught in it.

Effy's pulse juddered in her throat. The air had turned sharp and fragile and cold, as cold as the heart of winter. This frigid terror caught her by surprise—it was not the fear she'd known all her life, the fear of the Fairy King and his reaching hand. That was a danger she recognized.

This was nothing she knew. It was a novel horror, one that she could only parse once the ghost had vanished. At least—it had to be a ghost. Effy even took one cautious step toward the end of the hall, where the figure had disappeared. The door to the bedchambers was shut, and she had not heard it open. Whatever it had been had passed right through the wood.

It was fleeing something. The thought occurred to Effy as she retreated again, heart pounding crookedly. Watching a dress disappear around the corner and—impossibly—through the shut door was like staring at a dead crow in your path. Everyone, even the most skeptical Northerners, knew it was a death omen.

You didn't fear the bird itself. You feared whatever terrible, unknowable thing its death portended.

After Ianto's car had sped away and Effy had picked herself up off the road, she had swallowed one of her pink pills. The pills were meant to be a seawall against her visions, against the unreal world that always seemed to be blooming underneath the real one, like the beat of blood behind a bruise, waiting for its moment to break through.

Yet still, she had seen the ghost. And the Fairy King had appeared to her in the daylight, as he never had before. In the dark corner of her bedroom, his clawed hand curling around her closet door—but Effy had always believed the sunlight made her safe from him. In *Angharad*, the Fairy King had come for her at night, when her father and brothers were sleeping too soundly to notice.

There was something wrong here, in Hiraeth, in perhaps all of the Bottom Hundred. Old magic and wicked—or worse, ambivalent—gods. The Fairy King had more power here. The unreal world was close to breaking its fetters.

And Effy had walked right into the center of it, into this sinking house at the edge of the world. Her cheeks and brow were soaked in a cold film of sweat. Whatever reassurances the doctor had given her, they did not matter now. His pills were not enough to stop the waves from crashing over her.

When Effy was able to move her numb legs again, she ran down the stairs and hurled herself out the door, into the blackness of the night, heart pounding like church bells. She was not afraid of the ghost. But she was horribly, wretchedly afraid of whatever had killed the woman it had once been.

NINE

I can hear the mermaids singing
Beneath the rolling, wanton waves,
Their hair as lush as meadowsweet,
Their maidenheads as ripe for plunder
As the gold inside their sunken chests.

FROM "GREAT CAPTAIN AND HIS SEA-BRIDE,"

COLLECTED IN *THE POETICAL WORKS OF EMRYS MYRDDIN,*

196–208 AD

Morning was the pale gray color of a trout's belly, and the waves were lolling gently against the shoreline. Effy woke with a start slightly after dawn, the purple and green miasmas of her nightmares still swirling in the corners of her mind.

Her sleeping pills were meant to eliminate even her dreams, to plunge her into total, oblivious blackness, but they hadn't worked last night, either. She'd spent hours in the throes of nightmares, tossing and turning so violently that the moss-colored duvet slipped off the bed and onto the floor.

She had dreamed of him, of course. The Fairy King and his

bone crown. She could not remember a time when she had ever dreamed of anything else. Sometimes the nightmares were sliced through with images of Master Corbenic, but they flipped back and forth so rapidly that at some point, they appeared identical. It was all black hair and reaching hands and water rising to her throat.

Effy knew Preston would not be pleased with her being late. She hurriedly jammed her arms into her sweater sleeves and her feet into her boots. She hesitated at the door, fingers hovering above the iron knob. Now that she had seen the Fairy King in daylight, her old survival tactics could not be entirely trusted.

She slipped two of the pink pills into her mouth and swallowed them dry. Then Effy wrenched the door open and *ran*, skidding breathlessly up the path toward Hiraeth.

By the time she arrived, she was panting, her skin buzzing with adrenaline. She'd seen no flashes of damp hair in the gaps between trees. As she passed the front of the house, she looked in the driveway for Ianto's car, but—blessedly—it was gone.

Two seabirds were pecking at something in the tire marks instead. A run-over animal, mangled and flat. Effy didn't get close enough to tell what it was. She saw only the matted, bloody fur and her stomach turned over on itself. She clambered up the stairs into the house.

Preston was waiting for her in the study, a mug of coffee in his hands and a reproachful look on his face. "You're late."

Effy glanced out the window, which held a tender pink light. "It's still dawn. Besides, that's not fair. You slept here."

"And I had time to get coffee and everything." Preston looked down meaningfully at his mug. "If you'd been here at dawn, you could've gotten some, too."

She drew a breath and resisted rolling her eyes, but the utter predictability of his reaction was oddly comforting. After all the strangeness, her nightmares, Ianto's violently shifting moods, Preston's reliable fussiness was almost like a balm.

Not that she would ever tell him that.

"You asked me not to fight you at every turn, but you promised to be fifteen percent less condescending," she reminded him. "So you have to let me win sometimes."

Preston's lips thinned. "Fine," he relented. "You can win this one, whatever that means to you."

Pleased by his acquiescence, Effy considered what a suitable trophy would be. "It means you have to give me your coffee."

He heaved an enormous, persecuted sigh, but passed her the mug. Purposefully keeping eye contact with Preston over the rim, Effy swallowed a small sip and gagged.

Of course Preston Héloury took his coffee black. She put down the mug, trying to hide her grimace.

"Did you see Ianto leave?" Preston asked.

"No, he was already gone." Effy thought about the animal carcass in the road. It had been too small to be a deer but too large to be a rabbit, large enough that Ianto would have seen it through the windshield, and kept his foot pressed down on the gas pedal anyway.

The image of the Fairy King sitting there in the driver's seat blinked across her vision. Effy had to dig her fingernails into her palm to make it vanish again.

"We should hurry," Preston said. "I *think* Llyrian services only last an hour, but you would know better than me."

As they began walking toward the door, Effy said, "So my suspicions were correct—Argantians *are* heathens."

"Not all Argantians," he said, nonplussed, almost cheerful. "Just me."

"I'm sure your Llyrian mother is very pleased with you."

"She does her best to make me feel guilty about it." They started down the hall.

"But she can't really be that sanctimonious," Effy said as they rounded the corner to the bedchamber, "or else she wouldn't have married an Argantian."

"You'd be surprised how much cognitive dissonance people are capable of."

"Do you ever get weary of being so snootily unsentimental?"

Preston huffed a laugh. "No, it comes very naturally to me."

"You know, you *could* have said that love transcends petty theological squabbles."

"Love conquers all?" Preston arched a brow. "I suppose I could say that, if I were a romantic."

Effy snorted, but for some reason her heart thumped unevenly. She told herself it was nervousness about their assuredly ill-fated plan, and—as Preston reached for the door—the memory of the ghost surged forward in her mind. Her white hair lashing like a cut sail, her skin so pale it was almost translucent.

A similar coldness prickled Effy's skin, and she almost said, *Wait, stop.* But it would be useless to mention the encounter to Preston. She knew without asking that he was not the type to believe in ghosts.

Mrs. Myrddin, on the other hand, was perhaps worth bringing up. "Be quiet," she said tersely. "The widow must be in here."

"I *know,*" Preston whispered back. "I'm being as quiet as I can."

Effy held her breath as Preston turned the knob and pushed open the door to the private chambers. What spooled out in front of them was a narrow hallway, dust-choked and dark. The wooden floor was pocked with termite holes and the walls were bare, save for a small, rust-speckled mirror.

Effy was surprised to see it. Yet when she examined the mirror more closely, she realized the glass had been oxidized so thoroughly that there was no way to see a reflection in it. An odd disappointment settled in her belly.

She and Preston paused in the hallway and listened, but no sound echoed from either of the doors ahead. And just as it had the night before, even the thrashing of water against the rocks had gone silent. If Mrs. Myrddin was in her chambers, she must have been sleeping.

Or, a small voice nagged at Effy, *she might not exist at all.* It was not a thought she had any proof of, but when she thought of the ghost, her heartbeat quickened.

Keeping her voice low, she said, "Ianto's room is on the left."

"I hope he hasn't locked it."

There was something wrong with this section of the house.

It seemed to exist in another world, cold and silent and strange, like a shipwreck on the ocean floor. The rest of Hiraeth creaked and groaned and swayed, protesting its slow destruction. The air here was stiff and heavy, and Effy moved through it almost in slow motion, as if she were wearing sopping wet clothes. In truth, it was as though this wing of the house had already been drowned.

Ianto's door opened without so much as a shudder.

Effy didn't know what she had expected to see on the other side. A beached mermaid on the bed, a heap of selkie skins? The ghost herself? The bedroom was disappointingly ordinary, at least as far as Hiraeth was concerned. There was an enormous canopy bed, not unlike the one Effy slept in herself, with moth-eaten gossamer curtains and dark blue satin sheets that made the mattress appear waterlogged. As far as she could tell, there was no mirror.

There was a wardrobe, its doors firmly shut, between which the sleeve of a black sweater was caught like a badger in a trap. *A badger*, Effy thought suddenly. Perhaps that had been the animal in the road.

There were piles of yellowed newspapers, but none of them pertained to Emrys Myrddin. The headlines were very arbitrary: An article about an art installation in Laleston. One about a series of burglaries in Corth, a town not far east of Saltney. Another was about a pony that had become a hero for bravely facing down a mountain cat; in the end, the pony had succumbed to its injuries and died.

Effy let the newspaper drift back down to the floor. "Nothing."

"I'm not quite ready to surrender yet," said Preston. "Where was that white space in the blueprints?"

"Along the western wall." Effy pointed.

The western wall was just one huge bookshelf, only about half full. Silently Effy and Preston went about examining the spines, but they found no works of Emrys Myrddin there. Ianto's reading taste appeared to be more lurid. Mostly mysteries and romances, the sorts of books she knew Preston would call *pedestrian*.

One erotic title stuck out to her: *Dominating the Damsel*. Effy slid it back into place with a shudder.

"I don't understand," Preston said, letting out a heated breath. "There can't just be nothing. What sort of man scrubs a house so thoroughly of his dead father's memory?"

It was the second time Preston had brought that up, and she wondered why the fact seemed to bother him so much. "I don't know," she said. "Everyone has their own way of grieving. You can't know what you'd do until it happens to you."

"As it happens," Preston replied, "my father is dead."

He said it so casually, so conversationally, that it took Effy a while to react. She looked at him, half turned toward her, the meager light clinging to his profile. His eyes, which were a pale brown, seemed intense but steady, like he was staring at something he had been watching for a long time already.

"Look at us," she said finally. "Two fatherless children marooned in a sinking house. We ought to be careful that Ianto doesn't decide to slit our throats over the new foundation."

She'd meant to lighten the moment, but Preston's mouth went thin. "If there's anyone who would still believe in an old custom like that, it's Ianto. Did you see the horseshoe over the door?"

"No," she admitted. "But that's an old folk tradition, to keep the fairies out of your house."

Preston nodded. "And all the trees planted around the property are mountain ash. For someone who doesn't keep any of his father's books around, he certainly seems to have studied their edicts closely."

Mountain ash, iron. Effy had even noticed a crush of red berries outside the cottage. Rowan berries were meant to guard against the Fair Folk, too.

Ianto had his father's commissioned portraits of the Fairy King and Angharad hanging right above the stairs. Maybe that was another aegis. If he could keep the Fairy King trapped inside a frame, inside one of Myrddin's stories, it would stop him from slipping through the front door.

Effy wondered if perhaps that was what Ianto *truly* wanted from her: a house that could protect him from the Fairy King. What if he, too, had seen the creature in the road, with its bone crown and wet black hair?

But what would the Fairy King want with Ianto? He came for young girls with pale hair to gild his crown. Men slept soundly in their beds while their wives and daughters were spirited away. That was what the stories said.

And the shepherd had told her as much when he gave her the hag stones. *A pretty young girl alone on the cliffs up there . . .*

She shook her head to dispel the thoughts. Preston, who had been gripping the edge of the bookcase with both hands, stepped back, sighing.

The bookcase wobbled, not inconsiderably—enough to reveal a knife-slit of space between the shelf and the wall. Effy and Preston looked at each other.

Without needing to speak, they both went to the far end of the bookcase and pulled. It made a heaving sound that Effy was sure would disturb the mistress—if she was indeed in the next room—but her pulse was racing and her mind didn't linger on the possibility that they might be caught.

When they had gotten the bookcase far enough away, Effy could see that there was no wall behind it at all. Just an empty black space that became, as she stepped into it, a small room gouged into the side of the house.

"Be careful," Preston said. "Effy, wait. I'll get a candle."

She didn't *want* to wait. Her heart was pounding, but it was so dark that she didn't really have a choice. She stood there in the cold room, seeing nothing on all sides, and oddly she was not afraid. It was so silent, the air so still. Effy could only imagine that whatever was in the room with her, if it had ever been alive at all, was already dead.

Preston came back with a candle and slid into the room beside her. It was a tight fit, and their shoulders were pressed together. She could feel his arm rise with his breathing, just a little hitched, just a little quick.

He shined the candle around, revealing dust-coated walls

and cobwebbed corners, peeling plaster and gray spots of mold. Where the paint had been stripped away, a patch of brickwork was exposed, and the mortar was dyed black, as if with ink.

There was nothing in the room save for a single dented tin box. It was in the exact center of the floor, placed there with purpose.

Effy went to kneel beside it, but Preston thrust out his arm, pinning her back.

"What?" she demanded. "What is it?"

"Your knees," he said, lowering the candle to point at them. "I'm sure they're still raw and—" He looked flustered, one hand brushing through his untidy hair, and it took another moment for him to finally say, "Just let me."

"Oh." Effy watched as Preston knelt down on the floor. "I thought you were going to tell me the box was haunted."

She couldn't see his face, but she heard Preston's now familiar huff of laughter. "It does look a bit haunted, doesn't it?"

"I'm glad you don't entirely lack imagination."

Preston gave the box a gentle shake. "It's locked."

"No," Effy said, her voice edging on petulant. "Let me see."

Preston stood up, brushing off his trousers, and handed her the box. Like the rest of the room, it was covered in dust. Effy had to blow on the front to read the words stamped on it: *PROPERTY OF E. MYRDDIN.*

Her heart leaped. She tamped down her eagerness as she examined the rest of the box. Below his name was a little engraving of the same two saints, Eupheme and Marinell, their beards swollen like titanic waves. Effy got the same feeling she had felt while paging through those old books in the university library—like she was discovering something arcane and secret and special, something that belonged, in some small way, to her.

And to Preston, of course. She could tell from the dust that no other fingers had touched this box for a long, long time. There was a small keyhole in the front, but the metal felt very flimsy, no more substantial than the tin where Effy's grandfather kept his neatly rolled cigars.

She heaved the box against the wall, which it hit with a deafening clatter. There was the crush of metal as the corner of the box folded in on itself like a crumpled napkin.

Preston actually *yelped*. "Effy! What are you doing?"

"Opening it," she replied, which she thought was obvious.

"But Ianto," he choked out. "He's certainly going to notice that his father's box has been smashed and pilfered."

"The whole thing was covered in dust," Effy said. "I don't think he even knows that it's here."

Preston made another vague, strangled noise of protest, but Effy had already pried open the damaged lock. She flipped the lid of the box open, rusted hinges whining.

Inside was a small leather-bound notebook, wrapped up with a length of twine.

Her breath caught in her throat. Here it was, something Emrys Myrddin had actually *written in*. This was better than any obscure tome she'd ever found in the library. Better than any treasure a deep-sea diver could uncover.

She stole a glance at Preston, whose eyes were wide, mouth

slightly ajar, and found she didn't even mind that he was discovering it with her.

"I can't believe it," Preston said. "I never really thought we would find—well, I suppose we don't know what's inside yet. It could be a weather almanac. It could be a book of recipes."

Effy gave him a withering look. "No one keeps their recipe book locked away in a secret box, in a secret room."

"With Myrddin, I wouldn't be too shocked," Preston said dryly.

He picked up the diary and something slipped out from between its pages. Several things, in fact. Nearly a dozen photographs, washed out and worn thin with time.

Her fingers trembling, Effy took one. Through the pearlescent sheen of age, she could see it was a photo of a girl, no older than she was, with long, pale hair. She was curled on the chaise longue in Myrddin's study wearing a satin robe, which had slipped up to reveal a white calf.

Preston frowned. "Who is this?"

Effy found she couldn't speak. The air in the room suddenly felt very heavy, very thick.

She picked up the next photograph, which featured the same girl, on the same chaise, only she had changed position: her legs were straight now, bare feet dangling over the edge of the chaise, and her robe had rucked up farther, exposing the curve of her thigh.

Though Effy already knew what she would see, she needed to pick up the next photo. For so long the girl had been secreted away, gathering dust. That was why something might become a ghost— its life had meant so little, no one had even mourned it.

In the next photo the girl was on her back, robe cleaved open to bare her tight, round breasts. The buds of her nipples were small and pinched, as if it had been cold in the study that day. She was not looking at the camera. Her gaze was elsewhere and empty. Her arms were arced over her head but in a stiff and unnatural way, as if they had been positioned there by someone else's hand or whim.

Her body was as flat and bare as a butcher's drawing, all parts accounted for. Two legs and two arms, her head and her golden hair, her flat belly and perfectly symmetrical breasts. If you slit her down the middle like a fish, both sides would be identical.

Effy's grip tightened on the photo, crumpling its edges. A hard knot rose in her throat.

Preston had taken up another photo. His face was very red, gaze darting around hurriedly, trying to look anywhere else but at the naked girl. "Who do you think she is?" he asked again.

"I don't know." Effy's voice sounded slurred, like a reverberation from below water. "These could be Ianto's . . ."

"Ianto doesn't need to keep his, ah, adult materials under lock and key." Even the back of Preston's neck was pink now. "You saw his bookshelves."

Adult materials was the sort of euphemism only an academic would come up with. If the circumstances had been different, Effy might have laughed.

But the girl wasn't an adult, not really. She couldn't be. She looked Effy's age, and Effy certainly didn't feel like an *adult*.

The photographs made her dizzy, her vision blurring at the corners.

"They have to be Myrddin's, then." The certainty of it was like a fist against her windpipe. Her breath came now only in rough, hot spurts.

Preston looked at her, frowning. "Effy, are you all right?"

"Yes," she managed. But she couldn't bear to look at the girl anymore. She turned the photograph over.

There was something scrawled on the other side, in hasty but delicate script.

Preston read it aloud, his voice wavering slightly. "'I will love you to ruination.'"

It was what the Fairy King had said to Angharad, the first night they had lain together in their marriage bed. His long black hair had spilled out over the pillow, tangling with her pale gold.

The handwriting was not Ianto's.

There was a thump from downstairs, followed by the scrape of a door opening, and they both jumped. Effy felt her stupor lift. She put the box down on the floor and closed it, dented as it was, while Preston tucked the diary into his jacket pocket. They hurried out of the small room and shoved the bookcase back into place.

They left the photographs inside the box. Effy never wanted to see them again. She had no way of knowing, but she felt very certain that the girl in the pictures was dead.

By the time they made it back to the study, Effy was breathless. Her nose was itching with dust, her blood pulsing and hot, and when Preston removed the diary from his pocket, his hands were shaking.

He unwrapped the twine, long fingers working dexterously,

and Effy watched, oddly hypnotized. They were both huddled over the desk, close enough that their shoulders were nearly touching. She could feel the heat of his body next to hers and the frenetic hum of energy that radiated from him.

Behind his glasses, his brow was furrowed with consummate focus. The twine drifted to the ground.

Effy couldn't help herself; she reached forward and opened the notebook to the first page. In doing so, she brushed against Preston's hand, the nub of her missing ring finger grazing his thumb. He looked down for a moment, his attention briefly diverted, and then turned his gaze back to the diary.

The first page was dense with Myrddin's vexing, spidery scrawl. Both Effy and Preston bowed their heads, squinted, and read.

10 March 188

Visited Blackmar at Penrhos. He gave me some notes on The Youthful Knight, which were good. He also offered to introduce me to his publisher, some Mister Marlowe, in Caer-Isel. Blackmar seemed to think the head of Greenebough Books would be charmed by my impoverished upbringing—what he called, a bit too self-importantly, my "rough edges." Three of his daughters were there as well. The wife, I assume, banished.

That was the end of the first page. Preston lifted his gaze from the book and up to Effy. It was the first time she had seen him completely slack-jawed.

"I can't believe it," he said. "This is Myrddin's actual diary. Part of me hoped, of course, I could find some of his unpublished work, but I didn't even dare to imagine it would be a full *journal*. Do you know how valuable this is, Effy? Even if we don't discover any evidence of a hoax, this diary . . . well. Gosse is going to have a stroke—honestly, I think every academic at the literature college would amputate his left arm for it. As a museum artifact, it would be worth thousands. Maybe *millions*."

"I think you're getting a little ahead of yourself," Effy said. But her voice was weak, heart spluttering. "Ianto must not have known it was there. Or else he would've tried to sell it himself."

"Or," Preston said, his face darkening, "there's something in it he didn't want anyone to know."

They read on.

30 January 189

The Youthful Knight *will be published. Greenebough appears cautiously optimistic, but I do not expect much success. The youths themselves may read it, but I think it is too dry a tome. What do youths these days care for chivalry and modesty? Not very much, as far as I can tell. When I visited Penrhos I saw Blackmar's daughters again. The eldest is very fair, and took an interest in my work. But a woman's mind is too frivolous, and though she was an unusually sober example of her sex, I could tell she was more preoccupied with dance halls and boys. She has written a few poems of her own.*

Effy stared and stared at the line *a woman's mind is too frivolous*. It stung her like a snakebite, a sudden whiplash of pain. Angharad was anything but *frivolous*. She was shrewd and daring, her mind

172

always scheming, imagining, conjuring new worlds. She was strong. She had defeated the Fairy King.

If Myrddin really thought so little of women, why had he written *Angharad* at all?

"*The Youthful Knight* was Myrddin's first effort," Preston said, "but it was released to relative silence. Emrys Myrddin wasn't a household name until—"

"Until *Angharad*," Effy finished. Her chest hurt.

"Let's see what Myrddin had to say about that."

They flipped forward to 191, the year of *Angharad's* publication.

18 August 191

Blackmar delivered Angharad to me in the dead of night. The rain and humidity this time of year is unbearable. I don't take much stock in the fretting of the naturalists, but these summer storms are enough to make me mind their warnings about a second Drowning. Blackmar was happy to be free of her; she has been vexing him terribly of late.

    Publication is set for midwinter. Mr. Marlowe is greatly excited for the reinvention of Emrys Myrddin.

Preston let out a soft breath. His brown eyes were shining. "Effy, I can't believe this."

It did seem damning. But even though the words *a woman's mind is too frivolous* still gnawed at her, Effy wasn't willing to relent. "Who is Blackmar?"

Preston blinked, as if to banish the awestruck look from his face. "Colin Blackmar," he said. "Another one of Greenebough's authors. You probably know his most famous work, 'The Dreams of a Sleeping King.'"

"Oh. Yes," Effy said. "That awful, tediously long poem we all had to memorize bits of in primary school."

The corner of Preston's mouth lifted. "Do you remember any of it now?"

"'The slumbering King dreams of sword-fights and slaughter,'" Effy recited. "'He feels the steaming blood of his enemies through his mail, and his dream-self dreams of cool river water. He sees the dragon's long body uncoil, the flash of scales, the bright blades of its teeth, and oh, the sleeping King is foiled!—for he is both the knight and the dragon in the battlefield of his Dream-world.'"

She tried to make her recitation sound suitably dramatic, even though her head was spinning and her knees felt weak.

"You really do have the best memory of anyone I've ever met," Preston said. There was no denying the admiration in his tone. "Your schoolteachers must have all been very impressed."

"It's drivel," Effy said. "Surely you can't think there's any merit to it."

"Blackmar has always been a more commercial author. He was never a critical darling like Myrddin. No one in the literature college is studying 'The Dreams of a Sleeping King,' that's for certain." When Effy gave him a dour look, he went on: "And no, I've never personally been a fan. I find his work to be . . . well, tedious."

Finally, something they could agree on. "Did you know Myrddin and Blackmar were friends? Why was Blackmar bringing *Angharad* to him in August of 191?"

"I have a few ideas," Preston said. "But this is something big, Effy. Even if you're right and Myrddin was exactly who he said he was—an upstart provincial genius—there's so much else this diary could prove. So many things other Myrddin scholars have only been able to speculate on. Gosse is going to choke on his mustache."

"*If* it turns out Myrddin isn't a fraud," said Effy. But she was unable to imbue her words with the confidence she wanted. Her gaze kept darting back to the green chaise in the corner. She could imagine the girl there, robe flayed open like an oyster shell. "This proves that Myrddin was at least literate, but . . . it doesn't quite read like the thoughts of a once-in-a-lifetime genius."

Preston blinked rapidly at her, raising a brow. "Did I hear that correctly? Are you actually starting to come around?"

"No!" Effy burst out, face heating. "I mean, not entirely. It's just . . . the things he said about women. I don't see how you could write a book like *Angharad* if you really believed women were empty-headed and frivolous."

She tried to sound coolly rational like Preston always did, removed from emotion. But her throat was thick with a knot of unshed tears. The Myrddin from the photograph on the jacket of *Angharad* and the Myrddin of this diary were like two yoked oxen pulling in opposite directions, and as much as Effy tried, she could not hold them together.

"Cognitive dissonance," Preston said. When Effy glowered at him, he quickly added, "But you're right. *Angharad* isn't something your common misogynist would write."

To call Myrddin a common misogynist was strong language. It was probably the boldest, most unequivocal statement she'd ever heard Preston make. It made the lump in her throat rise.

"You can't write him off on just one line in a diary entry, though," she tried weakly. "Maybe he was just, I don't know— having a bad day."

The argument was pitiful; she knew it. Preston drew a breath as if about to argue, but then snapped his mouth shut. Perhaps he saw the look of misery on her face. They both stood there for a moment in silence, and Effy felt the pull of the chaise longue in the back of her mind. As if she might turn around and find the girl lying there, a corpse now, blue white and maggot ridden, buzzing with flies. The image made her want to retch.

"I like to hedge my bets," Preston said at last, and Effy was grateful to him for breaking the silence, the spell those photographs had cast over her. "But seeing all this, if I had to make a gamble . . . I would bet on us, Effy."

Behind his glasses, his eyes were clear. The determination in his gaze made Effy's chest swell. She had never thought she'd feel anything close to *camaraderie* with Preston Héloury—loathsome literature scholar, untrustworthy Argantian. Yet even *camaraderie* did not feel quite like the right word.

Meeting his stare, she realized what she felt was closer to affection. Even—*maybe*—passion. And Effy couldn't help but wonder if he felt the same.

"There's something here that someone has gone to great lengths to keep hidden," Preston said. His gaze never left her. "It's something others would—if I know my colleagues well enough— kill for. But if we're careful, we can—"

He was interrupted by the door banging open. Effy hadn't even heard any footsteps in the hall. But Ianto stood in the threshold, his clothes soaked, his black hair plastered to his scalp.

Preston's reflexes were impressively quick. He thrust the diary behind his back and under a pile of scattered papers on his desk.

Effy let out a soft, choked gasp, but no one else heard it over the sound of water sluicing onto the floor. It was dripping off Ianto's clothing and the barrel of the musket he held over his shoulder.

She was almost *relieved* to see him standing there, perfectly mortal even in his anger. Half of her had expected to see the Fairy King appear in the doorway.

"The storm started so suddenly," Ianto said. "As soon as I returned from Saltney I began my weekly patrol around the property—Wetherell swears he saw the tracks of a wolf—he keeps telling me to hire a groundskeeper, but I do like the fresh morning air. The two of you look cozy."

How had he found the time to traverse the grounds after returning from church? Surely they had not spent more than an hour looking for Myrddin's diary. But his car *had* been gone, and she had seen that dead thing decaying in the driveway.

Or at least, she thought she had. She had taken her pink pills this morning, two, for good measure, but after last night—after the ghost—she no longer trusted the medication entirely. Maybe there had been no animal at all, no blood.

She pressed her lips shut, skin itching.

Preston's face went very pale. "Effy was just, ah, telling me about her work. I have a passing interest in architecture. I was always curious about the differences between classical Argantian and Llyrian homes . . ."

He trailed off, and despite her dread, Effy was charmed to learn what an abysmal liar Preston was.

"We go to the same university in Caer-Isel," she said smoothly. "As it turns out, we even have some mutual friends. Small world."

The discrepancy in their narratives was obvious, but Preston hadn't given her too much to work with. Did he really expect Ianto to believe he cared about the difference between a sash window and a casement? Preston's fingers were curled tautly around the edge of the desk, his knuckles white.

Ianto just stared, as if neither of them had spoken at all. Very slowly he let the musket slide off his shoulder and hang parallel to the ground, its barrel pointed somewhere in the vague direction of Preston's knees. Effy's throat tightened.

"I believe," he said, each syllable staccato and deliberate, "that I have been quite generous in allowing you both into my home, and very patient in allowing inquests into my father's life and family history, things that are, of course, highly personal to me. If I were to learn that my patience and generosity were being exploited, for any reason—well. I suppose we would all rather not discover what might come to pass."

"Right," Preston said, too quickly, throat bobbing as he spoke. "Of course. Sorry."

Effy resisted the urge to elbow him. He had to be the most guilty-looking person alive.

"It's nothing like that," she said, trying to keep her voice even.

"We were just having coffee and chatting before getting to work. Did you enjoy your trip to town?"

"Mm," Ianto said vaguely. The end of his musket was a gaping hole, depthless black. Around him a puddle had formed on the wooden floor. "Perhaps you've done enough chatting for today, Ms. Sayre. Mr. Héloury. Effy, I'd like to see some new sketches by this afternoon."

It was as if he had forgotten everything from yesterday: their time at the pub, her jumping out of the car. His eyes were turbid again, unreadable. Even if Effy had felt brave enough to try, she could not have divined anything from staring into them.

Without another word, Ianto turned and slammed the door shut behind him. All that remained was the puddle of water on the floor.

The whole incident was enough to convince Effy that Ianto *was* hiding something, even if he didn't know about the diary. As she tried to work on her sketches downstairs at the dining room table, odd glass chandelier rippling overhead, she could not stop thinking about the photographs of the girl on the chaise. Each one was like a stake driven through her brain.

They were clearly old, though how old, Effy couldn't say. She thought again of the line scrawled on the back of the last one: *I will love you to ruination.* The handwriting matched the handwriting in Myrddin's diary.

And her mind turned even further on that line from Myrddin's diary: *a woman's mind is too frivolous.* Something was wrong with it, all of it—maybe not in the way Preston thought, but in a way that made her chest ache and her eyes burn. At this point, the best possible outcome was that the diary itself was a forgery. That Myrddin had never written those things about women. But that seemed highly unlikely, given the great pains someone—perhaps Myrddin himself—had gone to hide it.

That left her with two options: that Myrddin had believed all those things and still written *Angharad* (cognitive dissonance, like Preston had said), or that he hadn't written *Angharad* at all.

In that moment, Effy wasn't sure which would be worse.

She worked half-heartedly on her sketches, fingers trembling around her pencil. It was a good thing she had plenty of practice fumbling her way through architecture assignments with little enthusiasm. But strangely, Ianto never came down to check on her, even as the thin gray light bleeding in through the windows grew dimmer, and finally vanished.

Effy peered through the smudged glass. It was almost totally dark out now, the sun making itself small against the horizon. She folded up her papers and got to her feet.

She meant to return to the guesthouse—really, she did—but somehow her legs were carrying her up the stairs, past the portrait of the Fairy King, who blessedly remained trapped in his frame, past the carvings of the saints, past the door to the study where Preston was certainly poring over the diary.

It had been about this time last night that she had seen the ghost. Dusk, when the war between the waning light and the hungering dark made everything look shuddery and unreal. Effy told herself she only meant to bring the sketches to Ianto, like he had asked. But as she crept toward the door leading to the private chambers, she found herself moving stealthily, trying not to make a sound.

There was the same oppressive stillness she'd felt when she and Preston had entered the chambers earlier. But she did not see the ghost: no flash of a white dress or a naked calf, no curtains twitching. Effy was about to turn back, disappointed, when she heard a voice.

"Had to get out—"

She froze, like a deer at the end of a hunter's rifle. It was Ianto.

"I didn't have a choice," he said, and it was a low, moaning sound, as if he were in pain. "This house has a hold on me, you know that, you know about the mountain ash . . ."

He stopped speaking suddenly. Effy's blood turned to ice.

And then he spoke again: "I had to bring *her* back. Isn't that what you wanted?"

Effy waited and waited, her whole body shaking, but Ianto said no more. When she had the strength to move, she lurched unsteadily down the stairs, fear thrumming in her like a second pulse. It was like Ianto had been talking to himself—or talking to something that couldn't speak its reply.

Something like a ghost.

TEN

When the king was first interred,
He did not dream at all.
It was the abhorrent nothingness
That cast a dreadful pall.
That bleak and black oblivion
Was too much like death to bear.
And so the dreams came like a balm
For the half-dead king's despair.

FROM "THE DREAMS OF A SLEEPING KING"

BY COLIN BLACKMAR, 193 AD

The next day, Preston was jumpier than usual, flinching at every unexpected sound. He couldn't seem to get over the fact that Ianto had waved his rifle at them. But that was the least of Effy's concerns. Ianto's more overt antagonism didn't bother her—a man with a gun was an enemy she could easily recognize and comprehend.

No, she was far more concerned about the things she could only see out of the corner of her eye, the voices she heard when no one else was listening.

Ianto's threats had been vague, but she knew he didn't want to see her and Preston together again. So they began working only under the cover of night.

It would have taken days, if not weeks, to read through the whole diary with the careful attention it required. But the entries they *had* read pointed over and over again to Colin Blackmar. If Preston was to be believed, they didn't have much time to solve the mystery before the rest of the literature college came pounding at the door—or before Ianto banished him from the house.

"We could only have days," Preston said. "We have to focus on Blackmar now."

Effy knew nothing about Blackmar other than her memories of that one terrible poem, which she had a clear vision of reciting while wearing an itchy school sweater.

"He's about as patriotic a writer as you can imagine," Preston said. "Openly nationalist. There's a reason every Llyrian child has to learn 'The Dreams of a Sleeping King.' And the king is venerated because he slaughtered hundreds of Argantians."

Preston's voice tipped up at the end; he always sounded uncharacteristically nervous when he spoke of Argant, and his normally subtle accent became more pronounced.

"I bet the Llyrian government wishes they could put him in the Sleeper Museum too," Effy said. That was one thing all the Sleepers had in common: they had to be from the South.

"Oh, Blackmar is probably pitying himself that he had the misfortune to have been born north of Laleston. I suppose he could make up some story about how he was an orphan child, taken in by nobility, but with Southern blood running true in his veins. There you go—Sleeper Museum, eternal veneration, *magic*."

Preston's tone dripped with irony, and Effy rolled her eyes. "It must be immensely frustrating for you, to put up with all our Llyrian superstitions. Just because it's an archaic belief doesn't mean it's not *true*."

"Argant has plenty of its own superstitions, let me assure you. But I think magic is just the truth that people believe. For most people, that truth is whatever helps them sleep at night, whatever makes their lives easier. It's different from *objective* truth."

Effy laughed shortly. "No wonder you're such a terrible liar."

It did charm her to know that despite all his monologuing about good lies requiring a willing audience, he still flushed and stammered over his falsehoods.

"I don't *like* lying." Preston folded his arms over his chest. "I know it's not realistic, but the world would be a better place if everyone just told the truth."

It was a strangely naive thing to say. Effy had never thought much about the lies she told—she didn't feel *good* about them, but they didn't rend her apart with guilt, either. Lying was a form of survival, a way out of whatever trap had been set. Some animals chewed off their own limbs to escape. Effy just tucked away truth after truth, until even she wasn't sure if there was a real person left at all, under all those desperate, urgent lies.

But it had been a long time since she'd even tried telling anyone the truth. She just assumed no one would believe her. Preston especially, with his pretentiousness and disdain for anything that couldn't be proven. Yet even though he held to his principles, he wasn't as close-minded as she'd initially imagined him to be. He truly *considered* all the things she said, all the new information presented to him—and he'd even told her he was perfectly willing to be proven wrong.

Somehow, Effy found herself blurting out, "Do you believe in ghosts?"

Preston blinked at her. "Where did that come from?"

"I . . . I don't know." Effy had surprised herself with the words. "I'm just curious. I know you don't believe in Sleeper magic, but ghosts are different, aren't they?"

Preston's expression suddenly became very hard. "There's no proof that ghosts are real. No scientific evidence to support it."

"But there's nothing to prove they *aren't* real, is there?"

"I suppose not."

She expected Preston to say more, but his mouth had snapped shut and he wasn't meeting her eyes. It was uncharacteristic of him to be so withdrawn. Usually it took very little coaxing to get him to wax poetic on practically any subject.

"And there are so many ghost stories," Effy pressed. "So many sightings—I bet in a room full of people, half of them would claim they've seen a ghost. Every culture has ghost stories. That seems significant."

"I don't know what brought this up," Preston said slowly, "but if you really want to know what I believe—I believe in the human mind's ability to rationalize and externalize its fear."

"Fear?" Effy raised a brow. "Not all ghost stories are scary. Some are comforting."

"Fine, then." Preston's voice was tight, his gaze fixed stubbornly on some point above her head. "I believe in the emotions—grief, terror, desire, hope, or otherwise—that might conjure one."

It was not the dismissive answer Effy thought she might get. He hadn't laughed at her, like she'd been afraid he would. He hadn't told her she was childish or stupid. But she could tell from the way he'd spoken, how his whole body had tensed when she'd said the word *ghost*, that it was something he very much did not want to discuss. It was like she'd gotten too close to picking open a wound.

She found that she didn't want to hurt him, and so she resolved not to bring up what she had seen. What she had heard. Instead, Effy asked, "Blackmar is alive, isn't he?"

"Yes." Preston looked relieved that she'd changed the subject. "Ancient, but alive."

"Then let's go see him," she said. "He's the only one who can answer our questions."

Preston hesitated. They had both felt it too dangerous to keep the lights on in the study, so they were working by moonlight and candlelight, keeping their voices low. Right then the left side of his face was doused in orange, the right side in white.

"As it happens, I wrote to Blackmar already," he said at last. "His name crops up quite a lot in Myrddin's letters as well. I thought he might give me some insight into Myrddin's character, since Ianto won't talk about his father at all."

"Well?" Effy prompted.

"The letter came back marked 'return to sender,'" Preston said.

"But I know he opened it and read it, because the seal was broken and replaced with one of his own."

"Can I see the letter?"

Somewhat reluctantly, Preston produced it. Effy flattened the paper against the table, squinted in the candlelight, and read.

Dear Mr. Blackmar,

I am a literature student at the university in Caer-Isel, and my thesis concerns some of the works of Emrys Myrddin. I've recently become aware that the two of you maintained correspondence, and I hoped I might make a scholarly inquiry into the nature of your relationship, if you are amenable to answering some of my questions. I am happy to make the journey to Penrhos if you find face-to-face conversation preferable to written correspondence.

Sincerely,
Preston Héloury

Effy blinked up at him. "This is the worst letter I've ever seen."

"What do you mean?" Preston looked affronted. "It's brisk and professional. I didn't want to waste his time."

"He has to be in his nineties now, Blackmar. He has *plenty* of time on his hands. Where's the flattery? The beseeching? You could've at least *pretended* to be a fan of his work."

"I told you, I don't like lying."

"This is for a good cause. Isn't it worth lying a little bit, if it helps get to the truth?"

"Interesting paradox. Llyr doesn't have a patron saint of blessed liars for nothing. Do parents ever name their children after Saint Duessa?"

Effy's skin prickled. She didn't want to go down this dark road. "Some, I guess. But stop changing the subject. I'm making fun of your terrible letter."

Preston let out a breath. "Fine. Why don't you write one, then?"

"I will," she said with resolve.

That night, Effy wrote her letter, beseeching and full of flattery. They couldn't risk putting it in Hiraeth's postbox, since Ianto could easily check it, so Preston drove down to Saltney to send it.

"There's nothing to do now except wait," Preston said. "And I'll keep looking through the diary."

Effy found her mind lingering on a different mystery, the one she still didn't have the courage to tell Preston about. The Fairy King, the ghost, Ianto's strange conversation. The thoughts haunted her both sleeping and waking, and she found herself fleeing Hiraeth as quickly as she could at night, barreling toward the safety of the guesthouse.

It was almost a relief to not think about Myrddin for a while. She didn't want to remember the photographs, the diary entry where he'd called women *frivolous*. A part of her wished she'd never seen any of it at all.

At least distracting Ianto turned out to be easy. For him, Effy drew sketches that would never leave the paper, floor plans that would never be realized. She found that he was a willing audience for her lies. He wanted to believe, as she once had (as maybe a part of her still *did*) that the project of Hiraeth was more than just an imagined future. A castle in the air.

"I like the look of the second floor here," Ianto said, as they spread out her drawings over the dining table. "The bay windows overlooking the sea—it will be lovely for watching the sunrise and sunset. My mother will like it, too."

"Does your mother not want me to be here?" Effy had been holding on to the question practically since she arrived at Hiraeth, but after the odd half conversation she'd overheard, it was killing her more than ever not to ask it.

Now seemed like a good time. Ianto was in a jaunty mood. The sun was wriggling through the clouds. The Fairy King had not appeared to her since that day in the car, and Ianto had never brought up the incident. To him, it seemed, the whole event had never occurred.

Ianto leaned back in his chair and let out a breath. There was a long stretch of silence, and Effy worried that there was not, in fact, a good time to ask the question after all.

"She's a very private woman," he said at last. "My father made her that way."

Effy's stomach clenched. "What do you mean?"

"He grew up in dire poverty, as you know. He hardly had more than the clothes on his back, and his father's little fishing boat. When he finally did have something of his own, he was loath to let it go." Another beat of silence. "This house—he let it decay rather than have any stranger come to fix the leaking pipes or broken windows, much less the crumbling foundation. It's a good metaphor, I think, but I'm no literary scholar like our other guest."

He almost never mentioned Preston by name. He called him *the student* or *the Argantian*. Ianto's words reminded Effy of a certain passage from *Angharad*.

> *"I will love you to ruination,"* the Fairy King said, *brushing a strand of golden hair from my cheek.*
> *"Yours or mine?" I asked.*
> *The Fairy King did not answer.*

That made her think of the photographs again, and *that* made her cheeks turn pink. Maybe she didn't want to know about the ghost, about Myrddin's widow, about whatever secrets Ianto was hiding. It was all tangled up like catch in a fishing net, nearly dead things thrashing as they choked on air.

Maybe Preston was right about why people believed in magic. The truth was an ugly, dangerous thing.

"Well," Effy said, "I'll try my best to stay out of your mother's way."

"Oh, I doubt you've disturbed her," Ianto said. His colorless eyes had taken on a bit of that odd gleam she'd seen in the pub, and it startled her so much that she jerked back in her seat. "You're as demure as a little kitten."

Effy tried a smile. Fingers trembling, she gripped the hag stones in her pocket.

Only a day after her conversation with Ianto, there was a letter in Hiraeth's postbox. Effy and Preston had both been staking it out at all hours to intercept the letter before Ianto could see it. It happened to arrive on Effy's watch, and she seized it, clutched it to her chest, and ran up the stairs to the house. She didn't care that it was still daylight and Ianto might see her and be furious; she burst into the study, breathing hard, and slapped the envelope down in front of Preston.

He was sitting at Myrddin's desk, head bowed over the diary. The sunlight streaming through the window illuminated little flecks of gold in his brown hair, and highlighted the pale scattering of freckles across his nose. When he saw the letter, his face broke into a smile that, for some reason, made Effy's heart give a tiny flutter.

"He really wrote back," Preston said. "I can't believe it."

"You should have more faith in me. I can be very charming, you know."

Preston gave a huff of laughter. "I actually do know that."

Effy's cheeks grew warm. She picked the envelope up again and neatly broke Blackmar's seal. She pulled the letter out gingerly; it was written on very thin paper, almost translucent in the sunlight. She held it out so that Preston could read it, too.

Miss Euphemia Sayre,

I was pleased to receive such an admiring letter. You seem like a lovely, agreeable young woman. I would be more than happy to host you and your academic compatriot at my manor, Penrhos.

You already know the address, as the successful delivery of your letter demonstrates. You seem like quite a special young girl indeed, to be so interested in the work of two old men, one now six months dead. I will certainly entertain you for as long as it takes to satisfactorily answer your questions about my work and the work of Emrys Myrddin. He was a dear friend and even, in the end, family.

All my best,
Colin Blackmar

"I just went on about how much I loved 'The Dreams of a Sleeping King,'" Effy said, so pleased by the outcome of her letter-writing efforts that she was beaming and blabbering, words coming out fast and eager. "I barely mentioned Myrddin at all—I didn't want to offend him by even suggesting I might be more interested in Myrddin's work than his own. I told you all it would take was some flattery."

Effy looked at Preston expectantly, but he had gone silent, his brow furrowed as he stared at the letter. "I didn't know that was your full name."

In all her excitement, she'd forgotten that she had signed her letter to Blackmar as *Euphemia*. She'd done it intentionally. No one, not even her mother, not even her stiff and formal grandparents, called her Euphemia. But *Effy* had a childish, frivolous quality to it. She didn't want Blackmar to think of her as *frivolous*. She wanted him to take her inquiries seriously. So she had used her real name.

Now she could see Preston's mind turning, and her stomach shriveled. "Yes," she said. "That's my full name."

"Do you mind if I ask—I'm sorry, I don't mean to be unspeakably rude—" She had never heard him stammer like this. His face was flushed all the way to the tips of his ears. "You don't have to answer, of course, and honestly, please feel free to hit me or call me a twat for asking at all, but—were you a changeling child?"

Effy let the room sink into silence. She had gone by her nickname for so long, she had almost forgotten the significance of her real one: that a saint's name was the mark of a changeling.

She closed her left hand into a fist and opened it again. It really was an unspeakably rude question. No one asked. She was a good Northern girl from a good Northern family, and changeling children were a barbaric custom, practiced only by peasants in the Bottom Hundred.

"Yes," she said finally, and she was surprised by how easy it was, to say that single word.

"I'm really sorry. It's just that you mentioned being fatherless—" Preston ran a hand through his hair, looking positively miserable.

"It's all right," she said. That was easy to say, too. In fact, Effy realized, she could tell the whole story as if it had happened to someone else, and it would be completely painless. "My mother was my age, or somewhere near it, when she had me. My father was a man who worked at my grandfather's bank—older. There was no wedding or proper courtship. It was an embarrassment to my grandfather that she ended up pregnant. He fired my father, banished him back to the South. He was from the Bottom

Hundred—one of those upstart provincial geniuses."

"I'm sorry," Preston repeated desperately. "You don't have to say any more."

"I don't mind." Effy was elsewhere now, floating. Her mind had opened its escape hatch and she was gone. "My mother had me, but a child was such an inconvenience to everyone. To her and my grandparents. I was a terrible child, too. I threw tantrums and broke things. Even as an infant I wouldn't nurse. I screamed when anyone touched me."

And then she stopped. The escape hatch snapped shut. She hit that wall, the boundary between the real and the unreal. In her mind there was an even divide, a *before* and an *after*. Once she had been an ordinary, if imprudent, little girl. And then, in the span of a moment, she became something else.

Or maybe she had always been *wrong*. A wicked fae creature from the unreal world, stranded unfairly in the real one.

"There's a river that runs through Draefen," Effy said after a moment. "That's where my mother left me. I remember it was the middle of winter. All the trees were bare. I know she thought some sad and childless woman would come pick me up. She didn't mean to expose me, to let me die—"

Preston's expression was unreadable, but he had not taken his eyes off her face. She really should have taken the out he had tried to give her and stopped talking. Preston was the biggest skeptic she'd ever met. He didn't believe in magic; he didn't even believe in Myrddin. Why would he believe her, when no one else had?

But he had listened to her, when she had asked him about

ghosts. He had not dismissed her, laughed at her, though clearly the discussion had made him uncomfortable. And then she thought of the way he had dropped to the floor in front of her and cleaned her skinned knees and hardly even questioned why she had thrown herself from Ianto's car.

Effy opened her mouth again, and words poured out.

"No childless woman came for me," she whispered. "But *he* did."

Behind his glasses, Preston's eyes narrowed. "Who did?"

"The Fairy King," she said.

The old, barbaric custom was this: In the South, it was believed that some children were simply born wrong, or were poisoned by the fairies in their cradles. These changeling children were awful and cruel. They bit their mothers when they tried to nurse them. They were always given the names of saints, to try to drive the evil away. Effy always wondered whether her mother had picked her name, Euphemia, to be a blessing or a curse. The feminine variation of Eupheme, patron saint of storytellers. Most of the time it just felt like a cruel joke.

But if that did not work, it was the mother's right to abandon her child: to leave them out for the fairies to take back.

Preston would probably say that was just the pretty truth the Southerners told themselves to sleep easily at night—that they weren't leaving their children out to die, that a fairy would come to spirit them back to their true home, in the realm of fae. But Effy had seen him. Thirteen years later, and still the image was bright and clear in her mind. His beautiful face and his wet black hair. His hand, reaching out for hers.

Even thinking of it now, her chest tightened with panic. Before the true terror could take hold and plunge her under, Preston's voice shattered the memory.

"I don't understand," he said. "The Fairy King is a story."

She had heard it so many times that the words didn't sting anymore. Ordinarily she would have stopped talking right then and there, apologized, told him she was only joking.

But the words kept pouring out.

"He was there with me," Effy said. "He stepped right out of the river. He was still all glistening and wet. It was dark, but he stood in a puddle of moonlight. He told me he was going to take me, and he was terrifying, but when he held out his hand, I took it."

That was the hardest part to speak aloud. The ugliest confession, the black rotted truth at the very core of her. She had reached back. Any ordinary child would have shrunk away in fear, would have wept, would have screamed. But Effy had not made a sound. She had been ready to let him take her.

"But my mother returned," she said. Her voice was thick. "She snatched me up from the riverbank and pulled my hand right out of the Fairy King's grasp. I saw the look of fury on his face before he vanished. He hates nothing more than to be refused. My mother held me, but where I had touched him, my finger was rotted away. He took it with him, and said he would be back for the rest."

She held up her left hand, with its missing fourth digit. She didn't add the last of what the Fairy King had said: That he had taken her ring finger so that no other man could put a wedding band on it. So that she would always belong to him.

"You said it was winter." Preston's voice was gentle. "Your finger could've fallen off from frostbite."

That was what the doctor had said, of course. He had bandaged it and given her a brown syrupy medicine to stave off infection, just like, years later, he had given her the pink pills to stave off her visions.

It wasn't until years later, when Effy first read *Angharad*, that she had learned what *really* kept the Fairy King at bay. Iron. Mountain ash. Rowan berries. She had broken off a bough of mountain ash in the park in Draefen and kept it under her pillow. She had stolen her grandfather's iron candelabra and slept with it in her hand. She had even tried to eat rowan berries, but they tasted so bitter, she spit them out, gagging.

"I know you don't believe me," she said. "No one ever has."

Preston was silent. She could almost see his mind working, the thoughts scrolling behind his eyes. At last, he said, "I suppose that's why you're such a big fan of Myrddin's work."

"I didn't read *Angharad* until I was thirteen," Effy said, cheeks growing hot. "If that's what you mean. It wasn't a child's imagination—I didn't have some image of the Fairy King in my mind."

"That's not what I meant," he said. "I just meant . . . it must have been easier to believe that there was some magic at work—a childhood curse, the pernicious Fair Folk. Something other than ordinary human cruelty."

He didn't believe her. Maybe that was for the best. Her stomach was churning now. "I knew you wouldn't understand."

"Effy," Preston said softly. "I'm sorry. You didn't have to tell me."

"My mother did come back for me, in the end," she said in a rush. "And she felt so enormously guilty for leaving me. She even gave me a *good* saint's name. I feel sorry for the other changeling children, named after Belphoebe or Artegall."

"That isn't right, Effy." Preston's voice was low but firm, and he met her gaze unrelentingly. "Mothers aren't supposed to hate their children."

"What makes you think she hated me?" Now she *did* feel angry, not because he hadn't believed her, but because he had no right to judge her mother—a woman he'd never even met. "Like I said, I was a terrible child. Any mother would've been tempted to do the same."

"No," Preston said. "They wouldn't."

"Why do you always have to be so certain you're right?" Effy tried to imbue her words with venom, but she just sounded desperate, scrambling. "You don't know my mother, and you hardly know me."

"I know you well enough. You aren't terrible. You're nothing close. And even if you were a difficult child—whatever that means—there's no justification for your mother wanting you *dead*. How did your mother expect you to live with that, Effy? To go on as normal knowing that she once tried to leave you out in the cold?"

She swallowed. Her ears were ringing; for a moment, she thought it was the bells from below the sea, the bells of those drowned churches. If she had had one of her pink pills with her, she would have taken it.

Her mother had gotten her those pills for a reason, so Effy *could* live with it, so she could go on as normal knowing that she'd once been left for dead. Her mother had pulled Effy right from the Fairy King's grasp, leaving just a finger behind. That was love, wasn't it?

"You said you believe in ghosts," she said thickly. "What's so different about this?"

"I said I believed in the horror or desire that might conjure one," Preston said. His eyes shifted, a muscle pulsed in his throat. "I can't tell you I believe in the Fairy King, Effy. But I believe in your grief and your fear. Isn't that enough?"

She hadn't even told him the worst thing of all: that the Fairy King had never truly left her. If she told Preston she had seen the Fairy King in the car with Ianto, he would realize he had made a terrible mistake in trusting her to help him. He would never believe another word she said.

Her eyes pricked with tears, and she swallowed hard to keep them from falling. "No," she said. "It's not enough. You *are* being rude. You're being mean. It's not—no one believed Angharad, either. And because no one believed her, the Fairy King was free to take her."

Preston inhaled. For a moment she thought he might argue, but there was no petulance on his face, no vitriol. He looked almost grief-stricken himself.

"I'm sorry for being rude," he said at last. "I wasn't trying to be. I'm only trying to tell you . . . well, I was trying to say you deserve better."

With a sudden shock like a rush of cold seawater, Effy found herself thinking of Master Corbenic.

"You deserve a man, Effy," Master Corbenic had told her once. "Not one of these awkward, acne-spotted boys. I see the way they look at you—with their leering, mopey eyes. Even if it isn't me you want, in the end, I know that you'll find yourself in the arms of a man, a real man. You'd exhaust these spineless boys. You need someone to challenge you. Someone to rein you in. Someone to keep you safe, protect you from your worst impulses and from the world. You'll see."

She squeezed her eyes shut and shook her head, forcing the memory to dissipate. She didn't want to think of him. She would rather think of the Fairy King in the corner of her room.

But when she opened her eyes, there was no Master Corbenic. No Fairy King. There was only Preston standing before her, his gaze taking her in carefully, tenderly, as if he was worried that even his stare might chafe.

"I don't want to talk about this anymore," she bit out.

"All right," he said gently. But his eyes never left her.

She did not linger at Hiraeth that night. She did not want to speak to Preston, and she certainly didn't want to speak to Ianto. Instead, when the sun humbled herself to the encroaching darkness, Effy retreated toward the guesthouse.

The air was cruelly cold and the grass wet from an earlier sprinkling of rain. Effy buttoned her coat all the way up to her throat and wrapped her scarf around her neck three times, hiding her mouth and nose behind the wool fabric. Then she slid down against the door to the guesthouse until she was seated in the grass, knees pulled up against her chest.

Her sleeping pills and her pink pills lay untouched on the bedside table inside. It grew darker and darker. Over and over again Preston's words thrummed in her mind: *I believe in your grief and your fear. Isn't that enough?*

No. It wasn't enough. As long as that was the only thing he believed, she would always be just a scared little girl making up stories in her head. She would be infirm, unstable, untrustworthy, undeserving of the life she wanted. They put girls like her in attic rooms or sanatoriums, locked them up and threw away the keys.

Effy waited until it was black as pitch and she couldn't even see her own hand in front of her face. Then she lit a candle she'd brought from the house and held it out into the dense darkness.

I was a girl when he came for me, beautiful and treacherous, and I was a crown of pale gold in his black hair.

I was a girl when he came for me, beautiful and treacherous, and I was a crown of pale gold in his black hair.

I was a girl when he came for me, beautiful and treacherous, and I was a crown of pale gold in his black hair.

She repeated the line over and over again in her mind, and then she spoke it out loud, into the black night and its uncanny silence.

"I was a girl when he came for me, beautiful and treacherous, and I was a crown of pale gold in his black hair."

She was not afraid. She needed him to come.

And then, behind the tree line, a flash of white. Wet black hair.

Even a sliver of face, pale as moonlight.

All her fear came piling down again, and Effy's mind thrashed like something caught in the foaming surf. She staggered to her feet, dropping the candle. The wet grass instantly snuffed it out, and she was plunged into darkness.

She felt for the handle of the door, wrenched it open, and hurled herself through. She slammed it shut behind her, the iron brace scraping against stone.

Her heart was pounding against her sternum like a trapped bird. Effy's knees shook so terribly that she fell forward again, and had to crawl across the cold floor until she reached the bed. Her fingers were trembling too much to light another candle. She just heaved herself into bed and pulled the green duvet over her head.

He had come for her, just like he had promised all those years ago. She had seen him. He was real. She was not mad.

As long as the Fairy King was real, he could be killed, just as Angharad had vanquished him.

If he was not real, there would never be any escape from him.

Effy crammed two sleeping pills into her mouth and swallowed them dry. But even the pills could no longer stop her from dreaming of him.

ELEVEN

Most scholars of Myrddin view him as somewhat in conversation with Blackmar, though the extent to which their works bear any genuine thematic or stylistic similarities is still debated. While Myrddin, in what few interviews he gave, was adamant that he did not seek to be known as a "Southern writer," Blackmar, though a Northerner himself, was very much inspired by the aesthetic and folkloric traditions of the South. In this paper, I argue that Blackmar perceived the South as a fanciful realm of whimsy, trapped in a time long past, existing merely for Northern writers to project their fantasies upon. In that regard, I contend that Blackmar is indeed a Southern writer—but only in the South of his own imagining.

FROM *THE QUESTION OF THE SOUTH: COLIN BLACKMAR,*

EMRYS MYRDDIN, AND NORTHERN FASCINATION

BY DR. RHYS BRINLEY, 206 AD

When they met the next day, Preston did not bring up the Fairy King or changeling children. Effy was grateful to him. She did not want to try to justify herself, nor tell him that she'd spent the night in the cold darkness, waiting for the Fairy

King to show himself. Preston had treated her kindly—more kindly than anyone else she'd told the truth to ever had—but still, he didn't believe her. It stung, but the memory of him saying *Isn't that enough?* thrummed in her mind, and there was a small reassurance in it. At least he had not called her mad.

Instead, there was just the matter of convincing Ianto to let them go see Blackmar. It would not be an easy task. Preston had become so *jumpy* around him ("He did wave a *gun* at us, Effy," he'd said, in an oddly high-pitched tone, when she'd confronted him about it).

She did not relish the idea of beseeching Ianto to let her go away from the house. And Preston didn't like any of her proposed lies.

"Ianto isn't an idiot," he said. "I don't see how you can relate this to your project—and I don't see how you could convince him that *I* would need to come along, too. Saints, it would be easier to just tell him we were sneaking off for some midnight tryst."

Effy felt her face turn red. "I don't think he would like *that* at all."

Preston's cheeks were pink, too. "Surely not. He was clear that he didn't want to see us together again—but it would be a more convincing lie. I mean—well. He doesn't care where I go. He'd be happier if I just left and never came back. He only cares about you."

As much as she did not want to admit it, Effy knew it was true. But ever since the incident at the pub, Ianto had asked for nothing more than just a bit of perfunctory, chaste flirtation. She could do that.

"Then why don't we tell him you're bringing me somewhere?"

she suggested. "Dropping me off in Laleston. Dropping me off in Laleston so I can, I don't know, look at architectural textbooks. They have a library there. If everything goes to plan, maybe neither of us will ever come back. We can just take the diary with us."

She spoke with more confidence than she felt. Though at least half the time, she wanted desperately to leave this sunken house and its disturbing secrets, she still felt a strange pull that urged her to stay. This was the realm of the Fairy King, after all. Perhaps this was where she belonged.

"I suppose that's true," Preston said. "You never signed anything binding you to him, did you? Money never changed hands?"

She found it funny that he was so preoccupied with the technicalities. Effy's mind always skipped over those details. She let those small things slough off her; the small things were never what ruined you. If she were kneeling and examining the shells on the beach, she wouldn't see the titanic wave rising over her head.

What sort of things would she wonder about, if she weren't always waiting for the next wave to come? She didn't let herself linger on it. She had to speak to Ianto.

Effy found him sitting on the edge of the cliffs, a casually dangerous pose, draped over the white rocks like a lizard in the midday sun. It wasn't even particularly sunny that day, but even the weak, bleary light gave his hair an oily sheen. Wet. He always looked wet.

"Effy," he said as she approached, "come sit."

She went over to him but didn't sit. A mile down the face of the cliffs, the sea sloshed like dishwater, lazy and gray. "I have something to ask you."

"Anything," Ianto said at once. "Really, Effy, please come closer."

He was sitting so perilously close to the edge of the cliff, looking more like an outcropping of rock than a man. He had been born in the Bottom Hundred, in this very house. The danger of the sea was as familiar to him as breathing. Unexpectedly she felt a twinge of sympathy. He really did want to stay here, sinking foundation and all.

She wondered if you could love something *out* of ruination, reverse that drowning process, make it all new again.

Effy stepped closer, an arm's length from Ianto. His eyes were murky and colorless. Safe, for now.

"I have to go to the library in Laleston. They have some books I need—I'm sorry, I should have brought them with me from Caer-Isel, but I didn't realize what an involved project this would be."

"It's a long trip, to Laleston. Are you sure you need to go?"

"Yes." Her heart pattered; she was actually getting somewhere. "Quite sure. It's the closest library for miles. I don't want to have to take a train all the way back to Caer-Isel . . ."

"Let me at least give you money for the train," Ianto said. "It seems only fair, since you're here at my behest."

Effy drew a breath. "Thank you, but that won't be necessary. Preston has agreed to drive me."

Immediately a shadow fell over Ianto's face. In the silence, a seabird swooped and called, the noise echoing over the rolling sea. The wind picked up, carrying with it a faint sprinkling of salt water that dampened Effy's face. Ianto's colorless eyes shifted, a bit of the murk fading, and Effy's muscles tensed.

"I don't trust that Argantian boy," Ianto said finally. "He's been here for weeks now, and whenever I ask if he's made any progress, all he does is stammer out some academic jargon no ordinary person could understand. And I don't like the way he looks at you."

Effy almost choked. "He doesn't look at me any sort of way."

"He does," Ianto said. "Wherever you are in a room, he watches you. It's like he's waiting for you to trip so he can catch you. It's unsettling."

"It's nothing like that," she said, though she could feel her throat pulsing. "He's an academic, like you said . . . I don't think he has those kinds of, um, preoccupations. He's too focused on his work."

But of course Ianto's words made all manner of thoughts run through her mind, most of them inappropriate, many of them downright lascivious. Until now she had not wondered about Preston's *preoccupations*, if he had ever done this or that, maybe he even had a girlfriend back in Caer-Isel. All of it was distressing and flustering to contemplate.

"Regardless." Ianto held her gaze. "I can't have you going away for too long. Wetherell is pestering me for a final blueprint so we can discuss finances."

"It will only be two days," Effy said, carefully.

And then she saw the strange thing happen again: the murkiness vanished from his eyes, like sunlight beaming through clouds, and then abruptly it returned again. It happened several times— cloudy and then clear, cloudy and then clear—each time as quick as a blink.

It made her stomach knot. "It's just, you can't do the whole drive there and back in one day—"

Suddenly, Ianto rose to his feet. Effy shrunk back.

"You know," he said at last, "perhaps it will be good for you to have some time away. Being stuck up here in this house—it can be suffocating."

He spoke as if the words had taken great effort. All these shifts in him, like the trembling and crumbling of the cliffside under her feet, made Ianto impossible to read. He could swing a gun at her one day and be perfectly friendly the next. He could seize her hand and grip it so hard that it hurt and the next day keep himself at a noticeable distance.

The wind beat Effy's hair and the tails of her coat back and forth, snatching them up and then letting them loose again. She thought again of the ghost, of Ianto's one-sided conversation. *This house has a hold on me,* Ianto had said out loud, to no one. Effy was no longer certain of anything when it came to Hiraeth or Emrys Myrddin—but she was quite sure of that.

And if she remained here, it would take hold of her, too.

Ianto watched from the driveway as they packed their things into the boot of Preston's car. Wetherell stood beside him, looking as grave and disapproving as ever, his silver hair sparkling with the fine mist that had come over Hiraeth.

Preston was worried about the drive down the cliffs. Effy just wanted to leave as quickly as they could. Jagged tree branches snaked through the fog like witch's fingers, grasping at the air.

"I can't believe he agreed," Preston murmured as he lifted her trunk. His shirt came up a little over his abdomen, exposing a narrow swath of fawn-colored skin. Effy watched, transfixed, until his shirt came down again.

"You keep underestimating my charms."

"You're right," he said. "On the title page of our paper, I'll be sure to credit you as Effy Sayre, enchantress."

She tried to keep from laughing so Ianto wouldn't see, but her skin prickled pleasantly.

Preston walked around the car and unlocked her door. When he reached the driver's side, he pulled a cigarette from his pocket and lit it. After a beat, he asked, "Do you want one?"

The same warm pleasure pooled in her belly. "Sure."

Preston lit another and held it out to her. She took it, but she was no longer looking at Preston. Some force had pulled her gaze away from him, back to Ianto, standing in the gravel path, arms folded over his chest.

It was neither the cloudy-eyed, jovial Ianto nor the bright-eyed, dangerous Ianto. It took Effy a moment to decipher the look in his pale eyes as they skimmed from her to Preston and back again. But it was worse than she had ever imagined: worse than fury or loathing or wrath.

It was *envy.*

Even in winter, the Southern countryside was green: emerald-colored hills and patches of tilled farmland like plaited yellow hair. Coniferous trees stood in dense clusters along the hillsides in a darker green that gave a look of fullness to the landscape. There were streaks of purple thistle flowers and lichen-webbed rocks that jutted up from the grass. Some superstitious Southerners believed the hills were the heads and hips of slumbering giants.

Effy stared through the passenger window, everything crisp and sharp.

"It's so beautiful," she marveled, putting her fingers to the glass. "I've never been south of Laleston before."

"Me either," Preston said. "I'd never been south of Caer-Isel, actually, until I came to Hiraeth."

In leaving Hiraeth behind, it felt as though they had walked out from under the sea. Everything that had been blurry beneath the film of water was now bright and clear. No more fog on the windows or dampness dripping from the walls. No more mirrors clouded over with condensation. The sky was a magnificently bright blue, clouds drifting pale and puffy across it. Black-faced sheep speckled the hillsides, looking like tiny clouds themselves, the land a green inverse of the sky.

This did not feel like the realm of the Fairy King. She could not imagine him lurking here among the verdant hills, the flower fields and goats.

She certainly could not imagine him sitting in Preston's seat.

Preston had been driving for two hours now, up serpentine single-laned roads and down again, past villages that were no more than a clutch of thatched-roof houses, huddled together like bodies around a fire. They had only stopped once, for a farmer to cross his cows. Preston drove with consummate focus, his gaze rarely leaving the windshield, and only ever to look at her.

Effy shifted in her seat and squared her shoulders. "Do you need a break?"

"Can you drive?"

"No," she said. "My mother never let me learn."

There wasn't much of a point to it, in Draefen, where trams and taxis could take you wherever you wanted to go, and the houses were pressed together like piano keys, so wherever you wanted to go was never very far, anyway.

She'd once asked for lessons, and her mother had let out an irritated breath. "I can barely trust you to remember to turn off the stove. Why would I want you behind the wheel of a car?"

"That's all right," Preston said. "I'm fine to keep driving for a while."

Inevitably their conversation turned to Myrddin, Blackmar, and the diary. They had thumbed through the book to find all the references they could to Blackmar, and to *Angharad*.

Myrddin mentioned both quite often. *Blackmar struggled with A. tonight,* he wrote, the summer before the book's publication.

"I think Blackmar wrote it," Preston said at last, and then gave a huff, as though it had exhausted him to make such a bold assertion, with no hedging at all. "Myrddin talks about how Greenebough wanted to 'reinvent' him, to lean more heavily into the myth of the provincial genius. But Myrddin never mentions anything about penning *Angharad* himself. He only ever mentions it when he talks about Blackmar."

"But it's strange, isn't it?" Effy had already turned over this possible conclusion in her mind, and something about it just didn't feel *right*. She couldn't explain it. It wasn't just about Myrddin, not anymore. It was a bone-deep, blood-pulsing sense of wrongness that beat in her like a second heart. "The way they talk about her—about the book. They always call *Angharad* 'she,' or 'her.'"

Preston shrugged. "Sailors also call their ships by women's names. Myrddin's father was a fisherman. I suspect it's just a bit of cheekiness on Myrddin's part."

"Maybe." It still felt wrong, in no way that Effy could articulate. "I'm thinking about 'The Mariner's Demise' again. 'But a sailor was I—and on my head no fleck of gray—'"

"'So with all the boldness of my youth, I said: The only enemy is the sea,'" Preston finished. "It's a memento mori. It's about the hubris of young men."

"The sea is what, then? Death?"

"Not *death*, exactly. But dying."

She arched a brow. "What's the difference?"

"Well, in that earlier line, right before what you started reciting—'Everything ancient must decay.' I think it's about the sea taking and taking, eating away at you slowly, the way that water, say, rots the wood of your sailboat. The last thing the sea takes from you is your life. So. I think it's about dying, slowly. The mariner's hubris isn't necessarily in his belief that he won't die, but his belief that the worst the sea can do is kill him."

Effy blinked. The road ahead bunched and then flattened, splitting the hills like a furrow carved through an ancient hand. "I like that," she said after a moment.

"Do you?" Preston sounded surprised. Pleased. "I wrote a paper on it. I might incorporate it into my thesis—our thesis. Since you like it."

"Yes," she said. "I'll happily put my name to that."

The drive was very pleasant, the day green and blue and eventually, as evening came on, gold. After another hour they stopped at a small shop by the side of the road, and each got a sausage roll wrapped in waxed paper and coffee in a paper cup. Effy poured liberal amounts of cream into hers, and three sugar packets. Preston watched her with judgment over the rim of his own cup.

"What's the point," he began, as they climbed back into the car, "of drinking coffee if you're going to dilute it to that degree?"

Effy took a long, savoring sip. "What's the point of drinking coffee that doesn't taste good?"

"Well, I would argue that black coffee *does* taste good."

"I suppose I shouldn't be surprised that someone who drinks scotch straight would think that black coffee tastes *good*," Effy said, making a face. "Or else you're secretly a masochist."

Preston turned the key in the ignition. "Masochism has nothing to do with it. You can learn to like anything if you drink it enough."

The car rolled gently back onto the road. For a while they sipped their coffee and chewed their sausage rolls in silence. Effy's mind was stuck on the memory of Preston swallowing that scotch without flinching. He didn't strike her as the partying type, staying out until dawn at pubs or dance halls, stumbling back into his room and sleeping through morning classes. Those types of people milled around her at the university, but she'd never been one of them, never really known any of them—not even Rhia was so careless.

She looked at Preston, the golden light gathering on his profile, turning his brown eyes almost hazel. Every time he took a sip of coffee, Effy watched his throat bob as he swallowed, and let her gaze linger on the bit of moisture that clung to his lips.

She blurted out, suddenly, "Do you have a girlfriend? Back in Caer-Isel?"

Preston's face turned red. He had been mid-sip of coffee, and at her question he coughed, struggling to swallow before replying. "What put that on your mind?"

"Nothing in particular," Effy lied, because she certainly was not going to confess that she had been wondering about this since her conversation with Ianto—or admit how intently she'd been staring at him. "It's just that we go to the same university, but we didn't know each other there. I just wondered what sort of things you did . . ."

She was flushing profusely, too, gaze trained firmly on the coffee cup cradled in her lap. She heard Preston draw a breath.

"No, I didn't," he said. "I mean, I don't. Sometimes, you know, there are girls you meet, and—well. But it's never more than a night, maybe coffee the next morning . . . never mind. Sorry."

He was *phenomenally* red at this point, staring with stubborn attention at the road, though for a brief moment his eyes flickered to her, as if to gauge her reaction. Effy pressed her lips together, overcome by the inexplicable urge to smile.

She liked when she flustered him. It seemed to be happening more and more of late.

"Don't worry," she said. "I know what you mean. What a charmer you are after all, Preston Héloury."

He laughed, cheeks still flushed. "Not in the slightest."

"I don't know about that. I find you very charming, underneath all the smugness."

"You think I'm *smug?*"

Effy had to laugh at that. "You aren't exactly the most approachable person I've ever met. But I suppose that's because you're also the smartest, most eloquent person I've ever met."

Preston just shook his head. He was silent for a moment, staring through the window as the scenery passed by slowly. At last, he said, "There's a lot to compensate for, when you're the only Argantian in Llyr's most prestigious literary program."

All at once Effy was suffused with sympathy—and with guilt. She remembered how she had berated him on the cliffside, and then again in the pub, pricking at him, questioning his loyalties. "I'm sorry if people have treated you cruelly. I'm sorry for the things I said, when we first met."

"It's really all right," he said, turning to look at her. "It's just whispers and looks in the hall, mostly. I'm sure you've gotten your fair share as the only woman in the architecture college."

Effy tensed. She realized that, unintentionally, she'd created the perfect opportunity for him to ask about Master Corbenic. She still didn't know if that particular piece of gossip had reached the literature college.

"It's not so bad," she said. A lie. "I knew what I was signing up for."

Preston inhaled, and it seemed as though he wanted to say something more. In the end, though, he just snapped his mouth shut and turned back toward the road. They lapsed into a slightly uneasy silence as the green hills rolled past, looking as huge as waves at high tide.

Penrhos, Blackmar's estate, was not technically in the Bottom Hundred. It was still south of Laleston, and the nearest landmark was a busy market town, Syfaddon, where the lamplight pooled on damp cobblestones and storefront awnings flapped in the wind like dresses hung on clotheslines.

Preston's car inched through the crowded streets, jerking to a halt every few minutes so that a merchant could drag his cart across, or an errant child could escape her mother. The windows of the pubs and shops were bright with the glow of gas lamps.

"It's not far from here," Preston murmured. His knuckles were white around the steering wheel, brow furrowed with the immense concentration it required not to flatten an oblivious pedestrian. "Just up the road. Much less remote than Hiraeth."

Effy watched a fishmonger adjust one of his carp, mouth open so she could see its tongue and teeth. His fish were aligned perfectly on their bed of ice, as neat as bodies in crematory drawers. "Is Blackmar from Syfaddon?"

"No, he's from Draefen, actually. I think he's descended from one of those post-Drowning industrialists. Oil or railroads or something like that. Enough money he never had to work a day in his life, which doesn't make for a very interesting author profile."

"At least, not as interesting as an upstart provincial genius," Effy said, as Syfaddon's market shrank in the rearview mirror. "So you think the publisher—Greenebough—arranged for Blackmar to write *Angharad*, but publish it under Myrddin's name?"

"That's my working theory, yes. Blackmar had the best education money could buy, naturally—he studied literature at the university in Caer-Isel. There's even a scholarship named after him, or maybe his father?"

"But no one there is studying 'The Dreams of a Sleeping King,'" she said. "It's ironic, isn't it—that his best-known work is commercial tripe, but *Angharad* is beloved. I mean, why would Blackmar agree to it? It's not like Greenebough could have swayed him with *money*—you said he was rich enough already. And if he could write something like *Angharad*, why is his other work so . . . so middling?"

Preston was quiet for a moment, considering. "You're right," he said. "There's still plenty that doesn't add up. But that's why we're here."

With that, he turned onto a narrower road, more poorly paved, and lined closely with a fleet of enormous elms. The shadows between the trees looked dense and oily, like the dark itself was moving. It was evening now; the sun listing gently to the line of the horizon, the clouds a bruised violet. It was several more minutes down that dim, craggy road before the turrets of a house rose above the trees in the distance.

The black wrought-iron gates came into view, cutting the house behind them into slivers. *House* seemed insufficient, discourteous even—what stood before them was a mammoth construction of brickwork and groin vaults, marble columns and sash windows.

Effy hardly considered herself a real architect, but she could calculate the cost of each feature, each balcony and balustrade, and it amounted to a sum that made her dizzy.

Preston stopped the car in front of the gates and they looked at each other, the same unspoken question on their lips, before the gates began to slowly creak open.

He drove up the circular driveway, around an island of immaculately landscaped grass and a marble fountain in the shape of a maiden. Her arms were at her sides, hands turned out and fingers splayed, and water spurted from her open palms.

For a moment, Effy could swear she saw the woman's face change, sightless eyes shifting under marble lashes, but when she blinked, the statue was still again. It had never been a woman, had never been alive at all.

She dug her fingernails into her palm, and for some reason, found it appropriate to whisper, "This can't all be from writing, can it?"

"That's the family money, I'm guessing."

It was so different from Hiraeth, and that, more than anything, was what shocked her. Why did Myrddin's descendants live in such decaying squalor, all their once lovely things waterlogged and rotted and covered in a layer of sea salt and grime?

The bushes at Penrhos were groomed like equestrian steeds,

no ragged leaves or split branches. Even without a family inheritance, the Myrddins must have had money—there was no good reason for Ianto and his mother to have been living like *that* unless they were doing it out of some misguided, superstitious deference to their dead husband and father.

Preston parked, and they got out. The air was cold enough that Effy's breath floated out in front of her. She squinted in the evening light: there was a large stone staircase, and wooden double doors at the top of them.

In another moment, with a loud groan, the doors heaved open.

She couldn't see Blackmar very well; she could only hear the clacking of his cane against the stone as he came down toward them. When he was close enough that Effy could pick out details, she saw the flash of his red velvet dressing gown, the sharp ebony of his cane, and, when he smiled at them, the gleam of a gold tooth in his mouth. His feet were ensconced in matching red velvet slippers.

His face was like a rusted mirror, stippled with a million cracks. He was the most ancient-looking person Effy had ever seen.

"Euphemia!" he said, with a rattling, excited gasp. "I'm so glad you took me up on my invitation."

And then he seized her around the middle in a zealous but creaky embrace. Effy stiffened, unsure what to do, waiting for it to be over.

At last Blackmar let go, knifepoint eyes shining out of his shriveled-walnut face.

"Oh," Effy said as he released her, feeling breathless. "Thank you very much for having us."

"I'm always happy to entertain my admirers." Blackmar smiled. From that close, Effy could see that nearly a third of his teeth were missing, and that they had all been replaced with gold imitations. "Is this your . . . compatriot?"

"Yes," said Effy. "This is Preston Héloury."

Blackmar's wrinkled brow wrinkled even further. "Héloury," he repeated slowly. In his posh Llyrian accent, he made the Argantian name sound almost like a curse. "That name is familiar—you're a student at the literature college, aren't you? You've written to me before."

"I have." Preston's posture was stiff, arms folded over his chest. "I'm an admirer as well, just not as, ah, eloquent as Effy in expressing it. Euphemia."

He had a bit of trouble with the first syllable; Effy could see the small furrow in his brow as he tried, with his subtle Argantian accent, to pronounce it.

Hearing her full name in Preston's mouth for the first time made Effy feel strange. Not unpleasant, but distinctly odd, her skin prickling with unexpected heat. With the added effort that it took to articulate them, the vowels sounded softer somehow. Gentler.

"Well, Argantians are not known for their zeal or passion. Too cold up there in the mountains, I suppose." Blackmar chuckled, very taken with his own joke. "Come in, both of you. I'll get you some brandy."

He had two black-clad domestic workers take their trunks from Preston's car and carry them silently up the steps to the house.

Effy and Preston followed slowly. The low, flat clouds were

hanging darkly around the turrets of Penrhos manor, almost enveloping them, like a pair of gloved hands. The domestics set down the trunks briefly to heave the doors open, and then they all stepped over the threshold.

Inside was as grand as Effy had expected: a double staircase of white marble that led up to the second-floor landing, plush velvet carpets that matched Blackmar's slippers and dressing gown, damask wallpaper bulleted with gilt-framed paintings and portraits. A large tapestry rendered the Blackmar family tree, beginning with one Rolant Blackmar, who Effy assumed was that industrialist— oil or railroads.

Above it was an enormous taxidermy deer head, its black eyes gleaming emptily, staring at nothing.

"It's beautiful," Effy said, because she felt it was what she was expected to say, and because it saved Preston from having to lie again.

Penrhos *was* beautiful, in a particular way. It was perfectly ornate, the furniture and wallpaper and rugs impeccably matched, not a smear of dust or a cache of cobwebs in the corner. The portraits were all dour and unsmiling; the velvet curtains let in not a sliver of light. There were no audaciously kitschy lamps or brashly abstract paintings, no boldly ugly chandeliers that made you want to squint up at them, trying to gauge if they really were ugly or not.

It was a beautiful house, but not a *clever* one. It was a house with no imagination.

Effy found it almost impossible to believe that *Angharad's* author could live here.

"Thank you, thank you," Blackmar said, waving a hand. "But

you haven't even seen the best of it yet. Come into the study. I'm sure you'll want to relax after your long drive."

Effy did not feel that drinking with Blackmar would be relaxing at all, but she followed him into the study anyway, Preston just a pace behind her.

The study had the same cohesion: peacock-blue drapes and matching armchairs, which were lovely, but not exactly inspiring. Another taxidermy deer head was mounted over the doorway, and a grandfather clock ticked dully in the corner. It was around six fifteen.

The domestics had vanished; Blackmar poured the brandy himself, wizened hand trembling. He handed Effy and Preston each a cut-crystal glass.

Brandy was an odd choice. Effy had only ever seen her grandparents drink it, just one after-dinner swig of liquor served in a minuscule glass. It wasn't *rude*, precisely, to serve brandy without offering a meal first, but it gave Effy the distinct sense that something was slightly off with Blackmar.

Maybe the perfection of his furnishings was trying to compensate for something. A well-ordered house for a decaying mind.

"Cheers," Blackmar said, settling himself into an armchair with great effort. "Here's to a fruitful academic inquiry for you, and some good company for me."

He chortled again at his own joke, and they clinked glasses. Preston swallowed his brandy without flinching; Effy puckered her lips and mimed taking a sip. She didn't think Blackmar would notice. He sucked down half his glass in one gulp.

"Thank you," Preston said, not at all convincingly. "And thank you again for your hospitality."

Blackmar waved him off. "I'm an entertainer, you know. All great writers are. I entertain readers; I entertain guests. Once upon a time I entertained women, but those days are unfortunately behind me."

Out of grim obligation, Effy laughed. Preston just stared uncomfortably down at his glass.

"Well, I'd love if you could entertain a few questions," she said. "When did you first meet Emrys Myrddin?"

"Oh my. It was so long ago; I don't think I could give you a year. It must have been in the late one-eighties. My father hired him, actually, as an archivist for some of our family records. He was my employee, you know."

Effy glanced at Preston. That felt, somehow, significant. Preston's eyes had taken on a gleam of interest as well—even Effy had to admit this fact bolstered his theory that Blackmar was the real author.

"So he lived in an apartment in Syfaddon, just like our other domestics, but during the day he was here at Penrhos, sorting files and doing other drearily menial things. But I'm a curious man, and I've always been interested in the lives of my domestics. Their *backstories*. So, with little better to do, I began spending time with Emrys in the record room. It turned out we got along like a house on fire.

"I could tell he was a Southerner, of course, from his name and accent, but he was different from the other Southern transplants that we hired. Sharper. More ambitious. I was working on a very early draft of 'Dreams' at that time, and Emrys showed great interest in my writing. He eventually told me that he was a writer, too, and we exchanged some of our works in progress."

Effy's heartbeat picked up as she leaned forward, but Preston spoke before she got the chance.

"Myrddin must have been working on *The Youthful Knight* then," he said. "Was it bits of that you saw?"

Blackmar tilted his head contemplatively, eyes clouding. "I believe so. Saints, that was a long time ago. Another lifetime. Emrys was despairing—he thought no one would want to buy a book by a backwater peasant from the Bottom Hundred. But my family has connections with Greenebough Publishing, so I offered to make an introduction."

Effy nodded slowly. That all lined up with what they'd read in the diary. "But *The Youthful Knight* didn't do very well, did it? Myrddin wasn't a household name until—"

"Yes." Blackmar's voice suddenly became curt. He set down his near empty glass on an austere side table. "That's the part of the story everyone knows. *Angharad* made Myrddin famous."

Blackmar had gotten cagey, and Effy could tell Preston sensed it, too. Preston set down his glass, and in a challenging sort of way, asked, "Was Myrddin still your employee then?"

"No, no," Blackmar replied. "He'd made enough from royalties to rent an apartment in Syfaddon. And then he bought that dreadful house in the Bay of Nine Bells. I could never understand why he wanted to return to Saltney, of all places. But he said there was something about the bay that beckoned him. Like a lighthouse to a ship, calling him home."

"There's nothing quite like the place you were born," Preston said. There was a solemn but inscrutable look on his face. "So did the two of you correspond while Myrddin was writing *Angharad?*"

"You know," Blackmar said, his voice sharp, "my memory does not serve me as well as it once did. I think it would be better for you to speak to someone from Greenebough on these matters. As it happens, Greenebough's editor in chief, Marlowe, will be coming tomorrow evening."

Definitely cagey. But Effy was undeterred.

"That's wonderful," she said. "Thank you so much for letting us spend the night. I'm sure we'll be able to find everything we came for."

Preston shot her a look, and she gave him a silent, almost imperceptible nod in return.

Shakily, Blackmar rose to his feet. In the time it took him to stand, Effy watched a fly land on the taxidermy deer head and crawl into one of its nostrils. The deer was unperturbed. Dead, as it should be.

"I'm sorry," Blackmar said plainly. "I'm an old man now, and early to bed. I'll have the help show you to your rooms."

Their trunks had already been placed in two adjacent bedrooms upstairs. Effy's room had opaque black curtains and an enormous blue sea anemone sitting on the desk, frozen in timeless suspension. There was a full-length mirror but it had been flipped over

225

to face the wall instead. For some reason Effy felt it would be a bad idea to turn it forward.

The bed was, strikingly, unmade: a morass of sea-green sheets and an incongruous purple duvet, the color of wine straight from the bottle. In opposition to the rest of Penrhos, there was nothing stodgy about this room; it had a bit of chaos to it.

If Effy had been allowed to decorate her own room as a child, it might have looked a bit like this. She sat on the edge of the bed, letting out a breath.

Preston leaned over the desk, arms crossed. "Blackmar did get cagey, didn't he? The moment we brought up *Angharad*."

"He did." Effy chewed her lip. "There's something there. I don't know what it is. But we'll have a chance to talk to Greenebough's editor in chief tomorrow."

Although everything they'd learned so far appeared to be pushing toward Preston's theory of Blackmar as the true author, Effy just couldn't force herself to accept it. It wasn't just her allegiance to Myrddin, though she still felt it, that childlike admiration. There was something else. Secrets buried under years of dust. An emotion that was inarticulable.

"That still doesn't give us much time," Preston said. "If we don't get back to Hiraeth tomorrow night, Ianto will be very suspicious."

But it was not Ianto she was thinking about. It was the Fairy King, the creature with the slick black hair and the bone crown. Here at Penrhos she felt safe from him. Here that world of danger and magic felt properly chained and fettered.

"We'll just have to get back then," Effy said, voice shrinking. "I'm sorry I can't help drive."

"No, that's all right. I don't mind driving. We'll get back to Hiraeth before midnight, I promise."

Midnight was a fairy-tale thing. She didn't know if Preston had been thinking about that when he promised it, but Effy was remembering all the curses that turned princesses back to peasant girls as soon as the bell struck twelve. Why was it always girls whose forms could not be trusted? Everything could be taken away from them in an instant.

"Thank you," she said, trying to put those thoughts out of her mind. "Tomorrow we'll speak to Greenebough's editor and get the answers we need."

Preston nodded. "For now I suppose we'll just . . . sleep on empty stomachs."

Effy laughed softly. She found it odd, too, that Blackmar had offered them brandy with no food to accompany it, but who was she to question the man when he had been generous enough to entertain all their probing questions?

Up to a point, of course.

She reached for her purse and began to dig for her bottle of sleeping pills. She no longer minded if Preston saw them. He already knew she was a changeling child. He had learned her true name. He knew what she believed about the Fairy King.

But she searched and searched, and still her hand closed around nothing. Panic began to swell in her chest, her breaths growing rapid and short. And then, the flash of a memory: her bottle of pills on the bedside table in Hiraeth's guesthouse, forgotten there in her haste to leave.

"Oh," she whispered. "Oh no."

"What is it?"

"It's—" Her mouth was dry and it was hard to speak. She cleared her throat, vision blurring at the corners. "I forgot my sleeping pills. I don't know how to sleep without them."

Preston pushed off the desk and walked over to her. Still standing, he looked down at her with a furrowed brow. "What keeps you awake at night?"

It was not the question she'd expected him to ask. It rattled Effy from her panicked state, softening the sharp pulse of adrenaline. No one had ever asked her such a thing before, not since she was a child, babbling about the creature in the corner of her room.

It took her a few moments to find the words to reply.

"I get afraid," she said at last. "Not of anything specific, really—it's this bodily thing. Somatic thing. It's hard to explain. My chest gets tight and my heart beats really fast. In the end I guess I'm scared that something bad will happen to me while I'm lying there. I'm scared that someone will hurt me."

The words came out all at once—breathless, stammering. She hadn't mentioned the Fairy King by name, but the rest was true enough.

She tried to gauge Preston's reception. He was only looking at her with the same furrowed brow, the same concern.

"Is there anything that helps? I mean, aside from the sleeping pills."

No one had ever asked her that, either, not since the doctor had thrust the pills into her hands. Effy looked at him, feeling very small, but not necessarily in a meek, prey-animal sort of way. She said, "I suppose it helps not to be alone."

Silence fell softly over the strange room. Preston drew in a breath. And then he said, very carefully, "I could stay."

Effy blinked at him in surprise, her cheeks instantly growing hot. Preston flushed too, as if only just realizing his words had a certain implication.

"Not like *that*," he assured her, running a nervous hand through his hair. "I'll even sleep on the floor."

In spite of herself, Effy laughed. "You don't have to sleep on the floor."

The bed was easily big enough for two, even if they were not touching. The next few moments unfolded in silence as well: Preston turned around, face to the wall, so that Effy could strip out of her sweater and trousers and into her nightgown, and slip under the wine-colored duvet.

Preston turned around again and sat hesitantly on the edge of the bed. Effy gave him an encouraging look, though her cheeks were still splotchy with heat, and he shifted to lie down beside her. Her beneath the covers, him atop them. Facing each other. Not touching.

She had never been so close to him before. His eyes were fascinating from this vantage point, light brown ringed with green, gold daubs around the irises. His freckles were pale, winter-faded. She suspected they would become more prominent when summer returned. His lips were stained just a little bit from the brandy.

While Effy looked at Preston, he looked at her. She wondered what he saw. Master Corbenic had seen green eyes and golden hair, something soft and white and pliable.

Sometimes she wanted to tell someone everything that had happened, and see what they had to say about it. She had already heard the version of the story in which she was a tramp, a slut, a whore. She had heard it so many times, it was like a water stain on velvet; it would never quite come out. She wondered if there was another version of the story. She didn't even know her own.

Surely Preston couldn't guess at all the things running through her mind. Unlike Effy, he looked very tired. Behind his glasses, his eyelids had begun to droop. That was something funny: his left eyelid seemed to droop slightly more than his right. From far away, she never would have noticed.

"Sleepy yet?" he asked, his words somewhat slurred.

"Not really," she confessed.

"What else can I do?"

"Just . . . talk," she said. She had to lower her gaze, embarrassed. "About anything, really."

"I'll try to think of the dullest topics I know."

She smiled, biting her lip. "They don't have to be dull. You could—you could tell me something new. Something you've never told me before."

Preston fell silent, contemplating. "Well," he said after a moment, "if you want to know why I remember 'The Mariner's Demise' so well, it's because there's an old Argantian saying that's eerily similar."

"Oh?" Effy perked. "What is it?"

"I'll tell you if you promise you won't flinch at the sound of our heathen tongue." The corner of his mouth twitched upward.

Effy just laughed softly. "I promise."

"*Ar mor a lavar d'ar martolod: poagn ganin, me az pevo; diwall razon, me az peuzo.*"

"Is that really Argantian?"

"Yes. Well, it's the Northern tongue. It's what grandmothers speak to their eye-rolling grandchildren." Preston smiled faintly.

"What does it mean?"

"'Says the sea to the sailor: strive with me and live; neglect me and drown.'"

"That does sound a lot like something Myrddin would write," Effy said. It was the first time, she realized, that she'd heard Argantian spoken by a native. It was beautiful—or maybe just Preston's voice was. "Say something else."

"Hm." Preston frowned, considering. Then he said, "*Evit ar mor bezañ treitour, treitouroc'h ar merc'hed.*"

"What's that?"

Amusement crinkled his eyes. "'The sea is treacherous, but women are even more treacherous.'"

Effy flushed. "*That* doesn't sound like something your grandmother would say."

"You're right. She would clap me on the back of the head for that one."

"Tell me another," said Effy.

Preston pursed his lips, eyes glazing over for a moment as he thought. At last, he said, "*Ar gwir garantez zo un tan; ha ne c'hall ket bevañ en e unan.*"

"I like how that one sounds the best," Effy said. "Tell me what it means."

Behind his glasses, Preston's eyes fixed on her. "'Love is a fire that cannot burn alone.'"

Effy's heartbeat skipped. "It sounded a lot longer in Argantian."

"I'm paraphrasing." His voice grew lower, sleepier. "I promise I'm not secretly swearing at you."

"I didn't think that." Effy's own eyelids were beginning to feel heavy. "That helped, though. Thank you."

Preston didn't seem to hear her. His eyes had slid shut. After a few moments, his breathing slowed, his chest rising and falling with the rhythm of sleep.

Very gently, so as not to disturb him, Effy reached over and took off his glasses. He didn't shift at all.

A curiosity overcame her, and she slipped the glasses onto her own head for a moment. Effy had wondered, more than once, whether Preston really *needed* his glasses or if he just wore them to make himself look more serious and scholarly. But when she blinked and blinked behind the thick lenses, her vision blurring and head throbbing, she realized that he did need them after all, and quite badly.

Well. *Angharad* still eluded her, but that was one mystery solved.

She folded the glasses neatly and laid them on the bedside table. As she turned over, Effy saw one of the hag stones half sunk into the plush carpet. It must have fallen out of her pocket while she undressed. Effy fished it off the floor.

Preston still had not shifted. She turned back over, and held the hag stone up to her eye, holding her breath, pulse quickening.

But all she saw was Preston's sleeping face: his long, thin nose, winged with the tiny indents his glasses had left, his freckles, the slight cleft of his chin. His skin looked soft; there was a small furrow in his brow as if, even in sleep, his mind was turning on so many things.

Effy lowered the hag stone. Her heart was still pounding, but for a very different reason. She rolled over and set the stone on the bedside table next to Preston's glasses. Then she pulled the chain on the vaguely kitschy-looking lamp, settling them both into darkness.

Effy did manage to sleep, eventually. When she woke the next morning, Preston had already risen. He was sitting at the desk, Myrddin's diary open in front of him.

Hearing her stir, he turned around. His normally untidy hair had achieved an unprecedented level of anarchy; the brown strands seemed to all be rebelling against one another, and against his scalp. He had his glasses back on.

The first thing she said as she sat up was, "It's a good thing Blackmar didn't peek in."

Preston's face reddened. "There was nothing untoward about it. But I can imagine how it might have looked."

"No, you were very well-behaved." Effy let the covers fall off her. One of the straps of her nightgown had slipped down her shoulder, and she noticed Preston intentionally averting his gaze as she righted it again. "Thank you."

"There's nothing to thank me for," he said, still not quite meeting her eyes. "I slept well, actually."

"And you kept your hands to yourself." She couldn't help but try to fluster him more, just because she liked the way he looked blushing.

In that room, just her and Preston, she almost forgot they were at Penrhos at all. They could have been anywhere, in this small, safe place just for them, everything quiet and gentle and slow. Even the light crawling in was tender and pale gold.

Reluctantly, Effy got out of bed, and Preston turned around again, facing the wall so that she could dress.

He had stayed dutifully on his side of the bed all night, knees curled to allow for the too-short length of the mattress, even his breathing soft and unobtrusive. He hadn't touched her, but Saints, she wanted him to.

TWELVE

What defines a romance? All scholars seem to converge on a single point: it is a story that must have a happy ending. And why is that? I say, it is because a romance is a belief in the impossible: that anything ends happily. For the only true end is death—and in this way, is romance not a rebuke of mortality? When love is here, I am not. When love is not, I am gone. Perhaps a romance is a story with no end at all; where *the end* is but a wardrobe with a false back, leading to stranger and more merciful worlds.

FROM *AN EPISTEMOLOGICAL THEORY OF ROMANCE* BY

DR. EDMUND HUBER, COLLECTED IN THE *LLYRIAN*

JOURNAL OF LITERARY CRITICISM, 199 AD

After spending so long at Hiraeth, Effy had almost forgotten what it was like to live in a regular house. She bathed in Blackmar's perfectly proper and mundane claw-foot tub. She wrapped herself in a borrowed silk robe.

All of it was very pleasant. The floorboards were not particularly cold, and the windows let in no drafts of early winter wind. When she finished bathing, she went back into the bedroom, feeling clean and bright-eyed, and flopped down on the unmade bed.

She could hear the sounds of Preston running the water in the other room and felt, for some reason, suddenly flushed.

All that had happened the night before (though nothing had really *happened*—they hadn't even so much as brushed fingers) nearly distracted Effy from her task. While Preston bathed, she stood up and began to pick her way around the room.

She opened desk drawers and found, disappointingly, nothing. Someone had cleaned this room thoroughly a long time ago, and let it lie fallow after that. She wondered whose room it had been.

There were a number of musty-smelling dresses in the wardrobe, but no false back, no secret room behind it—Effy even pulled it out from the wall to check. She peeked behind the opaque black curtains. The immaculately manicured lawn of Penrhos looked as untouched as an oil painting.

It felt almost too silly to look under the bed, too facile and childish, but she dropped to her knees anyway. Instantly her nose itched. It was too dark to see beneath the bed frame, so Effy reached out her arm and felt around.

Her fingers closed around something: a scrap of paper. Two, three.

She snatched them up as quickly as she could, afraid for some reason that they might just vanish, float away. Effy held them to her chest, breathing hard. They felt like a secret, just the way the diary had, just the way she had felt when she paged through those ancient books in the university library. She was about to look at them when she heard the door open.

Effy whipped around, but it was only Preston, his hair damp and mussed from the bath, wearing one of Blackmar's dressing gowns. It was too short on him, and Effy felt, momentarily, very lascivious for taking notice of that at all. What young girl of this century was left feverish by the sight of a man's *calves*? She was like one of those protagonists from a novel of manners, swooning over a glimpse of their betrothed's bare ankle.

"Effy," said Preston, "what are you doing on the floor?"

"I found these," she said, holding out the papers. "Under the bed."

She had been planning to stand up, but before she could, Preston knelt on the floor beside her. There was still water glistening on the sharp planes of his face, one damp strand of hair curling down over his forehead. Even wet, it appeared untidy. Effy drew in a breath, now fully irritated at herself for becoming attuned to these inane details.

The papers were very old; she could tell as much right away, without even looking at the dates at the top. Their edges were curling, ink slightly faded, and they seemed overall as if they had been forgotten—as if someone running away had let them slip out of their grasp and lie gathering dust under the bed, or a maid who came in to clean had simply been unable to reach them with her broom.

Effy held the first page out so that she and Preston could both read it.

17 April 189

My sly and clever girl,
You must have gotten my address from papers in your father's
study, or else how would you know where to write me? I shall not

*underestimate your shrewdness again, and perhaps I shall even
expect you, one day, to show up at my door. I would not protest it.
I might be very happy to see you scowling at me in the threshold.*

*The poems you sent me were, I think, rather good. I par-
ticularly enjoyed the one about Arethusa. I did not think that a
girl of Northern blood would have any interest in our myths and
legends, but I suppose your father did not give you a Southern
name for nothing.*

*Please do send me more, should you feel so inclined. When I
am at Penrhos again, I would very much like to discuss Arethusa.
She is generally seen as an aspect, or rather, an equivalent, of
Saint Acrasia, who, as you know, is the patroness of seductive
love. A very interesting subject for your poem.*

Yours,
E.M.

"Arethusa," Effy said. Her mind was still reeling with the effort
of trying to understand all she'd just read, but Arethusa she knew.
"She's the Fairy King's consort, at the beginning of the book."

"Yes," Preston said. "She's initially presented purely as a foible
for the protagonist—seductive and active where Angharad is sub-
missive and passive. Like your two-headed goddess, Saints Acrasia
and Amoret. As Myrddin mentioned in the letter. But eventually
Arethusa becomes an ally. It's a very clever subversion of the trope
of the malevolent seductress."

"He didn't say who he was writing to." Effy stared down at

the page again, just to be certain. "He said she had a Southern name . . . one of Blackmar's daughters. Myrddin's diary mentions that Blackmar's eldest daughter showed him some of her poetry, remember?"

Preston nodded. "And the dates line up—that entry was in January; this letter is from April."

Effy's heart was pounding. It didn't help that she was very close to Preston, their shoulders nearly touching, the heat of his body against her. She took a breath to steady herself.

"Let's look at the next one," she said.

13 November 189

My foolish and lovely girl,
I fear your father has discovered us. He asked me, without euphe-mism or subterfuge, whether I had imperiled his daughter's purity, whether I had taken you to bed. I told him truthfully that we had NOT lain together. I don't know if you are a virgin, like your self-styled protagonist. And I don't know why your father has such a keen interest in his daughter's purity—you are a grown woman, for Saints' sakes.

Best not to see each other for a while—at least until I can speak with your father about this delicate matter. But if you do manage to slip away, I shall reward you lavishly.

Yours,
E.M.

Effy's stomach lurched like a ship in the waves. She didn't want to think about Myrddin this way. This was worse than the photographs. She had loved Myrddin's book so thoroughly that she'd left tear marks on its pages, so thoroughly that its spine was cracked from a thousand readings—she did not want to imagine him this way, ruminating on whether he should take some young woman's virginity.

Her breath was coming in short, hot gasps. She looked up at Preston, tears pricking the corners of her eyes.

He looked back at her in concern, and then said in a tight voice, "Let's just read the last one. It's short."

1 March 190

My beautiful and debauched girl,

You said something to me last night, as we lay together, that I shall not soon forget. I was near to sleeping, but you pulled the covers over your naked breast and sat up. Leaning over me, you said, "I will love you to ruination."

I sat up as if I'd been prodded, since neither of us had said those trite three words to the other before, and answered somewhat groggily, "Whose ruination? Yours or mine?"

You did not answer, and I still wonder.

Yours (in every conceivable fashion),
E.M.

"That's the line," Effy whispered. "From *Angharad*."

Preston swallowed. "*I will love you to ruination*, the Fairy King said, brushing a strand of golden hair from my cheek. *Yours or mine? I asked. The Fairy King did not answer.*"

"From the first time they lie together." Effy's voice was trembling. "On their wedding night."

"Spring of one-ninety," said Preston, and his voice was shaking a little, too. "That would have been around the time that Myrddin began writing *Angharad*—or allegedly began writing *Angharad*. It all lines up."

Effy shook her head. Her vision was crowding with blackness, panic surging up in her like a wave. "I still don't understand."

"*This* is the connection to Blackmar. Not friendship or employment—Myrddin had an affair with Blackmar's daughter, and somehow *Angharad* was born from it. No wonder Blackmar was so cagey when discussing it. I don't know how Greenebough factors in, or why the decision was made to have the book published under Myrddin's name—if indeed it was Blackmar's work, of course—but it's conceivable that the daughter was somehow part of the . . . negotiation process."

"You're saying they bartered her, like a piece of livestock." Effy wished she could drift from her own body, to slip out that secret door into the safe, submerged place. But her body seemed to be holding on to her mind with all its might: blood hot, stomach churning, terrible signs of life. "And if Blackmar was so concerned about his daughter's *purity*, and Myrddin clearly took it, then why would he let Myrddin have *Angharad*, too? That diary entry says

Blackmar delivered the manuscript to him in August of one-ninety-one."

She could hardly choke out the words. Preston was looking at her with even greater concern now.

"Effy," he said slowly, "are you all right?"

"That line." Her eyes were hot with unshed tears. "'I will love you to ruination.' That's one of *Angharad*'s most famous lines, and Myrddin didn't even come up with it."

Preston hesitated. When he spoke again, his voice was gentle. "Writers take things from their real lives all the time. It's not as though the phrase is copyrighted."

Logically Effy understood that. But it still felt wrong; all of it felt so wrong. "I wish we could talk to her. Blackmar's daughter."

"That would be the simplest solution," Preston conceded. "But we'll have to make do with speaking to Greenebough's editor."

The sense of wrongness sat in her belly like a stone. She could not evict the image of Myrddin from her mind: lying in bed beside a young girl while she spoke aloud *Angharad*'s most famous line.

She wished she could return to that day in her dorm room, when she had stared at his author photo in the back of her book, when this had been just a blank space upon which she could hurl her desires like paint on a canvas. She didn't want answers anymore. Every new clue she uncovered was like a blow to the back of the head: brisk, sudden, agonizing.

She and Preston searched thoroughly under the bed in case there were more straggling letters, but found nothing but dust.

Right before they were about to give up and go down for

breakfast, Effy's fingers closed around something hard and cold. When she brought it out, her palm and fingers were covered in tiny nicks. A knife.

It was as small as something you might use to cut fruit in the kitchen, but its handle was silver and there was a faint rust around the blade. She and Preston looked at each other as she gripped it close to her chest. Neither of them needed to speak to know that it was iron.

They dressed and went downstairs, Effy still feeling queasy. There they discovered that an entire buffet had been laid out in the dining room. The black-clad domestics looked even fancier and even more resolute than the day before, skulking around like somber monks, dusting furniture penitently. Finding no traditional breakfast food (much to Effy's dismay, as she'd hoped for tea to settle her stomach), they ate stuffed olives and tiny fruit tarts that dissolved in sugar on her tongue.

It was odd that Blackmar had left a banquet for them, with only supper food, but after last night's unaccompanied brandy, Effy supposed it was in character for the old man. She was reaching for a second tart when Blackmar himself strode in, wearing a suit with a sensible pocket square.

"What are you doing?" he cried in dismay. "This food is for the party!"

Preston choked on his pastry. "What party?"

"The *party*," Blackmar repeated impatiently, "that I am hosting tonight. I did tell you, didn't I—that's why Greenebough's editor in chief is coming. For the *party*."

"No," Effy said. She tried to swallow the rest of her tart without him noticing. "You didn't say anything about a party."

"Well, I do hope you'll join us, after coming all this way. It will be your opportunity to speak with someone from Greenebough. I believe he'll be able to give you better insight than I can. Like I said, my memory isn't what it used to be."

"But we don't have formal clothes," Effy said, gesturing to her trousers and oversize sweater.

"Nonsense." Blackmar waved a hand. The woman mopping behind him flinched, as if he'd cracked a whip that had struck her. "My daughter left behind plenty of things in her wardrobe. You two look about the same size. And Preston can borrow one of my suits. I have several I can spare."

And so it was settled. Blackmar sped off (as fast as anyone his age could get anywhere) and Preston and Effy trudged back to their chambers. She could not stop thinking about the letters, the last one in particular. It was swirling in her mind like dark water. Halfway up the stairs, her knees quivered so terribly that she fell forward, catching herself on the railing.

"Effy?" Preston turned around. "What's wrong?"

"I don't know," she managed. "It's just that last line. That last letter. 'I will love you to ruination . . .'"

She trailed off, fingers curling white-knuckled around the wood. Preston just looked at her in bewilderment.

"For all we know, it's something Blackmar's daughter read in one of her father's poems," he said. "I could look through them again and see if anything stands out to me. It's the beginning of something, isn't it? More evidence that Myrddin isn't as ingenious as he's supposed. More evidence tying *Angharad* to Blackmar—"

"No," she said quickly, surprising herself with the vehemence of her voice. "That's not what I mean. You don't . . . you don't need to attribute everything to Blackmar, necessarily. Maybe *Angharad* was a joint effort between the two of them." Preston opened his mouth to reply, and Effy hurriedly added, "This isn't me trying to defend Myrddin, just because I'm a fan. I don't even know if I am, anymore."

She pressed her lips together, eyes brimming. Preston just blinked at her.

"I wasn't going to accuse you of that," he said softly. "I think you have a point. We don't know exactly how this all shook out, and Blackmar refuses to speak the word *Angharad,* so we aren't going to get any answers from him. Tonight we'll probe Greenebough's editor as best we can."

Effy nodded, very slowly. She continued up the stairs, but her nausea didn't subside.

Blackmar's guests began arriving in the late afternoon, just before dusk, the waning orange-gold light pooling on the sleek hoods of their cars. They went up the circular driveway and parked in neat columns, like an arrangement of insects under an entomologist's glass. Effy watched from the window, counting the guests as they exited their cars, women trailing gossamer shrugs and men frowning under their mustaches.

There were at least thirty of them, and Effy wondered if that was better or worse for their purposes. Such a large affair might make it more difficult to get the editor from Greenebough alone, but a more intimate one would make her and Preston appear like awkward interlopers. Already their ages would make them stick out from the crowd: none of the arriving guests were younger than Effy's mother. It made her uneasy, and she drew the curtains shut.

She and Preston had found nothing about the affair in Myrddin's diary. In fact, every entry that should have appeared between April 189 and March 190 had been torn out right from the spine of the book. Preston looked more dejected than Effy had ever seen him.

Hoping to cheer him a bit, Effy said, "Even proving that Myrddin had a secret affair—that's something, isn't it? Was he already married at the time?"

"I'm not sure," Preston said. "There are almost no records of his personal life, no marriage certificates that I could find. A secret affair is something. But it isn't *enough*. Those letters are worth a salacious newspaper exposé, and maybe a paragraph or two of a thesis, but they don't constitute a thesis in and of themselves. We need more context, and we need more proof."

I don't want more proof. But Effy couldn't bring herself to say it.

Trying to put it out of her mind, Effy went to the wardrobe to choose something to wear for the party. She flipped through the dresses like they were catalog cards at the library, silk hissing between her fingers. She stopped when she found a dress of deep emerald green, with a corseted back, a low bustline, and cap sleeves made of shimmery tulle.

A memory invaded her with such intensity and suddenness that she felt almost blown backward by it. The photographs of the girl on the chaise longue, her empty eyes, her naked breasts—all of it came rushing back to Effy with the force of water thrashing against the cliffside.

"Preston," she said. "Do you remember those photographs?"

He frowned at her. "The ones in Myrddin's lockbox? You don't think—"

"I think that was Blackmar's daughter. It *must* have been. The writing on the back, that line—'I will love you to ruination.'"

"That certainly explains why Myrddin felt the need to hide them." Preston kept his tone subdued, but his eyes had grown bright.

"That's proof, isn't it? I mean, maybe it's not incontrovertible, but it's significant. Proof of the affair, and proof that Myrddin owed something to Blackmar. The photos were found in Myrddin's own house, tucked into his diary. What if—"

Effy stopped herself, drawing in a sudden breath. She had almost said something naive and fanciful, something that sounded as childish as believing in the Fairy King. Preston looked at her oddly.

"What if what?" he prompted.

"Nothing," she said. "Never mind."

"We have to go back for them," Preston said, voice urgent. "We'd need both the letters and the photographs to prove the affair. It's only one step after that to prove Blackmar wrote the book, or at least parts of it. We have to find them before Ianto does—"

He cut off, seeing the look of panic on Effy's face. She was remembering the envy in Ianto's eyes as he'd watched them leave. The idea of him finding the photographs was even more horrifying to her.

"Maybe we should leave now," she said. "To hell with this stupid party—"

"No." Preston shook his head. "We have to get something from Greenebough, whatever we can. Proving the affair is one thing, but proving it's connected to *Angharad* is another. We need Blackmar and the editor for that."

He was right, of course. Effy drew back, letting out her breath. She pulled the green dress out of the closet and laid it flat on the bed so that it looked like a headless, limbless body.

"Then I suppose we should get ready."

The dining room was bleary with the light of at least a hundred candles, and glutted with guests. The women moved about, graceful in their candy-colored dresses, taffeta skirts rustling like wind through river rushes. Their hands and forearms were consumed by long white gloves, graceful as the necks of swans. They knit themselves to the men's sides, their gloved arms curling through their husbands', which were blocky and stiff with black wool. When they laughed, they put their white hands up decorously to cover their mouths.

Effy had been to fancy parties like this before, with her grandparents, but only as a child in white stockings and patent leather shoes, pouting on couches and picking at the unappealing adult food. She felt equally out of place now, certain that every eye in the room would look at her and see that she was too young, that she did not belong.

Clouds of cigarette smoke ghosted through the air. The buffet table appeared refreshed; the domestics had succeeded in making it appear as if it had not been picked over by two oblivious guests earlier in the day. She looked for Blackmar's servants now and found them, still and silent, in each of the four corners of the room, like out-of-date family heirlooms you felt guiltily compelled to keep.

She was wearing the green dress. Blackmar's daughter's dress. It fit her perfectly, its sweetheart neckline dipping daringly low, cap sleeves tight against her shoulders without digging into her skin. In this light the color was more muted—forest green rather than emerald, like moss and earth and leaves.

She could have been one of the Green Men—not fairies, but something less sentient, more primal—who drifted through the forests of the Bottom Hundred with waterweed braided in their beards.

She could, Effy thought with no small amount of alarm, have been Angharad herself, dressed in the Fairy King's adornments.

No, she told herself with resolve. The Fairy King would not appear to her in this house. Penrhos was a place anchored firmly in the real world. The Fairy King's world was lying dormant, like a fallow field. She had not seen him since she'd left Hiraeth, and last night, sleeping beside Preston, she had not even dreamed of him. She had woken up feeling refreshed and safe, for the first time that she could remember. She hadn't needed the sleeping pills at all.

But the silk dress seemed like such a flimsy layer to put between her body and the world. She sometimes felt like her skin had been rubbed raw; whenever she exposed herself to the air, it stung and ached. And the dress, though lovely, was decades out of date. Surely she would be noticed, sneered at—Effy began to shrink within the crowd, voices running around her like water, her heart rising by increments into her throat.

Preston ducked his head to whisper to her. "Are you all right?"

He was wearing one of Blackmar's suits, again slightly too short in the arms and legs, but otherwise well fitting. He had forgone a tie, leaving the collar of his shirt open, and Effy was fascinated by the two leaves of white linen that unfolded to bare his throat to her, pulse throbbing in the candlelight.

There she was again: yearning miserably as if she were in some sort of Romance novel, with a capital *R*. Something Preston would probably also call *pedestrian*.

"Yes," she said finally, shaking the thoughts loose. "I'm fine."

"Good. Then let's find the man from Greenebough and get out of here."

Blackmar found them first, shouldering his way through the crowd, occasionally prodding someone rudely with his cane. He looked absurd in his expensive suit. It was as if someone had put a tie and jacket on a rotting pumpkin.

"Euphemia," he said, grinning widely to show his gold teeth. "Preston. I'm so glad you could join us."

"Of course," Effy replied. She raised her voice over the sound of the record player and added, "Thank you for inviting us. We're sorry about eating your food earlier. Would you please introduce us to Greenebough's editor in chief?"

She knew she was being a bit rude, but she didn't care. The grandfather clock in the corner had just ticked past six. They had to leave within the hour or they would never make it back to Hiraeth before midnight.

"In just a moment," Blackmar said. He looked her up and down, the wrinkled corners of his eyes wrinkling further. "My daughter's dress suits you well."

Effy's stomach turned. "Thank you. If you don't mind me asking, where is your daughter now?"

Blackmar just stared at her, for so long that Effy's blood began to turn cold. Preston cleared his throat, as if that might break Blackmar from his stupor.

At last Blackmar blinked, and then, as if he had never heard her—as if she had never even spoken at all—said, "I'll introduce you to Mr. Marlowe. He's Greenebough's editor in chief."

Without another word, he began to march back through the crowd. Perhaps there was some strangeness to Penrhos after all. Blackmar had behaved, temporarily, as if he'd been under an odd spell.

Effy and Preston followed bewilderedly behind him. For a moment Effy convinced herself she had just *imagined* asking the question. But no—she knew she had. And she knew Blackmar had rebuffed her in the most peculiar and awkward manner possible.

She looked up at Preston, who gave her a grim look in return. They needed answers, and quickly.

251

Mr. Marlowe turned out to be a man around forty, with a very thin black moustache. He wore a garish red tie and did not rise from the chaise longue when he saw them approach.

Instead, he swirled the gin in his glass and said, in a languid voice, "Blackmar, you scoundrel, I asked for dessert and you brought me a tart draped in silk?"

Effy's face turned scorching hot. She was too flustered and embarrassed to say even a word in her own defense. Preston made a choked sound, his brow furrowed with indignation—no, anger. She had never seen his expression transform so quickly. He opened his mouth to speak, but before he could, Blackmar dropped into the chaise beside Marlowe and said scoldingly, "My friend, it's not yet six. You've got to slow down if you don't want to end up strewn all over my carpet again."

"I'll end up wherever I please," Marlowe said in a petulant tone, though he did put down his glass. He looked between Effy and Preston, eyes cloudy and vague. "I suppose you're the university students, then. Come on, sit down and ask your questions."

Effy didn't want to sit. Preston lowered himself into one of the armchairs, gaze dark as he regarded Marlowe.

Her fingers curled, nails digging into her palms. The armchair next to Preston's was a muted shade of green. Her head started pounding and she felt herself slipping into that deep-water place. Preston's eyes darted up at her with concern, and when the silence had stretched too long, she finally sat down. Her face was still burning.

"Thank you for entertaining us," Preston said, but his voice

252

was stiff. Cold. There was no effort at friendliness, and Effy was afraid that even in his less-than-lucid state, Marlowe would be able to tell. "We're doing a project on Emrys Myrddin, and we would like to get the perspective of his publisher. Specifically on the process of publishing *Angharad*."

"I inherited the company several years ago from my father," Marlowe said. "I had nothing to do with publishing *Angharad*. But it's our most profitable work to this day—you could buy seven versions of Penrhos with the annual royalties, isn't that right, Blackmar?"

Blackmar looked distinctly uncomfortable. "That's right."

"And after you published *The Youthful Knight*," Preston went on, "did you solicit another book from Myrddin immediately?"

Marlowe picked up his glass again. "As far as I know from my father's stories, it was a great effort to publish. They say it takes a village—well, that's about a child, isn't it?" His gaze was faraway. "But a book is much the same."

"So it was a *joint* effort?" Preston arched a brow. Effy felt her heart skip. "Interesting, given that *Angharad* famously has no dedication, no acknowledgments."

Marlowe shrugged. "Myrddin was an odd fellow. Perhaps it was my father's decision. He liked to sell *authors* just as much as he liked to sell books. The author is part of the story, you know. It helped that Myrddin was from some backwater hovel in the Bottom Hundred. He writes rather well for an illiterate fisherman's son."

Even now, even after everything, Effy felt anger flare in her chest. She dug her fingernails deeper into her palm and, fighting to keep her voice level, asked, "When did Myrddin present the first draft to Greenebough?"

"Sometime earlier that year, I imagine." Marlowe yawned and made a show of appearing very bored. "These are awfully mundane questions, you know."

"Sorry," Preston said unconvincingly. "When your father did receive the draft of *Angharad*, was it postmarked from Myrddin's estate in Saltney?"

Now Marlowe seemed irritated. "How on earth am I supposed to know something like that? I was barely out of the womb myself then, and Blackmar here still had most of his teeth." Blackmar gave a forced laugh, his wizened brow beading with sweat. "Saints, I don't want to spend my evening discussing the history of a book that was published half a damn century ago."

Effy's palms were slick. She rubbed them against her bent knee, the silk of her dress bunching under her palms. She could feel the danger that spread from Marlowe like a mist, the same cold, paralyzing mist that had come over her when Master Corbenic had slid his hand up her thigh for the first time.

She drew a breath and gritted her teeth. She had not come this far only to be thwarted by her own memories, her own weakness. She moved farther forward to the edge of her seat and said, "Did you ever meet Mr. Blackmar's eldest daughter?"

Blackmar spoke up at last, voice sharp: "Enough now, Euphemia. It's a party, after all. Let the man breathe. You have all night to discuss our dear old friend Myrddin."

Marlowe's gaze grew suddenly clear and bright. Just like Ianto's, it had a hard, broken-glass glint. He, too, shifted forward in his seat.

"I'll tell you what, love," he said to Effy, voice low. "Have a dance with me, and I promise—I'll give you everything I've got."

No. The word rose in her mind like a steep and powerful wave, one that darkened the whole shoreline. But it crashed against an invisible seawall, a barrier as stubborn and unrelenting as the face of a cliff.

The world was lost to her entirely, swept up in the snarling riptide. She closed her eyes, and when she opened them again, she swore she could see the shape of the Fairy King over Marlowe's shoulder. His cold white fingers curled, reaching for her—

And then, inexplicably, Preston took her hand. His touch wrenched her out of the black water, and the Fairy King vanished as quickly as he had appeared.

"My apologies if it wasn't clear to you, Mr. Marlowe," Preston said icily. He lifted their joined hands and gave a thin smile.

Marlowe leaned back, huffing in surprise. "Well. I didn't expect . . . I mean, you don't quite look the type—never mind. You ought to take the lady to dance, then. That's what women want, isn't it? Dancing and idle chatter. I'm sure she's had enough of this men's talk."

"I will," Preston bit out. "Effy, come on."

He helped her to her feet and led her through the crowd into the middle of the room, amid the other swaying couples. She blinked furiously, still trying to make sense of it all. Her lost voice, the Fairy King. Through it all she grasped onto Preston like an anchor, her head held just above the foaming water, the drowning place.

Somehow, in that time, her other hand had found its way to Preston's shoulder, and his had found its way to her waist.

"I'm sorry," Preston said in a low voice. "I couldn't think of another way to get Marlowe off of you. Men like him don't seem to respect anything besides another man's claim on a woman, and sometimes not even that." His voice grew coarser, angrier. "He wasn't going to give us a single goddamned answer anyway. He's sloshed and useless."

Effy managed a shaky laugh. "I've never heard you swear before."

"Well, sometimes the situation warrants it." The anger in his voice began to ebb, slowly. "I can't believe we came all this way—forget it. I'm sorry. I didn't mean to force you out here. Just one song and then I think we can slip away without Blackmar noticing."

"Just one song," Effy echoed. For some reason, it felt like a very sad thing to say.

She became acutely aware, in that moment, of Preston's grip on her waist. The warmth of his palm through her dress. The silk was very thin and very tight; she was certain he could feel the curves of her body under it.

Her own hand could feel the taut muscles of his shoulder through his jacket, the sudden jut of bone. Their faces were close, closer than they had been even last night, lying chastely in bed together.

The song was slow, achingly so, the singer's voice almost mournful. Effy knew it would end soon. She didn't want it to.

She realized right then and there that she did not want Preston to let her go. If anything, she wanted him to pull her closer. She wanted to loosen the buttons on his shirt. She wanted to feel the pulse at his throat against her lips.

Miserably, and against her will, Effy realized that she was in a Romance after all. Pedestrian as it might be. She wished desperately that it wasn't so—because what would a man like Preston Héloury want with a frivolous, flighty, untethered thing like her?—but this was the story she had found herself in, the narrative built up around her like the walls of a great house.

The song, of course, did end. But Preston didn't let go. He allowed his arm to drop from her waist, yet he held on to her hand. He kept his gaze trained on her, unblinking. It wasn't until Effy remembered the clock, ticking closer and closer to midnight, that she reluctantly slipped her fingers from his.

Together they hurried out of the dining room, down the hallway, and through the door, out into the cold, damp night. They had already packed their trunks, with the letters and diary safely inside. Effy never even felt the chill prickle her bare arms; she was all adrenaline and heat as she opened the passenger-side door and fastened her seat belt.

The gates of Penrhos creaked open, and Preston sped them away down the gravel road.

THIRTEEN

It is theorized that the goddesses Acrasia and Amoret were once a single female figure, rather than the two-headed goddess worshipped in Llyr today. When did Llyrians begin to see love as strictly dichotomic, rather than of a vast and multitudinous quality? Why was this dichotomy characterized by submission versus dominance? I put forth the argument that this doctrinal transformation is tied to the evolving role of women in Llyrian society, the fear of female advancement, particularly in the decades immediately following the Drowning.

FROM *THE SOCIAL HISTORY OF A SAINTHOOD*

BY DR. AUDEN DAVIES, 184 AD

Preston drove fast down the unlit roads, the green hills invisible in the dark, only fat smudges like thumbprints on a windowpane. They passed by with dizzying speed, the blackness racing alongside them. Effy did not sit in cars often, and when she did, they were almost never going at such a pace. She leaned back in her seat, feeling vaguely nauseous.

She couldn't blame Preston for not taking notice; he was staring straight ahead with intense, almost unblinking focus, headlights carving tunnels through the dark. She trusted him, of course, but this had to be the most reckless thing either of them had done so far—including sneaking around right under Ianto's nose and, for her, jumping out of a moving car.

That car had been going a lot more slowly.

Effy closed her eyes. Again and again, in the theater behind her eyelids, she watched the progression of the photographs, the satin robe pulling apart, the girl's breasts bared to the cold room. She watched the letters trembling in her shaking hands, Myrddin's hasty scrawl rolling past: *My sly and clever girl. My foolish and lovely girl. My beautiful and debauched girl.*

Call her by her name, Effy wanted to shout, but at no one in particular, because Myrddin was dead. The girl probably was, too. Blackmar's daughter. Myrddin's . . . conquest. She had been lost to the ages, just like those drowned churches.

In all her time at Hiraeth, Effy had never heard the bells.

Suddenly she was crying. The tip of her nose burned, her eyes grew fierce with water, and a strangled sob forced its way out of her throat. She clapped her hand over her mouth, trying to stifle the sound, trying not to distract Preston from his task, but her breaths were coming hot and fast, and tears were running paths down her cheeks.

"Oh, Effy," Preston said. And then, absurdly, he pulled the car over. "I'm sorry. There's very little worse than when our heroes fail us, is there?"

"I didn't know Myrddin was your hero. I thought you didn't like him."

"I do like him," Preston said. "I mean, I *did*. I still like the words that are attributed to him. I like that he wrote about death as decay. Deaths that last years and years, the same way the Drowning—well, never mind. Those words still mean something, even if Myrddin didn't write them. Even if he did."

"It's just . . ." Outside the darkness settled around them, slowing like low tide. "Preston, I've read *Angharad* a hundred times. You know I can quote it word for word. It saved me, believing all the things Myrddin wrote—or didn't write. Every story is a lie, isn't it? A story about a girl who's kidnapped by the Fairy King, but defeats him through her courage and cleverness . . . if that's not true, then everything I've always believed is a lie, too. You told me that the Fairy King never loved Angharad. That he was the villain of the book. I think you were right."

"Effy." Preston drew in a breath, but he didn't go on.

"There's no Fairy King at all," she said. Speaking the words aloud terrified her. They felt like walls closing in, crumbling on top of her. "I thought *Angharad* was some ancient story made new, and Myrddin was some otherworldly genius, magic like the rest of the Sleepers. But he was just some lecherous old man, and *Angharad* was just some shrewd attempt by his publisher to make money. There's no magic in it at all. Or at least there isn't anymore, because I've stopped believing in it. Now it's just another lie."

And what of all the times she had paged through *Angharad*, trying to discover its secrets, taking heart in the way Angharad's life so clearly mirrored her own? What of all the nights she had slept with her iron, with her mountain ash, seeing the Fairy King through her slitted eyes?

None of it was real. She was a mad girl, one whose mind could not be trusted, precisely the kind of girl her mother and the doctor and her professors and Master Corbenic had said she was.

That was the truth at the very center of everything, the truth she had tried her whole life to evade: there were no fairies, no magic, and the world was just ordinary and cruel.

She ought to have been embarrassed, with how much she was whimpering and blubbering, her vision blurred with tears. But Preston only looked at her in concern, his brows drawn together. He shrugged out of his jacket and held it out to her.

"Here," he said. "Sorry I don't have any tissues."

It was all so absurd. Effy blew her nose on a sleeve. "Why are you being so nice to me?"

"Why wouldn't I be?"

She huffed a pitiful laugh. "Because I've been awful to you. Pestering you just to pester you, trying to get under your skin, being foolish—"

"You don't see yourself very clearly, Effy." Preston shifted in his seat so that they were facing one another. "Challenging me isn't *pestering*. I'm not always right. Sometimes I deserve to be challenged. And changing your mind isn't foolish. It just means you've learned something new. Everyone changes their mind sometimes, as they should, or else they're just, I don't know, stubborn and ignorant. Moving water is healthy; stagnant water is sickly. Tainted."

Effy wiped her eyes. She still felt embarrassed, but her heartbeat was returning to its ordinary rhythm. "Which one of your heroes failed you?"

Preston sighed. It was a very weary sigh that could have belonged to someone thrice his age. "I told you before that my father is dead. Well, plenty of people have dead fathers; it's hardly an uncommon backstory. But the manner of his death—I can't really imagine anything worse."

"You don't have to talk about it." The sadness in his tone made her feel bad about asking.

"No, it's all right. My mother is Llyrian, as I've said. Her family is from Caer-Isel, quite well-to-do, seven advanced degrees among her immediate family. Scholastically inclined people. My father is from very far north, up the mountains—it's a bit like the Bottom Hundred, a very rural place, but sustained by mining rather than fishing. It was a torrid story of forbidden love, as far as I can tell. They moved to a suburb of Ker-Is—Caer-Isel—on the Argantian side of the border, close enough that we could visit my mother's family often. My father could never go—no Llyrian passport. Anyway. He worked as a construction manager, nothing prestigious or glamorous."

Preston was a good storyteller. He paused in all the right places, and his voice grew grave whenever it was appropriate. Effy tried to stay as silent as she could, hardly even daring to breathe. It was the first time Preston had spoken so openly about himself, and she didn't want to risk shattering the delicate moment.

"He was working late one night, during a bad storm. It was summer; I was sixteen. The roads were slick and deadly. His car skidded out on a sharp turn."

"Oh," Effy said. "Preston, I'm so sorry."

"He didn't die then," said Preston. He gave her a flimsy half smile. "He survived, but he hit his head hard on the dashboard, and then on the pavement. He wasn't wearing his seat belt—he was always reckless like that. It drove my mother mad. The ambulance arrived and took him to the hospital, and by the next morning he was awake and talking. Only the things he said didn't make any sense.

"My father wasn't from some well-heeled family, but he was a brilliant man. Self-taught, literary, very thoughtful. He easily held his own at the dinner table alongside my uncles with all their advanced degrees. He had a library in the basement with hundreds of books. What else? He loved animals. We never had any pets, but he would point out every rabbit he saw on the lawn, every cow we passed on the side of the road."

Preston's voice became smaller and smaller as he spoke. The grief in it made Effy's heart wrench.

"I'm sorry," Effy said again, but he didn't seem to hear her.

"A traumatic brain injury, the doctors said at first. He might return to his old self eventually, but there was no way to tell. Day after day, and he hardly recognized us, my mother and my brother and me. Sometimes I could see a rare moment of clarity in his eyes, when he remembered someone's face or name, but it would be gone again in just a blink. His body, externally, was unharmed—he could do all his regular things, supposedly. So the doctors let us bring him home, only it was like living with a stranger.

"He was intractable, combative. He broke glasses and shouted at my mother; he had never done that before. He tore all the books from their shelves. He was nothing like he'd been. Eventually we confined him—or rather, he confined himself—to the upstairs bedroom, where he spent every hour of the day watching television, sleeping. We brought him his meals on trays. I was the one who found him, in the end. Dead right there in the sheets. His eyes were open, and I remember the light of the television still flickering over his face."

"Preston," she started, but she couldn't think of what to say. He gave her a tight nod, as if to indicate that he wasn't quite done yet.

"When they did the autopsy, they found out that the doctors' initial diagnosis had been wrong. It wasn't a traumatic brain injury, or at least not the kind they had been envisioning. That we had been thinking of all along. It was hydrocephalus. Fluid in the skull and spinal cord that can't be flushed out. The pressure builds and builds. If the doctors had known, they might have been able to put in a shunt, drain it out. But no one knew until the end, until he died. Hydrocephalus. Water on the brain."

Preston's voice was nearly inaudible now. Hollow-sounding. Resigned. Effy wanted to reach out and hold him to her chest, but she settled on laying her hand over his instead.

For a moment they both froze; she waited to see if she'd done something wrong, stepped too far over some invisible line. But then Preston turned his hand over and entwined their fingers.

"I wish I remembered," he said very quietly, "the last time he pointed out a rabbit on the lawn. When I found him that day in the bedroom, all I could think of were the rabbits. That gentle, brilliant person he'd been—that person was dead long before he was. Sometimes I feel guilty even doing what I do, studying the things I study . . . because my father never had the chance. And he won't even get to see me graduate, or read any of my papers, or . . ."

He trailed off, and Effy squeezed his hand. The wind rattled the car windows, and it was like they were awash in a churning river, clinging to each other so that the water wouldn't drag them down.

Preston lifted his gaze, eyes meeting hers.

"Thank you," he said.

"For what?"

"I don't know. For listening, I suppose."

"You don't have to thank me for that."

Preston was silent. After a beat, he said, "And, well, I suppose that's partly why I don't have much faith in the notion of permanence. Anything can be taken from you, at any moment. Even the past isn't guaranteed. You can lose that, too, slowly, like water eating away at stone."

"I understand," Effy said softly. "I understand what you mean."

With great gentleness, Preston untwined his fingers from hers and placed both hands back on the steering wheel. "Let's get back to Hiraeth," he said. "I think we can still manage it before midnight."

Somehow, even bereft of her sleeping pills, Effy managed to fall asleep. It was Preston's presence that soothed her, just like it had the night before, his mere proximity enough to make her feel safe. The next thing she knew, the car had stopped, and her head jerked up from where it had been leaning against the cold window, her lashes fluttering blearily. Through the rain-speckled windshield, in the valley of the headlights, she could see the vague shape of the guesthouse. Her vision was still black at the edges, and her head felt very heavy.

"Hey," Preston said. "We made it. Eight minutes to midnight."

"Oh," she said, her voice thick. "I'm sorry. I can't believe I fell asleep."

"There's nothing to apologize for. I'm glad you got some rest."

Effy scrubbed at her face, scraping off some of the salt tracks left on her cheeks. Her eyes were puffy. Preston got out and walked around the car to open her door for her. She stood up unsteadily, and he offered her his arm for support.

She took it, fingers curling into the fabric, feeling the lean, corded muscles through his shirt, pressing against him for warmth. She let him lead her up to the guesthouse. The night was damp and wreathed in mist, and there was no sound save for the crickets and their feet shuffling through the grass.

When they reached the doorway, Preston said, somewhat awkwardly, "You must be relieved to have your sleeping pills again."

"Yes. I suppose I can't expect you to lie chastely next to me every night."

Preston gave a soft laugh and removed his arm from her grasp. "Good night, Effy."

Effy's stomach felt hollow with disappointment. But she said back, quietly, "Good night."

She watched him as he walked back to the car, and watched the car until it had vanished into the darkness, taillights blinkering away. Only then did she go into the guesthouse and lie in the green bed.

If she went back outside, would she see him? The flash of white between the trees, the long, slick black hair? He had appeared to her so clearly, so many times, since that very first night on the bank of the river. Now she knew it was truly just her imagination. A sad little girl's effort to make sense of a world that was insensibly cruel.

She felt her eyes start to brim again, and she squeezed them shut to stop the flow of tears. There was nothing left to do except try to be good now. To swallow her pills dutifully. To simply look away if she saw the Fairy King in the corner of her room. No more iron, no more mountain ash, no more fanciful girlish tricks.

No more *Angharad*.

Myrddin was dead now, in more ways than one. It was time to let him rest—or rather, it was time to bury him. They had the letters, the diary, and soon, the photographs. The truth would fall on top of his lifeless body like grave dirt, and maybe then she would be free.

Effy fumbled for the pill jar on the bedside table. When she closed her fingers around it, she felt a searing sense of relief.

Only this time, she didn't take the sleeping pills to stave off thoughts of the Fairy King, or Master Corbenic, or Myrddin's letters, or the girl from the photographs. She took them because otherwise, she would have lain awake all night, wondering what might have happened if she had refused to let Preston go.

❦

Even though Ianto had initially encouraged her to leave, and even though they had technically made it back before midnight, the next morning, he was not pleased. He glowered at them over his coffee as water dripped steadily from the ceiling, over the glass chandelier, and pooled on the dining room table.

Seconds ticked by, punctuated by the falling of those large droplets.

"There's a big storm coming, you know," Ianto said at last, setting down his cup. "Two days from now. The biggest in a decade, the naturalists are saying. The road down to Saltney will be washed away until Saints know when."

"I thought winter was meant to be the dry season," Preston said.

"Not in the Bottom Hundred. Not anymore."

Silence again, save for the water falling. Effy wondered what was leaking from upstairs, how the water had gotten in. She had forgotten how strongly Hiraeth smelled of the sea—salt and rot, sodden wood.

She thought of the time she had turned over a fallen log in her grandparents' back garden: the wood had disintegrated right there in her hand, and she'd stared down at the slimy dead leaves, the white mold, the fungi that had sprouted up like flower heads, each one shaped and striated like an oyster shell.

Trees didn't die when they were cut down, did they? Their dying took months, years. What a terrible fate to endure.

"I suppose you'll want to board up the doors and windows," Effy suggested mildly.

"I don't need a Northern girl to tell me how to weather a storm, my dear," Ianto said. His tone was light despite the bitterness of his words, but there was the faintest gleam in his eyes—something knifing through the muddled paleness. Effy's skin prickled. "What I do need are your blueprints. Wetherell has been hounding me for days. Where are they?"

She exchanged a look with Preston that she hoped Ianto didn't see. Two days until the storm meant they had two days to discover the house's secrets. They could not allow themselves to be trapped up here on the cliffs indefinitely.

Trying to keep her voice cheery, Effy said, "They ought to be done in two or three more days."

Ianto let out a low breath. "Once the blueprints are done, we will still need to hire contractors, builders, search for supplies . . . I had hoped to begin construction before the end of the year."

For all that she'd teased Preston, Effy felt a bit guilty lying to Ianto now. "That's definitely still possible," she said. "I promise. Two days, and it will be done."

"All right," Ianto said. But his pale eyes had grown sharper. "I hope you both had a . . . gratifying trip."

He was trying to goad them into confessing something, but Effy wasn't sure what. Could Blackmar have called Ianto and exposed them? Or did Ianto merely have a vague suspicion that they might be lying, and hope to hit a target just by chance?

Effy remembered the look of jealousy on Ianto's face as he had watched them drive away. It was somehow the most sinister emotion she could imagine. Her heart pattered in her chest.

"I think we both found what we needed," she said uneasily. "If you don't mind, I ought to get back to work now . . ."

But Ianto didn't shift. He kept staring at her with his glass-sharp eyes, his enormous fingers curled around the handle of his coffee mug.

"Mr. Héloury," he said. "You can leave us. I'd like to speak with Effy alone."

For a moment, it looked like Preston might argue. Silently Effy begged him not to. They were so close to proving *something*, and they only had to survive Ianto and this house for two more days. Now was not the time to prod the serpent.

Preston appeared to have reached the same conclusion. "Fine," he said, rising to his feet. "I have my own work to do, anyway."

He left, but he watched Effy over his shoulder until he was through the threshold. Effy held on to his gaze for as long as she could, until the tether snapped and she was forced to look at Ianto again.

"What did you want to talk to me about?" She tried to sound serene, pleasant. Tractable.

"I hope that Argantian boy didn't do anything untoward."

Effy couldn't manage to keep herself from blushing. "No! Of course not."

"Good." Ianto inclined his head. The water had finally stopped dripping; the pool on the dining table was murky and stagnant.

He was silent for so long that Effy felt she had to say something. "Is that all?"

Ianto looked back at her at last. "You know, I've spent all this time trying to pin down what sort of girl you are, Effy. All women are either an Acrasia or an Amoret. Patroness of seduction or patroness of submission. But some women are far more one than the other. I believe you're an Acrasia. A siren, a temptress. Men can't help what they do when they're around you."

She tried to choke out a laugh, hoping she could brush off his words—but Ianto's face was deadly serious, colorless eyes bright, no more murk.

Her heart ricocheted in her throat. She had her pink pills in her pocket. If she took one of them now, would it convince her he had said nothing wrong at all, that it was just her imagination that made her blood pulse with prey-animal panic?

In the pale mirror of Ianto's eyes, Effy saw herself reflected back, only she was a child again, red-nosed and whimpering, as she had been on the riverbank. Impossible—a trick of this wretched house and her addled mind. She blinked and blinked until the image was gone, yet Ianto did not for a moment lift his stare.

She had disavowed Myrddin. She had left behind her hag stones in the pocket of her other trousers. She had sworn to herself she would be sane and safe without them. But that was the problem with annihilating her imagination. Her mind could no longer conjure that escape hatch, that crack in the wall. There was nothing for her to slip through.

Effy stammered her way through the rest of the conversation, then fled upstairs.

Preston was perched on the chaise, holding Myrddin's diary, when she walked in. He looked up at her, with joy and relief, and said, "I got them."

"Got what?" Effy was still breathless from her desperate scramble up the stairs, and Ianto's voice was pulsing in her ears.

"The photographs," Preston said. "I decided to take advantage of the opportunity when you were with Ianto downstairs, and—Effy, are you all right?"

"Yes," she said, but her voice was shaking. Her legs threatened to give way beneath her. "Ianto just, well . . ."

Preston's back straightened with attention. "Did he threaten you?"

"No—not really." How could she explain it to him? She could barely explain it to herself. Ianto hadn't brandished a knife; he hadn't even tried to shift closer and slide a hand up her thigh.

As if conjured, Master Corbenic's face appeared before her, rippling like a reflection on water. He had said to her once: *You need someone to challenge you. Someone to rein you in. Someone to keep you safe, protect you from your worst impulses and from the world. You'll see.*

The words now felt like prophecy. If a story repeated itself so many times over, building itself up brick by brick, did it eventually become the truth? A house with no doors and no windows, offering no escape.

I was a girl when he came for me—
I will love you to ruination—
My beautiful and debauched girl—
Men can't help what they do when they're around you—

"Stop it," she whispered, too low for Preston to hear. "Stop it stop it stop it—"

"Effy," said Preston gravely, rising to his feet. "Please. Sit down. You look pale."

Too numb and too queasy to refuse, she let him lead her to the chaise. He sat down beside her. They were not touching, not quite, but she was close enough to feel the heat of his body, and see those two little grooves that his glasses carved into the bridge of his nose. She still wanted to ask him if they hurt. Or if they had hurt once, but he'd grown so inured to the pain that he didn't even notice it anymore.

"I'm sorry," she said meekly. "I'm—I'm fine. I just haven't eaten in a while."

A mad girl, like the doctor had said. Like her mother had always believed, like the other students whispered in the halls. She tried to catch her breath, gulping down huge mouthfuls of air. Preston sat tensed next to her, fingers curling and uncurling in his lap. As if he wanted to reach out and touch her but didn't quite dare.

At last, Effy lifted her head. *Stop it,* she told herself again firmly. *It's not real. None of it is real.*

"You said you got the photographs?" she managed finally.

Preston hesitated, still looking very worried. "Yes. And something else occurred to me. If the pictures were indeed taken on this chair, then it means that Blackmar's daughter was here at some point, at Hiraeth. Which means that the affair went on for more than just a year. Blackmar said that Myrddin didn't move here until after *Angharad* was published."

Effy frowned. She felt dizzy, unsafe in her own skin. "So that diary entry of Myrddin's where he mentions Blackmar dropping off the manuscript—that was just to his apartment in Syfaddon?"

"It must have been. Part of me began to think, well, maybe it's something as simple as Blackmar doing some light editing of the manuscript and then bringing it back to Myrddin to send to Greenebough? There's nothing exceptional about that. But then why is Blackmar so uncomfortable at any mention of *Angharad* and his daughter? He was sweating when you asked Marlowe about it. I keep running it all over in my mind, paging through Myrddin's diary, but there's something we're missing, something—"

"Preston," she cut in. "We need to get into the basement."

She had been thinking of Ianto, of course, which made her think of the key, which made her remember that dark locked door, the wood rotting and speckled white with barnacles. She remembered the water, shifting and seething, so black that it had seemed impenetrable, that it had seemed like a floor she could have walked on, like something she would have to break in order to slip through.

And then she had been thinking of her own theory, her mind turning on in the silence like a record player in an empty room, though it still felt too fragile to speak aloud. She was thinking of the girl in the photographs. Effy had once thought her gaze empty, but now she realized that the girl had simply escaped her own body, her spirit wandering elsewhere while Myrddin's camera flashed over her naked breasts.

Effy knew that trick well. It was almost like magic. If you tried hard enough, you could believe yourself out of the cold and banal world.

The color drained from Preston's face. "We can't go down

there—it's all submerged, and we don't even know if there's anything of use . . ."

"We have to *try*," Effy urged. "What else can we do? The storm is coming, and we're out of options."

Preston drew a breath. "Even *if* we can get the key—and that's quite an *if*—what are we meant to do? Swim through the dark until our hands happen to touch something? Something that could be too heavy, something that could drag us down? That seems like an awfully good way to drown."

His voice was wavering like it never had before, and his hands were fisted so tightly on his lap that his knuckles had turned white.

Effy frowned. "Are you scared?"

"Of drowning? Of the dark? Yes. Those are very reasonable things to be scared of," Preston said tersely.

Hydrocephalus. Water on the brain. How could she blame him for being afraid?

"Then I'll do it," she said. "You can just hold the flashlight."

"Effy, this is all mad. We don't even have the key."

"I can get it," she said. And even though a part of her wished she didn't, Effy felt quite sure of that. "I promise you I can. And then I'll swim. I'm not afraid of drowning."

She meant it. Well, in some primal way, maybe she would be afraid once she was under, her lungs throbbing and burning, the light slowly waning overhead. But in an abstract sense, drowning didn't scare her.

She wasn't afraid of dying, not really. It was the ultimate act of flight, an escape artist's tour de force. Drowning did not seem

275

like a particularly easy way to go, if Ianto was to be believed, but it wouldn't matter once she'd already taken the plunge. Fear and pain could be endured if you knew that eventually, they would end.

"Stop it," Preston snapped. "Just—just stop being so reckless. That's the one terrible thing about you, you know. You jump out of moving cars and dive into dark water."

He sounded as angry as he had when they'd confronted Marlowe at the party, and it shocked her. But his anger had a different edge now, something tense. Something desperate.

Effy was silent for a moment, letting his words settle over her and then slip off, as if they were that dark water itself.

"You don't understand," she said. "You weren't there in that car with Ianto. When I jumped out I wasn't doing it to be *reckless*—I was saving myself. What you think of as recklessness, I think of as survival. Sometimes it's not very pretty. Skinned knees and a bloody nose and whatever else. You told me I don't see myself clearly, but I do. I know what I am. I know that, deep down, there's not much else to me but surviving. Everything I think, everything I do, everything I *am*—it's just one escape act after another."

Believing Myrddin's stories had become an escape act, too, her greatest and most enduring one. But it had made her unstable, untrustworthy, a fragile, flighty thing. That was the cruelest irony: the more you did to save yourself, the less you became a person worth saving.

Effy held Preston's gaze, undaunted, challenging him to reply. Her chest was heaving. She heard herself swallow hard.

"You couldn't be more wrong about that," Preston said. His

throat was pulsing. His eyes, once pale brown, had somehow turned dark. "You're not just one thing. Survival is something you do, not something you *are*. You're brave and brilliant. You're the most real, full person I've ever met."

Effy's breath caught, and when she tried to speak, she found that no words would come. She wanted to say *I don't believe you.* She wanted to say *thank you.* She wanted to say *tell me more about who I am because I don't know anymore.*

If Myrddin had not written *Angharad*, if he really had just been some lecherous old man, if there was no Fairy King, then who *was* she? Just a mad girl, thrashing about in black water. A part of her only wanted to cry.

She didn't do or say any of that. Instead, in one swift, decisive maneuver, she swung her leg over Preston's hips, straddling him, and bore him down onto the chaise. She pinned him there, their faces closer than they had ever been before, noses near enough to touch. Where their chests were pressed together, she could feel their hearts pounding in frenzied tandem.

For a long, long moment, neither of them moved or spoke.

"Effy," Preston whispered at last. His hand slid under her skirt, his fingers folding around the curve of her hip. "We can't."

"Don't you want to?" *Don't you want me?* she'd meant to ask, but she couldn't quite find the courage to make that small substitution.

"Of course I do." He shifted, and Effy *felt* him, hard and urgent against her thigh. "And if you were just some girl, at some party, I would. But I know you. I know what's been done to you—"

Her stomach fluttered. "What's that supposed to mean?"

With his other hand, Preston reached up. At first Effy thought he was going to stroke her face, but instead he gathered up the golden hair that was falling over both of them, tickling his cheeks, twisted it into a knot, and tucked it over her shoulder.

It was a neat and gentle motion, the tendons on the inside of his wrist flexing. Effy let out a quivering breath.

"I know about that professor at your college," he said softly. "What he did to you—I'm so sorry."

She felt as if she'd been slapped. She recoiled, sitting up, now perched awkwardly in Preston's lap.

"You never told me," she said, voice trembling. "You never told me that you knew."

"You never brought it up. I didn't want to be the one to mention it." Preston sat up, too, arms braced around her so she wouldn't topple backward. "At first I wasn't even sure it was you—there were just whispers about a girl in the architecture program who slept with her adviser. And then I learned you were the only girl in the architecture program . . ."

"I never slept with him." Her stomach lurched as if she might vomit. "I've never even—it's not fair. Men just say whatever they want and everyone believes them."

"It's not fair." Preston's voice was low. "I know."

"We did other things, but not that." The tip of her nose grew warm, the way it always did when she was going to cry. She tried desperately not to cry now. "And everyone thinks I started it but I didn't. I never got anything from him. That's what all the boys at

278

my college said. But he just touched me and I let him."

"Effy," Preston said. "I believe you."

She blinked, half in bewilderment, half to keep the tears from falling. "Then why won't you . . . ?"

Preston flushed lightly. "I didn't mean it like that at all, that you were some fallen woman and I—never mind. But I won't be another man who uses you. I don't want you to think of me that way, just a shag on a chaise. I don't want to be something else that keeps you from sleeping at night."

Effy felt a sob rise in her throat. She pressed the heel of her hand to her eye. "I would never think of you like that. I thought you were . . . cold, frigid, like the stereotypes say. Really. I didn't know you felt anything at all when you looked at me."

"I did. I do." Preston's grip on her tightened, knuckles folding gently against the small of her back.

She remembered the way he had scrawled her name repeatedly in the margins of that paper: *Effy Effy Effy Effy Effy.* She wanted to hear him *say* her name like that, over and over and over again.

She was halfway to begging—fallen woman indeed. What sort of temptress was she if she couldn't seduce the man she *really* wanted?

"I'm sorry," she said miserably. "I'm so, so stupid."

"Stop it. You're not." Preston swallowed, and Effy allowed herself, at last, to put one hand to his throat, feeling it bob under her palm. "I wanted you, too. For so long. It was terrible. Sometimes I could barely eat—sorry, I know that sounds like the strangest thing. But for days I didn't feel hungry at all. I was . . . occupied.

You took away all the other wanting from me."

She held her hand there against his throat, and Preston held her that way in his lap, and outside, the sea roared against the rocks with a sound like nearing thunder. All the papers, Myrddin's diary and letters, the photographs, spilled out on the floor, their edges lifted by an uncommon breeze. And still something slid between them, like water through a crack in the wall.

FOURTEEN

Water finds its way through the smallest spaces and the narrowest cracks. Where the bone meets sinew, where the skin is split. It is treacherous and loving. You can die as easily of thirst as you can of drowning.

FROM ANGHARAD BY EMRYS MYRDDIN, 191 AD

The rain had already begun the next morning, just a light spray of it, enough to cloud the windows of the guesthouse with condensation. Outside, the green world had gotten greener: dripping with rainwater, the leaves and the grass turned jewel-toned and the moss on the trees and rocks looked richer. Well-fed. The wood had turned almost black, damp and breathing. The pieces of sky that showed through the tree canopy were densely gray.

Effy walked up the path toward the house, wind tossing her hair every which way, the sea churning and churning below. The rocks jutted through the slosh of foam like sharp teeth. She squinted and peered down the side of the cliff, but the seabirds had all gone, their nests and eyries abandoned.

Once Effy had read a book about the Drowning that said

animals had sensed it coming. The penned sheep had bleated in desperation in the days before the storm, the yoked cattle straining and straining against their binds. In the end, they had all perished, too. Her skin chilled.

That was when she saw it, the flutter of something dark like a piece of fabric caught in the wind. But as her eyes adjusted to the muddled light and she blinked rainwater off her lashes, it took a more solid shape: damp black hair, scraggly as kelp, bone-white skin, and a jagged crown of antlers. Its face was blurred and featureless, as if it were a painting, not yet dry, that had been run over and ruined with rain.

It spoke to her, but it was a language not meant for human ears, something unfathomably ancient, or perhaps she simply could not make out the words over the thrashing rain and wind. It extended its hand, long fingers uncurling, claws at their tips. Effy stood there frozen in terror, water pouring off them both.

And then she ran. The path to the house had already turned mostly to mud, sucking at her boots, the air so fiercely cold she regretted her choice of a skirt and stockings instead of trousers. She ran until she was short of breath, and then she stopped, panting, and looked over her shoulder.

There was nothing but the rocks and the rain, and her own sodden footprints in the mud. Effy curled her cold fingers into fists and squeezed her eyes shut.

She had taken her pink pills dutifully this morning. She had resolved not to believe in such things anymore. What had gone wrong? Had she lived in the unreal world so long it was impossible to pull herself out of it? Had she spent so long believing the stories, the lies, that her mind now rejected the truth?

Perhaps she was beyond saving. Perhaps no pink pills or wheedling doctor could rescue her from drowning.

Effy stood there in the shadow of the enormous house, swallowing her tears. There was one thing left, her last desperate resort. Something she could still hang her hopes on. Maybe when they uncovered the truth about Myrddin at last—unearthed the final, irrefutable clue—the Fairy King would die with him, with his legacy.

It was all she had to believe in, or else the rest of her life would be locked rooms and padded walls and pill after pill after pill. She would sink to the seafloor like one of Myrddin's selkie wives and never surface again.

So she tried to narrow her mind like the edge of a knife, focused on one singular thing—*the key, the key, the key.* But her thoughts kept wandering to Preston. Specifically the memory of his fingers cupping her hip. She had replayed the moment over and over again in bed the night before: his hand sliding up her thigh, under her skirt. He had wanted her, too, she had *felt* it, the proof of his wanting right there between her legs. And yet—

She shook her head, smoothed her hair back from her face, and forced herself to think of anything else. Anything but the Fairy King she did not want yet could not escape, and the boy she *did* want but could not have.

As she approached the house, Effy heard a ringing sound. At first she thought it was the bells, the fabled bells she'd been longing to hear, but it was something clearer, something above the surface. Metal against metal.

Above her, Hiraeth itself seemed to sway and groan, rocking perilously against the bruise-colored clouds. Effy picked her way around the house, her boots completely waterlogged now, in search of the ringing sound.

To her surprise, she found Ianto there, kneeling at the base of a large black tree. He had a hammer in one hand and he was striking a small piece of metal repeatedly, driving the stake into the root of the tree. His hair was loose and wild around his face, his brow drenched with rainwater and sweat.

He didn't see or hear Effy until she cleared her throat and said, "Ianto?"

He turned around, colorless eyes murky and depthless. "Effy."

"What are you doing?" She had to raise her voice to be heard over the wind.

"The trees have to be staked down," he said. "Or else the wind will tear them up by their roots and hurl them right through the north wall of the house."

Effy looked around. There were hundreds of trees, branches whipping violently, their leaves coming loose and curling up into the air. "Do you need any help with that?"

Ianto gave a mirthless laugh. "Not from you, my dear. This isn't women's work." But his voice was light, and there was no cruel, glassy gleam in his eyes. There was a long metal chain on the ground beside him, coiled like a snake ready to strike. "Well. I suppose you could bring me my jacket. It's draped over one of the chairs in the dining room."

"Of course," Effy said. She was trembling already, overwhelmed by the opportunity she'd been given. Where Ianto's collar slung low, she could see just a glimpse of the leather cord.

She hurried up the stairs to the house and heaved the door open, breathing hard.

The foyer seemed darker than usual, one rusted candle stand in the corner giving off a bubble of filmy light. Effy splashed through the puddles on the floor, ignoring the water dripping from above and the ceiling sagging like an old man's jowls.

Wetherell stood in the threshold to the dining room, looking even grimmer than usual.

"What will you be doing to weather the storm, Ms. Sayre?" he asked. His lips barely moved as he spoke.

She did not want to tell him that she planned to leave; he might warn Ianto. "What is there to do?"

"Board up the windows. Tie down the trees." Wetherell's eyes shifted under their heavy lids. "If you were smart, you would leave now, while you still can."

Effy blinked in surprise. "You're going to leave? You're in charge of Myrddin's estate . . ."

"Myrddin's estate is more than just this house. It's all the money in his Northern bank account, the royalty checks owed by his publisher, the letters that I gave Mr. Héloury. This house is nothing but an ugly, rotting testament to the late Myrddin's cruelty, and the price Ianto is still paying for it."

"Cruelty? What do you mean?"

"This is no place to bring a wife, to raise a family, living always with the fear of destruction. Myrddin did it on purpose, building the house here and holding his wife and son within it. He wanted them to be afraid—afraid to stay, and afraid to leave, in equal measure."

Suddenly Effy remembered the one-sided conversation she'd overheard.

I didn't have a choice, Ianto had said, groaning as if he were in pain. *This house has a hold on me, you know that, you know about the mountain ash . . .*

She remembered the look of envy in his eyes when she had left Hiraeth with Preston. She remembered how desperate Ianto had been to get back to the house after their meal at the pub, desperate enough to leave her stranded on the side of the road.

If she was not supposed to believe in magic, how could she explain any of it? She had no choice but to think Ianto was mad, miserable, chained to this house and to his father's legacy out of guilt and grief and enduring terror. Myrddin wanted Ianto to be afraid, and so he was, even after his father was gone.

Perhaps the truth would free Ianto, too. They just had to get to the basement.

Effy drew in a breath and met Wetherell's eyes without contrition.

"I'm not afraid," Effy said, even as the wind made the window glass ripple like paper. "I'm not leaving until I get what I need."

When she went back out to bring Ianto his jacket, it was already raining more furiously, the droplets hard and fat, almost painful as they hit her skin. Ianto scarcely looked up as she reemerged; he was coiling the large chain around the trunk of the tree, looping it through the stakes with a bitter, teeth-gritted concentration.

He shot her a brisk look and said, voice tight, "Lay it on my shoulders, please."

Slowly Effy approached, blood pulsing with adrenaline. If she failed now, it was unlikely she would get another chance. With great care and deliberation, Effy laid the jacket over him. One shoulder, and then the other. And then, as he began to shrug into it, she slipped the cord from around his neck with a gentle and innocuous tug.

Sucking in a sharp breath, Effy stumbled back, shoving the key quickly up the sleeve of her coat. Ianto didn't even twitch.

He looked up for a moment, at the tree that he'd draped with chains and fastened to the ground, like a sorceress tied at the stake. His eyes were half-closed. His expression was unreadable.

"Ianto," Effy said, against her better judgment. She knew she ought to just flee to the basement now, knew that Preston was waiting for her, that they couldn't afford to waste any more time. But her chest felt tight with an unexpected grief. *This house has a hold on me*, Ianto had said out loud, to no one.

Despite his odd, shifting moods, despite his occasional cruelty, Effy had finally realized they had more in common than she'd thought. "Are you sure you want to stay?"

He choked out something that Effy thought was a laugh, but she couldn't quite be sure. Ianto turned around at last, strands of black hair plastered down his face like the long claw marks of some wild beast.

"'But a sailor was I,'" he said, "'and on my head no fleck of gray—so with all the boldness of my youth, I said: The only enemy is the sea.'"

The sound of the rain blurred his recitation, striking out syllables. But Effy knew the words by heart. Ianto, with his cloudy, turbid gaze, had no intention of leaving Hiraeth.

Effy could barely bring herself to nod at him. She staggered back up toward the house, heart roaring in her ears. Ianto had omitted the poem's first line: *Everything ancient must decay.*

Preston was waiting for her outside the basement door, pacing nervously. One hand was curled around the back of his neck. Effy pulled the key from her sleeve and held it out, dangling it in the air.

Behind his glasses, Preston's eyes grew wide. "You really got it?"

"When will you finally stop underestimating me?"

He huffed out a laugh, but it was shaky with fear. "You don't have to do this, Effy. Really. We can come back later. We can hire a dredge crew to clear the water—"

"Preston," she said curtly, "we both know that we're not coming back."

Wetherell had vanished from the threshold. Effy hoped he'd packed his things and driven down the road, away from this house, while he still had the chance. Had he turned the car's mirrors rightside out again before he went?

She imagined the bartender at the pub in Saltney nailing boards over her windows, all the fishermen battening down their hatches. How many more houses would this storm take? How many stories, how many lives, crumbling into the oblivious, uncaring sea? With trembling hands she fitted the key into the lock and turned it.

The rotted door swung open without a sound.

Behind it, the dark water rippled and seethed. It sang a wordless song of depths, of danger. Effy took one step down the stairs, then another, until she had reached the very last stair that was not submerged.

Preston stood in the threshold above her, his shoulders actually *trembling*.

"It's all right," she said, and she was surprised by how calm her voice sounded. "Turn on the flashlight."

Whispering something unintelligible, Preston clicked it on. Light grafted onto the damp stone walls and illuminated the faded engraving above the water. *The only enemy is the sea.*

Effy had liked swimming as a child, when her grandparents had brought her to the natatorium at one of the hotels in Draefen. They had gone on weekend mornings, while her mother slept until noon, obliterated by last night's bottle of gin. In her bright yellow bathing costume, Effy had splashed and played, and even made it a challenge for herself to see how long she could stand to hold her head underwater. Her grandfather had noticed her enthusiasm and paid for lessons, and though they had tapered off by the end of secondary school, Effy considered herself a stronger swimmer than most.

She had practiced holding her breath last night, to see how long she could last before her lungs started to burn and panic set in. Thirty seconds, forty, sixty—but Effy knew it would be different once she was under. It always was. When there was only the bleary, distant light from Preston's flashlight, when the cold sank into her bones. She knelt down on the slick, barnacle-ridden step and began to slide her boots off.

"Just give me one last chance to convince you," Preston said in an urgent, quavering voice. "We can find some other way . . ."

Effy set her boots down and stood there in her stocking feet, shivering at the feel of the wet stone. She shrugged off her coat, tied back her hair with its velvet ribbon. She stared down into the dark and impenetrable water.

Almost impossibly, a sliver of her reflection rippled up from that black mirror. A pale crescent of face, a puff of dark blond hair. The flash of high cheekbones and the feather of yellow lashes.

It made her feel both more and less afraid. She felt the way she had when she had seen the ghost in the hall—fear not of the thing itself, but of the dark water closing in around it.

She turned around to face Preston. She said, "Don't be afraid. I know that I can do this."

He curled his fingers around her arm, anchoring her there for just one moment. He looked her right in the eye, gaze steadier now, fierce with determination.

"Remember what we talked about," he said. "Keep one hand on the left wall so you don't get lost. The first dive is exploratory. Try to see how far the cavern goes, then come back for air and we'll reassess."

Under his collar, his throat was pulsing. Effy wanted to touch it again, to touch *him*, but she knew that if she did, she would never want to let go. Very gently, she extricated herself from his grasp.

"I know," she said. "I'm ready."

And then she turned back and began her descent. The water was cold and the initial shock of it made her gasp, rolling up to her waist and then higher, until her arms were submerged. She was buoyant now, having lost the sensation of the slippery ground under her feet.

She reached out, movements made sluggish by the turbid water, and found the left wall. It, too, was slick with algae and she could feel the crevices where the brick had crumbled away, letting the water in.

Effy heard Preston's breathing quicken, but she was determined not to look back. Her hair drifted out around her head like pale flotsam. She took another deep inhale, and then ducked under.

Instantly the light dimmed; it turned the water a murky green in front of her, nearly opaque. Effy kicked, propelling herself forward. There was the dark shape of *something* in the distance, but she couldn't tell what, and already her throat was growing tight.

She let herself drift a little farther, carried by the inertia of her initial kicks, until her fingers brushed against something hard and solid. The dark thing, whatever it was—she could reach it.

She wanted to keep going, to get her hands around it, to *hold* something, but she remembered her promise to Preston and turned back, kicking up toward the bleary light. She surfaced again, gasping, and saw that Preston had moved farther down the steps, now submerged up to his knees.

He grasped her wrist and hauled her up the steps, out of the water.

"Effy," he choked out. "Are you all right?"

It took a few moments of labored breathing before Effy could speak.

"I'm fine," she managed at last. "I saw something—I *touched* it. I don't know what it is, but I need to get to it. I know that I can . . ."

Her teeth were chattering, but she didn't even feel the cold. Adrenaline had cloaked her in a haze of numbness, all her blood pulsing and hot. Preston kept his grip tight on her wrist.

"Are you sure?"

She nodded, and with every passing second, she felt more certain. The beam of the flashlight flickered against the stone walls, against the water, dappling the black surface with gold.

Effy slipped away from Preston, and for a moment she saw herself through *his* eyes, drowning in increments as she retreated back down the steps, vanishing like a selkie beneath the waves.

It was nothing like swimming at the natatorium, where the water was clear and chemically blue. This was a dense and exquisite darkness. Her body, too, was heavier now. She no longer had the lightness of a child, all spindly limbs and easy faith. Her arms and legs felt so burdensome now.

Effy pressed her left hand to the wall and kicked, the black shape materializing slowly, like something moving under ice. She reached out and touched it again, trying to get a sense of its size. Rotted, ancient wood fell away under her hand.

There was a low noise, a thrumming sound that seemed to come from the water itself, and Effy remembered, suddenly, all the fairy tales that warned children away from the edges of oceans and lakes. Kelpies, selkies, fairy women wrapped in seaweed who took you to the water and strangled you with their long hair. Arethusa, the consort of the Fairy King, who seduced men with her beauty and then drowned them while singing to cover up the sounds of their desperate, doomed thrashing.

A tense and terrible fear gripped her. She brushed her hand along the wood, quite sure now that it was a shelf. She was as much a fool as the mariner in Myrddin's poem—if it really was Myrddin's poem at all—who believed the only thing he had to fear was the might of the sea itself. There were a thousand dark creatures in it. There were a thousand ways to drown.

Effy had once read, in one of those ancient tomes on the sixth floor of the library, about a method of torture practiced in the south, in the pre-Drowning days. The victims were strapped down and forced to drink and drink and drink, until their stomachs burst, until their bodies gave out from the weight of it all. The water cure, it was called. For days after she could not stop imagining all those swollen bodies. Sometimes, she had read, the victim was forced to vomit up all the water and then drink it down again.

Effy's lungs were starting to burn.

Her fingers found the edge of something, something with a handle she could grasp. She tried to pull but it was too heavy, and her chest felt close to bursting.

Yet somehow she knew that if she broke for the surface now, she would never have the courage to return. So she let her left hand leave the wall, and used both hands to grasp the heavy metal thing and *pull*.

She tried to swim for the surface, but the thing in her hands—feeling it now, she knew it was a box—weighed her down. Panic loosed itself from her chest. She felt the cold, and the fear, the awful fear that stilled her and pulled her down even farther. Her vision grew black at its edges.

Yet Preston had been wrong about her, in a way. Perhaps she realized it only now. Even though she was afraid of living, she didn't want to die. Effy was no architect, and she might never be a storyteller, either, no heir to magic and myths and legends, but one thing she knew was survival.

Effy escaped the water and surfaced into a world of stubborn light.

Her eyes were still filmy with blackness, so she couldn't see Preston. But she felt him as he grabbed her around the middle and hauled her up the stairs, both of them gasping and coughing, and Effy spitting the fetid water out of her mouth.

They lay there for a moment, Effy clutching the box to her chest and Preston clutching her. The water lapped tamely at their feet.

"I—I did it," she stammered, voice hoarse. "I told you I could."

"Effy," Preston whispered, his breath warm against her ear. "Look."

For a moment she wasn't sure what he meant; her brain still felt waterlogged, churning like surf break. Her numb fingers curled and uncurled around the edges of the rusted metal box that now felt as if it was a part of her, a fifth limb.

A great daunting padlock jangled as she shifted. But printed at the top of the box, in steadfast black letters, was one word. A name.

Angharad.

The rain was falling in thick sheets as they stumbled down the path toward the guesthouse. Wetherell's car was gone, frantic tire tracks gouged in the deep mud of the driveway. All around them, as the wind howled, there were the terrible twisting, wrenching sounds of branches being stripped from trees, of leaves being blown away in great swirling gusts.

Effy would have been afraid, but she was too busy concentrating on not freezing to death.

Layered under two coats—hers and Preston's—she staggered through the mud, holding tight to Preston's arm. In his other arm, he held the metal box.

Effy was trembling all over, her vision blurring in the half-light, the shadows oily and slick between the trees. For a moment she thought she saw him again, wet black hair flashing, bone crown shining, but when she blinked it was gone. She felt no fear. Whatever was inside the box was the truth, and it would vanquish the Fairy King for good. It would evict him from her mind. It would chain him in the world of myth and magic, where he belonged.

Her own hair was stuck to her forehead and cheeks, freezing there like seaweed in slushy water. Her numb legs trembled under her, and she was afraid that her knees might give out.

Somehow, without her speaking, Preston knew to hold on tighter. He hauled her up to the threshold of the guesthouse.

As he rammed open the stone-and-iron door, a deadly tangle of branches blew by them.

Preston shut the door, muffling the horrible sound of the wind. He took out his lighter and went around lighting the oil lamps and candles, while Effy stood there, clothes dripping onto the floor. Everything felt very heavy, dreamlike.

She looked at the box, which Preston had set down on top of the desk, reading that word, that name, over and over again. *Angharad Angharad Angharad Angharad Angharad.*

"I'm sorry," Preston said, jolting her from her reverie. "There's not much wood in the fireplace, and I don't think I can get more, since it's so wet outside . . ."

He trailed off, looking despairing. Effy just blinked at him and said tonelessly, "It's all right."

"You should, um, take off your clothes."

That, at last, made Effy's heartbeat quicken, cheeks flooding with heat. Preston flushed, too, and quickly added, "Not like that—I just mean, you're soaking wet."

"I know," she said. She slipped out of his coat, then hers, letting them puddle on the floor.

Preston turned around, facing the wall, as she took off her wet top and wet skirt and wet stockings. She dug through her trunk for the warmest sweater she could find and pulled it on. Then she walked over and got under the covers, pulling the green duvet up to her chin.

Preston turned back around, face still pink. "That's better."

Yet still she felt so cold. She felt like she might never be warm again, even under the covers, even with the four solid walls around her. She wanted to feel safe, anchored. She wanted to live in a world where there were no antlered creatures outside, where there was no need for iron on the door.

Was this the unreal world, or the real one? It all felt muddled now, like there was no longer a rigid border between them. There was black water rising and she could barely keep her head above the surface.

"The storm," she managed. And then Effy could not think of what to say. Her mind was a knotted sea net and foaming waves.

"It'll be all right," Preston said. His glasses were speckled with rainwater. "We can still make it down to Saltney. You just need to get warm first." He paused, lips quivering. "But you did it, Effy. You really did it."

She made a choked sound that she hoped sounded enough like a laugh. "Even if I lose a few more fingers."

Preston just ducked his head, as if he wanted to scold her but couldn't. Preston, who had delicately picked all the rocks from her wounded knees and washed away the blood, back when they both still barely trusted each other. A surge of sudden, desperate affection swelled in her chest.

"I should go back to the house," he said. "We—"

"No," Effy cut in, heart pounding. "Don't."

He frowned at her. "We still need to get the letters and the photographs."

"Please," she said. "Please don't leave. I think I'll die if you leave."

She really meant it, right then and there, with the wind trying to tear through the door and no way of knowing what was real and what wasn't. He was the only thing that felt solid, stable, and true. Without him she would slip under and never resurface.

Preston let out a soft breath. For a moment she thought he might leave anyway, and her heart tumbled into the pit of her stomach.

But instead he moved toward her slowly, and sat down on the edge of the bed. His clothes were wet, too. His shirt stuck to his skin, translucent with rainwater.

"All right," he said. "I'll stay."

The heat of his body bled through the blankets. Effy sat up and inched closer. She rested her chin on his shoulder very carefully, as if she were setting a glass down on a table and didn't want it to make a discordant sound.

She felt him breathing slowly, shoulders rising and falling. He turned his head toward her.

He kissed her, or she kissed him—it mattered only as much as it mattered whether the house was sinking or the sea was rising. Once their lips touched, Effy could think of nothing else.

Preston took her face into his hands and, with exceptional gentleness, lowered her back down onto the pillows.

They broke apart for a moment, Preston half on top of her now, propping himself up on his elbows. A bit of water trickled down from the back of his neck, past his collarbone. He said, "Effy, are you sure?"

She nodded. She wanted to say *yes*, but somehow the word got tangled up in her throat. Instead she said, in a small voice, "I've never been with anyone before. I've kissed boys—and then there was Master Corbenic, but that was just . . ."

"This won't be anything like that, Effy. I promise. I'll be kind to you."

She believed him. It almost made her want to cry. Carefully she began to work at the buttons on his shirt, baring his throat and then his chest, his abdomen and navel. She had never seen someone stripped down like this before and she was momentarily stunned by the *vitality* of him—the signs of life in every clench of muscle, every shift that made his bones move under his skin.

Effy couldn't help but touch him all over, there and there and there, his rib cage and sternum and, finally, the triangle of skin above his belt buckle.

Preston shivered under her touch; she heard him swallow hard. His hands slid under her sweater. "Can I?"

"Yes," she said, finding the word at last.

He took her sweater by the hem and pulled it over her head. *She* was bare then, and he kissed her again, softly dragging his mouth along her jawline, down her throat. Effy gave a quiet gasp as his fingers found her breast, but he only moved his hand over it and held it, as if to protect her from the coldness of the air.

Her own hands had stopped at his belt buckle, vexed by it, heart suddenly skipping beats. She felt him again through his trousers, stiff and urgent. It thrilled her and scared her in equal measure. She'd wanted him for so long, and now she knew—there was no doubt—that he wanted her back.

She managed at last to undo his belt and free him of his pants, and he lifted the covers and slid into the bed beside her.

The only thing remaining between them was his glasses. She plucked them off his face and laid them on the bedside table. He blinked at her, as though readjusting his eyes. Effy saw the two little nicks winging the bridge of his nose and ran her thumb over them, feeling where the small bits of metal had made his skin give way.

One corner of his mouth curved. "What are you doing?"

"I've always wondered if these hurt."

"Not really," he said. "Most of the time I don't even notice. I wish I could see you more clearly right now. But even blurry you're so beautiful."

She felt her cheeks grow warm. There was no cold left in her now at all. "Please be gentle."

"Oh. I will. I swear it." He shifted, slowly parting her thighs.

There was a little bit of pain, but it was like a breath that was tightly held: it gave way to seemingly infinite pleasure upon release.

She whimpered quietly into his shoulder, a sound that was half surprise, half surrender. The yielding was easy when the assault was so tender. The land would never protest if the sea washed over it with what could not be called anything else but *affection*.

They matched each other inhale for inhale, Preston's mouth close to her ear. When his breathing sped up, Effy could tell he was very close, but then he slowed again, strokes long and deliberate.

"Don't," she whispered petulantly against his throat. "Don't *stop*."

"I just wanted to tell you," he said, "when this is over, I'll take care of you, too. If you want me to."

Effy closed her eyes, and even the blackness there behind them was bright with false stars. "I do."

When it *was* over, Effy lay beside Preston, both of them concealed by the green covers. She lay on her belly, he on his back, but they faced each other with their cheeks pressed against the pillows.

The four walls around them seemed impenetrable. Effy scarcely heard the rain at all.

"I don't want to go back out there," she said, in a tiny muffled voice. "Not ever."

He didn't ask if she meant back into the storm, or the house, or the world entirely. "That seems, unfortunately, impossible."

"Why should I believe that? You can't even see two feet in front of you."

Preston laughed. "I'll put my glasses back on if that gives me more credibility."

"No. I like knowing more than you for once."

"You know plenty of things that I don't." He brushed back a damp strand of hair from her forehead. "There's an Argantian saying about that, too, actually."

"Oh? What is it?"

"*Ret eo anavezout a-raok karout.* 'One must know before loving.'"

It was such a terribly *Preston* thing to say that Effy almost laughed herself. He loved nothing more than the truth, and she had loved nothing more than her imagined world. Somehow, in spite of that, they had found each other.

"You Argantians are a very poetic people after all," she said.

"As much as Llyrian propaganda would have us believe otherwise."

"You told me I was *smug*."

A smile tugged at her lips. "Well, some stereotypes have a bit of truth to them."

Preston snorted. Effy shifted closer to him. She ran one gentle finger along the crook of his elbow, just to see how he tensed and shivered. A sign of life, like tiny green shoots that grew up stubbornly out of the hard winter earth.

In her peripheral vision, she could see the locked box.

"You're right about one thing, though," she said at last. "We *will* have to leave eventually."

Preston must have heard the grief in her voice, the tremor of fear. He took her into his arms, her naked back against his naked chest, her head tucked neatly under his chin. His heartbeat sounded like the rhythm of a steady tide.

"The only reason anything matters is because it ends," he says. "I wouldn't hold you so tightly now if I thought we *could* be here forever."

"That makes me want to cry." She wished he hadn't said it.

"I know. It's not the most original argument, and I'm hardly the first scholar to make it—that the ephemerality of things is what gives them meaning. That things are only beautiful because they don't last. Full moons, flowers in bloom, you. But if any of that is evidence, I think it must be true."

"Some things are constant," Effy said. "They must be. *I* think that's why so many poets write about the sea."

"Maybe the idea of constancy is what's actually terrifying. Fear of the sea is fear of the eternal—because how can you win against something so enduring. So vast and so deep. Hm. You could write a paper arguing that, at least in the context of Myrddin's works. Well, it might have to be an entire thesis."

"Oh, stop it. You're being so relentlessly *you*."

She felt his laugh against her back, making them both tremble. "Sorry. I'll be quiet now. I'm so tired."

"Me too." Effy yawned. "But please go back to being you when I wake up. Don't go anywhere."

"You don't have to worry about that."

As inevitably as the sea rose up against the cliffs, sleep washed over them both.

FIFTEEN

I passed so many sleepless nights wondering how I could ever escape him. And yet I found the true fetters were ones of my own creation. Those nights I kept circling the same ancient questions: Why had the Fairy King chosen me? What had I done to deserve this? Those questions were powerful magic indeed, for they kept me trapped there, motionless, my husband slumbering beside me. Until I broke the spell my mind had cast, I could not ever be free.

FROM *ANGHARAD* BY EMRYS MYRDDIN, 191 AD

Effy woke in darkness, her heart clanging like a bell. Thunder rolled against the stone walls of the guesthouse, and rainwater made the windows ripple. All the candles had burned down to puddles of wax. When she sat up and spoke, her breath clouded out in front of her face.

"Preston," she said. "The storm—we have to go."

He sat up with a start, as if he'd been prodded. She watched him blink into the filmy darkness, searching for his glasses on the bedside table, as lightning turned the windows a pure, stark white. He grasped them at last and put them on.

She could feel the pulse of fear that radiated from him, a skin-prickling heat.

They both dressed in silence. Nothing could be heard over the sounds of the wind and rain, but Effy was afraid to speak anyway, afraid to voice how dire everything felt. When she couldn't stand it anymore, and when she had tied back her hair with shaking fingers, she said, "What if it's too late? What if we can't make it down?"

"We *can*," Preston said, his voice fierce. "We are *not* getting trapped here."

"I'm so stupid. I shouldn't have asked you to stay. We shouldn't have slept—"

"Effy, stop it." He reached her, took her hand. "What's done is done, and I don't regret—I would *never* regret . . . it doesn't matter. We're taking this box and we're driving down to Saltney. We'll get some locksmith to break into it, and . . ."

He trailed off as another peal of thunder reverberated through the little house. Effy glanced over at the box, chin quivering. It looked so huge and heavy, and the padlock gleamed faintly under layers of algae and rust.

Something occurred to her then, with a terrible start. "The letters. The photographs and letters. They're still up at the house."

Preston's face paled. His chest swelled and then deflated again as he drew one heavy, steeling breath. "Damn it. All right. That's fine; I'll go up and get them. You just wait in my car."

"Now you're being stupid." Lightning flashed. "I'm coming with you."

At least Preston had learned not to argue with her. They put on their coats and went to the door.

For some reason, Effy felt a pull of grief as she considered leaving the guesthouse behind. It had served her well, in her time at Hiraeth. The iron on the door had held; the four walls had not come down, even as the water trickled in. Whether he was real or not, it had kept the Fairy King at bay.

A last-minute thrill of fear compelled Effy to grab the rest of the hag stones off the desk and shove them into the pocket of her trousers.

Preston did not even appear to notice. His teeth were clenched, a muscle feathering in his jaw. When she joined him at the door again, he slid his hand into hers.

"I meant what I told you, before," he said softly. "I want to take care of you. When we get back to Caer-Isel, the horrible professors and the horrible students . . . I never want you to have to weather it all alone again."

Effy's throat tightened. "They're cruel. They'll be cruel to you, too."

"It doesn't matter. I'm not afraid to care about you, Effy."

If there had been more time, she would have folded into his arms and let him hold her there until the storm passed. Instead she only squeezed his hand. Together, they pushed open the door.

At first it seemed impossible to take a single step forward. The wind blew past them with such fury that Effy had to close her eyes and put up her hand in front of her face, and even then it felt so brutal and sharp that she thought it might chafe her skin.

The rainwater drenched her an instant, soaking through her coat. Leaves and branches were flying through the air at dizzying speeds.

Preston put his hand up, too, and he had to yell to be heard over the wind. "We have to hurry! I won't be able to drive down if it gets any worse."

Effy wondered how he would be able to drive down *now*, but it seemed too defeatist a thought to be worth speaking aloud. Fingers still locked, they charged through the storm, up the path, which was now covered over with fallen trees and which had turned, mostly, to mud.

It was only Preston's tight grip on her that kept Effy from falling down. When she had to stop because the mud was sucking desperately at her boots, he hauled her forward again and up the small incline.

But reaching the edge of the cliff was worse. From there Effy could see the sea, and the sky, almost indistinguishable in gray-white rage. Together they rose up, and then bore down on the rock, and at last Effy understood why the Southerners, in the very ancient days before the Drowning, believed that there were only two gods: the Sky and the Ocean. The land itself was just something caught and pressed between their warring furies.

She remembered, suddenly, what Rhia had told her: that the Southerners believed the Sleepers were the only thing stopping the second Drowning. That Myrddin's consecration was keeping them safe. Had she and Preston done this, somehow? Had uncovering Myrddin's lies whittled away at the magic of the Sleepers, just as Effy had initially feared it would?

Preston yanked her back as a bit of the cliff crumbled beneath her, swallowed up in an instant by the foaming mouth of the sea. Effy couldn't help but stop and watching while something else— even if it was just nameless, weatherworn stone—was lost to the ages.

Yet in the midst of the chaos, no dark figure stood in the house's shadow. Of all times, Effy thought it was now that he might come, with the seal between reality and *something else* broken.

As they stumbled up the path, Hiraeth appeared in the distance, a black bulwark against the gray sky. Maybe Ianto was right; maybe her task had not been insurmountable after all. Maybe there was some old, silent magic protecting it, something not even their discoveries could shatter.

The trees, the mountain ash—despite Ianto's best efforts— were being torn from their roots. The rowan berries were stripped off their branches and smashed into pulp. All the wards obliterated. Yet still the Fairy King did not appear.

Effy was too bewildered to know whether she should feel relief. Shingles blew off the gabled roof like birds taking flight.

Just as they reached the steps, an enormous tree went flying past them, trailing its chains. Effy staggered back, gasping, and Preston stammered out a curse.

"Saints," he said over the wind. "I'm starting to think the naturalists were right about the second Drowning."

Effy didn't mention the Southern superstitions, or the Sleepers. Her mouth had gone dry and her stomach was roiling with the same ferocity as the sea.

They clambered up the steps and through the door. Preston heaved it shut behind them, while Effy leaned back against the wall, trying to catch her breath.

"If this is a second Drowning," she said, each syllable carefully and painfully rendered, "what are we meant to do?"

Preston wiped the rainwater from his glasses. "Get out of here as quickly as we can."

There was nothing else to say. They charged upstairs as around them, the house groaned deafeningly, water bleeding through every crack in the walls and ceiling.

Some of the paintings along the stairwell had been shaken down; the glass holding the Fairy King had shattered, and he stared up at her with his colorless eyes from among the broken shards.

The frame no longer bound him. Effy felt a jolt of fear before Preston hurried her along again, beneath the archway carved with the faces of Saint Eupheme and Saint Marinell. The archway was crumbling, their wooden faces rotted. No saints to protect her now.

Your prayers are no use, the shepherd had said. *They won't protect you against him.*

The second floor was worse. The walls were drenched with water, wallpaper peeling away in long tongues of faded green. All the naked glass bulbs had broken, and the floorboards creaked beneath them with every step.

Perilously, they made their way toward the study, while half the ground behind them fell away, ancient wood finally crumpling under the weight of so much water.

"It's all right," Preston was mumbling, more to himself, Effy thought, than to her. "It's all right, it's all right . . ." He flung open the door to the study.

Ianto stood in front of Myrddin's desk. He had a length of chain thrown over his shoulder, and his musket was lying on the desk behind him. He was drenched, shirt sticking to his body, black hair dripping puddles onto the floor.

Effy froze, stomach lurching with dread.

Ianto said, very calmly, "Welcome back."

"Wh—what are you doing here?" Preston stammered out.

"*Well*," said Ianto slowly, "just last night, as I was about to crawl peaceably into bed, I got the most unexpected phone call from an old friend. Blackmar is ancient and half-demented, and at first I thought I was going to have to silently nod along to the ramblings of a toothless lunatic. But he actually began to tell me that recently he had hosted some unexpected guests, two students from the university in Caer-Isel. He said they told him that they had been working on a project centered around Emrys Myrddin, and had asked him quite a lot of suspicious questions. Specifically about the publication of *Angharad*."

Effy's legs began to go numb. Then her arms, then her whole body. She could scarcely feel Preston's fingers gripping hers.

"How curious," Ianto went on, putting one hand under his chin in an exaggerated gesture of perplexity. "Curious, curious, curious—that's what I said to Blackmar, when I told him that I was *also* playing host to two students from the university in Caer-Isel, one of whom professed an interest in my father's life and his works. I was utterly taken aback by Blackmar's insistence that these wholesome students, whom I had graciously allowed into my home, could have any nefarious intentions. I don't like to assume the worst of people, you know. But I also don't like being taken for a fool. So I decided to come over to the study myself and ask—and oddly enough, I found it empty."

His eyes. They were crisp and translucent, no more murk. They were sharp enough to cut and clear enough to see her reflection.

"I warned you away from him, Effy," he said.

"Ianto . . . ," she started, but her voice was trembling too much to go on. At its edges, her vision was rippling, fear thickening her belly.

He shifted, rattling the chains that he'd thrown over his shoulder. "Saint Acrasia is your patroness indeed. I see the mark of his mouth on your throat. Defiling yourself, and for an *Argantian*, of all people—I expected better from a good Northern girl like you."

This was the Ianto from the pub, the one who had grasped her hand and held on to it until it hurt. If there was any trace of the genial, lighthearted, hopeful Ianto, she could find none of it in his gaze.

"Please," she said. Bile was rising in her throat. "Please stop."

It was as if Ianto didn't hear her, as if she hadn't spoken at all. "And you, Preston Héloury—well. I don't know how you managed to seduce Effy into your little scheme, but now I know why you're really here. You claimed you had nothing but respect for my father, for the legacy of Emrys Myrddin." Ianto reached onto the table behind him, and Effy let out a small, strangled noise of terror, thinking he was reaching for his musket. But instead he picked up a scrap of paper. "'Execution of the Author: An Inquiry into the Authorship of the Major Works of Emrys Myrddin.' This is an assault on my father's legacy."

"It's not like that," Preston tried hoarsely. But Ianto only shook his head and held up his hand, rattling the chains again.

"I might have believed your wheedling lies, had I not found these." With a flourish, he gathered up the photographs of the girl and then dropped them, letting them flutter to the ground. Effy saw a flash of the girl's naked calf, her pale hair. "You're no better than a sleazy tabloid journalist, looking for evidence my father was leading some lascivious double life. I don't know where you got these, or where you managed to find his *diary*, but it ends here. This is my father's house. This is *my* house. And you've come here to wreck it, to ruin it—"

His words were cut off by an enormous crash of thunder, so loud that Effy winced, and a fantastic bolt of lightning that cast the entire room in a clear white light.

The house groaned miserably around them, and from somewhere far below, there was a further crashing sound: more rocks crumbling into the sea.

"Ianto," Effy said, once the thunder ceased and there was only the howling of the wind. She tried to make her voice low, pliant. What else was left but to try to reason with him? She had really thought the truth might save him, but perhaps it had not come soon enough. "Please—this house isn't going to survive the storm. We all need to leave, now."

312

"Shut up," Ianto said savagely. His pale eyes were darting back and forth between them, manic and wild. "I called the university in Caer-Isel. It took a bit of convincing, but eventually the dean's office pulled their files on both Preston Héloury and Effy—excuse me, *Euphemia*—Sayre."

It was the first time she'd heard her full name, her *true* name, in Ianto's mouth. There was another clap of thunder, and something large and black slammed against the window, hard enough to form an enormous fissure in the glass. A tree branch. Rainwater trickled in.

"It appears you were a bit of a problem for the architecture college, Euphemia," Ianto went on. "Some funny business with your adviser—you start to think that's why the university used to bar women from attending at all. They're all temptresses or blushing maidens, unfit for higher thinking."

Effy squeezed her eyes shut. "Stop it."

"Perhaps I didn't peg you right. Perhaps you're Amoret, not Acrasia. Perhaps you lay there limp as your adviser had his way—"

It was Preston who shouted then, over the sound of the wind and the thunder. "Stop it! You don't have any idea what you're talking about, you—"

"They pulled your file, too," Ianto cut in. "Preston Héloury. What an odd, in-between name. Your mother is a blue-blooded Llyrian, but your father is some Argantian mountain peasant. *Was.* It took a while, searching through all those newspaper records in Argantian, but I found the obituary. So unpleasant. I can't think of a much worse way to go, a mind decaying, bleeding water."

Preston's grip on her hand tightened. Behind his glasses, his gaze grew hard.

At last the window at Ianto's back shattered entirely, letting in the rain and wind. The shards of glass were swept up and Effy's hair blew around her face, tears stinging her eyes.

"Please," she said. If the truth could not save Ianto, perhaps burying it would at least save her and Preston. "You can keep the diary, the photographs, *everything*. We'll never write a single word about your father. Just please—we all have to go or we'll die here."

"Oh no," Ianto said. "This isn't a place for leaving. Things live and die here, but they don't leave."

Another deafening howl of wind, lightning crackling across the sky. "You're mad," Preston said.

And Ianto *did* look mad, in a way—his eyes glassy and over-bright, his wet hair sticking to his scalp and shoulders, the enormous chain rattling with every movement. But in another way, Effy could tell that what he said made sense in his own mind. There was a logic to it—a sick logic, perhaps—that someone like Preston would never understand. That only people who believed in fairy tales and magic and ghosts could see.

People like her and Ianto.

Effy remembered a ghost story her grandfather had told her once, about a prisoner who had been forgotten about and left to starve in a dungeon cell. For all the rest of the lord's life, he heard the rattling of chains at night, moving down the halls of his castle. With each passing night, the sound grew closer, until at last, one morning, the lord was found dead in his sheets, the bloody marks of strangulation around his throat like a garish ruby necklace.

If he stayed here, Ianto would become a ghost, too. Only there would be no house left to haunt.

She had to leave him here, in his madness, or she would be dragged down with him.

"Preston," Effy said urgently. "Let's go."

Hands still joined, they took a cautious step backward. But before they could flee toward the door, quick as a flash Ianto had his musket in his hands, the black mouth of the barrel staring down at them. Effy's throat went dry. She froze in place.

And then, most unexpectedly, Ianto asked, "Do you know the tale of Llyr's very first king?"

Neither of them managed to speak, but that did not deter Ianto. He took another pace toward them, musket still aimed high. His chains shook like lots being cast.

"Llyr's very first king was just a tribal chieftain who won all his wars," he said. "He had the beards of all his enemies to prove it, and he wove them together into a great cloak of hair. He had tents and huts and even houses, but when his kingdom was at last united, he wanted to build a castle. He found the best builders among his new subjects, and they began to dig a foundation. But every night when they went to sleep, they would find that the foundation was flooded with water, even though they could not remember hearing any rain.

"The king, understandably, was bewildered and vexed. Angry. But his court wizard, a very old man who had seen many tribal chieftains live and die, told the king that the land was angry with him in return. All the trees he had cut down in his quest, all the grass he had burned—why should the land allow him to build anything, when he had treated it so cruelly? The court wizard told the king that if he wanted his castle to grow tall and strong, he would have to give something back to the land. A sacrifice.

"And so the king ordered his men to go find him a child, a fatherless child. He tied the orphan boy to a stake within the foundation of his castle, and then went to sleep. When he returned in the morning, he found that indeed the water had come, and the boy had drowned, but when his builders went to repair the foundation, the next night it stood strong and dry. The castle was thus built, and to this day no storm or conqueror has been able to tear it down."

All through Ianto's speech, the wind had not ceased its wailing, and rainwater pelted his back. From somewhere down below, Effy had begun to hear creaking, crashing sounds: floorboards crumbling inexorably against the cliffside and into the sea.

"That's a myth, a legend," Preston said, voice edged with desperation. "It isn't true; it isn't *real*. But death is real, and we're going to die if we stay."

Ianto gave a low and bitter laugh. "All this time spent in the Bottom Hundred and you still don't understand. What your scientists and academics call myths are as real as anything else. How else could a land and a people survive Drowning?"

Effy shut her eyes against the stinging wind. When she first came to Hiraeth, she had believed that, too. Believed in *Angharad* and rowan berries and mountain ash and girdles of iron. But stories were devious things, things with agendas. They could cheat and steal and lie to your face. They could crumble away under your feet.

"You *are* mad," she said, opening her eyes to the barrel of the musket hovering ever closer.

"Call me mad if you like," Ianto said, and as he stepped forward, the chains rattled, "but all I see before me are a drowning foundation and two fatherless children."

The gun was jammed against her back before Effy had even made sense of his words. Preston was stammering out protests as Ianto herded them back out into the hallway, around the holes where the floorboards had at last given way, and down the stairs. Water was dripping down the ruined faces of Saint Eupheme and Saint Marinell, making it look as though they were weeping.

A torrent of water slid down the steps beside them, carrying the shattered painting of the Fairy King with it. The glass had cracked, but the painting was untarnished behind it, the features of his face still sharp and clear. It was as if the water couldn't touch him at all.

Ianto stopped them in front of the door to the basement. He shook the end of the musket as if he were giving a reproachful wag of his finger. "I noticed that my key was missing, Euphemia," he said. "You hardly needed to be so deceitful about it, you know. I would have given it up to you, for a price."

His hand grasped at her face then, cupping her chin and turning it up toward him. His eyes were cloudless, crystal clear. He held her face so tightly that it hurt, and Effy gave a quiet whimper.

"Don't touch her," Preston snarled.

Ianto let go of her roughly, fingernail scraping down her cheek and drawing blood. "I've heard quite enough from you. Smug and smarmy since the first day I let you into my home. I think this will be a fitting way to go—just like your father. A death by water."

"No!" Effy cried as Ianto swung the door open. Black water was pouring in from all the cracks in the wall, inching farther up the steps.

Without letting go of his musket, Ianto shifted the chains from his shoulder. Effy saw now that there was a stake tied to the end of them. He seized Preston by the arm, swinging him forward toward the dark water. Preston's boots scrabbled against the slick stone, hands flying out to catch himself on the threshold, but Ianto grabbed the front of his shirt and held him so he didn't fall.

Effy realized only then that he wasn't going to hurl Preston down. Instead, he began wrapping the chains around Preston's wrists.

"Stop!" Effy threw herself against Ianto's back, but she was like a small wave lapping at solid stone. He shrugged her off with a mindless twitch.

Though Preston struggled against his bindings, Ianto's grip was tight, and the musket was still aimed at his chest, barrel gleaming in the half-light.

Ianto jerked Preston by his chains down the steps, where he took the stake and drove it into the wall, then began hammering it into place with the blunt end of the musket. Time seemed to bend and slow around Effy, like river water around a rock, and there were no thoughts in her mind, nothing but the pure and brilliant surge of adrenaline in her veins.

She splashed down the stairs after them and took hold of Ianto's wrist, making him fumble with the musket and stumble backward, nearly plunging into the dark water.

"You stupid girl," Ianto growled as he righted himself. Water was pouring through the walls, between the cracks in the brickwork, like hundreds of weeping eyes. "You have no idea what you're playing at."

And then, with one huge, sweeping arm, he hurled her against the wall, so hard that her head hit the stone with a terrible crack. Effy felt the pain in her teeth and jaw, and then a hot, blooming agony seeped throughout her skull and down to her throat.

She managed to reach up with one numb hand and feel the back of her head. Her fingers came away smeared with blood.

Ianto was a large man, but not *that* large. Not large enough that two people couldn't wrest the gun from his hands. The strength he had was impossible. Inhuman.

Preston was shouting, but she couldn't hear him. She was deaf to everything but the roar of blood in her ears. Legs trembling beneath her, Effy slumped down onto the steps, submerging her lower body in the sleek, dark water.

"Please," she heard Preston say, when her hearing briefly returned to her. "I'll do anything—just let her live." His voice was shaking, syllables dropped between his sobs.

"Oh, don't worry about that," Ianto said. "The foundation only needs one fatherless child. I have no intention of letting her die."

Effy tried to pull herself back up, but the pain was obliterating. Her vision was starry and fading. She heard the sounds of the musket beating against the stake again, grim metallic clangs, and the brief rattle of chains.

And then everything but the water was silent.

He took Effy by the arm and dragged her up the steps, as if she were as light as a doll, some child's plaything. The water sloshed around them, and upstairs the house was groaning and groaning.

Effy's last glimpse of Preston was through half-shut eyes. She saw only the rusted chains around his wrists, binding him to the wall, and his gaze flashing fearfully behind his glasses.

She tried to cry out his name but couldn't, and then Ianto slammed the door shut after them.

Ianto dragged her into the dining room. Effy's vision returned in increments, enough to see that the doorway had half collapsed on their way through, splintered wood sticking out at strange angles like the branches of a stripped pine tree.

It took her a moment to realize it wasn't just the blow to her head: the entire room *was* slanted, tipping down toward the sea. The dining table had slid against the far wall, the chairs crammed up alongside it, and against all odds the glass chandelier still swung perilously overhead, like the heavy pendulum of a grandfather clock.

She was propped up in one of the moldering chairs, gaze still fuzzy. Ianto moved with graceless determination around the room, hurling furniture, flinging open cabinet doors viciously. As if he were looking for something. The musket still gleamed at his side.

"Please," Effy managed, around a mouthful of blood. "I'll do whatever—whatever you want from me. Just don't let him die, please don't let him die . . ."

She couldn't tell if Ianto heard her at all. He didn't turn around again for several moments, and when he did, there was something clutched in his fist. A crumpled piece of paper and a pencil. He thrust them at her, and in her bewilderment, Effy took them.

"Here," he snarled. "Finish the damn blueprints."

Effy just stared at him, mouth hanging open. "This house is going to fall into the sea."

Ianto laughed, and it was a terrible, rasping sound, like stone scraping against stone. "When the water fills your lover's lungs, when he turns pale and swollen with it, when his body floats like the carcass of a dead fish—this house will stand. It must."

Her heart was throbbing in her throat, hatred burning a hole in her belly. "Then why should I draw anything for you, if you're just going to let him die? I won't do it. I *won't*."

Fury rolled like dark clouds over Ianto's face. He jammed the end of the musket under her chin. "I don't want to have to kill you, Effy. You do know that, don't you? I have always wanted to keep you here. Safe from the world."

"I don't know that," Effy said. Her vision was still black at the corners. "I don't know what you mean."

Ianto gave a laugh that, this time, was remarkably soft—almost tender. "You can't really think that the most qualified person for this project was a first-year architecture student failing half of her classes. Didn't you ever question it, why the estate of Emrys Myrddin would hire a mewling little girl, with nothing to offer the world but a pretty face?"

Effy tried to reply, but her voice failed her. She managed only a small whimper.

"I didn't need to read your file, Effy." Ianto's voice grew softer now, and he lowered the musket, bringing up his hand to cup her chin instead. "I knew what sort of girl you are. I've always known. A beautiful girl, but a weak one. One that no one would miss. Who would ask after you, if you vanished from your classes, from your dorm room? You were the perfect choice for this house. For me. A girl who could so easily slip away."

Once upon a time, Effy had believed herself to be that girl. She had been terrified of anything that might hold her where she was, that might chain her where she couldn't flee. She had fashioned herself into an escape artist, a magician whose only trick was vanishing. Permanence was dangerous. It had always felt like a trap.

Only now things were different. Perhaps her classmates would not ask after her, nor her professors. Perhaps even her mother would be glad to finally be done with her. But if she did slip away, through one of those tricky little holes in the foundation of the world, Effy knew that Preston would spend the rest of his life searching for her. She could not leave him alone. She could not let him drown.

And yet—she didn't know how she could stop it.

Slowly, Effy unfolded the paper in her hand. Her fingers shook as she put the pencil to the page.

"There," Ianto said, somehow even softer than before. "That's a good girl. Build something beautiful for both of us. I don't want to wait much longer. I've spent twelve mortal years looking for you, and now, finally, you've come home."

Tears bloomed in the corners of her eyes. That old fear sensation was starting in the tips of her fingers and toes, the somatic terror that gripped her at night, that had hunted her like a dog all her life. It was the fear that her body felt before her mind could comprehend it.

"Ianto," she tried, even as she moved the pencil tremulously against the paper, "please. I don't . . ."

"No whimpering now," he said, clucking his tongue. "You're a girl, not a child."

And then there was a sudden, immense groaning sound. A wrenching rattle. Behind Ianto, the chandelier at last loosed from the ceiling and fell to the floor. In one splendid, brilliant moment, it shattered, bits of glass flying out in all directions. A shard of it cut her cheek; another lodged itself in her calf, cutting right through the nylon of her stocking.

Effy gave a quiet utterance of pain, but Ianto scarcely seemed to notice at all. The whole floor was a constellation of shattered glass, glittering like hoarfrost. Even as blood tracked down her cheek, all she could think of was Preston, downstairs, drowning.

"I can't do it," she whispered. "Please, Ianto, *please*. Just let him go."

"Love is terrible, isn't it?" Ianto said, over the sound of the churning water below. "That's why the one line became so famous.

'I will love you to ruination.' I think we all understand what it's like to be wrecked by it. Even me."

Ianto leaned close to her, so close that she could smell the salt and rot that wafted from him, the damp-earth scent of something not quite human.

His fingers gripped the back of her neck, fisting handfuls of golden hair. He jerked Effy's face toward his and pressed their lips together with such violence that it was like seawater striking stone.

Time slowed around her again. Effy sat silent and still, green vines growing around her wrists and ankles, trapping her in that chair.

She knew that if she tried hard enough, she could escape this: she could go somewhere into the deep caverns of her mind and hide until it was over, until her body was hers once again.

But Preston was downstairs. Drowning. While Ianto took her lower lip between his teeth and bit hard enough to make her bleed, Effy reached into the pocket of her trousers and found the hag stones.

When Ianto broke their kiss for just a moment, Effy crammed the stones into his face, into his mouth, with as much brutality as she could muster. He staggered backward in shock, choking on the rocks, garbling curses.

"You little whore," he spat, hag stones dropping to the floor. "You were meant to have kept yourself pure for me."

She had one last hag stone, gripped between her index finger and her thumb, in the hand that was missing its fourth finger. Trembling, Effy raised it to her eye.

The world around her rippled, as if it were a reflection on water. And then a shuddering metamorphosis took place: Where Ianto's torn white shirt had been, there was now a vest of black bramble, and under it just muscle and sinew and pale, pale skin, all wrapped around bone. His hair had grown longer, sleeker, reaching the middle of his back. His face had been handsome before, but too rugged somehow, too obviously weatherworn and human. Now it was impossibly, unreasonably beautiful, cheekbones as sharp as blades, eyes so pale they almost looked like they had no color at all, just the white and a black iris, like an eclipsed sun.

His fingers ended in claws, and he reached out to Effy with one hand, beckoning.

The shock of it nearly stopped her breathing. Effy lowered the hag stone, yet there the Fairy King still stood. He wore a coronet of bone. His hair was dripping with fetid water. She blinked and blinked and blinked, but nothing could erase him from the room.

"I really am mad," she managed, choking on the words.

"No," the Fairy King said, and his voice was the sound of shears through silk. "You are seeing truly, the way you always have, Euphemia. You were offered to me on the riverbank, and then withdrawn. I don't like to be forsaken. I have spent twelve years chasing you, but you hid yourself from me with your banal mortal tricks. No more. I come to claim what is mine by right. Once offered, a sacrifice cannot be revoked."

It could not be real. And yet Effy knew that it was—it must be. There was no escaping this. It was what her entire life had been lurching toward. She had hidden behind her pink pills, behind her saints, behind the scolding of the doctor and her mother. She had convinced herself out of it. And it had almost worked.

But here in the Bottom Hundred, in this ancient, sinking house, there was nowhere left to hide.

"Why?" she cried out, over the sound of the thrashing water below. It was the question that had plagued her more terribly than anything else. "Why me?"

The Fairy King laughed, a lovely and awful sound. "I am not as cruel a creature as all the stories say, Euphemia. I do not come for girls just because they are beautiful. You were a pretty young child, with your golden hair, but there are many pretty children, safe in their beds, who I cannot touch. I come for the girls who are left out in the cold. They cannot belong anywhere else but with me."

Somehow, her missing finger began to throb, as if she had only just remembered that the loss of it was painful. A phantom pain, eerie and old, but a pain nonetheless. Effy gripped the hag stone, even though she knew it would not save her.

"The world has not been kind to you, Euphemia," he went on, in his silk-sharp voice. "But I can be. If you obey, if you give yourself over to me entirely, I will be so kind, it will make you weep. When you were young, all I could take was your finger. Now I will have the rest."

"No," she said, even as her breath came in rough, panicked spurts. "No. I don't want to go with you."

The Fairy King cocked his head, and for a moment he looked quizzical. Almost human. "And why not? What is tying you to this insipid mortal world? Here you are just another beautiful girl who has been treated meanly. With me, you could be something so much greater. With me, you could be a queen."

Part of her had waited her entire life to hear those words, fearing them and yearning for them in equal measure. Effy let out a tremulous breath, the phantom pain of her missing ring finger still throbbing.

The belief, the hope and the terror both, had kept her alive. At last Effy understood the magic of Hiraeth, its curse and its blessing. Hiraeth Manor, the grand thing that Ianto had wanted her to build, would always be an imagined future, a castle in the air. The magic was the impossibility of it. The unreal could never disappoint you, could never harm you, could never falter under your feet.

But now the real and the unreal had snarled together and it no longer mattered which was which. Effy was staring down the Fairy King in all his immense power, and she was just a girl clutching a hollow stone.

"I'll do it if you save him," she blurted out. "Save Preston, and I'll go with you. I'll do whatever you like."

The Fairy King looked at her with a treacherous fondness. "I don't make slanted deals with mortal girls. Mortal girls make their desperate bargains with me. You have walked into my world already, Euphemia. You took the bait and sauntered right into my trap. I will have you no matter what, my darling girl. You will not elude me again. But it would make me so much happier if you took my hand and came with a lovely smile on your face."

It would have been painless. Effy knew that. If it was a kind of death, it would be much quicker than drowning, easier than falling into the sea along with this ruined house.

In some way, she had always yearned for this, to slip through the final crack in the world. But she had a rope to tether her now, and walls that stood, and a foundation that was strong.

A seed of something began to bloom in Effy's mind.

"How would you have me?" she asked carefully, trying to make her voice sound low and sweet. "Would you have me on my knees?"

The idea seemed to surprise the Fairy King, if he were a creature capable of feeling such a thing. He smiled his beautiful smile.

"Yes," he said. "It would make me very happy, to see you kneel."

Very slowly, Effy lowered herself to the ground. The broken glass dug into her knees, but she swallowed the pain of it. As the Fairy King stalked toward her, she scrabbled through the wreckage until her hands closed on a long, broad shard of glass, about the size of a small dagger.

"Euphemia," the Fairy King said, his voice a warning.

"Don't," she bit out. "Don't speak my name."

And then she held up the shard, the bit of mirrored glass that took in the Fairy King's form and reflected it right back at him.

He stared at himself for a long moment, seeing, for the first time, his own lovely face, his black hair, his bone crown. The moment felt so heavy that Effy nearly let her arm drop from the weight of it.

Just as she was about to give up, there was a second shuddering metamorphosis: in the mirror, the Fairy King changed. His beautiful face turned waxy and sallow, cheeks hollowed like porcelain bowls. His hair grew silver and brittle and then fell out.

His skin sagged around his bones, creasing with wrinkles, and in the span of seconds he became a very, very, very old man, pitiful and mortal after all.

The Fairy King opened his wizened mouth, but he could not speak a word. He crumbled away like a sandcastle on the shore, run over by the mindless tide. His eyes shriveled in his skull. Even his bone crown splintered into tiny pieces.

And then, at long last, he was nothing more than dust.

With difficulty, Effy got to her feet. She staggered over to the ruin of him, her knees aching and her stockings spotted with blood. For a final time, she raised the hag stone to her eye.

But through the hole, all was the same. The Fairy King was still ash on the wind. And Hiraeth was still crumbling around her. Effy let the stone fall from her hand, but if it made a sound, she didn't hear it. There was only her own heartbeat, her own breathing, the gentle but ceaseless reminder that she lived.

Effy let the shard drop, too, some of her blood falling along with it. Then she limped through the ruined threshold of the dining room, back to the rotted basement door.

SIXTEEN

No man escapes his primal fault,

That silent seep of black decay.

Decay is one thing, danger another, I said—laughingly.

But the wise man laughed right back at me, and said—

The sea is a thing no sword can slay.

FROM "THE MARINER'S DEMISE"

BY EMRYS MYRDDIN, 200 AD

The Fairy King was gone, but the house was still sinking, and now there was no *time*. Preston could have drowned already. The mere thought of it threatened to destroy her, the notion of his floating corpse—

But when Effy flung open the door to the basement, she saw him there, his face pale in the tepid light, his glasses flashing like two beacons.

She nearly collapsed in relief. He was drowned up to his shoulders, the walls still weeping, but he was alive. Effy stepped down into the black water and swam until she reached him. She threw her arms around him, holding on to him like a buoy, as the water eddied around them, creeping upward toward the open door.

"Effy," he gasped. "I thought you were—"

"I thought you were, too." She touched every part of him that she could reach—his cheeks and his long, narrow nose, his forehead and chin, the line of his jaw that she'd kissed last night, the throat that pulsed beneath her hand. Her head throbbed, but she paid it no mind. *Signs of life*, she thought. They could both still survive this.

Eventually, her hands wandered down his arms until she reached the manacles holding him fast to the wall. Effy grasped the chains and pulled. Preston pulled, too, desperately straining forward against his bindings, until both were breathless. The stake had not budged an inch.

Panic began to seep into her. "It won't move."

"I know." Preston's voice trembled, his breath against her cheek. "I've been pulling this whole time—I'm held fast. Effy, you have to get out of here."

She let out a low, shaky laugh, a sound that contained no humor at all. What else could she do but laugh? It was absurd.

"Don't be stupid," she said. "I'm not leaving you here. I'll find something to break the chains—"

She was interrupted by another terrible crashing noise— thunder, glass shattering, floorboards cracking? Effy couldn't tell anymore. There was so much destruction around them that it had all begun to sound the same. Plaster and dirt rained from the ceiling. The water had risen to Effy's chin.

"There isn't any time," Preston said quietly. "You need to leave."

"No." Effy locked her arms over his shoulders again, digging her fingernails in. "*No.*"

"If you don't, we're both going to die here, and what's the use in that? You can still make it down to Saltney, take the car keys out of my pocket and—"

She hated him then, well and truly hated him, for trying to be so damned *reasonable.* The Fairy King was real, which meant they were far beyond the point of reason.

And besides—there was no reasoning with the sea.

"You're not being fair," Effy choked out. "Do you really think I can just walk up these stairs and close the door behind me and *leave?* After everything . . ."

A sob drowned out the rest of her words. It had risen in her throat without her noticing, and she wasn't aware she was crying until she tasted a bitter tang in her mouth. Tears, blood, seawater— all of it tasted the same. Salt and salt and salt. Preston was now submerged to the chin.

"I wish we could have stayed there," Preston whispered into her hair. "Forever—impossibly. I'm sorry for saying all that inane nonsense about things only mattering because they don't last. That was hubris, I think. I don't want to die here. I want—"

His voice broke, and Effy was wrecked all over again. Tears rolled down his cheeks, and Effy reached up and tried to brush them away, because how could he do it when his hands were tied? She lifted his glasses and kissed his nose, then his mouth, tasting nothing but salt. Preston choked against her lips, a strangled sob wrenching itself from his chest. The water was past their chins now, leaking into their mouths.

"I love you." Effy pressed her forehead against his.

"I love you," Preston said, voice wavering. "I'm so sorry it's ruined us both."

A part of her wanted to smile, wanted to laugh, even, but if she opened her mouth, the water would pour in. She closed her eyes, then opened them again. Preston stared back at her, gaze unblinking behind his wet glasses. She wanted him to be the last thing she saw.

Yet—familiar words rose up in her mind. *If there's one thing I know, it's survival.* She had stared down the Fairy King, vanquished him at last. She could not let it end like this. If that was all she was—a survivor—she would be one until her very last breath.

Effy reached down and began to yank furiously at Preston's chains again. She pulled so hard she could feel her skin tearing, and Preston strained, too, as the water rose to the bridge of his nose. But still the stake held fast.

And then—impossibly—another pair of hands closed over hers.

I have to be dreaming, she thought. Perhaps she was already dead. Perhaps her escape had been an illusion after all. Perhaps Ianto had killed her, or the Fairy King had taken her; it didn't matter which. But she kept pulling, driven only by instinct now. Preston strained. The phantom hands pulled, too. At last, where two pairs of hands had not been enough, three sufficed, and she felt something give, the stake shifting loose from the wall.

As soon as Preston broke free, Effy grasped him, still trailing his chains, and hauled them both to the surface. When Effy had blinked the film from her eyes, she saw someone floating in the water beside them—a woman, white dress and white hair spreading out like a gauzy jellyfish caught in the surf. Her skin was pale and furrowed with age, but her hands, where they had touched Effy's, were as soft as a girl's.

Effy choked out a laugh, as all three of them staggered up the steps. How absurd, to be rescued by a ghost.

Yet if the Fairy King had been real, who was she to question it?

Everything else felt very real, from Preston's arm draped over her to the cold, slick stone against her palms and knees. Lightning flashed, illuminating the face of the ghost, wrinkled in some places but familiar, so familiar it was almost like looking into a gilt-edged mirror.

Effy had seen that face trapped in photographs, attached to a nude torso. She had thought the girl dead, erased from time, but now she stood right there before her.

As the whole house shook with the howling wind, Effy was struck by a bolt of knowledge.

"It's you," she whispered. "Angharad."

The woman who was not a ghost led them swiftly through the foyer, deftly avoiding the holes in the floor, as if she had done this a hundred times before. Her feet were bare and Effy wondered how they didn't bleed for all the splintered wood and shattered glass on the ground.

Effy and Preston limped after her, hand in hand. When they

reached the threshold, it took all three of them, sopping wet and breathing hard, to heave the door open.

The wind had its claws in them immediately. It wrenched Effy's black ribbon from her hair and nearly swiped Preston's glasses from his face. It blew up Angharad's white robe, sheer with dampness, until Effy could see her bare ankles and knees, and the blue veins pressing up from underneath her skin like striations in the cliffside. She stopped for a moment, even in the midst of the deadly gusts, just to stare.

Angharad's hair shuddered around her face. Aging, Effy realized, was the opposite of alchemy. What was now silver had once been gold.

"Come on, then," she urged them, in a fine and proper Northern accent. "We need to get to shelter."

Preston's car was still in the driveway, but leaving Hiraeth was a distant dream now. It would be impossible to drive in this storm, impossible to see through the windshield. As they clambered down the steps, Effy saw the muscle in Preston's jaw clench and unclench. His hand in hers was freezing.

"Where are we supposed to go?" he asked, voice raised over the shrieking wind and the rain that pelted them ceaselessly.

Effy knew. "The guesthouse," she said. "It will keep us."

Preston looked at her as if she were mad.

"The four walls will stand," Angharad said. "And we don't have another choice."

At the very least, Preston could recognize the logic in that. His hand gripped hers more fiercely.

There was no path now; it was all mud and sucking water. They skidded along the edge of the cliff, limbs flailing, Preston's other arm flying out to catch them both against the trunk of a tree. The mud had risen nearly to the cuffs of his trousers. Overhead branches flew like clumsily loosed arrows, aimless and deadly.

The hem of Angharad's gown was black. She said, "Don't stop walking."

Effy felt as if she'd been struck by a switch. "I won't."

They waded through the mud, through a wasteland of uprooted trees, their trunks split and their roots splayed to the air like men struck down in the heat of battle. The guesthouse was in sight now, its four stone walls seemingly unperturbed by the storm.

When at last they reached it, Angharad threw her weight against the iron-girded door and forced it open. Effy and Preston shuffled through, and Preston shut the door behind them, muffling the sound of the wind.

Effy leaned against the desk, trying desperately to catch her breath. She could not feel her legs under her. When she looked down at her hand, she saw that the tips of her fingers were blue and trembling.

And yet she could not bring herself to care. She stared at the woman in the white dress as she wrung out her hair. Water dripped from her slim body and pooled decorously on the floor.

Of all things to do, Preston had begun *pacing*. He walked back and forth between the door and the desk, stopping to look Effy up and down, and on his second trip, when he noticed Effy's blue fingers, he took both of her hands in one of his, raised them to his mouth, and blew on them.

"I won't let you lose another one," he said.

There were quite a few more pressing injuries, including the torn skin around Preston's wrists and the wound on Effy's head, but none of that seemed to matter in that moment. Effy still felt mostly numb.

"Well," Effy said at last, a bit dizzily, "when things are meant to rot, they will."

The strangeness of what she'd said made Preston's brow furrow, but Angharad's head shot up, as if she'd been called by name.

This movement seemed to alert Preston to her presence again, and he stopped blowing on Effy's fingers long enough to say, "Thank you. I—thank you."

Angharad nodded once, lips pressed thin.

"It really is you." Preston hesitated, lowering his hands, and Effy's, down from his mouth. "The mistress of the house. Myrddin's . . ."

He trailed off, and for a moment everything was silent, even the sound of the wind beating against wood and stone. It was as if the guesthouse, improbably, had been blanketed in a layer of snow.

At last, Angharad inclined her chin.

"Yes," she said. "I am Angharad Myrddin, née Blackmar. My husband has been dead for six months. My son, I imagine, has died along with his father's house. But in truth, like his father, he died months ago."

The grief in her voice was hard to bear. Effy thought of what had become of the Fairy King, now just a heap of dust and ash. Ianto had perished along with him, like wine bled out of a smashed vessel, possessor and possessed both ruined by that one shard of mirror.

Inside Preston's grasp, her numb fingers curled.

"I didn't mean to," Effy said despairingly. "I didn't mean to kill him, too, I just . . . I didn't know. Not until it was over. Well, I didn't believe myself."

To Preston it must have sounded like nonsense. But Effy knew that Angharad would understand. The older woman hugged her arms around her chest and replied, "There was nothing else to be done. As I said, my son has been dead for a long time. To become the Fairy King's vessel is to lose yourself, little by little, like water wearing away stone. Ianto fought it as best he could."

"I'm sorry," Preston said, blinking. "Do you mean to say that the Fairy King is real?"

Angharad gave him a weary look. "Northerners never understand until they see something with their own eyes. I don't blame you—I was a naive Northerner once, too, who thought that the stories were just stories and the Fairy King was nothing more than paper and ink and Southern superstition. Real magic is just cannier, better at disguising itself. The Fairy King is devious and secretive, but he *is* real. *Was*."

To hear someone else say it out loud at last—Effy's knees almost gave way under her.

"I've seen him my whole life," she whispered. "Ever since I was a little girl. No one ever believed me."

Angharad looked at her steadily. "No one believed me, either. Not about the Fairy King. Not about him using my husband and then my son as his vessels. And certainly not about the words I wrote. About my book."

"We believe you," Preston said. "We, ah, read your letters."

"Which ones? I thought Greenebough had them all burned."

"We found them under your bed," said Effy. "We went to visit your father at Penrhos—it seemed like they'd just gotten left behind somehow, gathering dust . . ."

All of this, she only now realized, was very humiliating to recount. Her cheeks heated. Angharad's wrinkled brow wrinkled further.

"Hm," she said at last. "It sounds like you two are going to be a bit of a problem for Marlowe and my father."

"Ianto tried to kill us for it," Preston said. "Or it wasn't him, I suppose, if—"

He trailed off again, appearing somewhat hopeless. Effy didn't precisely blame him for being unable to take the revelation about the Fairy King in stride. Of all the skeptics she had ever met, he was the most skeptical by far.

"My son." A look of devastation crossed Angharad's face. "He has too much of his father in him. *Had.* The Fairy King can sense weakness and wanting in men. It's like a wound, a gap that he can use to slip inside."

Effy tried not to think of Ianto in his final moments, his mouth smearing against hers so hard her jaw still throbbed. There had been another Ianto, too, one she'd seen emerge in particular moments, like a seal briefly surfacing from the water. He'd been kind to her when they first met, hopeful about the house she would never build and the future he would never see.

The best parts of him were all too familiar to her. He, too, had liked to believe in impossible things. It was not his fault that the Fairy King had used him.

"I'm sorry," Effy said, and it still felt like not nearly enough.

Angharad waved a hand, though her green eyes looked damp and overly bright. "Well," she said after a moment, "I suppose you have quite a lot of questions. Let's sit."

Angharad lit a fire with what little dry wood there was, and they all sat down on the floor in front of it. The blue death shade had receded from the tips of Effy's fingers, leaving them tender and pink. She pressed close to Preston as the wind shook the walls, rain turning the window glass marbled and opaque.

"I was eighteen when I met Emrys Myrddin," Angharad began. "I cannot say I had any idea back then that one day we would be wed, that we would have a son together, that all of this would come to pass. *This*." She laughed hollowly. "My life. Back then Emrys was just a handsome stranger, an employee of my father, and all I knew was that when I asked questions, he answered them. I could not see the Fairy King behind his eyes."

Preston leaned closer. "How old was Myrddin then?"

"Thirty-four." Angharad looked into the fire. "When I was young, I believed I had invited all that came to pass. I believed that I wanted it."

Effy's stomach lurched. "The letters we saw . . . your father wasn't happy that you and Myrddin, um . . ."

"Had an affair," Angharad said, her voice clear. "That's what we all called it then. An illicit thing, all parties equally to blame. Myrddin was unwed, but it was still terribly scandalous, to have relations with a young girl, your best friend's daughter. That was another thing no one believed—that it had all begun so innocently. I was a young girl and my father had no time for me. I wanted him to look at some of my poems, but he waved me off. He said that girls' minds were not fit for storytelling; we were too capricious and inconstant. Those were his words exactly—banal and redundant, if you ask me. That's why the only enduring work of Colin Blackmar is a dull poem children read in primary school."

It was such a shock to hear her deride her own father that Effy let out an inappropriate and too-loud laugh. "'The Dreams of a Sleeping King' really is terrible, isn't it? Why did Greenebough Books pick it up?"

"Oh, I'm sure he saw a gap in the market for rote poetry that can teach nine-year-olds about metaphor and simile. The elder Marlowe was very shrewd. I've heard no similar praises sung of his son."

"No, I expect not," Preston said. "We met him, at one of your father's parties. He was a lecherous sot."

"Well, so was my father," said Angharad, still staring into the flames. "He's too old now, I think, to be much of a philanderer, and my mother is dead, so I suppose it's not technically *philandering*, but he is vile. I'm sorry you had to meet him."

She raised her head and looked directly at Effy when she said this, green eyes hard and bright. Effy felt herself caught in that gaze, like flotsam in a sea net. Angharad's eyes were so clear, they were like twin mirrors—nothing like the murky green sea glass that the tide left strewn across the sand. Effy saw her own wavering, miniaturized reflection staring back from them. Her blond hair was a mess and her pale cheeks were splotchy with heat.

"He's not yours to apologize for," Effy said, tearing her gaze away from her own face. It had been so long, she realized, since she had seen it.

Angharad gave her a small smile. "Well. Regardless. There are three men in this story, and none of them ever said they were sorry for anything. They never expressed as much as a twinge of guilt."

"Guilt," Preston repeated. "Guilt over what?"

The fire crackled. Thunder rolled like waves against the shore. Angharad's eyes held the firelight.

"Our *affair* began slowly," she said. "At first it was nothing more than elbows brushing. The touch of a knee. Then a kiss, apologetic and rueful. Another kiss, penitent. Then another, heady and stolen and not regretted at all. Emrys feared my father's wrath, but nothing more."

Effy felt a phantom hand brush against her skull, raking its fingers through her hair. The whispers of her classmates hummed in the back of her mind, her surname scratched out on the college roster and replaced with *whore*. "Can you really call something an affair if the man is nearly twice your age and you're just, well . . ."

"A girl?" Angharad arched her brow.

"Yes." The word felt heavy in Effy's mouth.

"I was eighteen," said Angharad again. "That meant I was a woman, in some people's eyes. Well—I was a woman when it was convenient to blame me, and a girl when they wanted to use me. Everyone thought that I wanted it. I convinced myself that I wanted it, too. Emrys was always kind to me. At least, before the Fairy King took him over entirely. I suppose it was a bit of youthful rebellion on my part, too. I hated my father and wanted to spite him."

At first Effy had imagined Master Corbenic's hand, with all its rough black hair, palming her skull. Now, with a roil of nausea that made her want to retch, she imagined it was Myrddin's hand instead, grasping the back of her head and holding it like a fish he expected to try to wriggle free.

"Emrys read my poetry," Angharad went on, "and he told me what was good and what was rubbish. He encouraged me to write more; he said I had a talent. I wanted to be published, too." She gave a dry, humorless laugh. "I suppose my dream did come true, in a way."

Effy's stomach knotted with grief. Preston said, gently, "The book—*your* book—it's the most famous book in Llyrian history. Perhaps that's cold comfort. I'm sorry."

Angharad shook her head. "For a long time, I stopped even thinking of it as *my* book. It's very hard to believe something when it feels like the whole world is trying to convince you otherwise."

I know, Effy thought. And then, because she could, she said it out loud: "I know."

343

"My father despaired of me," Angharad said with a small smile. "My sisters all hated to read. They played harp and baked tarts and were eager to find husbands who worked at banks. I was the sort of girl who, in the old stories, caught the eye of the Fairy King."

Effy drew a shaking breath as Angharad said this. Even though she had seen him crumble into dust, the fear of him had not yet faded. Her body remembered what it felt like to be afraid so well that it would take time, a long time, to teach it something new.

"Emrys was the one who told me that." Angharad's smile was almost sincere now. "Back then, I didn't understand that it meant he would come for me. I was a Northern girl. The Fairy King was a legend—Southern superstition, as I said. But those words planted the seed.

"I went to the library in Laleston and read all the tomes I could find about the myth of the Fairy King. Yet I found that the stories were always about how to keep him at bay, how to hide from him: the horseshoe you could place over your door, or the necklace of rowan berries you could wear. They were about the girls he stole and how he killed them. I thought, what if there was a girl who *invited* the Fairy King to her door? Who did not weep when she was taken? Who fell in love with him?"

"So it *was* a romance," Effy said. Preston gave her a dour look.

"At first," Angharad replied. "You know, I never changed a word from the beginning of the book. I didn't want there to be any *signs*. I wanted to preserve the way I felt when I wrote it, when I thought it was going to be a romance. I wanted the audience to be convinced that they were reading a romance as well."

Effy opened her mouth to speak, but Preston was quicker. "So we were both right," he said, "in a way. It *is* a romance—until it's not."

Angharad dipped her head. "The protagonist doesn't know—and I didn't know, then—what it would all become. I wrote the first part before I knew. Before that night I spent with Emrys in his apartment. That—"

It was the first time Angharad had stopped so abruptly in her telling, and the sudden silence felt as hard and rough as a rock dropping from some great height. It was a long and unbearable silence, during which Effy's blood turned thick with despair.

The rain beat down on the roof. At last, Angharad opened her mouth again.

"I had a little hand mirror," she said, voice low now. "After we made love for the first time, we lay in bed together, and Emrys nodded off to sleep. But I felt like there was a fire in my veins, a humming in my fingers and toes, and I couldn't get myself to sleep. So I sat up and combed my hair in the mirror; what else was I going to do? I felt as bodiless as a ghost. I could not trust my own form any longer. I was there in bed beside him, and when the mirror caught Emrys's sleeping form, I saw the Fairy King behind me instead."

Effy's breath caught. Even in the recounting, decades later, Angharad's fear was so palpable and so familiar that her own stomach lurched with it. Preston's grip on her hand grew tighter.

"I didn't believe it, of course," she said. "I thought my own eyes were lying to me. How long had I been hearing that a woman's mind couldn't be trusted? I dropped the mirror in shock and it shattered all over the floor. I remembered the books I'd read at the library—how if the Fairy King saw his own reflection, it would destroy him. But Emrys was sleeping, and only I had seen the truth.

"What I had seen occupied my whole being for weeks afterward. The rest of the book flowed out of me like no story or poem ever had. I finished it in no more than a fortnight. It was a book made of my own fears and hopes, about a girl who had seen terrible things but, in the end, defeated them."

"How did Myrddin get his hands on it, then?" Preston asked. "And how did it all . . . become his?"

Angharad smiled ruefully. "I was so caught up in the world I had created inside my mind that I forgot the real one existed, for a while. I suppose that's why I became careless enough to be caught. My father found one of Emrys's letters to me. He was furious, of course. Not that he cared for *my* sake, but because it undercut his power. Like someone planting on your land without your permission, or putting up a fence around what used to be yours."

The words made Effy's blood roar in her ears, like water rushing down the cliffside. She wanted to clap her hands over them, to drown it out, but she didn't. She couldn't. All the hurt was what made it real. The hurt that transcended all the years stretched between them, tying together two different girls on two different shores, half a century apart.

"At the same time we were discovered, I was discovered. Emrys found the manuscript, newly completed, in the drawer of the desk I used when I visited him. I still don't know if it was Emrys who read it or the Fairy King. Either way, he recognized that the book could bring him money, fame. Even eternity."

"A place in the Sleeper Museum," Effy said.

Angharad nodded. "The next thing I knew, I was dragged into my father's sitting room, with my father and Emrys and Marlowe all gathered around me in their armchairs, looking solemn. Their brows wrinkled as they laid out the architecture of my future."

Architecture. The word caught at Effy like a thorn. She and Angharad had been caught in the same trap, muzzled, made silent by the brick walls built around them. "And what did they say?"

"That I had been very bad, of course." Angharad gave a thin smile. "Lying to my father, seducing his former employee and friend. What sort of licentious, depraved girl would do a thing like that? Certainly not one who could be trusted to live her own life. Certainly not one who could have believably authored a book like the one I had written."

Effy heard Preston's breathing quicken, but he didn't say a word.

"So all was decided," Angharad said, "by these three stern men in armchairs. Emrys could have me. Greenebough could have the manuscript. And Emrys could have the glory, but in exchange, my father would receive all the royalties. 'Consider it a dowry,' Marlowe said."

Now Effy understood the opulence of Penrhos, the obvious discomfort Blackmar had displayed when they had questioned him about *Angharad.* "So Emrys never earned anything from the book at all?"

"Not a penny. He, my father, and Marlowe had all done their leering calculations and figured out the worth of my book and the worth of my life. And what did I get in return? I was not turned out of my father's house, disinherited for being a loose woman. A disgrace to the Blackmar name."

"That's unbelievable." Preston huffed and shook his head. And then, realizing his error, hurriedly added, "I don't mean to say I don't believe you. Just that it's so egregiously unfair."

Angharad arched a brow and turned further toward the fire. The firelight pooled in all the crevices of her face, her crow's-feet and smile lines, the marks of passing time. Her hair, dry now, feathered lightly over her shoulders. Pure silver, save for a few enduring strands of gold.

"I never named the narrator, you know," she said. "The book is in the first person, as of course you're aware, and she's never referred to by name. The Fairy King only calls her—"

"'My darling girl,'" Effy quoted. The same thing Myrddin had called Angharad in his letters. The words felt terribly heavy.

"So the omission of the main character's name was intentional?" Preston shifted forward eagerly. "I always thought it was meant to reflect the universality of Angharad's experience, how her story reflected the stories of thousands of other girls and—sorry. I don't mean to be rude. I just have so many questions."

"I know." Angharad drew her knees to her chest, and she did look almost like a girl then, very small in her white dress. "I'll answer them. Eventually. But it's so much to remember. The weight of a memory is one thing. You get very used to swimming with it dragging you down. Once it's loosed, you hardly know what to do with your body. You don't understand its lightness."

A memory sparked in Effy's mind. "In Myrddin's letters," she said, "he mentions that Blackmar was bringing Angharad to his house. We thought he was talking about the manuscript. But really he must have meant you."

Angharad nodded. "My father delivered me to Emrys like a horse that had been bought and sold. We were married in a matter of weeks. The book came out not long after that. Marlowe decided the title."

"I thought it was just cheekiness on Myrddin's part, calling the book *she* and *her*." Preston flushed. "And I thought, initially, that Blackmar wrote it. I thought *that* was the conspiracy we were trying to uncover."

"The letters." Effy blinked, as if newly prodded from slumber. "Preston, remember? There were some strange letters, allegedly from Myrddin, only his name was spelled wrong. It's what made you think at first that they might be forgeries."

"Oh," Angharad said. "About a decade after the book was published, some intrepid reporters began sniffing around. In a fit of paranoia, Emrys burned all of his letters and ripped pages from his diary. Marlowe was even *more* paranoid, so he drafted some letters that would be proof of Emrys's authorship, if it ever came to that. It never did, of course. No one cared to look further. Until . . ."

"Until me." Preston swallowed, a muscle feathering in his jaw. "And it still took far too long. I'm sorry. Now it feels obvious, like I should have known."

"Well, you came to the answer in the end," Angharad said. "Even with the world against you—Marlowe and my father and my son, who was far too much like *his* father. I must sound as innocent as a child now. But for all my life, those three *were* my whole world."

Effy's voice wavered when she asked, "What about the Fairy King?"

"The Fairy King was all of them," said Angharad. "Every wanting man has that same wound he can use to slip in. It wasn't until we were back in the Bottom Hundred, in Hiraeth, that the Fairy King's hold over Emrys became unshakable. His power was at its peak here. Still, there were years of wondering—would the man entering the threshold be my husband, imperfect as he was, or would he be the Fairy King, cruel down to his marrow? It was almost easier when the Fairy King took him over entirely. Then I knew to expect his viciousness, and I had my little mortal tricks."

"The mountain ash, the rowan berries, the horseshoe over the door," Effy recounted, realization dawning on her. "All of that wasn't to keep the Fairy King away. It was to keep him trapped here."

That was why Ianto had so hurriedly rushed her back to Hiraeth the day they visited the pub, back to the fetters that Angharad had placed on the house, before the Fairy King could take him over entirely. Effy felt another wave of sorrow. Ianto really had been fighting the Fairy King, as best he was able.

I had to bring her *back*, she remembered Ianto saying. *Isn't that what you wanted?*

He hadn't been talking to a ghost at all. He'd been talking to the Fairy King, to the voice inside his own head, invisible and inaudible to anyone else. And he'd been talking about Effy: the Fairy King could not allow Ianto to let her slip from his grasp.

"Emrys—or the Fairy King—smashed all the mirrors," Angharad said. "And of course forbade me from buying new ones. His power was enough to keep me here, and my mortal trickery was enough to keep *him* here. When my husband died, I thought I might at last be free of him. But the Fairy King found a new vessel. My son."

Grief entered Angharad's voice again, like the sea flooding a tide pool.

"I'm so sorry," Preston said again. "For that . . . and for everything you've endured."

Angharad's smile was sad and gentle. "I'm sorry, too. For what my son did, for what the Fairy King did, for what I couldn't stop them from doing. He did fight, you know—Ianto. He could loosen the Fairy King's bonds sometimes, long enough to leave the house, but eventually, always, the Fairy King would begin to take over again and Ianto would have to hurry back. To trap him here again, in my little web, in my orchard of mountain ash."

Ianto had driven up the cliffs in such a vicious hurry, even as he had been losing the battle. She *had* seen the Fairy King in the car beside her. It had not been her imagination, a hallucination. The pink pills could not have stopped him—and neither, in the end, could Ianto.

"I could tell he was fighting it," Effy said. "He wasn't entirely a monster."

351

Angharad lowered her gaze. "There were times, I confess, that I could have gotten my hands on a mirror. Yet I knew I could not bring myself to use it against my own son, even as I saw the Fairy King's hold on him grow more complete with every passing day. I invited you here, Preston, in hopes that you might uncover the truth. But you . . ." She turned toward Effy, eyes dim. "The Fairy King wanted a bride, and I didn't know how to keep you safe from him."

"The guesthouse," Effy realized, and it seemed almost a silly thing now, with the storm battering the walls and the embers burning with their waning light. "You did protect me. You ordered Ianto to have me stay here."

Angharad appeared almost bashful. "I thought you might take it as an offense. I wasn't sure it would be enough to keep you safe—but still, it was something."

It had not been Myrddin protecting her as Effy had initially thought; he had not put the iron on the door. It had been Angharad this whole time—everything had been Angharad.

Effy felt tears prick at her eyes. Just as Angharad had said, she felt like some enormous weight had been lifted, and the lightness of her limbs was unfamiliar. Like the buoyancy of water. "Thank you."

"There's nothing to thank me for." Angharad turned to Effy now, green gaze meeting green gaze. "I had decades to learn."

"It's not just that," Effy said. "You have no idea—I've read your book a hundred times, maybe more. It was a friend when I didn't have any. It was the only thing that said I was sane when the whole world was telling me I was mad. It saved me in more ways than I can count. Because I knew no matter how afraid I felt, I wasn't truly alone."

Angharad's eyes were shining now, too. "That's all I wanted, you know," she said. "When I was young—when I was your age. I wanted just one girl, only one, to read my book and feel that she was understood, and I would be understood in return. Writing that book was like shining a beacon from a lighthouse, I suppose. Are there any ships on the horizon? Will they signal back to me? I never got the chance to know. My husband's name was all over it, and his was the only ship I could see."

"I saw it," Effy whispered. "I see it. And it saved me."

"Well," Angharad said, "you saved me, too. The Fairy King is gone. No matter what happens now, I'm free."

Tears were falling down Effy's cheeks, and even though she tried, she couldn't stanch them. The warmth in her chest spread through her blood, all the way to her fingers and toes. Her missing ring finger didn't ache anymore. That phantom, too, had been banished.

"I'm so sorry," Preston said quietly, "but we couldn't get it in time—Myrddin's diary, the letters. The, uh, photographs." His cheeks reddened. "The two of us know the truth, but the rest of it has been lost with the house."

"You found Emrys's diary?" Angharad's voice tipped up in disbelief. "My son didn't know that secret room was there. The Fairy King might have, but I put iron on the back of the wardrobe, so he couldn't get at it even if he wanted to. How did you find it?"

Preston glanced over at Effy, with a look of great admiration and affection. "She's very clever, this one. Effy."

"Effy," Angharad repeated. It was the first time she had spoken Effy's name. "I cannot begin to explain how grateful I am for all that you've done for me. Both of you. It's enough, I think, to be free from this house. And to have even two people who know the truth."

But Effy just wiped her eyes, feeling wretched. Feeling *angry*. It was an uncommon feeling, unexpected. Her weightless limbs suddenly strengthened, as if filled with purpose.

It was not enough. Not enough to justify a life spent in obscurity and repression, a girl and then a woman and then a ghost, alone in that ruined house, tormented endlessly by the Fairy King. It wasn't fair, and Effy could not bear it. She would shout the truth to the world, even if it was only her voice, and even if it turned her throat raw. She could not bear to be silent any longer.

And she would not return to Caer-Isel only to lower her gaze to the ground every time a classmate snickered at her, every time she saw Master Corbenic in the hall.

She would not go back to that green chair.

As Effy's gaze traveled across the room, it landed on something she had forgotten about until now.

She lurched to her feet, so abruptly that Preston looked frightened and startled, and Angharad blinked in bewilderment. Heart beating fast, Effy grabbed the heavy box from the desk and brought it over to them, its enormous padlock thumping.

"We have this," she said, a little breathless from the effort. "We couldn't open it, of course, but . . ."

Angharad looked up at her, eyes wide and disbelieving. "How?" she managed. "I thought it had been lost, drowned . . . that silly line. Emrys did write that one, sort of. He wrote all his poetry, more or less, at least when he was *himself*. It was after an argument we had, when my husband was still my husband some of the time. I wanted us to move, before the Fairy King took his body back, but Emrys was as deluded as his possessor, driven mad by those cycles of possession. He said there was something *important* about living in Hiraeth, no matter how close it was to ruin. I snapped at him, 'Well, everything that's ancient must decay.' 'You can't fight time,' I must have said. And Emrys snapped back, 'It's not time I'm worried about, darling girl. The only enemy is the sea.' How did you manage to recover it?"

Effy and Preston looked at each other. At last Preston said, "Brave, too. Brave and clever, Effy Sayre."

"I can see that," said Angharad. Very slowly, she drew her hands up to her throat. She pushed her hair back over her shoulder and dipped her fingers below the collar of her gown. After a few moments, she produced a thin chain and, at the end of it, a key.

The key slipped into the lock like a sword at last returning to its sheath. Effy saw a little leather-bound book tucked inside, and yellowed letters wrapped in twine. She saw Angharad's decorous script, her name and Myrddin's bracketing every page. His at the top (*dear*), hers at the bottom (*yours*); him beginning, her ending.

But Effy also saw that the top of the box had been fitted with a mirror, and in that mirror she watched her own lips parting, her lashes fluttering, her golden hair curling in the firelight. She saw her face there beside Angharad's, and right above the old letters, past and present and future all coiled into one moment that felt as tight and tense as a held breath.

Effy reached up and felt her own face, watching her movements in the mirror. She traced the bridge of her nose, trailed gently along the planes of her cheeks and the line of her jaw. The numbness had receded, and warmth radiated from her skin.

Signs of life, as her muscles twitched and jumped at the feather-light touch. Signs of life, everywhere.

SEVENTEEN

What wisdom do you want from a death-marked girl? I can say only this: In the end I learned that the water was in me. It was a ghost that could not be exorcised. But a guest, even uninvited, must be attended to. You make up a bed for them. You pour from your best bottle of wine. If you can learn to love that which despises you, that which terrifies you, you can dance on the shore and play in the waves again, like you did when you were young. Before the ocean is friend or foe, it simply is. And so are you.

FROM *ANGHARAD* BY ANGHARAD MYRDDIN
(NÉE BLACKMAR), 191 AD

It took some time, of course, for Effy and Preston to compile and index the letters, to copy the pages of Angharad's diary using the wheezing mimeograph in Laleston, and for Preston to write it all up on the old typewriter that Laleston's chief librarian grudgingly permitted them to use. They had spent two weeks in Laleston, and had now been away from Caer-Isel more than a month.

Preston had a cigarette in his mouth while he worked, smoke curling out the window of their hotel room. Sometimes he got up to pace, mussing his already mussed hair, muttering about omniscient narration and melodrama. Effy understood all the theory only vaguely, but she offered insight where she could.

She felt, as did Preston, that she understood *Angharad* on a level that was almost inarticulable: it was as primal and unconscious as her lungs pumping and her heart beating.

"Why don't you take a break?" Effy offered as she perched on the edge of the hotel bed, mug of coffee in hand. "I can write for a while."

"You don't have to." He had told her, at the beginning, that he thought it might be difficult for her. To read all the words, to write in such a stilted, formal manner about a life that so neatly mirrored her own.

"I want to," Effy said. She handed him her coffee. "I want it to be finished. I want it all to be done."

What she meant was that she wanted it all tied up neatly. No more questions, no more doubting. No more scolding about how what she knew and what she believed weren't real.

Preston frowned. "I don't think scholarship is ever really *done*," he said. "If anything, this is only the beginning. Academics and tabloid journalists alike are going to be hounding us, hounding *her*. There are going to be a hundred papers, even books, arguing against our thesis. Not to mention the Sleeper Museum . . . are you ready for all that?"

It didn't make her happy. But Effy knew he was right.

She nodded as she slipped into the seat he had vacated. "Yes," she said. "Let's just get it all down." Seeing the look of alarm on

Preston's face, she added, "Not *all* of it. But the parts the academics will believe."

If she and Preston published a paper arguing for the literal existence of the Fairy King, they would be laughed out of the university. Effy accepted that. It was enough—for now—that she and Angharad knew the truth.

And of course, though she had seen the Fairy King, Preston had not. Effy knew he believed her, in his own way, in a way that didn't compromise his cynicism. She wasn't exactly sure how he made sense of it in his head. There was plenty to believe in—Ianto's possession, the details in Angharad's diary—but there was plenty to doubt, as well. Ianto's demise *could* have been ordinary. And Effy had never heard the bells. There was a small prickle of grief when she thought about it, how perhaps she and Preston would never *quite* see eye to eye.

But he believed her fear, her grief, her desire. That had to be enough.

Two weeks later, they had a finished draft. The title page bore both of their names in bold, unequivocal black lettering: *Euphemia Sayre and Preston Héloury*. Her true name, stark against the white paper. If there was anything to attach her true name to, it was this. Her true name held so much sorrow and suffering, but it also held strength. Hope. The yearning to make the old saint's name mean something new.

Effy picked the title. *Uncovering Angharad: An Inquiry into the Authorship of Major Works Attributed to Emrys Myrddin.*

❧

Angharad had rented an apartment nearby in Laleston, with flowers in the window boxes and a view of the bustling street below. From every room you could hear horns blaring and cars braking, people shouting. It was not a quiet apartment. Effy sensed that Angharad had known enough silence to last the rest of her life.

She and Effy sat together, right by the large windows that let in the deep golden light of late afternoon. Angharad's silver hair had been cut; it was no longer the gossamer, slightly wild locks of a young maiden. It was a bit severe, the cut, like that of a schoolteacher or a governess, someone with quiet authority. Effy liked it.

"Preston says that they'll come to you," she said. "As soon as our thesis is out there—reporters and scholars will start hounding you."

"Let them come. I have spent long enough being silent."

"They'll press you. They could be cruel."

"I have nothing to hide," she said. "And who do I have left to embarrass? My son is dead. My father will be soon. My sisters and I haven't spoken in decades. There's no story to memorize, no lines that need repeating. There's only the truth."

The truth. Effy nodded. In the street below, a cart rattled past, wheels knocking against the pavement. "And what about Marlowe? Preston says he may try to sue . . ."

"He can try. Greenebough has nothing left to take from me. And I never signed anything; only Emrys did. The secret was so precious that there was no contract, no paper trail, nothing bearing my name."

Someone shouted in the road. "Have you set your accounts in order?" Effy asked.

"Wetherell has," Angharad replied. "Marlowe still owes me royalties from Emrys's other works. That's in my husband's will. You don't have to worry so much about me, Effy. I know I'm an old woman now, but I'm not looking for *peace*. I've spent my whole life fighting, even if no one knew about it. The daily battles I waged in the privacy of that house, making sure the mountain ash was blooming and the iron on the doors held fast . . . if I can survive that, I can survive journalists and academics."

"I wish I had fought." Effy surprised herself by saying it. The words had leaped out of her throat, unbidden. "I know I beat him in the end, but for so many years all I could do was run and hide. I just sat there and let the water pour in around me. I didn't know that I could fight back. I didn't know how to do anything but wait to drown."

"Oh no, Effy. That's not what I meant at all. You don't have to take up a sword. Survival is bravery, too."

As if she could tell Effy was going to cry, Angharad laid a soft hand over hers. Effy wiped at a few burgeoning tears and said, "There's something else."

Angharad arched a brow, and Effy reached into her bag. She pulled out her old and battered copy of the book, its pages dog-eared and water-stained, its spine cracked from so many openings.

The cover still bore that dead man's name, but Effy opened the book to the page that held the first line.

I was a girl when he came for me, beautiful and treacherous, and I was a crown of pale gold in his black hair.

Effy held it out to her. "Will you sign it for me?"

Without words, Angharad took it. She scrawled her name forcefully on the page in black ink. When she was finished, she said in a low voice, almost like a confession, "I've waited so long to do that."

"This way I'll always remember," Effy said. "I'll always know. A lighthouse, like you said."

"I know you have to leave now," Angharad said, dabbing at her face. "But Effy, you can always come back. It's safe here. I'm growing rowan berries in the window boxes. You know what they say about old habits."

They both cried a little together, after that. Angharad's green eyes were shining and bright. Like two lighthouse beacons stretching over dark water, telling her there was safe harbor ahead.

There was so much to *do* when at last they returned to Caer-Isel. Preston fretted a bit over all the coursework he had missed, but Effy had no such concerns. Her life in Caer-Isel had been so small, so wretched and run-down, it had been easy to slip through the cracks. She had left it all behind so quickly, escaped through its crumbling walls.

Now she wanted to tear it down to the foundation. She wanted to start anew.

Rhia performed exaggerated shock when she saw Effy, even mimed swooning. "Thank the Saints," she said. "You're back now. I thought you might've turned into a fish after all."

"No gills or fins," Effy said. "But you were right about the Bottom Hundred. It's a strange place. It changes you in other ways."

Rhia frowned, looking her up and down. "You do seem differ-ent. I can't put my finger on it. Maybe it's your hair. No offense, but have you brushed it at all since you left?"

"Barely," Effy said with a small smile.

"Well, since you didn't have the decency to *call*, I'm going to have to throw together a very last-minute welcome-home party. It won't be up to my usual standards. I apologize in advance."

"Oh no," said Effy.

"Oh yes," said Rhia.

Effy set her trunk on the floor and hung up her coat. "And how are the spiders?"

Rhia let out a long, exhausted breath. "The war is at a stale-mate, for now. Thank the Saints. Generations have lived and died in your absence."

Effy laughed. She began the work of unpacking, as Rhia went on about all that she had missed. Effy rolled up her thick sweaters and woolen socks and stuffed them in the drawer, letting Rhia's voice fade a little into the background. She touched her copy of *Angharad*, gently running her fingers over the well-worn spine.

Then she tucked it under her pillow. Old habits.

"Hey," Effy said. "Can I invite someone to the party?"

Rhia's brows shot up. "But of course. Who is it?"

"He's someone you've never met before. I think you'll like him, though." Effy paused, considering. "He's a bit smug, until you get to know him. Very pedantic. Very smart."

"Well, you're painting quite a picture." Rhia flopped onto Effy's bed, a scheming smile on her face. "I can't wait to torment him."

Effy could easily imagine it. "Be careful. He's a very stubborn arguer."

After that, it was another week before Effy and Preston were able to present their thesis to the dean. Effy had only met Dean Fogg once, when he'd given her permission to go to Hiraeth, and he had not changed at all in the weeks since. He was a narrow man with blindingly white hair and no smile lines. His expansive office had a sitting area with five armchairs gathered around a coffee table, and his assistant served them tea and biscuits in clinking silver dishes.

Master Gosse, Preston's adviser, was also present. He was Dean Fogg's opposite in many respects: short and broad where the dean was tall and thin, with an ebullient mustache and maniacally curling black hair. He stood rather than sat, and refused the tea and biscuits. His dark eyes were leaping swiftly from one thing to the next, like a kitten following a stuffed bird on a stick.

The first few moments progressed in silence. Dean Fogg sipped his tea. He held a copy of their thesis on his lap. Preston bounced his leg, an anxious tic, and Effy's fingers curled and uncurled against her thigh. Master Gosse paced, a bit Preston-like. His brisk footsteps against the wood floor were the only sound in the room.

At last, Dean Fogg set down his teacup and said, "I think it's rather good."

Effy almost let out a highly inappropriate laugh of relief. She clapped a hand over her mouth to stop it from coming out, while Preston said, "I know the theory and criticism sections could use some work. We could have cited more sources, delved deeper into alternative theories. But as a whole, do you think the argument is there?"

"Well, there's certainly an *argument*. And, of course, you've furnished it with evidence that no other academic has any access to, presently . . . this diary and these letters. I suspect there's quite a bit more than what made it into your paper. But it won't mean much until they're widely released."

"What?" Effy managed. "What do you mean, 'widely released'?"

"Any thesis needs to be *vetted*, my dear," Master Gosse said. He had stopped pacing. "You can make an argument based on your interpretation of the evidence, but if no one else has read the evidence—well, it's just mythmaking, at that point. No one has any reason to believe you."

Preston nodded. "I know it seems a bit counterintuitive. But we'll have to give everyone else a chance to read the letters and the diary before we can prove our thesis is correct."

Effy glanced over at the chair beside her, the empty fifth seat in the office. It felt *conspicuously* empty. It felt as though it should have been occupied by Angharad. She remembered Angharad's fixed determination when she had spoken of these potential inquiries. If she were here, she would say again: *Let them come.*

"So let's say we do release it all," Effy said slowly. "We're going to war with every other academic, aren't we?"

"Oh, not just academics," Master Gosse said. "Tabloid journalists, the Sleeper Museum, the Myrddin estate, Greenebough Publishing . . . they all have a vested interest in preserving Myrddin's legacy. The Southerners will riot, which will cause the Llyrian government to go into a panicked frenzy. Personally, I expect them to sue the university. They might even sue *you*."

Preston made a nervous sound. Dean Fogg frowned. "The university has ample legal counsel," he said. "But this mention of 'we' perturbs me, Euphemia. You are not, to be blunt, an *academic*. You are not a literary scholar. You are a first-year architecture student—"

"With all due respect, sir," Preston cut in, "this paper is as much Effy's as it is mine. It couldn't have been written without her. We wouldn't have found the diary or letters if not for her. And she's more brilliant than any of my colleagues at the literature college, so if you're planning on trying to leave her out of this somehow, I'm more than happy to take *my* paper elsewhere. To a tabloid journalist, perhaps?"

Dean Fogg's thin lips thinned further. "You make a very sorry scholar yourself, Mr. Héloury, if you would leave this discovery to a newspaper gossip column."

"It's not my first choice," said Preston, "or else we would be in the offices of the *Llyrian Times* right now instead, meeting with their editor in chief. But if you object to Effy's inclusion, well, that's just what I'll have to do."

Effy gave him a grateful smile as she rubbed the abrupt end of her ring finger.

"You've always been such a stubborn lad." Master Gosse looked amused. "I never thought you would try and *extort* the university, though. Good on you." He seemed to mean it genuinely.

Dean Fogg gave a disgusted snort. "How do you think it will

look for the university to publish a groundbreaking thesis with a *woman's* name on the cover sheet? There's never been a woman at the literature college before. It's unprecedented."

"It's an absurd, archaic precedent," Preston said. "It should embarrass the university."

"Watch yourself, Héloury," Dean Fogg said.

Effy looked around the room again. Angharad had been here before: three men arguing over her work, laying a framework for her future. She had been silenced then.

But Effy would not be silent now.

"This thesis is a story about a young woman who was taken advantage of by powerful men," she said. "She was bartered like a head of cattle, traded by men who tried to claim her work as their own. How do you think it will look for the university to do precisely the same thing? If we do hand over the thesis, and you publish it without my name, I'll go straight to the offices of the *Llyrian Times* and tell them yet another story about men using young women. If that's the sort of legacy you want for yourself as dean."

It was impressive how quickly Dean Fogg's face turned red, then purple. Effy had determined, upon further inspection, that the thick white hair was in fact a wig, and in his shock it slipped incrementally to one side.

He took a decorous sip of tea, as if to calm himself, and then said, "So you would have me admit you as a student of the literature college? There's no other way to justify it, the name of some obscure architecture student on the title page."

Effy's breath caught a little bit in her throat, but after a moment she was able to answer. "Yes," she said. "I'll be the first woman in the literature college, but not the last."

Dean Fogg nearly choked on his tea, but Master Gosse gave a delighted chortle. "Oh, I like this," he said. "The university will finally be catching up to the times . . . and it will make a good story, won't it? A story in which the university is a beacon of progressivism, and its dean a fierce but benevolent advocate for the rights of women."

Yet something stuck in Effy like a splinter. Her mouth had gone dry, and she had to swallow hard before she could manage to speak.

"You can't tell the story unless you fire him," she said, voice wavering.

"Fire *who?*" Dean Fogg demanded.

She drew a breath. "Master Corbenic."

And then Dean Fogg *laughed*, a hacking sound of disbelief. "Now, you listen to me, Euphemia," he said. "Master Corbenic is a tenured professor. He's esteemed in his field, and a personal friend of mine. If you think we're going to fire him at your behest, because of some schoolgirl's grudge—"

"'Some schoolgirl'?" Effy's voice suddenly became hard, her blood running hot in her veins. She had just interrupted the dean of the whole university, but she didn't even care. "That's all Angharad was, too. A girl. Unless you fire him, you'll never see a page of these letters."

There was a long silence, during which Effy's heart pounded so loudly she could scarcely hear anything else, and during which

Master Gosse looked quickly and eagerly between the two of them, as if waiting to see who would flinch first.

Preston's jaw was set, his hand moving to grip the edge of her armchair.

It was too late to save Angharad. Perhaps it was too late to save herself. But it was not too late for another girl who might wander into Master Corbenic's office and sit down obliviously in that green chair.

"I will consider it," Dean Fogg said at last, every word wrenched out through gritted teeth. "We have a great deal more to discuss, as it is. If it puts your mind at ease, once you are officially enrolled at the literature college, you will never have to see Master Corbenic again."

Once upon a time, she would have taken that as enough of a victory. She would have left, escaped that awful stuffy room and just hoped that she would never have to catch a glimpse of Master Corbenic in the halls. But that could not be guaranteed, and she was not going to enter any more slippery, slanted bargains with men who believed themselves to be beyond burden or blame.

Effy got to her feet. She had done enough sitting.

"No," she said. "It's not enough. And I'm not bluffing. If you don't fire him, I'll tell the whole country. I'll tell the whole world."

Dean Fogg just stared at her, his eyes turned to angry slits. A mere month ago she would have shrunk under his gaze, her mind slipping out of her and her body following, fleeing the room as quickly as she could.

But she had faced down the Fairy King in all his eldritch power.

She had made him crumble into a handful of dust. This battle was easy by comparison.

"All right," he said. His voice was a low snarl. "I'll acquiesce to your terms, ludicrous as they are."

Master Gosse chuckled. "I enjoy this girl, Fogg. I look forward to instructing her."

Preston stood then, too. "We'll have to speak about a publication schedule, make revisions. And of course sign the papers to transfer Effy from architecture to literature."

"Of course," Dean Fogg said sourly. "My office will be in touch. Now, both of you, get out of my sight."

Effy kept her lips pressed shut until they had left the dean's office, gone down the hallway, and burst from the building into the cool afternoon. Everything was bright, drenched in sunlight, making Preston squint behind his glasses as he looked at her.

There was a wonderful tightness building in her chest, and at last it bubbled out in a laugh.

"We did it," she said. "We really did it."

The promise he had made to her all those weeks ago, that they would write a paper that gained her admittance to the literature college, that he would stare down Dean Fogg and fight for her, had finally been fulfilled. It was the foundation upon which Effy could build a new life.

And then, unexpectedly, Preston pulled her into an embrace and lifted her into the air. He spun her around for a brief moment before putting her down again, his cheeks flushed, looking bashful.

Effy laughed again. "I thought you weren't a romantic."

"I wasn't," Preston said, cheeks still pink. "Until you."

Now he was making *her* blush. Effy cupped his face. "I think we should celebrate."

When they arrived back at Effy's dormitory, she realized Rhia had been underselling herself. For a last-minute party, there was an impressive selection of liquor, an impressive number of guests, and even a hand-lettered *WELCOME HOME* sign that had been stuck to the wall using hairpins and a bit of thread.

Rhia dragged Effy and Preston into the center of the kitchen and immediately barraged him with questions. Effy could only watch in quiet amusement as he stumbled to answer them. This was not the kind of test that any amount of studying or natural intellect could help him pass.

Rhia had borrowed (*stolen*, she confessed, after two rounds of drinks) a record player from the music faculty. It turned on and on, needle wearing very gently against the vinyl. When a slow song came on, Preston took Effy's hand. They danced (which was mostly just swaying, as Preston, too, was several drinks deep), her head on his shoulder. When the song ended, she felt only a twinge of grief.

Then Preston encountered a fellow literature student, and Effy saw him truly in his element for the first time. He was more patient than she remembered him being, when they'd met that day on the cliffs. Even as the other student argued that "The Dreams of a Sleeping King" was unfairly maligned, Preston listened, and made his counterarguments without a trace of smugness.

All around her Effy could feel walls coming up, rising out of the earth like a tree from its roots. But they didn't feel stifling. The architecture of her new life was taking shape, and there were windows and doors. She did not need to slip through cracks in order to escape. If she wanted to leave, she could. If she wanted to stay, there were repairs that could be made. The foundation would be strong. Effy was sure of that.

After several hours, Preston brought her back to his dorm room.

As soon as they arrived, he fell into bed without even taking his shoes off. Effy lay beside him, eyelids heavy. Moonlight was streaming through the window, as clear and bright as the beacon of a lighthouse.

Nighttime was still scary. Ordinarily it was when the Fairy King would appear as a vague, dark shape in the corner of her room, his pale hands reaching, his bone crown gleaming. If she did manage to sleep, Master Corbenic waited for her there: the glint of his gold watch and the enormity of his hands. And now her dreams were lurid with images of drowning houses, of the thrashing, uncaring sea.

And the Fairy King, always the Fairy King, in Ianto's body or his own. She had defeated him in Hiraeth, but would he ever be gone for good? When she closed her eyes, she could still see him. His ghost lingered—or at least, the grief and fear did.

Preston shifted in his sleep, arms circling her waist. His heart thudded softly against her back, with a rhythm as constant as the tide. The walls here were strong. They would hold against anything. There was no need for iron, for rowan berries, for mountain ash.

The danger was real. Effy and Angharad had both proven that, with their wits and their mirrors. The danger lived with her; perhaps it had been *born* with her, if the rest of the stories about changeling children were to be believed. The danger was as ancient as the world. But if fairies and monsters were real, so were the women who defeated them.

Effy did not have her copy of *Angharad* under the pillow, but she thought of its last lines, which she knew by heart.

I know you think I am a little girl, and what could a little girl know about eternity? But I do know this: whether you survive the ocean or you don't, whether you are lost or whether the waves deliver you back to the shore—every story is told in the language of water, in tongues of salt and foam. And the sea, the sea, it whispers the secret of how all things end.

At first the morning was a bit miserable, both of them groggy and Preston nursing a headache. The sun was too bright on their faces. Effy pulled a pillow over her head and groaned as Preston tried to urge her out of bed.

"Coffee," he reminded her in a lofty, plying voice, and at last she threw off the covers, blond hair plastered to the side of her face.

Coffee was a necessity. They went to the Drowsy Poet and got paper cups, holding them in two hands as they walked down the street along Lake Bala, breath coming in white clouds. It was very cold that morning, but the sunlight was strong, and some of the ice on the lake had melted, veins of blue water showing between the cracks.

Effy tugged her gray coat around herself, the wind raking through her hair. She had forgotten her ribbon, or perhaps it had gotten lost somewhere over the course of the night. They paused at one of the lookouts, leaning over the railing to watch the sluggish tide moving ice along the surface of the lake.

Behind them, the white stone buildings of the university cast broad shadows, as huge as the Argantian mountains on the other side.

Looking at Preston's homeland across the water made her think of something. "Have you told your mother everything?"

"I called her yesterday, before we went out. She was happy for me, of course, but I think secretly she was a bit glum. She was a fan of Myrddin, too. Even though she lives in Argant, she's still Llyrian at heart."

Right when they'd gotten back to Caer-Isel, Effy had gone to the Sleeper Museum. She told no one about it, not even Preston. She took one of the brochures and walked around the crypt, passing by the other Sleepers, wizened men whose alleged magic kept their bodies from decaying.

At last she had come to Myrddin's glass coffin, and stared at his slumbering face.

It was the first time she had seen it. It was a long and slender face, rather unremarkable, marred by wrinkles and age spots. When their thesis went to print, Effy had wondered, would the magic vanish with it? Would the museum close off the exhibit in shame, would the curators meet in their smoke-filled rooms and decide, grimacing, to remove his body?

Even after everything, the thought had filled her with grief. The truth was very costly at times. How terrible, to navigate the world without a story to comfort you.

But Effy had learned. Or at least, she was trying to. Better to pen a story of your own. Better to build your own house, with a foundation that was strong, with windows that let in plenty of light.

At least some people, she figured, would always be convinced that Emrys Myrddin had written *Angharad*. Effy had left the crypt behind, slipping out within a crowd of other visitors, and threw the brochure in a rubbish bin outside.

Now, Effy blinked into the wind, the memory leaving her as Preston's face came back into focus.

"I still think his poetry has some merit," she said. "'The Mariner's Demise,' at least."

"Oh, certainly," Preston said. "He wasn't a terrible writer, even after all this. I don't know exactly what his legacy will be. Maybe when we're dead, some other scholars will come along and rehabilitate his image."

Rehabilitate meant literally to make something livable again. As if Myrddin's legacy were an old house that they were trying to tear down.

They hadn't gone to look at the ruin of Hiraeth, but Effy could imagine it as easily as she had once imagined the beautiful manor it could have been. The wreck of wood and stone along the cliffside, the furniture smashed against the rocks, the gabled roof rent in two, its shingles flung off into the distance. And, of course, the sea, swallowing everything it could reach.

"I can't decide if I want that." Effy chewed her lip. "I don't know if I want him to be forgotten in obscure shame, or for his works to still be appreciated for what they were. The real ones, that is. A part of me still loves him, I think. The *idea* of him."

Preston gave her a small smile. "That's all right," he said. "You don't have to know. For what it's worth, I've stopped believing in objective truth."

Effy laughed softly. "So all this has left its mark on you, too."

"Of course it has. You have." The wind tousled his already tousled hair, and as he pushed his glasses up the bridge of his nose, Effy was suddenly overwhelmed by affection. A sign of life: tender, almost anguished, but real. "There's something I've been wanting to ask you."

Just as suddenly, her stomach lurched. "What is it?"

"Oh, it's nothing important," he said quickly. "Don't look like that. For a while I didn't know if it was worth mentioning at all . . . it's the strangest thing, really. Maybe just my imagination. When we were at Hiraeth, and I was sleeping in Myrddin's study, some mornings I would wake up to the sound of bells outside the window. They sounded like church bells, but of course the nearest church is miles away, in Saltney. Once or twice I even went outside to investigate, but I never saw anything. The sound was coming from down the cliffs, which is impossible, I know. But I just wanted to ask, to be sure. Did you ever hear them, too?"

ACKNOWLEDGMENTS

Thank you to my lifesaving, miracle-performing agent, Sarah Landis: every step I've taken on this journey has been lighter with you by my side. Thank you to my brilliant, insightful, and compassionate editor, Stephanie Stein: you have helped me tell the best version of this story. Thank you to Sam Bradbury, my fairy godmother across the pond: three down and hopefully many more to come.

Thank you to Sophie Schmidt, editorial assistant extraordinaire, and to the rest of the team at Harper for helping to bring this book into the world. Thank you to Katie Boni, Sabrina Abballe, Julia Tyler, James Neel, Erin DeSalvatore, Mark Rifkin, and Chloe Bollentin. Thank you to everyone at Del Rey UK for yet another one. I'm incredibly lucky to be surrounded by some of the best people in the industry.

As always, to my GSJ, Allison Saft and Rachel Morris: I could not have dreamed up more wonderful friends. The hive mind is real. Thank you for filling my life with humor and unconditional love.

To Manning Sparrow and Sophie Cohen: every day I'm grateful that, by some propitious internet algorithms, we were able to find each other. Manning, thank you for more than ten years (!) of loving, funny, through-and-through friendship. Sophie, thank you for coming into my life at just the right time and holding my hand through some of my bleakest moments.

Thank you to Grace Li, one of the brightest things under the California sun—here's to a million more coffee dates. Thank you to Courtney Gould for always being a shoulder to lean on and a reason to smile.

To all the absurdly talented authors who have held my hand and shared their wisdom with me throughout this journey: I'm still pinching myself that I get to count you as colleagues and friends. Melissa Albert, Rory Power, Kendare Blake, Erin A. Craig, Vaishnavi Patel, Rachel Griffin, Isabel Ibañez, Sasha Peyton Smith, Alix E. Harrow, and Rebecca Ross: thank you for reading, blurbing, and loving.

Thank you to the booksellers, bloggers, and influencers for sharing their enthusiasm and helping this book reach its audience. I'm forever grateful especially to Joseline Diaz, Kalie Barnes-Young, Brittany Smith, and Bridey Morris.

To James. Thank you for not being afraid to love me, for always believing me, for reminding me what's real. I don't know how to begin unraveling everything my head thinks and my heart feels. Hopefully this book is a good start. I love you.

And to Zelda: I remember you. I believe you.